JUDGED

ELISE NOBLE

Published by Undercover Publishing Limited

Edited by Nikki Mentges, NAM Editorial

Cover design by Abigail Sins

www.undercover-publishing.com

www.elise-noble.com

Qui audet adipiscitur.

CHAPTER 1

RO

"Mr. Robert, would you like tea?"

I checked my watch. The Omega Seamaster was a relic from my past, and even though it had been with me through hell and high water, it never lost time. The engraved words on the side of the case —a motto I'd followed in a previous life—caught the light streaming in through the window beside me.

Always a little further.

Having daylight in my office was nice, don't get me wrong, and also a change from London City University where my allocated workspace was in the basement, but whoever designed the campus of Kabul International University hadn't been a local. The floor-to-ceiling windows might have been appropriate in a country like England, but in Afghanistan, with its forty-degree summers and minus-twenty-degree winters? We had the choice between baking and freezing. At the end of February, I was wearing a wool sweater inside, and half of my colleagues kept their coats on all day.

For the last seven months, I'd been seconded to Kabul as a teaching assistant while I performed the field research for my PhD. My timetable was flexible, allowing me scope to travel to the tribal areas as well as taking a couple of trips back to England each year for activities that definitely weren't part of the sociocultural anthropology curriculum.

Forty minutes until my next seminar, and I'd already prepared my notes on the ethnography of nineteenth-century Pakistan. I'd also developed a taste for Afghan tea over the past few months, which didn't bear much resemblance to the milky brew I'd grown up drinking in deepest Wiltshire.

"*Chai* sounds great. Thanks, Faruq."

"I will bring it to your office."

First, Faruq would boil cinnamon, cardamom pods, and sugar, and then he'd add green tea and saffron and let it steep. An old family recipe, apparently, and he always served it with almonds. I'd brought some PG Tips into work once and made him a cup, and although he thanked me politely, whenever I'd offered to make the drinks since, he'd immediately leapt up and run to the kitchen. Now I saved Britain's finest for those times when I was home alone in the evenings.

Faruq had been working as the anthropology department's Man Friday ever since I arrived. He assisted with paperwork, helped to organise our travel and schedules, and ordered stationery supplies. But the best part? He gathered all the gossip in Kabul and dished it out over tea and almonds every chance he got.

"Good morning, Robert," Francois called. He was a

fellow PhD student, although a year ahead of me. "We'll be playing basketball later—want to come?"

"*Bon matin.*" It was a habit in the department to greet each other in our native languages, a tradition that started because we had staff and students from every corner of the world. "Sure, why not? What time?"

"We leave at five."

I joined in whatever team games were on, plus hiked in the parks most weekends. Sometimes in the mountains too, although they weren't particularly safe, especially for foreigners. Every Monday evening, I lifted weights at the university gym, and occasionally I ate lunch at one of the big hotels so I could use the pool. I wasn't as fit as I used to be, but I'd stayed in shape after I switched to academia.

"See you there." I spotted another colleague at the door to the common room. "Marieke, are you coming?"

"Coming where?"

"Basketball."

"Tonight? No, I'm watching a movie with Sabrina."

I couldn't say I was heartbroken. Last month, Marieke and I had shared an awkward moment after Faruq's birthday dinner when she'd had one too many drinks and I'd offered her a ride home. After she stumbled over a chair in the restaurant and nearly went arse over tit, I'd half carried her out to my car, whereupon she'd misread the signals and tried to kiss me. Quite apart from the fact that she'd been paralytic at the time, I wasn't interested in anything more than friendship—relationships were far from compatible with my job—and my evasive manoeuvre had been hasty rather than subtle. I'd shovelled her into the passenger seat of my Toyota Corolla—everyone in Kabul drove a Toyota bloody Corolla—and taken her home, but she'd avoided me for a fortnight afterwards.

Now we were speaking again, but with the overly polite gingerness of two people who didn't want to make another fuck-up.

"Maybe next time," I muttered, then backed into the hallway that led to my office.

Someone had left fingerprint smudges on the brass door plaque, and I paused to rub a handkerchief over my name. *Mr. Robert Kemp.* I shared the cramped space with Bashir, a London-educated researcher who originally hailed from Islamabad. He specialised in object-based learning while I focused on social and cultural aspects, which meant our noticeboard was covered in photos of people we'd met and places we'd visited, and the shelves underneath held trinkets as well as textbooks. Bashir was back in Pakistan visiting his family this week, which had I been any other man on the planet would have meant a peaceful day working on my thesis, but instead...

"Morning, old chap. Turned out sunny again."

Instead, I got Peregrine Sumner III, who guffawed at his non-joke and put his feet up on the desk as he leaned back in Bashir's chair.

"Yes, it did."

"I overheard Faruq saying you plan to visit Kandahar?"

"Some of the outlying villages, yes."

"Did I ever tell you about the time I went there? It was right before the Battle of Maiwand, and one of my men was run down by an elephant when the damned thing got startled by a field gun."

You know the old saying that dead men tell no tales? It was bullshit. To those unfortunate enough to be able to hear them, dead men talked incessantly, and even earplugs couldn't block out the sound. Perry was a former British officer, shot in 1880 during the second Anglo-Afghan War in the very spot where my office had been built. He'd been stuck there ever since.

"You've mentioned it once or twice."

"Raj, that was the elephant's name. Surly old fellow, he was."

"I need to work, Perry."

"Work?" he snorted. "A man needs to get outside and use his hands, not stare at a magic box."

I'd tried to explain computers to Perry many times, but he still viewed them as a cross between witchcraft and science fiction. Same with mobile phones and TV. What was wrong with a good old telegraph?

Sometimes, I wished I'd never started speaking to him. When I kept my mouth shut, the spirits, ghosts, souls, ghouls, whatever they were, never knew I could see them. After all, nobody else could. I never used to be able to either, but one day when I was six years old, I woke up and there they were. Wilbur at the far end of the garden near the swing set, Jamal on the way to school, Harry beside the playground. It never occurred to me that talking to them wasn't normal until my foster mum sent me to a psychiatrist. Then I got sent to a group home, and I quickly worked out that if I didn't want to spend the rest of my life there, I needed to keep my mouth *shut*.

And so I did. In the twenty-seven years since, I'd only discussed spirits with one person—Shaykha Bushra, an old Afghan mystic who seemed to know me better than I knew myself. I hadn't mentioned my own experiences, obviously, but she'd told me change was coming. And she'd been right —I'd left my old job, I'd moved halfway across the world, and her granddaughter had ruined me for all other women. Almost unconsciously, I touched the string of turquoise beads encircling my right wrist. Ziya had put it there four and a half months ago, and I hadn't taken it off since. Probably never would.

"Yes, work. I have a thesis to finish," I told Perry.

"You live in the past, you old codger." Perry spread his arms. "Look to the future. There's so much out there waiting to be discovered."

Said the man who flatly refused to believe we'd sent a man to the moon, even when I showed him a video.

While I did embrace technology, the past fascinated me, and I wanted to save our history for future generations before it was too late. Every day, ancient artifacts got destroyed by war or razed to the ground to make way for modern development. And all the little pieces of knowledge locked up in people's heads faded, important facts lost with the elders before they could pass them on to the next generation.

"The future and the past are linked," I told Perry for the hundredth time. "We need to learn from our mistakes so we don't make them again."

Although considering the current situation in the Middle East, we seemed hell-bent on ignoring everything we should have known. My research on how past conflicts had shaped life in Pashtunistan, the area covering modern-day Afghanistan and Pakistan, probably wouldn't have much of an impact—I knew that—but at least I'd have done what I could.

And I had one significant advantage that other anthropologists didn't—I could talk to people who'd died in those conflicts as well as those who'd survived the years that followed. I just had to be extremely careful how I worded my findings.

"Man will always make mistakes," Perry told me. "There'll always be war. Survival of the fittest, what ho."

"I understand that." And I accepted it. But we still needed to be smarter if humankind was to have a long-term future.

"Say, did you find out what that explosion was yesterday?"

"A car bomb."

"Another one?"

The security situation had improved in recent years, but terrorist attacks were still unfortunately a part of daily life. Sometimes, it felt as if the city was teetering on a knife-edge of tension and one wrong move by the wrong people would push it into war again. Shaykha Bushra had told me the world had bad energy.

"Yes. Near the French embassy."

"How many is that this year?"

"Three so far."

Plus a dozen shootings and a kidnapping. A journalist for *Natural World* magazine had vanished along with her photographer, bodyguards, and translator near Tangar, which wasn't a million miles away, and the story had been all over the news. Did I worry living in Kabul? Of course, but I'd learned how to look after myself, and besides, crime levels were rising everywhere. Last week, a guy had blown himself up inside Madame Tussauds in London. The internet was already full of bad-taste jokes about the melted exhibits in the World Leaders' area being an improvement.

Footsteps sounded on the tiled floor outside—Faruq, if I wasn't mistaken. He took short, quick steps and insisted on wearing flip-flops all year round. Even when it was bloody snowing. A lesser mortal would have got frostbite in winter, but not Faruq. He was the only person in the department who wasn't affected by the shifts in temperature, and he hadn't deviated from his favoured shalwar kameez during the whole time I'd lived in Kabul. His hair had grown longer —he'd gone from slightly unkempt to man bun—but his wife liked it that way so he wasn't allowed to cut it short. And I could hardly comment. I'd grown a beard to fit in with the locals, and I hadn't bothered trimming it for at least two weeks.

"Here is the tea." The cups clinked on the silver tray as he set it down on my desk. "And my wife made baklava."

"She's an excellent cook. You're a very lucky man."

Faruq nodded, pleased, and took a seat on Perry's lap. Well, not so much on his lap but right *in* him. At first, I'd been disconcerted by seeing one person pass through another, but I'd grown used to it over the years.

"Did you hear Simon is returning to the United States?"

"Really? When? I thought he was here for two more years."

Simon was another of the lecturers, specialising in dirt, excrement, and decay—DEAD for short—and what decomposing matter meant to anthropology. I'd sat in on one of his talks last month, and it was more interesting than I'd imagined, although I couldn't say I fancied studying the subject myself. I'd seen enough shit to last a lifetime in my previous job.

"His mother is sick. They say it is the cancer."

"Fuck." Faruq glared at me. He wasn't fond of cursing. "Shit, sorry. Uh, are we organising some sort of collection?"

"Yes, I am doing it. I will purchase a card and gifts for his family."

I grabbed a handful of afghani notes from my pocket—a hundred afghanis equalled roughly one pound sterling— and passed them over.

"Here you go. Did you hear any more about that bomb yesterday? Anything from your brother-in-law?"

Faruq's sister was married to a lieutenant in the Afghan National Army, and the whole family ate together most evenings. I suspected half of Faruq's non-university-related tales came from talk over dinner.

"Six men died and nine are in the hospital. It was the Khyber Liberation Army."

Again? The KLA had been responsible for the last bomb too. For decades, they'd been an obscure little group based in the Khyber District of Pakistan, but thanks to a charismatic new leader and funding from various overseas organisations, the ragtag collective had transformed into a force to be concerned about. The Pakistan Army was having a crackdown, which meant the KLA had spilled over the border to cause chaos in Afghanistan instead. They opposed westernisation and enforced a strict moral code that bordered on barbaric. For the past few years, foreign money had been flowing into Kabul's regeneration, giving the city new malls and cinemas, wedding-cake-style housing estates that sat among the shanty towns, and a diverse group of cultures at the new university—everything the KLA abhorred.

"The army's no closer to rounding up the ringleaders?"

Although people knew the self-styled KLA general's name—Dayyin Rouhani—nobody had seen him for months, and he remained as elusive as the bomb-maker himself. Whoever *he* was, I had to grudgingly admire his skills, even if I hoped he'd blow his fingers off someday soon.

Faruq shook his head. "They are ghosts."

Perry chortled, which looked bizarre since his mouth was superimposed over Faruq's.

"If only he knew," Perry said.

Let's not go there, eh?

The KLA leaders definitely weren't ghosts. I knew that for certain. Not only were ghosts stuck in one place with limited communication skills, but they also seemed to be victims rather than aggressors for the most part. Every single one I'd spoken to had met a nasty end, and they usually displayed the evidence to prove it. Bullet wounds, shrapnel damage, streaks of blood—the scarlet trail down the front of Perry's jacket was a case in point. He'd died in his army uniform, and now he'd wear it for eternity.

Did ghosts stick around forever? Most of them, it seemed, but I wasn't sure *all* of them did. One or two had told me the same fantastical tale, of a spirit guide that visited them right after they breathed their last to tell them about the Electi, a group of magical assassins who'd work with the spirit to avenge their death. Only once the Electi had bumped off the spirit's killer would the spirit be allowed to leave earth.

No matter how many times the tale was relayed, it always sounded far-fetched. Perry swore every word was true, but I'd never met a ghost who'd so much as heard an Electi—the air crackled when they got near, apparently— let alone spoken to one. In any case, the soldier who'd shot Perry was long-since dead and buried, so I was stuck with his chatter until I left Kabul, come rain, come shine. And I'd admit to feeling a little envious that ghosts couldn't sense temperature. Perry was probably the most comfortable man in the whole damn building.

"The KLA are human," I told Faruq. "Although their actions aren't."

They'd killed two children with last month's bomb. Two young boys whose siblings would mourn them, whose friends would miss them, whose parents would never see them grow up. I'd walked past the spot where they died, and there they were, limbs missing and faces burned, more confused than anything else. Ghosts didn't feel pain either, and that was a blessing, but seeing them stuck there made me question once again why I'd come to Kabul.

Because you wanted to help, Ro.

But stemming the violence was like trying to stop an arterial bleed with a Band-Aid.

"They are animals."

"Animals? No, they're not. Animals tend to follow unwritten rules. They adapt to their environment through positive and negative feedback and act out of necessity rather than desire. Humans are far more unpredictable. The logic behind their actions is often warped."

"Yes. Yes, it is. Like what happened at that village you visited earlier in the year. Balaguri? Remember I helped you to type up your notes from there?"

A chill ran through me, icy crystals that started at the base of my spine and needled their way upwards to the nape of my neck. It wasn't the first time I'd had that feeling. My gut was well-honed to sense trouble.

"What happened at Balaguri?"

"Didn't I tell you?"

I made an effort to unclench my teeth. "No, you didn't."

"It got burned. Half of it was razed to the ground, and many men died."

No. No, that shouldn't have happened. *Couldn't* have happened, not now. A deal had been made. Balaguri was meant to be under the protection of Tabesh Siddiqui, a neighbouring opium producer and all-around asshole. The man who'd married the woman I felt drawn to like a moth to a flamethrower. Dread settled in my gut like second-hand musket balls.

"Why? Who did it?"

"A man from Balaguri stole a cow from the next village and would not give it back. So the *lashgar*, they burned a house, and then more houses caught fire, and there was a small war."

The *lashgar* was a local militia, often sent to dispense justice at the behest of a jirga, or tribal council. The practice of burning down an offender's home was disturbingly common, but to wipe out half a village over a fucking cow? Why hadn't Siddiqui stepped in? And more importantly, had Ziya's family survived?

"I'll need to postpone today's seminar. Could you let the students know?"

"Huh?"

Faruq's expression said he hoped I was joking. I wasn't. His mouth turned down at the corners as realisation dawned.

"You are serious about this?"

"I need to take the afternoon off."

"Why?" Five seconds passed as Faruq came up with his own thoughts. "Balaguri? You are going to Balaguri?"

"Yes."

"But why?" Faruq was understandably puzzled. Attacks were a common occurrence in that corner of the world, and I didn't usually drop everything to investigate. "You want more information? I will ask people."

"Ask, please. But I still need to go to Balaguri."

CHAPTER 2

ZIYA

Have you ever carefully weighed up the pros and cons of a decision and gone with head over heart? Chosen the option you thought would be the least painful for everyone concerned, even though you hated it?

I had, and it turned out to be the dumbest thing I'd ever done.

I'd fallen in love with one man, then married a different one, and now I was stuck in a slightly colder version of hell. Although if I waited a few months until summer, the two would be virtually indistinguishable.

"Ziya, why haven't you swept the hallways?"

Because I'd been busy doing the laundry, and I'd only just hung up the last of the shalwar kameezes. But I didn't say that. Pointing out the obvious didn't go down well with my husband's other three wives. Theoretically, under Islamic law, we were all meant to be equal, but the reality was vastly different. As the new girl, I got the worst chores, the thinnest mattress, and a sharp word whenever I did anything wrong. Dina, Delal, or Daneen screaming at me in Pashto was an hourly occurrence.

I cast my eyes down, avoiding Dina's gaze. Non-confrontational was definitely the best approach with this one. More than once, she'd slapped me for some perceived slight.

"I'll do it right now."

Perhaps I should have been happy. After all, I was considered by many to be fortunate. Afghanistan was the most challenging country in the world to be a woman—and that wasn't just my opinion, it was a fact. Two-thirds of Afghan girls didn't go to school, three-quarters faced forced marriage, and ninety percent lived with domestic violence. The country's maternal mortality rate was among the highest in the world, sixty percent of girls got married by age sixteen, and constant conflict left thousands of widows struggling to bring up children alone. My own cousin had been married at the age of twelve and died on her seventeenth birthday.

Me? I might have escaped the village where I was born, but I'd never escape my roots or my gender.

And despite all that, I was *still* considered to be one of the lucky ones.

I had my parents to thank for that. Mostly my mother, but my father had been open-minded enough to listen to her on occasion in a country where women were treated as property. Free will was just a dream—a wife belonged to her husband, a daughter belonged to her father, and a sister belonged to her brother. But my mama, she'd refused to take her fate lying down. Each morning after my father went to work in the fields, she used to sneak me out of the house and we'd walk the three kilometres to the nearest girls' school. If my father noticed us leaving, she used to lie

—say we were going to the mosque, or to Quran studies, or to the market—and in the time it took him to realise the truth, I learned how to read and write. Art became an escape, and I drank in science and maths as if they were the freshest spring water.

"School isn't a place for girls," my father had contended.

Mama always spoke softly, but she didn't quit. "But Adil, if Ziya learns, she will be able to teach her sons. Don't you want your grandchildren to have good jobs? Buy new clothes? Drive cars?"

"Yes, but..." There really wasn't a "but." My father hated farming. Months of back-breaking effort made barely enough money to feed us, let alone buy the Toyota he'd always wanted. "School takes up time. What about the cooking? The cleaning?"

"It will get done."

And it did. It always did, even if my mama stayed up half the night.

It took a tragedy to send me down the next path in my life. As I got older, I helped with the chores, and when Mama grew frail, I took over completely. I didn't mind the work. The part I hated was watching my mama in agony as the tumours ate away at her. At first, she brushed off the symptoms. A little discomfort was normal as the years passed, was it not? When she finally accepted that there might be a problem, there was no doctor for her to see, not one female doctor within fifty miles. And visiting a male doctor was out of the question.

By the time my father had saved enough money to take her to a hospital in Jalalabad, it was too late. She faded away three days before the appointment.

But before she died, my mama planted a seed. What if

there *was* a female doctor near our village? What if other women could be saved?

Like most couples in Afghanistan, my parents had an arranged marriage. But unlike many others, they grew to love each other over time. And after my father buried Mama, he decided that I should become that doctor, and he moved mountains to make that happen. I wasn't joking. One of his side jobs had involved digging tunnels into the hills for the Khyber Liberation Army to hide things they weren't supposed to have.

Since at that time, I'd still answered to my father, I was able to work because he allowed it. In Jalalabad, where I'd studied at Nangarhar University, I got a job as a tailor's assistant to pay some of my living expenses. Did I miss my family? Of course, but I liked living in the city. Occasionally, my baby brother would come to visit, and I always welcomed him even though I suspected he harboured a hint of bitterness that I spent most of my time studying while he had to look after the animals at home. I'd promised to help him to follow his dream of being an artist as soon as I earned enough money.

And then life fell apart.

You're still one of the lucky ones, Ziya.

I whispered those words more and more often now, always too softly for anyone else to hear, as if by saying them out loud, I could convince myself they were true. I lived in a nice house—one that might even be described as fancy—and I wasn't about to go hungry. We had running water, ceramic everywhere, and even AC in the living room.

But no amount of furnishings could change the fact that my husband was an arsehole. Or that I'd had to abandon my studies a year before I graduated to marry him.

I bent to pick up a broom, and as I swept, the thought of

the baby growing inside me brought a rare smile to my lips. He gave me something to live for. And it would be a boy, of that I was quite certain. Not that I'd had a scan or anything —because I hadn't graduated, Balaguri and the surrounding areas were still woefully short of healthcare facilities. Every few months, an NGO ran a mobile clinic, but prenatal care was inadequate, and if there was an emergency...

Don't think about it, Ziya.

So, how did I know my baby was a boy? Because my grandma had visited in a dream and told me so. Most people had thought she was crazy, and perhaps I was too for believing in the vision, but since Grandma had also foretold my father's death, and my broken heart, and guessed that our neighbour was going to have twins, I was inclined to believe her. The only prediction of hers that hadn't come true was the first. When I was eight years old, she'd sat me down, poured me a glass of sweet tea, and told me that one day, I'd help to save mankind. Although even that guess hadn't been way off base. "Mankind" had been an exaggeration, of course, but I'd come so, so close to finishing my medical studies, and I would have saved lives if I'd qualified.

Almost unconsciously, I reached to my neck, to the gold charm that hung on a cord at the base of my throat. She'd given it to me that day and said... Well, I'd forgotten her exact words, more focused on the shiny gift as any child would have been, but she'd said that not only would the charm bring me luck, it would mark me too. Mark me, because one day he would come.

The traveller.

I'd always wondered who exactly the traveller was, but whenever I'd asked her, she'd just smiled her toothless smile and shaken her head. "One day, you will not need to ask that question anymore, little Ziya," she told me. I was always "little Ziya," even when I grew taller than her and changed from a girl into a woman. But now Grandma was gone too, passed to *jannah* with my mama and my father.

And I was alone, in spirit at least.

Dina hadn't swept the hallways for days, and dust puffed up as I brushed dirt and stray leaves into a pile. Tabesh's house was huge, a maze of rooms that had been added to over the years without any thought for planning. And even indoors, I still needed to wear a veil because his men were often around.

Wait... What was that sound? I'd heard a quiet whimper. A stray kitten? If it was, I needed to find it and move it before Tabesh did. At least if I put it outside in the shade of a tree, it might stand a chance of surviving. Tabesh hated cats. And dogs. All animals, really. And most people.

The soft cry came again, and this time, I wasn't so sure it was a cat. The sniff that followed sounded more like a human. Had Tabesh beaten Daneen again? She was the youngest of his wives, even younger than me, and she wasn't too horrible when we talked on our own. Dina had corrupted her. Perhaps I could offer some comfort?

Then I heard footsteps. Heavy footsteps, and I knew at once who they belonged to.

"Ziya, why are you sweeping here?" my husband asked.

Of course, he would have told Dina to do it, but he didn't understand that Dina was a lazy *gaday bacheeay* who would make trouble for me if I didn't follow her instructions. And he also didn't understand jealousy. Dina had been married to Tabesh for the longest, almost twenty years, which put her in her early thirties. And in that whole time, she hadn't given him a son, or in fact any children at all. Neither had Delal or Daneen. Yet I'd fallen pregnant immediately. Tabesh had celebrated the news by forcing himself on me again, then pushing half of my workload onto the others so I'd give him a healthy child. The baby was a miracle, he said. A gift.

"I can still sweep," I told him. "Dina's feeding the horses."

"Don't sweep this part of the house. You should rest."

"But—"

"Rest!" He snatched the broom out of my hands and threw it on the floor. "Sit in the living room. And don't answer me back."

His face twitched, and I was certain that if I hadn't been pregnant, I'd have felt the palm of his hand. Last week, he'd given Delal a black eye when she burned dinner. I might have felt sorry for her if she weren't so nasty to me.

Tabesh's gaze burned into my back as I left. With his quick temper and imposing size, it wasn't difficult to see why everyone feared him—not just his wives, but men from Kabul to the Khyber Pass. And that was the only reason I didn't cry myself to sleep every night.

This marriage hadn't only been about me, you see.

Balaguri, the village where I grew up, my home, had always been volatile. A tinderbox that was constantly embroiled in some trouble or another. Whether it was the Taliban throwing their weight around, or a petty squabble with a rival tribe, or a battle between the US Army and whatever militia happened to be on the rise... Balaguri suffered. And after my father's death, the fragile truces he'd negotiated fell apart, and people died. Too many people. Grandma. Gulab, who'd worked with Baba to grow food for their stall at the market. My best friend, Quaseema. Her cousin and her aunt. We'd needed help, and the only person who'd offered it was Tabesh.

Of course, nothing in life was free. My uncle negotiated Tabesh's protection as my mahr—the price for my marriage. A dowry, if you like. Under Islamic law, the mahr should have been money paid to me, but laws got bent, laws got broken. And if sacrificing my freedom would save Balaguri and the people I cared about, then it was a price I'd gladly pay. I still had a brother. Yafir had just turned fifteen. Our father's death had cut Yafir to the core, and I didn't want him to suffer the same fate.

So there I was. A wife, a prisoner, and soon to be a mother. The only problem? I was almost certain that Tabesh wasn't the baby's father.

CHAPTER 3

ZIYA

Rest, Tabesh said, but how could I?

At first, I tried watching TV. When I'd lived in Jalalabad, back when I still had dreams of working in England for a year to further my medical career, I'd spent the evenings studying British entertainment programs, but not anymore. Not only was I stuck in Nangarhar province forever, but all the good channels had been banned too. Now I had the choice of state-run news or corporate news, which were basically the same thing from different angles. I didn't trust either of them. On the only other station that worked properly, Hoda TV was having a phone-in. Women with problems would call for advice, which was the most pointless thing ever. Everything was haram. Forbidden.

Don't be so ungrateful, Ziya. Tabesh's ridiculously ornate home was the only house in the area with reliable electricity, thanks to a set of solar panels in the yard, and it also had running water supplied via a pump from its own well. And there was a satellite dish on the roof for the internet, although Tabesh constantly complained about the download speed.

Yes, I *should* have been grateful, but I still preferred my shared apartment in the city. Four of us had lived there, two to each bedroom, and for my last year, I'd shared with Nancy, who came from Essex but planned to get a job in London after she returned to England at the end of her placement. When I'd asked why on earth she'd chosen to come to Jalalabad of all places, she said she'd been seeing a right tosser who cheated on her with, like, everyone, and she only found out when he matched with her hairdresser on Tinder. As a consequence, she'd taken the first job the nursing agency had offered, and until she landed in Afghanistan, she'd thought Jalalabad would be a resort kind of like Sharm el Sheikh, where she'd once been for a friend's hen do although most of that trip had been a blur.

I really missed her and the way she talked at a hundred miles an hour in sentences that went on forever. In the beginning, I'd had to constantly ask her to slow down, but by the time I left, she'd assured me I could totally get a job as an extra on *The Only Way is Essex*. Which I most definitely shouldn't have been watching, but Nancy had a Netflix subscription and a VPN. Yafir had caught me once. Season two, episode three, right before yet another power cut. I'd been terrified he might tell our father, but he'd promised to stay quiet, and he hadn't broken his word. I missed him too.

Life in Tabesh's home sucked.

Plus I couldn't stop worrying about the kitten. And I was sure now that it *was* a kitten because I'd heard Daneen walk past in the hallway with Delal, and they'd both been laughing. Should I try sneaking back again? I tiptoed over to the doorway, but a pair of Tabesh's men strode by with rifles slung over their shoulders, and I hastily retreated.

Losing the little freedom I'd once enjoyed had been the hardest part of adapting to my new life. My grandma and mama had shared a rebellious streak, and I didn't doubt that I'd inherited it too. Grandma especially had always encouraged me to ask questions. To walk my own path as far as the boundaries of our society would allow. Which for the next four and a half months would let me wander around Tabesh's dusty compound and no farther. After that, who knew? The baby growing in my belly was a ticking time bomb.

The best-case scenario was that it *did* belong to Tabesh, but I put the chances of that at slim. The timing didn't quite fit, and then there were the fertility problems he wouldn't admit to.

What would he do if I gave birth and the baby looked nothing like him? Tabesh had a round face, a broad, flat nose, big sausage lips, and protruding eyes. Robert Kemp? His face was squarer, his nose narrow and straight. When we first met, he'd been clean-shaven with a strong jaw and a hint of a dimple in his chin, but on his last visit to Balaguri, he'd grown a beard and could have passed for a local if you only gave him a quick glance. His eyes revealed the truth, though, those intense blue eyes with flecks of silver in the irises. They were kind. Too kind for this part of the world. And in four and a half months, there was a good chance they'd reveal the truth about my baby's parentage too. Both Tabesh and I had dark brown eyes. Yes, there was a chance of two brown-eyed parents giving birth to a blue-eyed child, but the probability was tiny when compared to the fifty-fifty odds with a blue-eyed father. And Tabesh didn't really believe in science. If he saw blue eyes, he'd ask questions, and if those eyes came coupled with lighter skin and finer features, I wasn't sure I could come up with a plausible answer. On our wedding night, I'd sprinkled sheep's blood on the bed to make him think I was a virgin, but would it be enough?

Robert—he'd told me to call him Ro—was yet another thing I missed about my old life. I'd first met him eleven months ago when he came to Balaguri as part of a volunteer project to drill a well. Until then, we'd had to either fetch water from a small river three kilometres away or buy it in bottles from a supplier. Not only did a trip to the river and back take an hour, but carrying a heavy jerrycan in each hand also made my back ache. And because animals shared the water source, people in the village often got sick. Bottled water avoided those problems, but it was expensive, and the mountain of plastic bottles left after we'd used the contents was a blight on the landscape. The well had changed everything. Now it took five minutes to fill up a can, and the water was clean.

I'd been back in Balaguri for a year at that time, called home by Uncle Shafiq after my father passed away. My uncle, he wasn't a bad man, but he firmly believed that my place was in the home and not a doctor's clinic. Unlike my father, Uncle was guided by faith rather than science. If somebody was ill, it was Allah's will whether they survived or not.

But he did appreciate having fresh, cool water, even if he wasn't keen on foreigners, and I'd been tasked with translating for the charity's team. Ro was nearly fluent in Pashto thanks to his childhood best friend being an Afghan refugee, but nobody else spoke more than a few words of the language. Due to my time in Jalalabad, I'd spoken Pashto, Dari, and English, and so I'd been busy that month. But not too busy to sneak away from the house to talk to Ro late every evening. If my uncle had caught me, I'd have been punished, but it was worth the risk.

So we talked, and I found out what it was like to have a man actually listen to my side of the conversation. Ro told me he worked in project planning for a waste disposal company back in England, but he'd become disillusioned with the organisation and he was planning to make a change. He wanted to see the world. To understand more about people and their different cultures. We discussed life in Afghanistan, the challenges and also the small joys it could bring.

Although I felt drawn to him, nothing had happened between us, not then. The only time he touched me was when our fingers brushed as he handed me a handkerchief to wipe away my tears. My father's death still weighed heavy on my soul even now, but back in those days, it had been a boulder pressing down on my shoulders.

Ro had helped to lighten the load.

After he left, I thought I'd never see him again, but he'd shown up in Balaguri several months later with gifts for all the children, wanting to talk to Grandma about the village's history as part of his research for an anthropology doctorate. He'd finally quit his old job and taken a big step towards realising his dream. Except by then, Grandma was dead, and I was dead inside. I'd lost half of my little family, and I'd also been promised to Tabesh.

But Ro had stayed to talk to the other villagers, and our nightly chats resumed under cover of darkness. Then he came back again, and again. Every time I crawled into bed, my emotions grew more and more jumbled, confusion mixed with regret mixed with a strange fondness for a man who was firmly off limits. And out of that murky soup, a germ of an idea had sprouted.

During my medical studies, I'd learned the mechanics of human reproduction, but Nancy had no shame, and she'd educated me further. According to her, there was more than one kind of sex, not that she'd called it sex because why use a technical term when she could substitute a more vulgar one in its place?

Anyhow, what I'd begged Ro for definitely fell into the "pity fuck" category.

He hadn't wanted to do it. At first, he'd told me "no way," but when I turned to run, he pulled me into a hug instead. And I confessed my fears, how I knew Tabesh wouldn't be kind and that I hated the thought of my first time being with a man I disliked so much. How badly would it hurt? My eyes had stung just from thinking about it.

So Ro acted against his better judgement and that night, we'd fumbled around in an old goat house on the hill behind my uncle's home, and yes, it *had* hurt, but Ro was so kind about the whole thing that I'd cried again. He hadn't come inside me, just as he promised he wouldn't, but I knew from my studies that pulling out wasn't necessarily foolproof. I'd taken a gamble—which of course was also haram—and I'd lost.

Lost twice over. Ro had asked me to leave with him that night, and I'd stayed. In my country, love before marriage was a sin, and a girl who showed affection for a man who wasn't her husband could be killed, sometimes even by her own family. So out of fear and loyalty, I'd stayed. And now I was trapped.

When I woke up the next morning, Ro had gone, and two days after that, I'd been married in a three-day ceremony that turned into a funeral when one of Tabesh's relatives shot Dina's cousin. And that wasn't even the worst part. No, the worst part came when Tabesh led me to the bedroom and I saw he had what Americans would call a cocktail wiener. It barely even touched the sides. The huge risk I'd taken with Ro, it had been unnecessary.

Every day, I felt sicker, and it wasn't all from hormones.

I leaned my head back against the wall. What was the point in thinking about my past? I needed to focus on the future, not that I had much of one.

There were so many things I loved about my country— the people of Balaguri and the sense of community there, the desolate yet beautiful landscape and the way the sun kissed the mountains every morning, the fact that people focused on their families rather than material things, and the decency of the majority of Afghans, who'd always help out if you needed a hand.

But there was no getting over the widely held belief that women were second-class citizens, or the constant destruction caused by people who couldn't accept that different people might hold different views. And then there was the indisputable fact that my husband was a slug with the cunning of a fox and the ethics of a mosquito.

I had to go and look for the kitten, didn't I? If I left it to fend for itself, it was as good as dead, just like the dreams I'd once had.

CHAPTER 4

ZIYA

"Here, kitty," I murmured.

I didn't expect it to answer, of course, but I hoped that maybe the creature would react to the sound of my voice. Move a little or make a noise. If I found it, I planned to put it into a basket and sneak it out to the barn behind the house. The men didn't go in there much.

Footsteps sounded in the hallway outside, and I froze. This part of the house was off limits to women unless we were cleaning. Some of the rooms were used for storage, but Tabesh's men often gathered there to eat because the thicker stone walls kept it cooler than their own mud-brick-and-straw accommodation block. That was on the other side of the compound near the long, low building Tabesh used for business.

The opium trade was both a scourge and a necessity for Afghanistan. At the hospital in Jalalabad, I'd come face to face with the horrible effects of addiction, but I'd also seen people starving in the villages of Nangarhar amidst the periodic clampdowns by whoever's turn it was that year.

Sometimes it was the Taliban wanting to drive up prices, other times corrupt politicians fighting for control or foreign troops trying to curb addiction in their own countries, but it never stopped. Afghanistan was always somebody's battleground, and its citizens just had to do their best amongst the fallout.

So I couldn't honestly criticise Tabesh for trafficking drugs, but I could criticise him for being a horrible human being.

The footsteps carried on past, and I let out the breath I'd been holding. If anyone caught me, I'd claim I'd come to the storeroom to fetch more cooking oil, but Tabesh would still be angry if he found out I'd disobeyed his order.

There it was! A soft cry. I tiptoed out into the corridor, and the sound came again, followed by a sniffle that sounded more female than feline. Was it a person after all? If so, who?

The next door was closed, bolted from the outside. The bolt looked new. Were my eyes playing tricks on me? Had it been there before? I rarely ventured into this area, only when Dina sent me.

Beads of sweat trickled down my back as more footsteps approached. At least two men this time, maybe three or four. I scuttled to the next open room and pressed myself against the wall behind the door. Why hadn't I gone in the other direction? This room contained nothing but dusty old furniture, and I had no plausible reason for being here whatsoever.

The bolt rattled. I heard a *thunk* as it shot back, followed by a muffled scream and the sound of an open hand on flesh. My spine stiffened. In all the time I'd been at Tabesh's, I'd been miserable and fearful for the future, but never had I felt I was in immediate danger. Now? I didn't know how to feel. What was I listening to? That scream had sounded decidedly feminine, but there were only three other women in the house, and I knew it wasn't any of the D-Team. Part of me wanted to creep forward and look, but the sensible part, the tiny kernel of my brain concerned with self-preservation, longed to curl into a ball and cover my ears. Finally, my knees decided for me. When I tried to take a step, they buckled.

Then the men were in the corridor again, and I heard scuffing sounds. Another sniffle. A few mutterings.

"They're late."

"On their way to collect...going to Deraz."

"Let me go, you—"

The woman's protest was quickly followed by another slap, harder this time. But not before I'd heard her accent. She was American?

No, no, my ears must have been playing tricks on me. Even Tabesh wouldn't be crazy enough to lock up a foreigner.

"*Dere qrrate ma kawa!*" a man ordered. Shut your ugly mouth!

Who was she? Why was she here? Were they taking her to Deraz? Deraz was a village to the north, bigger than Balaguri because it had better soil. We used to trade with the people there, but since it became a stronghold for the Jala Mujahideen, we'd stayed far away.

The footsteps receded along the corridor, and the outside door slammed. The house fell silent. Stay or go? Stay or go? My legs were shaking, but if I stayed, the men might come back, and that was a risk I didn't want to take.

I hugged the wall as I hurried back towards the main part of the house, but when I walked past the makeshift prison, I glanced inside. The room stank of urine, and I spotted a bucket in the far corner as well as a tray with an empty glass and a half-eaten flatbread. How long had the woman been in there? A day? Two days? The only other evidence of her presence was a grubby pink scarf near the door, and I guessed it had come off in the struggle. I stooped to take a look. Several long blonde hairs clung to the fabric, and I couldn't hold back my gasp. Tabesh *had* kidnapped an American? That could cause a freaking war!

I plucked a strand of hair from the scarf and held it up between my fingers, praying I was mistaken. But no, the strand was too fine to have come from a horse's mane and too long for a dog. What should I do? What *could* I do?

Then I felt it—tiny bubbles popping in my belly. At first, I thought it might be gas, but then it came again, the soft flutter of a butterfly's wings. The baby was moving. My child had kicked some sense into me, and I fled along the corridor, only slowing when I got back to the living room.

I was safe.

For now.

An engine started out in the yard, and I hurried over to the window in time to see a battered red Jeep sputtering off along the track that led to the road three kilometres away. *I* was safe, but another woman was in danger. Grave danger. And there wasn't a thing I could do about it. Even if I'd had access to a phone, who would I call? The police? The government? They were as corrupt as each other, and who would believe me anyway?

This was the part of my life I hated the most. The helplessness. The feeling of being completely and totally alone despite my living arrangements. I wasn't even allowed to visit my family. Every time I asked, Tabesh said, "Maybe tomorrow," but tomorrow never came.

My heart was still pounding from my narrow escape,

and I couldn't breathe under my veil. I needed air, and the only place I could get that was in the bedroom I shared with the other three women. Tabesh summoned one wife to his room each night on a rota system. Not me, though—the absolute best thing about being pregnant was that I'd been missed off the schedule. Tabesh said sex would harm the growing baby, which it wouldn't, but he always knew best and I wasn't going to correct him.

The mattresses and quilts were all folded up in the corner during the day, leaving only thin woven carpets on the floor to sit on. Our room was comfortable, but nowhere near as opulent as Tabesh's. Next door, the colour scheme was maroon and navy blue with gold fittings that twinkled against walls yellowed from cigarette smoke. So tasteful. I half collapsed into a cross-legged heap and tore off my veil. Even though the air was stuffy, I sucked in lungfuls as I tried to calm my racing pulse. *Why* would Tabesh abduct a woman? What did he have to gain from it?

I still hadn't come up with any answers when the door flew open and Dina marched in. Great. Exactly what I didn't need at this particular moment. I scrambled to my feet, but any hopes I might have had that she was just there to drop off laundry or change her clothes were soon dashed when she stopped in front of me, hands on her hips.

"What did you say to Tabesh?"

"Huh? Nothing."

"You did! He yelled at me and told me to sweep the whole house."

"I only told him you were feeding the horses. He wanted to know why *I* was sweeping."

"You should have stopped when he came near."

"I would have stopped if I'd heard him."

"It's not fair that you get to watch TV all day. You're pregnant, not ill."

"I don't *want* to watch TV all day."

Dina's eyes narrowed, and she looked me up and down. She might have been pretty if she didn't hold her face in a perpetual sneer. I wanted to face up to her, to meet her gaze with my own, but I knew from experience that would only bring trouble. So I stared at the floor.

"What's this?" she asked, slender fingers reaching out. "Did Tabesh give it to you?"

For the second time that day, my heart threatened to give out. *This can't be good for the baby.* My gold pendant, the one I usually kept so carefully hidden under layers of clothes, had popped out when I removed my veil. Now it lay against my chest, glinting in the late afternoon sun that streamed through the tiny window high in the wall.

"N-n-no. It came from my grandma."

"Don't lie! This is expensive, and your family has no money." Dina folded her arms, and even though I couldn't see her mouth, I knew it would be arranged in a smug smile. "You believe you're so much better than the rest of us, but do you think Tabesh will still treat you like a queen once you've given him a son? He doesn't even like you."

"Oh, and he told you that?"

"He didn't need to. Tabesh hates defiance."

Just for a second, I saw a glimmer of pain in Dina's eyes. As if she was remembering the past. Had she once been the defiant one? Quite possibly. Life in Tabesh's compound had a way of wearing you down—I'd aged a decade in less than five months—but any sympathy I might have felt quickly ebbed away when she snatched my pendant on its thin leather cord and hung it around her own neck instead.

"Hey! Give that back!"

"You don't deserve trinkets. You don't even do housework."

"I told you it—"

Dina's hard shove caught me by surprise, and I staggered backward with my arms windmilling. My heel caught under the edge of a rug, and I landed hard on my butt. That daughter of a defective donkey!

"Wait one hour, then finish the sweeping. And this time, make sure you listen for Tabesh."

I wanted to chase after her, to take my necklace as she'd taken it from me, but I had to protect my baby. Who knew what she'd do next time? Pregnancy was my shield right now, and I had to admit that Dina was right in one respect —if I couldn't give Tabesh a son, I was dead weight in the household. Emphasis on the "dead."

I needed to get my talisman back, but I'd have to bide my time. Plan things out. Letting it go wasn't an option. When Grandma gave it to me, she'd said it was important. That it belonged to the man who'd restore balance to the earth—this traveller, this...wandering spirit—and one day, it would find its way back to him. That she'd looked after it for her lifetime, but now I was the guardian. Honestly, I wasn't certain I believed the story—Grandma had said a lot of crazy stuff over the years—but the talisman was the only thing I had left to remember her by. In terms of sentimental value, that "trinket," as Dina called it, was priceless.

CHAPTER 5

RO

Bloody hell. Quite literally.

I stopped the Land Rover as I got my first glimpse of Balaguri. The village nestled in a gently sloping valley in the shadow of the Safed Koh mountain range, a cluster of houses surrounded by shared grazing land and small fields of crops. On the four other occasions I'd made this journey, sheep and cows had dotted the scrubby grass in the distance, but today, the only sign of life was a pair of goats nosing among the charred remains of the dwellings. One building farther up the hill was still smoking.

For the whole journey, I'd been hoping for the best, keeping my fingers crossed that Faruq had been exaggerating about the village's fate—after all, it wouldn't have been the first time he'd embellished a tale. But this was beyond even the worst scenario I'd modelled in my head as I drove.

Was *anyone* left alive?

I reached under the passenger seat for my binoculars

and scanned the area, moving slowly from left to right, keeping an eye on the far end of the village where the road —such that it was—wound high into the mountains that divided modern-day Pakistan from Afghanistan along the Durand Line. That road was Balaguri's greatest enemy. In years gone by, it had been an important link between the tribes of Pashtunistan, but today, it led to opium country. And opium meant trouble.

Apart from the goats, nothing stirred in Balaguri, nothing with a pulse anyway. The ghosts were easy to pick out. They moved differently, which was to say they barely moved at all. A group by the well I'd helped to build shimmered in the morning light, one or two talking to each other, but mostly they just stood in silence. On my last visit, there had been five men in that little cluster. Today there were eight.

The woman by Shafiq's home was new too, and most notable because she wasn't wearing a veil. Could that be Ziya's aunt? She looked to be the same size, but I'd never seen her with her face uncovered. I refocused and saw a young boy nearby. Ah, fuck. That was either Ziya's cousin or his doppelgänger. What the hell had happened in Balaguri? Faruq said there'd been an argument over a cow, but there was a damn crater where a house had once stood. The only people in the area with enough firepower to do that sort of damage were the coalition forces or possibly the Jala Mujahideen, a group of junior jihadis with fewer ethics than the Taliban.

I needed to take a closer look at the village. Should I take the Land Rover or go in on foot? The vehicle would present a larger target if there were any undesirables still hanging around, but I'd also be able to make a quicker getaway if the need arose. On foot, I could sneak right up to the front door, but I wasn't exactly dressed for the situation. With so many checkpoints between Kabul and Balaguri, both the official army posts and the unofficial stops manned by locals that occasionally popped up, I'd worn a brown shalwar kameez with oversized pants baggy enough to cover my ankle holster, plus a traditional white skullcap—a *taqiyah*—and a thick sleeveless jacket for warmth. If a foreigner ventured too far outside Kabul, their progress was liable to be noted and transmitted along the way, just in case anybody wanted to ambush them. Blending in was definitely the way to go. The Land Rover looked the part too—I'd sourced it from an old acquaintance soon after I moved to Kabul, and while the outside resembled something out of the Soviet era, the engine and chassis were top notch. So was the heater, thankfully. If I'd tried to drive the Corolla to Balaguri, it would have rattled its wheels off before the nondescript buildings of Jalalabad faded in the rear-view mirror.

Oh, what the hell—if somebody planned to shoot me, they'd have done it by now. I turned the engine over and trundled down the hill, keeping my eyes peeled for any flashes of light that might indicate a rifle scope. But there was nothing. I parked the Land Rover behind the ruins of what had once been a barn and let out a long private sigh. I should have known better than to come back to Afghanistan, shouldn't I? Damn the Mansfield Foundation and their fucking "research grant."

If I stopped to draw a gun from my waistband while wearing a kameez, I'd be dead before I hoicked the tunic halfway up. So my Glock 17 went into my waistcoat pocket, and I checked the Colt Officer's ACP was securely fastened into the ankle holster. The Colt had been a good-luck gift from my case officer at the Foundation—or asset manager, as she liked to call herself—complete with custom walnut grips because "they'll match the leather elbow patches on Robert's tweed jacket." When I'd told her I wouldn't be needing the Sig, she'd just laughed. She'd laugh even harder if I actually used it to shoot someone.

But I didn't have time to think about Marina Carrigan's warped sense of humour right now, not when I'd potentially painted a bullseye for the Taliban on my arse.

I slipped out of the driver's side of the Land Rover, keeping the vehicle between myself and the nearest building. A ghost near the crumbling wall watched me with mild curiosity but didn't attempt to speak, which was hardly surprising seeing as I'd steadfastly ignored the spirits on my previous visits. I'd spent years perfecting my poker face, but today, it was time to reveal my hand.

"Is anyone still here?" I asked quietly.

He didn't answer, just turned to peer over his shoulder.

"Yes, you with the bullet hole in your chest. I'm talking to you." What was his name? I recognised him from my first trip. "Are you Pamir's son?"

"You...you see me?"

"Yes, but I don't have time to have a conversation about it. Is there anybody alive in the village?"

"You are here to avenge my death?"

Clearly the spirit guide had already reeled off her spiel.

"No, I came to sightsee. Who else is here?"

"I don't understand."

For fuck's sake, I'd be a ghost myself before I got a straight answer. I gave up on maybe-Pamir's-son and crept to the edge of the building, gun in hand, using the wall as cover. A clatter made me whip around, heart rate jumping, searching for the threat. But it was only a plastic bottle, one of thousands that had been tossed into the ten-foot-high pile behind the house. Recycling hadn't yet caught on in Afghanistan.

Another ghost watched from thirty metres away, wide-eyed. Did he recognise me? Possibly, but I wasn't worried about my cover being blown, not now. The dead might tell tales, but not to the living. At least, not unless they were talking to me or possibly one of these Electi people who may or may not have existed.

Out of the Land Rover, I was able to get a better feel for my surroundings. My former colleagues used to say I had a spooky sixth sense—oh, the irony—but today, nothing pinged my radar. Balaguri's soul was dead. But even so, I moved from house to ravaged house, clearing each property as I went. There was nobody left. If anyone had survived whatever happened in this village, they'd fled before I arrived.

An engine sounded in the distance, and I ducked into a house before the vehicle came into sight. A broken red plastic car lay on the floor beside scattered cushions, and the tragedy that had struck here punched home like a mortar round. For years, I feared I'd lost my humanity. This was proof it had only been mislaid, but as I studied what had once been a family home and felt my eyes start to sting, I wished I'd never had to find out the truth.

The garishly painted truck outside slowed as it passed, the driver just one more ghoulish onlooker travelling through the valley of death to deliver supplies. Who should I talk to next? The men at the water pump seemed the best bet—they'd have had a good view of whatever happened last week.

I was about to cross the open space between the houses

when a loud rumbling sent me fumbling to get my gun up. The enemy? Another attack? I dived behind a crumbling wall and waited.

CHAPTER 6
RO

The rumbling turned into a splintering *crash*, and I peered carefully around the end of the wall, keeping low. No, it wasn't an attack, just the roof of a house collapsing inwards onto the floor below. Fuck, I was jumpy. I never used to be that way, but a lack of backup and nearly a year as a semi-civilian had messed with my mind. Training battled with misplaced instincts and an inbuilt sense of self-preservation.

The spirits had all turned to watch me now. I squinted at the taller of the newcomers, a skinny guy with half his face missing and blood dripping down his white shalwar. Well, I'd found Pamir. Plus Amu and Ghazan, two brothers who'd lived in the farthest house in the village. Ghazan had been a tailor. Several of the shirts he'd made me were still hanging in my closet. The other five men, I had no idea about. I'd never spoken to them before. Guess they were going to get a shock today.

Pamir recognised me first and turned to Ghazan. "Is this Robert? The man who came with the water pump?"

"Yes, and the pencils."

"And the writing paper, and the toys."

Okay, so I might have got a little carried away buying gifts for kids. Like that red plastic car, for example. What had happened to the young boy who'd carried it everywhere?

"But why does he have a gun?" Ghazan asked. "He is a teacher."

"So? Teachers carry guns. Remember Gedi, Ahmed's cousin? He taught at the boys' school during the day, and at night, he fought with the Jala Mujahideen."

"You call that a gun?" one of the other men scoffed, a hunched old gent with a bushy white beard. "It is too small."

They were so busy talking, they hadn't noticed me watching them. I cleared my throat.

"Can anyone tell me what happened?"

Eight mouths dropped open. Synchronised gawking.

"You...you see us?" Amu asked. He was the youngest, just eighteen or nineteen, his life snuffed out by what looked like assorted shrapnel.

"Yes, I see you."

"How? You are one of those people...an Electi?"

Pamir nodded knowingly. "A man? Now this makes sense. The fog-being, she said the avenger would be a woman, so we thought she was making a joke."

"I said you heard wrong," White-Beard told him. "Clearly the avenger has to be a man. You are here to avenge our deaths, yes?"

No, but under the circumstances it seemed easier to agree.

"Absolutely."

"Why are you not glowing?" Ghazan asked. "We were told you would be glowing."

"Because my batteries ran out."

Which was obviously a joke, but they all nodded in understanding.

"Why did you not talk to us before?" White-Beard asked. "You came twice."

Hmm... How could I put this without insulting them? I didn't make a habit of lying, but when I did, it was for good reason. Like that memorable time when I'd been stationed at AAC Middle Wallop and invited the receptionist from the officer's mess out for dinner. Well, room service. I'd reserved a junior suite at the White Hart Hotel, a delightful establishment that was just about affordable on a lance corporal's salary.

I'd been thinking with my dick rather than my brain that evening, more concerned with getting laid than checking my fuel gauge, which was the reason we'd run out of petrol on the A343. Not a huge problem in itself, and I'd been ready to schlep to the nearest petrol station while Helen—who'd dressed for the occasion in three-inch heels —sat back and listened to the radio. But then I heard the car tooting behind us.

As luck would have it, Captain Thomas had recognised my piece-of-shit Honda thanks to the "I Love Beavers" sticker affixed to the back bumper by the previous owner, and he'd stopped to help. Again, that wouldn't have been a problem if Captain Thomas hadn't been best buddies with the station commander. Why was that such an issue? Because as well as being the receptionist, Helen was the station commander's daughter, and he'd have cut my bollocks off with a rusty butter knife if he found out how I planned to entertain her that evening.

So I'd told a porky-pie, aided in no small part by Helen.

"Helen and I bumped into each other in the Melton Arms, and I offered her a lift home."

"A blind date," she said. "The chap was a terrible bore."

Captain Thomas looked at us, and then he looked at the car. "Why are you driving away from the base?"

Ah. The fatal flaw in the argument. "Helen left before the main course, so we decided to go back via the chippy."

"I ran out the rear door," she told him. "Honestly, the man talked about nothing but himself for an hour. Thank goodness Rohan was there."

"I didn't want to abandon Colonel Wilson's daughter to the local minicab firm."

Finally, Captain Thomas nodded. "You did the right thing, Keyes. I'll be sure to let the colonel know."

I got a free can of petrol out of the subterfuge, courtesy of the captain, plus the colonel's profuse thanks the next day. And I also got the pleasure of Helen sucking tiramisu off my dick as it stood to attention two hours later, because of course we snuck out again. For a moment, I wondered how she was. The last I heard, she'd moved to Stratford-upon-Avon and shacked up with a thespian her father couldn't stand.

Those days seemed a lifetime away now. The only constant was that I could still fib creatively when the need arose.

"I've only just completed my training," I told White-Beard and his buddies. "Until we graduate, we're not allowed to talk to spirits without supervision. Can you tell me what happened here?"

Pamir glared at Amu. "Amu took a cow."

"I did not take the cow. I found it near my house."

"But you did not give it back."

"Because the man who said it was his, he lied. He

claimed the cow walked here from Deraz, but it was too weak. Too thin."

I didn't have time to argue over the definition of theft. "How did a dispute over a cow lead to a thirty-foot crater in the middle of the village?"

"The man came to get the cow, and Amu said it was his cow now. So the next day, the man brought his friends."

Wait, wait, wait. This sort of shit was precisely what the agreement that Ziya's Uncle Shafiq had made with Tabesh was meant to prevent. The threat of his protection should have kept invaders at bay.

"Did you call Tabesh Siddiqui?"

All the neighbours knew about the deal that had been done. I very much suspected that the entire village had helped to pressure Ziya into accepting the terms.

"Yes, we tried."

"So why the hell is the hole there?"

"Akif, he drove to get a phone signal to call Tabesh, but he didn't return. And Tabesh never came."

"Akif went to call, not Shafiq?" Akif was a kid. Shafiq had done all the negotiation with Tabesh. "Where was Shafiq?"

"Shafiq died."

"What?"

"Three months ago."

"How?"

"He crashed his truck and broke his head."

Of course he did. Nobody around here ever wore a bloody seat belt. They preferred to trust their fate to Allah rather than actual safety devices.

"So Tabesh stayed away, and the men came back. Then they...what? Set off a bomb?"

"No, they burned the houses and shot at us. And then

some foreign soldiers came past, and they shot at them too."

"So did Pamir," Amu piped up.

"They broke into my house and saw my wife without her veil," Pamir snapped back. "What did you expect me to do?"

Night-time raids had always been a big sticking point in Afghanistan. From the point of view of the Americans, the Brits, the French, and so on, it was the best time to drag jihadists and drug dealers out of their homes, but it also presented problems. For a male stranger to see an unveiled woman was the greatest insult, and a Pashtun man had to fight back or he'd disgrace his tribe.

The war was just one culture clash after another.

The coalition had waded into the fight with good intentions—few sane people would argue against their initial objective of destroying Al-Qaeda's presence in the region—but they'd stayed on with a second goal in mind: to turn Afghanistan into a modern state. Opinion was split on that one. The coalition troops thought they were doing the Afghans a favour, while the Afghans resented the occupation and thought the foreigners didn't respect their values. Then in came the Taliban to distort the natives' beliefs into a jihadist ideology. Add in a corrupt government, and this was what you got. A bloody great hole in what had once been a thriving village.

Life was cheap in Afghanistan.

"The coalition called in an air strike?"

"Boom." White-Beard waved his arms over his head. "Everything blew up."

"Did anybody survive?"

"A few," Pamir said. "They left yesterday. I heard my nephew say they were going to Jalalabad."

I sucked in a breath and asked the question I dreaded hearing the answer to. "What happened to the Khalizai family?"

"Ziya is still with Tabesh, that father of all dogs."

"You think he stayed away on purpose?"

A shrug.

"What about the others? Her brother? Her aunt? Her cousin?"

"Her cousin and aunt, the soldiers buried them behind the house. Yafir wasn't here."

"Where was he?"

"After Shafiq died, Yafir began to work for the KLA as his father once did. At the Tangar Caves. He sent money to his family."

This went from bad to worse. Ziya was hitched to a traitor and her brother was in the clutches of a group of madmen? Someone up there was having a laugh, possibly the same arsehole who allowed me to talk to the dead in the first place.

The question was, what should I do about the situation? I wasn't going to travel to Deraz and start a fight with the owner of a cow that had now disappeared, and nor did I plan on steaming up to the Tangar Caves and getting myself shot. I *could* put feelers out among my contacts to find out what had gone on with the air strike. "Condolence payments" were available if the coalition leaders felt them "culturally appropriate," and although the amounts were meagre, they might help the villagers who'd fled to Jalalabad, assuming somebody could find them.

That left Ziya.

And no matter how dangerous or how utterly fucking inappropriate it might have been to go to her, I couldn't leave without at least checking that she was okay.

CHAPTER 7

RO

Something crawled over my leg as I hunkered down beneath an overgrown honeysuckle bush high up on the hill behind Tabesh Siddiqui's hideous house. A cockroach? A gecko? Whatever, I didn't move a muscle as two guards strolled past, AK-47s slung across their backs.

Better not be a fucking scorpion.

When I quit the military, I'd thought I was done with all this. Eleven years of service had taught me we were fighting a battle we'd never win, not using current tactics. With every day that passed, each side had grown more bloodthirsty, their tactics more extreme, the death tolls higher. How could I carry on fighting for a government I no longer respected? For leaders I no longer trusted?

In hindsight, I'd carried on for longer than I should have, thinking that this tour, this operation, could be the one that made the difference. I should have listened to my gut. But the darkness had crept up on me like a slow-rolling fog, malevolence seeping from the world's pores. And then it pounced.

First, one of my best mates met his maker in Syria. Jake

and I had gone through training together, then visited every hellhole imaginable. We'd survived dawn raids, night-time insertions, and even a bloody helicopter crash before shrapnel from an IED severed his brachial artery. A freak accident. An inch either way, and we'd have been laughing about it over dinner. In all honesty, I should have quit at that point, but my commanding officer had convinced me that my talents were too good to waste.

So I'd kept going. More fool me.

My last mission in Afghanistan had involved a jaunt into opium country not too far from here when my four-man team was tasked with retrieving a fool who'd decided to backpack from Kabul to Islamabad and found himself the recipient of free room and board courtesy of the Taliban. We'd found the hapless hippie, liberated his sorry arse, and begun making our way back when we got stuck at an American roadblock.

An old truck had been first in line, its bed piled high with bulging sacks. An American soldier had the driver out of the cab, his M16 pointing at the man's chest. *No, no, no.* This wasn't how checkpoints were supposed to work. The soldier looked more nervous than the driver, and when I saw the slight tremble in his hands, I got out of our minivan to hear what he was saying. That day, I was dressed as a local—we all were. We'd found the easiest way to hide was in plain sight, so we turned the radio up, waved our rifles out of the windows, and generally acted like arseholes. Regular Afghan civilians and even the police gave us a wide berth. All that meant I couldn't simply wade in and offer to help.

"What's in the truck?" the soldier shouted. Four cars back, I could still hear every word.

And the Afghan kid didn't understand the question,

that much was clear. He tried answering, and I caught the words, "*Za na poheegum.*" I don't understand.

The soldier didn't understand either, and when he asked the same question again, the driver just shrugged and smiled, which only made things worse. As a wise woman once said, insanity is doing the same thing over and over and expecting different results.

"Don't grin at me—answer the question."

How long had this been going on? Another soldier stood behind the first, but he was only watching. Both men seemed way, way out of their depth, a symptom of a greater problem. An increasing number of deaths in service, poor recruitment figures, and cost-cutting had all led to young privates being sent to war before they were ready. They were badly trained and they were scared—the worst possible combination.

An older man climbed out of the passenger side of the truck, also smiling as he approached the soldiers. He was wearing similar clothes to those I'd worn to Balaguri, except his shalwar kameez was white and his waistcoat brown.

"Stay back," the soldier warned.

The man stepped forward, and so did I.

Then things happened in a heartbeat. The newcomer reached into his pocket, and I saw the soldier tense. His eyes widened as he swung the muzzle of the M16 around.

Instinct took over, and I broke cover. "Stop!"

Both soldiers looked over at me, but the guy with the gun, his trigger finger was already squeezing. And the safety was off. The bullet just missed me as it exited, and the Afghan man stayed standing for a few seconds before he crumpled, permanent surprise etched onto his face as the ID card he'd been trying to present fluttered to the ground beside him. The younger guy, the driver, he acted on instinct too, but attacking an American soldier carrying a gun was never going to have a good outcome. Two lives had been lost that day, quite unnecessarily.

The truck? It was full of onions. The older man? He'd been Ziya's father. The teenager, the one who'd died on the way to the hospital, he'd come from Balaguri too.

That night and every night since, I'd relived the moment. If I hadn't shouted, would the grunt have pulled the trigger? What if I'd broken cover sooner? What if I'd offered to translate? What if, what if, what if?

Later that week, when the roadblock had gone and rain had washed away the last of Adil Khalizai's bloodstains, I'd driven back to that desolate spot, now home to a spirit destined to watch over the rutted road for eternity. As darkness fell, I'd sat alone on a boulder and talked to Adil. Told him I was sorry. Sorry that I'd stood by, sorry that I'd played a role in Afghanistan's troubles. He said he forgave me. But he also begged me to do one thing: help his people. His family, his tribe, and his country.

I'd given him my word that I'd do what I could.

But never in my wildest dreams did I think I'd fall for his daughter.

As soon as I completed the mission, I flew home and handed in my year's notice. I couldn't stay in the army any longer. And then I began making plans to return to Afghanistan, to see if education could win where war had failed.

The constant guilt eating away at me had led me to raise money for the well and water pump in Balaguri, that and a desire to fulfil the promise I'd made to Adil. I'd done a sponsored climb up Mount Kilimanjaro with a mate, and the army had even given us time off to do it.

Curiosity sent me to the village to help with the installation, and Ziya had lured me back for a second visit under the guise of research for my studies, then a third visit, and then a fourth. The last trip had been four and a half months ago. Honestly, I didn't understand why I felt so drawn to her. Before the day we first met, I'd been attracted to self-confident women who wouldn't get broody or clingy or go into hysterics when I walked away. And I always walked away.

Ziya? She radiated fragility, her inner strength masked by the weight of cultural expectations. Vulnerably beautiful, beautifully vulnerable. Even if she wasn't married, a fling would be out of the question, and yet for her, I'd walk right into the lion's den.

The woman screwed with my head as well as my dick.

Tabesh's guards disappeared from sight, but still I didn't move. Who knew when the next ones would appear? So far, I'd seen fourteen men, all armed, and sure as shit there were more. The compound was laid out around a large courtyard surrounded by ten-foot-high walls. Tabesh's house took up the whole of one side and was possibly the ugliest building for a hundred miles. No, definitely. It was as though he'd beamed up the Afghan equivalent of a McMansion from downtown Kabul, dropped it in the middle of the wilderness, jerry-built extensions on either side, and painted it duck-egg blue. Two long, low buildings behind the house appeared to be a barracks and a drug-processing facility respectively, and there was also a barn with a few animals wandering around. Goats and chickens mainly, but I'd heard neighing, so there were horses somewhere too.

By the time night fell, I'd been bitten by creepy-crawlies despite having tucked my trousers into my socks, and my legs itched like mad. But the wait was worth it. I knew now that there were two guards on duty in the compound at all times, and I also knew that they didn't take their jobs seriously. Right now, one was dozing while his pal fiddled with his phone, and the radio crackling out folk music beside them would cover the sound of my approach.

How was I going to get in? Easy. Tabesh had grown complacent and allowed the branches of a willow tree to spread up and over the wall. Getting out would be trickier —I'd have to pick the right moment and sneak through the side gate, which was bolted from the inside. The only problem? It was just ten metres from the guards' resting place.

Still, I'd faced bigger challenges.

An advantage of Tabesh living in a secure compound with a collective of mercenaries lounging outside was that he didn't feel a need to lock his doors. Once I'd hopped over the wall, it only took five minutes to get inside the house. This was when the major problem with my plan became all the more evident—how the hell was I meant to speak to Ziya? Afghans didn't like to sleep alone, so it wasn't as if I could sneak into her bedroom for a quiet chat. Worst-case scenario was that she was with Tabesh. I clenched my teeth just from thinking about it. Statistics said there was a twenty-five percent chance of that, but maths didn't take into account the fact that Ziya was by far the most attractive out of Tabesh's wives. *Wives*. What kind of selfish bastard needed four women, anyway?

Okay, I might have done a little research when I found out who Ziya planned to marry. Tabesh Siddiqui was the son of a carpet dealer who, rather than following in his father's footsteps, had worked out that shifting drugs was far more profitable than flogging prayer mats. Over the years, he'd stayed reasonably neutral as he built up his business, walking a fine line between warring tribes. He paid lip service to Islam. His religion was capitalism, his first love was the almighty dollar, and his vice was laziness. I suppose it shouldn't have surprised me that he'd betrayed the people of Balaguri, given that ammo cost money and negotiation took effort.

Silently, I slipped along a hallway lined with closed doors. No light seeped out from under any of them. Were they bedrooms? A kitchen? A handy space to store weapons or surplus opium? I turned the first handle slowly, a millimetre at a time, and found a storage room—shelves stacked high with sacks of rice and drums of cooking oil and a pile of old-style body armour. Next to that was a prayer room with mats lined up on the floor, then a large empty room that smelled like shit. Actual shit. Moonlight glinted off the bars across the window, and I dreaded to think what might have happened to the last occupant.

The layout of the place was diabolical. Had the architect been paid in product rather than cash? The next hallway came to a dead end, and I stilled as footsteps passed outside the open window. A mesh screen kept bugs at bay but didn't stop a cloud of smoke from enveloping me. Tobacco mixed with hash. No wonder the guards weren't as alert as they could be.

I carried on through the house, mapping it out in my head. I had to play the long game here. Ziya's safety trumped everything else, which meant treading softly until I found a way to talk to her privately. Perhaps once I knew her routine, I could find somewhere to leave her a note? Faruq had promised to cover for me at the university, so I figured I wouldn't be missed for a week or so. A sudden bout of food poisoning was a perfectly plausible excuse in this part of the world.

Of course, that plan meant not getting caught, and when a light blinked on nearby, I swore under my breath. Who was awake? Not Tabesh. One of my sources had told me he was fond of a tipple before bed, usually smuggled Russian vodka. In Afghanistan, being drunk was a sign that you had money.

With footsteps coming closer, I ducked into the nearest room—a bathroom I'd just checked out. I'd intended to leave via the window, but when I tried to open it, the frame stuck halfway.

Fuck.

The footsteps stopped right outside the door.

Double fuck.

I had two options—recreate the shower scene from *Psycho* or hide behind the door. The former offered a chance of escaping detection, but the latter meant I'd have more control. Silencing somebody from a foot away was infinitely easier than doing so from across the room. I'd be able to subdue the insomniac and escape, but discovery would make returning a hell of a lot harder. If Tabesh increased security, I might have to wait for months until he let his guard down again.

But I was a patient man.

The handle turned, and self-preservation kicked in. Better to take a short-term setback and live to fight another day.

CHAPTER 8

RO

A figure clad in a pale abaya glided in, one arm outstretched towards the light switch. I wrapped one arm around the woman's chest—it was definitely a woman—and clamped my other hand over her mouth. Quick as a flash, she bit my finger, and I clenched my jaw to keep from cursing.

"Stay still," I murmured in Pashto. "I won't hurt you."

She went stiff in my arms, then relaxed. I risked loosening my hand.

"Ro?" she whispered.

Bloody hell. "Ziya?"

I spun her around and hugged her tight against me. Then it was my turn to freeze. Last time I saw her, she'd been slender, a touch too thin, but now? She'd definitely put on weight. Was Tabesh providing better food, or...?

I raised her chin so she looked at me. The moonlight filtering through the high window let me see her shy smile.

"How did you get in?" she asked. "There are guards."

"There are? I climbed over the wall, and I didn't see anyone. Guess I must've got lucky."

Would Ziya buy the story? She'd always been trusting, too trusting. I'd used that to my advantage before, something that had bothered my conscience at the time and now left me mired in guilt. But I had no choice other than to rely on her naivety again. To carry on with the charade I'd started eleven months ago.

Luckily, she nodded, accepting my explanation. "What are you doing here?"

"I wanted to check that you were okay," I said, sticking with Pashto. Ziya's English was good, but she didn't need the added stress of trying to translate my words tonight. "Ziya, are you pregnant?"

A quick nod. Shit. My first thought? *This changes everything.* But did it really? Secretly, I'd harboured hopes of getting her out of there, but she'd already turned me down once.

And if I was honest, her rejection had been a lucky escape. When I took a step back, away from the weird pull Ziya exhibited, I understood that our being together would have been a logistical nightmare. She didn't have a British passport, so I would have had to stay in Afghanistan for the foreseeable future. Her family wouldn't have condoned the relationship, not in a million years, plus Tabesh would have put a price on my head and probably hers as well. Oh, and I'd lied to her about almost everything.

Sometimes, I wished I'd been truthful from the start. But I'd been selfish. I'd felt a desperate need to atone for what happened to Ziya's father, to keep my promise to him that I'd help, and that meant digging the well in Balaguri. Ziya and her family hated foreign soldiers with a passion— something I couldn't blame them for—and if they'd found out my background, I'd have been run out of the village before we'd even unloaded the truck. A few white lies had seemed the obvious solution. I'd never imagined things might spiral this far out of control.

So yes, Ziya's decision to marry Tabesh had been for the best. No, nothing *had* changed, not for the two of us. Nothing except the crack in my heart—that grew a little deeper.

At least she's all right, Ro. Physically, at least. The question was, did she know about Balaguri?

"Uh, congratulations."

"You shouldn't have come. Are you crazy? Tabesh will kill you if he finds you."

"Tabesh is sleeping off his hangover. Is he treating you well?"

Again, she nodded, but the moon revealed her lie. I wiped away the single tear with my thumb, leaving a shiny track down her cheek.

"If he's laid a hand on you..."

"At the moment, it's okay. He makes me rest. For the baby. The others do the work."

"Right, the other wives. I guess that's sensible with your condition. Uh, how pregnant are you? I mean, how far along?"

I'd felt heartache once before. The gouging Ziya had given me on my last night in Balaguri had hurt worse than a bullet—I knew that from experience. But now that painful throb in my chest, the one I thought had dulled with time, started afresh. Ziya had a family now, even if her husband was an arsehole of the highest order. *Had* he abandoned Balaguri? Decided not to honour a deal made with a dead man? Or had Akif simply failed to call him? I didn't know what to think, but even if Tabesh *had* broken his word, what could I do about it? I was just a washed-up soldier turned part-time spy who should have stayed in Kabul.

Ziya wrapped her arms around my waist and burrowed her face against my chest. "I thought I'd never see you again. I wish... I wish..."

"You wish what, Zizi?"

"I wish I'd never come here."

"You do?"

"The other women are mean." Ziya switched to English. "And Tabesh is a right tosser."

I chuckled against her hijab, even though it was no laughing matter. The way she stuffed the most British of insults into conversation never failed to amuse me. Her former flatmate had a lot to answer for. During our evening tête-à-têtes, Ziya had confessed the details of her time in Jalalabad, including her friendship with Nancy and their secret Netflix marathons.

But I quickly grew serious again. How much had Tabesh told Ziya about recent events in Balaguri? Did he know the village had been destroyed? I had a hard time believing he didn't. Tabesh's spies lurked everywhere.

"Sweetheart, Tabesh might be even more of a tosser than we originally thought. Has he mentioned Balaguri in the past few days?"

Ziya shook her head. "Last week when I asked if I could visit my family, he said maybe next month, but he won't let me. He never does."

"You haven't been back at all?"

Another shake of the head. "Have *you* been there? I'm worried about Uncle. Remember how he hurt his ankle before I left? I told him he should rest, but he always knows best."

What the fuck? Tabesh hadn't even told her that Shafiq

was dead? I took Ziya's "tosser" and raised it to "traitorous maggot."

"Oh, sweetheart." I held her just a little bit tighter. "I don't... Where should I start?"

She must have caught the dread in my tone. "What? What happened?"

"I came here from Balaguri. Ziya, there's nobody left there. A few days ago, the—"

"What do you mean, there's nobody left? My family would never leave."

"Shh," I reminded. "Keep your voice soft."

"Sorry. I'm sorry, but what happened?"

I laid out the basics as succinctly as I could, but there was no way of making the news sound anything less than horrific. Tonight, Ziya was wearing a simple scarf over her head, and I used one end of the cloth to wipe away her tears. Her entire life had been one tragedy after another.

"They're gone? *All* gone? This marriage was for nothing? Why didn't Tabesh tell me that Uncle had died? I missed the *funeral*. And my aunt, she would have been alone with no money."

"I heard a rumour your brother is still alive." Although I couldn't say who I'd heard it from, of course. "He was providing for your aunt."

A tiny note of hope sounded in Ziya's voice. "Yafir is alive? I need to see him."

"That might not be so easy. He wasn't at Balaguri, and my source said he might have joined the KLA."

"The KLA?" Ziya sagged in my arms, and I took her weight, all too aware of Tabesh's child sandwiched between us. I suppose her pregnancy shouldn't have surprised me, but it did dash any residual fantasies I'd had of snatching Ziya and disappearing into the sunset. Being spurned by a wife would infuriate a thug like Tabesh, but losing a child would turn him positively homicidal. He'd send his entire army after us, and while he might kill me relatively quickly, Ziya would suffer the consequences until the baby was born.

And then there was the small matter of Her Majesty's Government. The powers that be wouldn't be too pleased if one of their sleeper agents abandoned his post to start a war with a drug trafficker.

When I handed in my resignation from the army, MI6 had tried to recruit me, but I'd rejected their advances in favour of going back to school. I'd had enough of that world. But then they came up with a compromise. The Mansfield Foundation, which was basically a bunch of spooks with a slush fund disguised as a charity, would provide training in espionage as well as funding my studies at an institution in a mutually agreed country if I'd only keep an ear to the ground and pass along any tidbits of information that happened to come my way. And possibly, just possibly—if an urgent need arose—get my hands dirty in an emergency.

Heaven help me, I'd accepted. The package they offered was too good to turn down, and deep down inside, I still agreed with the coalition's loftiest goal—to bring peace to the Middle East and Asia—even if I didn't agree with some of their methods. And I knew first-hand that intelligence could save lives.

The transition had been seamless. One day I was a soldier, the next, a spy. I'd been meeting with Marina while I was still in the army, and my cover was established and ready to go. To give the people at the Foundation their credit, they'd mostly left me alone once I got to Afghanistan. I checked in with Marina every few weeks and focused on my research. So far, she'd asked me to do one sneak-and-peek—a snoop around a house in downtown Kabul—and that was all.

And that snoop had been worth the effort. Under cover of darkness, I'd slipped into a three-storey home that would have been considered luxurious by Afghan standards but nondescript in any western country. Nondescript apart from the pile of Kalashnikovs in the lounge and the anti-tank guided missile in the downstairs bathroom. I'd passed the information on, and then it was out of my hands. Somebody else got to do the tricky part. Easy money, and if I was honest, it hadn't been a bad arrangement until now. I got on okay with Marina. She was an irreverent, no-nonsense former MI6 agent who'd moved to the Foundation after an accident in the field left her reliant on a wheelchair. And unlike many spooks, she tended to give it to you straight rather than talking in riddles.

"I'll ask around about Yafir. I heard the people who survived the…" What did I call it? "Massacre" was an appropriate descriptor, but Ziya was upset enough without hearing such a stark term. "…the events at Balaguri fled to Jalalabad. I'll see if I can find them. Someone might know how to contact your brother."

Ziya hadn't let go of me since I arrived. So many nights, I'd dreamed of having her in my arms again, but not under these circumstances. I'd much rather Balaguri was still standing even if it meant staying away from her forever.

She nodded and swiped at her face with a hand. "Why are you still helping me?"

"Because I care about you. I'll always care about you, treasure."

"Treasure?"

"You're very precious to me."

"I wish I'd gone with you that night. I thought... I thought I'd be protecting my family, from shame and from harm, and now... It's too late, isn't it?"

My turn to nod. "Tabesh might be a tosser, but he's your husband and the father of your baby. He'd kill both of us."

"I think... I think he'll kill me anyway, because I'm almost certain the baby isn't his."

Every atom in me froze as I processed Ziya's words. Was she saying what I thought she was saying? The night we'd slept together, she'd been a virgin, and she'd married Tabesh two days later. If he wasn't the father, then...

"It's mine?"

"Tabesh is infertile. Either that or all of his other wives are. And the timing fits."

"Are you...?" I trailed off. Ziya was practically a doctor. Of course she was sure, or as sure as she could be.

Bloody fucking hell. Now this, this *did* change everything. My birth mother had abandoned me—in a Selfridges carrier bag on a church altar, no less—and I wouldn't, *couldn't*, do that to my own child. And Ziya was right—if Tabesh even suspected she'd been unfaithful, she was a dead woman. This wasn't the UK. I couldn't wait until she gave birth and then have a custody battle. If I wanted my child to have a chance, I had to fight now. Plus I'd promised Adil that I'd help his family, something I'd failed at spectacularly until today.

I closed my eyes and pressed my lips to Ziya's forehead. "I'll get you out of here."

"Tonight?"

"No, not tonight. I have to plan things."

Hand in my notice at the university. Come up with a story for the Mansfield Foundation. Cash in some investments.

Work out how the hell I was going to get Ziya out of Afghanistan because sure as hell neither of us could stay here. I still had a contact or two left from my military days. Favours owing. Then somehow, *somehow* I'd have to rearrange my life to resemble the one I'd foolishly described to Ziya. Trade in my motorcycle for the hatchback I'd claimed to own. Get to know Robert Kemp's home town of Swindon. Rent a house. Buy some fake tennis trophies and a racquet or two. Add a few fake photos of my fake dog, the one who'd passed from old age last year. Fuck, I couldn't even remember its name.

"You'll really come back?" Ziya asked.

"I will, I promise. We'll need to work out a way to communicate. If I give you my phone, is there somewhere safe you can hide it?"

The phone's battery was almost full. If Ziya turned it on for a couple of minutes each day at a set time, it should last for weeks.

"I can hide it with the chickens. Tabesh lets me collect the eggs in the afternoons. We don't have a cell signal here, but I can connect to the Wi-Fi for messages. Will you be able to get another phone?"

I had a spare plus a secure satellite phone in the Land Rover. "Yes."

Hell, were we really doing this? Cold dread settled in my stomach, a heavy weight on top of the horror that had taken up residence the moment I'd crested the hill to Balaguri, but there was something else too. A frisson of excitement, the same buzz I used to feel at the beginning of a job in the good old days at Stirling Lines.

And also an interloper: fear.

I tried to stay positive as I talked her through a basic code. Each morning, I'd message her a number. A one meant stand down, nothing was going to happen that day. A two let her know she had to meet me in the bathroom again—apparently the baby made her pee all the time, so nobody would think her nocturnal wanderings were unusual. A three? She needed to pack her belongings because we'd be leaving that night.

A quick check of my watch told me we'd spent almost half an hour together, which was both too long and not long enough. But at least we had a plan, and the baby wasn't due for four and a half months. As long as I could get her out in three, that should give us enough time to get out of Dodge.

"I need to make a move."

She stood on tiptoes to kiss my cheek. "There's something else before you go."

"What, treasure?"

"There was another woman here yesterday. An American."

"A visitor?"

"A prisoner. She was locked in a room."

Holy fuck. Tabesh was kidnapping foreigners now?

"What did she look like?"

"I didn't see her, but I heard her speak. And I found some of her hairs afterwards. Blonde hairs."

There was only one American woman missing in the area that I was aware of. The wildlife journalist. Her picture had been on the news, and her hair was practically platinum.

"She's gone now?"

"A guard said she was going to Deraz. Men came to collect her, and they left in a truck. Can you tell someone? The police?"

Marina. "Yes, I can tell someone. Did the guard say anything else?"

A quick shake of the head. "I ran away."

"Good. That's good, Zizi. You need to stay safe. Don't take any risks."

"Okay."

"Go back to bed, and I'll contact you tomorrow."

"Uh, I still need to..."

To pee. Of course she did. Fuck, this was a disaster waiting to happen. Quite apart from the logistical challenges, I'd never lived with a woman before, and I'll admit that I didn't entirely understand them. My relationships, if you could call them that, were usually measured in days if not hours. Hell, I'd never even kissed Ziya properly. The sex had been a fumble in the dark where I'd struggled to stay hard while waiting for Uncle Shafiq to come out and shoot me, and she didn't even know my real name. Or my former occupation. I'd told her I worked for a waste disposal company before transitioning to academia, which wasn't a total lie, but I might have been a little hazy about the type of waste I disposed of.

Yes, I'd asked her to leave with me before, but I'd known in my heart of hearts that she'd never accept. And I'd never thought I'd see a day where things would be any different, so coming clean hadn't exactly been a priority. The only option I had was to engineer a plan where I'd become Robert Kemp for good. The Mansfield Foundation had given me the option of studying in Iran or Pakistan instead of Afghanistan, so it looked as if a move to Tehran was on the cards unless I could talk them into a less volatile posting.

I brought Ziya's hand to my lips. Now wasn't the time to try any fancy moves. "I'll see you soon."

"I'll miss you."

That was the first time I'd smiled in two days. "I'll miss you too."

But not for long. Because "soon" came a lot quicker than either of us anticipated.

CHAPTER 9

ZIYA

I felt the slightest draught as the bedroom door opened. My chest seized. Who was it? A guard? They weren't meant to be in here. But what if someone had realised I'd been with Ro and come to punish me? I felt for the phone hidden beneath the long dress I wore in the house. Should I message Ro to return? *No, stupid, you can't because he gave you his phone.*

If it hadn't been for the phone, I'd have thought I was dreaming. Which would have been both a good thing and a bad thing. Ro had come back for me, but my family was dead and my brother was missing. The grief hadn't hit me yet. At the moment, I was still numb inside, but I knew that in a day, or maybe two days, the pain would roll over me like a slow wave. That's how it had been before, first with my mother and then with my father. And each time, the wave washed away pieces of my soul, fragments of my heart that I'd never get back.

The man's shadow passed in front of the window. Dina liked to sleep with the curtains open so she could watch the sunrise, and when I saw his silhouette outlined against the moon, my whole body jolted. I recognised that outline. The straight nose. The messy hair I'd just been running my fingers through. Why was Ro in our freaking bedroom? Daneen was snoring, but Dina was a light sleeper, and if she opened her eyes...

Ro hesitated, studying each mattress in turn. When his gaze landed on me, I raised my hand, and he crossed the room, his footsteps totally silent. What had happened? He wouldn't be here unless there was a problem.

He crouched beside me, and his lips brushed my ear as he whispered, "We're leaving right now."

What? Why? I wanted to ask, but I couldn't. Beads of sweat popped out on the back of my neck. This was soon, too soon. I hadn't packed. Hadn't even planned what I'd take. And Dina was still wearing my treasured necklace.

But Ro wasn't kidding, and if I didn't go with him, I might lose my only chance to escape. I had no choice. And I trusted him. Apart from my father and occasionally my brother, he was the only man in my life who'd ever shown me any respect.

I peeled back my quilt and quickly slipped the photos I had of my family into my bra, then reached for my burqa. The only thing stranger than a woman creeping around the countryside at night would be a woman creeping around the countryside at night without a veil. But Ro shook his head and pulled the burqa away.

What? Why?

He flipped through the small stack of clothing on the shelf at the end of my mattress and tossed me a different robe, dark grey instead of light blue. Right. Of course. If we were trying to sneak out, blending into the darkness sure would help. At least one of us was thinking straight. Perhaps we'd even live to see the morning?

Or not. As I went to tug the new burqa over my head, Dina stirred, and I froze. Was she waking?

No, but moonlight glinted off my gold pendant, and I gritted my teeth. I couldn't leave it behind. No way. It was my only connection to my grandma. To Balaguri. I crawled towards Dina on my hands and knees before Ro could stop me, trying to work out how on earth I could get the necklace over Dina's head without her noticing. The gold piece hung on a new leather cord, knotted at the ends, and Dina had a lot of curly hair. Maybe I could undo the knot?

Ro's foot landed in front of me, and he frantically shook his head. I nodded in response. Yes, I had to do this. Even if I could speak, he'd never understand why the necklace was so important to me, so it was best to just get on with the task.

I carefully felt my way along the cord until I found the knot and started picking at it. It was tight, too tight. Dammit! Perhaps if I lifted Dina's head an inch?

The softest *snick* sounded right next to me, and I realised Ro had a knife in his hand. A knife? Since when had he carried a knife? In Balaguri, he'd always borrowed my brother's. But the knife sliced through the cord, and I tugged gently, my heart pounding against my ribcage. I didn't need anything else, just my gold piece and my shoes, which were by the door. I could practically taste freedom.

Then Dina's eyes popped open.

I froze. She froze. Then her lips parted, and I knew she'd scream or yell and everyone in the house would come running with the possible exception of Tabesh because he was both lazy and drunk. Yes, alcohol was haram, but he only paid attention to the parts of the Quran he liked and ignored the rest.

So I panicked. I panicked and I grabbed the wooden bowl Dina kept her jewellery in, tipped out all the trinkets, and whacked her over the head with it. She slumped back onto the mattress, her head lolling to one side.

Son of a motherless goatherd, what had I done?

I didn't have a chance to think because Ro picked me up and carried me out of the room. In the hallway, he pressed a warning finger to my lips, but I'd already got the message. Stay quiet. He clearly knew his way around the house, and we headed straight for the side door, the one nearest to the chicken coop. Ro paused, listening before he turned the handle, and I took the opportunity to whisper in his ear.

"My shoes."

He lowered me to the floor but kept hold of my hand as I slid my feet into a pair of plain slippers. Flip-flops would make too much noise. Ro shook his head and pointed at Dina's sneakers instead. I was about to tell him they weren't mine, but what did it matter? I'd hit her on the head with a freaking bowl. Stealing her shoes paled into insignificance beside that. I tried the sneakers on for size— a little loose, but at least I could run in them if it came to that.

"Stay behind me," Ro instructed. "Keep your eyes on the back of my head. Don't look anywhere else."

I nodded because when a man gave me an instruction I *always* nodded, but when we got outside, of course I cast my gaze sideways. One of the chickens was still out. Susu— she was a pain in the neck who hated being locked away at night. I usually coaxed her into the coop with bread, but Daneen couldn't be bothered and just left her free instead. Now Susu was pecking at something in the dirt beside a bush. Leftover corn? I squinted through the mesh panel in my veil. No, a foot.

Wait. A...what?

I followed the line of the man's leg into the darkness, and the pale, lifeless eyes of a guard stared back at me. I recognised him as Azeez, who was a spiteful man the size of a water buffalo. Holy horse poop, he was dead? Pieces of the puzzle slammed into place. This was why Ro had come back, wasn't it? He'd tried to escape the compound but Azeez had spotted him, and somehow, the guard ended up dead. Was it an accident? Or had Ro killed him?

I felt sick at the thought. Horrified. Surely Ro wasn't capable? He'd always been so kind, so gentle. But how else could Azeez have died? A heart attack? An aneurysm? No, I just wasn't that lucky.

Should I turn back?

All the daydreams I'd had about Ro, all the fantasies I'd lost myself in, they'd been little more than wishful thinking. Fairy tales I'd created to avoid the realities of life in the compound. If I added up the moments we'd spent together, the total was measured in days rather than weeks. Had I misjudged his character? Maybe. But he *had* come back for me. And I knew for certain that Tabesh was a monster. He'd lied to me about Uncle Shafiq and then stood by while Balaguri was destroyed.

Hadn't he? I realised I only had Ro's word for that, but coupled with Tabesh's evasiveness... Yes, I believed Ro.

And even if Ro had played a part in Azeez's death, I could hardly judge, could I? Not when Dina was lying motionless inside. Was *she* dead? I hadn't meant to hurt her. I'd just panicked.

Ro tugged at my hand, and I forced myself to move. To follow him to the front gate. *To accept the lesser of two evils as my fate.* The gate opened silently, and for once, Tabesh deserved my thanks because he complained about the squeaking every other week and kept sending guards to put more oil on the hinges.

Then we were outside, and I hadn't been that side of the walls in four and a half long, long months. But there was no time to savour my freedom because Ro wrapped an arm around my waist and half carried me along beside him, staying in the shadows at the side of the rough track that led towards civilisation, such that it was.

"Do you have a vehicle?" I asked.

"Yes, a mile away. Are you able to walk?"

"What other option do I have?"

"I can carry you."

"No, I can walk."

We set off at a fast march, but I'd have run if it meant getting away from that place quicker. Neither of us spoke for at least ten minutes, but when the lights of Tabesh's home had faded away and only darkness surrounded us, I risked a question.

"Did you kill Azeez?"

"Shh."

I took that to mean "yes." Otherwise, why wouldn't he have said "no"? It had the same number of syllables. How did that make me feel? The fact that I might be on the run with a killer? It made me feel...confused. Not scared, because I didn't think Ro would hurt me. But I'd truly never thought he had it in him to take a life. In Balaguri, he'd even insisted on relocating the long-legged spiders from my aunt's home rather than squashing them. How did an office-worker-turned-student know how to kill a man efficiently? There'd been no noise. Not even the other guards had noticed Azeez's demise.

How well did I really know Ro?

The thought of finding out the answer, that worried me.

But no matter what, I couldn't change the situation. There was no backward, only forward. Almost certain death versus a glimmer of hope.

Fuck.

Fuck, fuck, fuck.

I'd told Ziya to keep her eyes on me, but she hadn't listened. Usually, I liked her rebellious streak, but not tonight.

Had that damned chicken attracted her attention the same way it had drawn the guard's? I'd ducked down beside a bush when I heard his footsteps heading in my direction, only for the thing to start squawking. Of course, the goon had turned to look straight at me. I should have snapped the bird's scrawny neck when I'd had the chance. Going soft in my old age? Instead, instinct had taken over and I'd hooked an elbow around the guard's windpipe, squeezing with an iron grip until I'd choked the life out of him.

Can't change the past, Ro. I sighed as I skirted around a tree.

"It was him or me, Ziya."

And perhaps her as well, if Tabesh's men had realised

why I'd been there. But I didn't say that. No point in piling guilt onto a woman who didn't deserve it.

"I know," she said softly.

"I'd never hurt you."

I wanted her to say she knew that too, but she stayed silent. And in all honesty, I couldn't blame her. Tonight had been a clusterfuck from the start, and it wasn't over yet. Because of my cock-up, we were left running with no plan, and as soon as the guards discovered their colleague's cooling body, we'd have a drug dealer's psycho army after us. Maybe sooner if wife number one woke up. I'd been tempted to give her another tap on the head, but that would hardly have endeared me to Ziya.

I checked our six again. That necklace better have been worth the sacrifice. Yes, it had belonged to Ziya's grandma, and I understood how much Bushra had meant to her, but if it cost us vital time, if it meant the difference between freedom and hell on earth, I'd curse it for eternity.

Ziya tripped, and I shot out an arm to catch her. The full implications of what I'd done were beginning to hit now. My carelessness meant I could kiss my job goodbye—both my official post at the university and my shady side hustle. Somehow, I had to get Ziya to safety. No easy task in a land where foreigners were eyed with suspicion and loyalty was to clan, tribe, and country in that order, and I had to do it more or less alone. I say "more or less" because I had one bargaining chip, but to play it would mean making a deal with Marina, and I had no faith she'd play ball. Especially after I told her I was leaving Afghanistan and thereby rendering moot all the time and effort and money the British government had put into training me.

Oh, and on top of that, I was quite possibly going to be a father. If I lived that long, anyway.

"Are you okay?" I asked Ziya.

"Mmm."

Did that mean yes or no? I wasn't sure. And that was another problem—I really didn't know Ziya all that well. Yes, I was drawn to her, pulled in by an invisible thread I still didn't understand despite the number of nights I'd spent lying awake trying to unravel the mystery. But I had no idea what made her tick. How she might react in any given situation. Whether she'd come with me tonight because she genuinely liked me or just because she saw me as a slightly better option than Tabesh. And that made me mildly nervous.

She shrugged my arm away and kept walking.

Great.

My former commanding officer once told me that my impetuousness was a blessing and a curse. That although it had paid off so far—like the day I'd "borrowed" a helicopter and flown through a hail of bullets to rescue an injured colleague with only fumes left in the tank—one day the trait would bite me in the arse. Was today that day? Quite possibly. The distant sound of a vehicle engine reached my ears, and I pulled Ziya into a scrubby clump of trees. Traffic was almost non-existent at this time of night, and the road led only to Tabesh's compound and a handful of small farms. Was he calling in reinforcements?

"What is it?" Ziya whispered.

"Engine."

No vehicle travelled fast over this terrain, so rather than wait for an indeterminate amount of time for the car or truck to appear, I motioned to Ziya to follow me through the undergrowth. Every second counted, and we needed to put as much distance between us and our soon-to-be pursuers as possible.

Movement ahead caught my eye, and I grabbed Ziya's arm automatically as the shape took on a human form. My gun was in my other hand before my brain caught up with my instincts. Ziya pulled back, but I couldn't afford to lose focus, not with a potential enemy ahead. I clamped my left hand around her wrist. Having to chase her back to Tabesh's compound was *not* in tonight's game plan.

The figure ahead turned to look at us, his stance relaxed, his movements unhurried. Empty hands hung by his sides. When I squinted, I could just about make out the bullet hole in his forehead, the congealed blood tracking down one cheek. Ah, fuck. Another bloody ghost. I put the gun away and turned my attention back to Ziya.

"Sorry, false alarm."

"You have a gun."

It came out flat. A statement.

"I do."

"But you said you didn't like guns."

Well, I wasn't exactly an enthusiast. I didn't have a hand-tooled leather holster or a subscription to *Guns & Ammo* magazine. Even when I was a new recruit, eager to right wrongs and serve my country, I hadn't been all that gung-ho. I'd much preferred flying. Now that I was old and jaded, I saw firearms as tools, nothing more.

"Sometimes, they're a necessary evil."

"You know how to shoot?"

"Yes."

"How?"

Should I tell her the truth? I wanted to, but if she got upset, that would put us both in danger. Once we were in the Land Rover, I'd have to confess, but coward that I was, I didn't mind putting off the inevitable for a few more minutes.

"Let's discuss this when we're safe."

I might not have been able to see her eyes through the burqa's mesh panel, but I sure did feel her glare searing into me. For all Ziya's fragility, she had an inner fire that had proven difficult to extinguish. I had a feeling I might get burned very soon.

We carried on through the scrubby woodland, Ziya tripping every so often because she couldn't see very well. Part of me wanted to suggest taking off the veil, at least temporarily, but I wasn't sure how she'd react. Yes, I'd seen her briefly without it in the bedroom at Tabesh's folly and she hadn't seemed upset, but her mind had to be in turmoil right now. Would stress harm the baby? Every step I took, I cursed myself for putting us in this position.

We reached the Land Rover as the first glimmer of sunrise fought its way over the Safed Koh, a thin white band where rock met sky, where freedom met oppression. I breathed a long sigh of relief and trepidation. We could start the next stage of our journey, but I also had to confess my sins to Ziya. I felt her wary gaze on me as I helped her into the passenger seat.

Where should I begin?

By driving away, that would be a good start. I turned the engine over, thankful that there was no traffic in sight when I pulled out onto the unpaved road. Ziya hadn't said a word since the gun/ghost incident, and I wasn't sure whether to take that as a good sign or a bad sign.

Half an hour of silence later, we'd put ten kilometres between us and Tabesh's digs, and I'd decided the lack of communication was definitely a negative. Ziya sat with her arms wrapped around herself, defensive, her frostiness a far cry from the cosy reunion we'd shared in the bathroom. Had that really only been two hours ago? I'd aged at least a decade in the time since. Eleven years, I'd been in the army, nine of them in special forces, and yet it was a woman who'd brought me to my knees.

"So..." I started.

Ziya's head swivelled in my direction.

"So, I guess I'd better start at the beginning."

CHAPTER 11

ZIYA

What had I done? What had I done? *What had I done?*

Two hours ago, I'd been happy. Happy that the man I loved had come back to me. Now I realised that Robert Kemp wasn't the man I'd thought he was. His sweet words, his kind gestures, they'd all been erased when we left Tabesh's house.

Not only because of Azeez—I realised from my own actions with Dina that anyone was capable of lashing out in a panic—but also because of what happened outside the gates. Ro had changed. Literally morphed into a different person. The way he'd moved, quick, confident, and stealthy, told me he'd lied. Ro had no more worked in an office than I had. Everything about him screamed "military."

And then he'd produced a gun. A pistol. How many people had he killed with it? How many of my people had he fought against?

How had I been so stupid?

I'd fallen for his lies. Believed him when he said he

wanted to help Balaguri. And worst of all, I'd begged him to take my virginity.

Life with Tabesh had been like sitting in a pot of water over the fire, unable to climb out while it slowly warmed, just waiting for death. Then Ro had offered me a ladder, but instead of escaping to freedom, I'd landed in the flames themselves. And now I was trapped. Trapped beside him as we drove along the narrow road that clung to the side of a mountain. I couldn't go back to Tabesh, I wouldn't survive alone, and the man I'd thought I loved had betrayed me. Let's start at the beginning, Ro said. Why? To remind me how foolish I'd been? Grandma had always said I was too trusting, and she'd been right, hadn't she? If it weren't for the baby, I'd have jumped out of the moving truck and prayed for a swift end.

"Ziya, I didn't mean for it to be this way."

For once, I was glad to be wearing a burqa. It meant Ro couldn't see my tears. But I could see his eyes in the mirror. Those beautiful blue eyes I'd once thought were so kind. Now they were two hard chips of cobalt.

"You lied."

"Yes." He paused. "And I'm sorry, Zizi."

"Don't call me that!" I snapped, then recoiled on instinct. In my world, speaking my mind meant punishment, from Tabesh and from my uncle before him. Even my father would have been unimpressed.

But Ro's only reaction was a tightening of his jaw. "I'm sorry, Ziya."

I let out the breath I'd been holding and made an effort to soften my voice. To be polite, even though Ro didn't deserve it.

"Then why did you do it?"

"Because if you knew who I was, your family wouldn't

have accepted my help, no matter how much the village needed a well." He turned to look at me, just for a second. "Would you?"

Would we? Back when the well project had been proposed, Uncle Shafiq had still been going on nightly rants about foreign invaders and how he'd strangle any soldier who set foot in Balaguri with his bare hands. Even when they passed through in trucks, he'd made a point of shaking his fist at them. No, Uncle would have refused the well on principle. After all, it wasn't him who had to fetch the water.

But that didn't excuse Ro's lies.

"Why didn't you just build a well in a different village?"

"Because..." Ro let out a long sigh. "Because I promised your father I'd help Balaguri. I promised him I'd help his family."

"You...you knew my father?"

"Not knew him, exactly. I met him just before he died."

All the little pieces fell into place. My father... Shot... Soldiers... *Just before he died.* I let out a gasp.

"You were one of the men who killed my father, and Malyar too!" I fumbled with the seat belt Ro had made me wear.

"I didn't—"

"Stop. Stop! Let me out!"

"We're not stopping."

"I'm not staying!"

"Ziya, listen—"

How dare he? My whole life, men had told me what to do. They'd beaten me down, stolen my free will. Well, they could all become black dust along with me. If I was going to die, I'd at least do it on my own terms. I grabbed the steering wheel and yanked, but Ro's grip was tighter than I thought, and instead of sailing off the side of the mountain, we skidded into a rock. Dammit. Dammit! I couldn't even get that right.

"May lightning strike you dead and dogs devour the pieces!" I cried.

"Bloody hell, woman."

"I hate you."

Ro grabbed my hand, leaned across me, and before I could breathe or think, he'd attached me to the seat belt with a thin band of plastic.

"Get that off me! What are you doing?"

"What am I doing? Thanks to your efforts, we've got a puncture, and I'm stopping you from jumping off this cliff while I change the wheel." He shook his head sadly as he opened the door. "I didn't kill your father, Ziya."

"Perhaps not with your own hands, but you helped."

"I was stuck in traffic behind him at the checkpoint. I tried to stop the man who pulled the trigger, but I didn't act fast enough. That's something I'll always regret."

Ro climbed out and slammed the door behind him. A moment later, I heard him scraping around in the cargo area, and the truck jostled as he began to jack it up. He seemed to be taking this calmly. Too calmly. A girl I'd gone to school with had married a man from three villages away, and he never used to yell at her. Never, not once. We all thought she was the luckiest girl in the world until we received word of her funeral. She'd left the house without permission, and he'd gone crazy.

Had *I* gone crazy? I had, hadn't I? I'd lost my mind and nearly killed two people. No, three people. My belly fluttered again, reminding me of my son's presence. Only Ro's strength had saved us. Now the tears came thick and fast, and I began shaking. My whole world had spun out of control. In some ways, life as a woman in Afghanistan was easy. Not pleasant, but easy. We had no choices to make. No responsibilities other than to raise our children and please our husbands. No need to think, just do, do, do. But now I was adrift with Ro, who didn't act like any other man I'd ever known.

I had no idea how to behave.

Outside, he was crouching a cat's length away from the cliff's edge, undoing the damaged wheel. I felt sick looking out the window, and not only because of the sheer drop. Now that I knew the gun was in his pocket, I couldn't unsee it. The way it pulled at his waistcoat. Weighed it down. A necessary evil, Ro had called it, but who else did he plan to kill?

The truck dipped as he climbed back in, and I could hardly look at him. But I didn't miss the glint of the knife he pulled from his other pocket.

"If I cut you free, are you going to test out your driving skills again?"

"No."

"Put your seat belt on."

"Is the truck okay? Apart from the wheel, I mean."

"Thankfully, yes."

"I'm sorry for what I did."

"Aren't we all?" Another sigh, and he started the engine. "Ziya, I won't beat about the bush here. We're in a world of trouble, and we'll only survive if we work with each other rather than against each other."

"I know that."

"I understand why you're angry. Hell, I'm angry with myself. But I can't turn back the clock. If I could, there are a hundred things I'd do differently, but I'm not sorry I went to Balaguri because otherwise I'd never have met you. Do I regret the circumstances of my visit? Yes. But not the visit itself."

Ro pulled back onto the rock-and-mud road as I digested these latest snippets of information.

"My father really asked you to come?"

"I'll spare you the details, but there came a point when he understood he wouldn't make it back himself. And yes, he asked me to help. That was also the moment I realised I couldn't keep fighting, not the way I had been. War's not the answer. I don't know what *is* the answer, but sending poorly trained armed teenagers into a situation they don't understand and aren't equipped to de-escalate isn't it. Bombing from afar with drones isn't it. Pulling SAS operatives off precision raids to hold local forces' hands isn't it. Commanding officers paying more attention to politics than to conditions on the ground isn't it."

"Are you really a student?"

Ro nodded. "Only by making an effort to understand each other can we achieve peace."

"The Taliban don't want peace. Only war."

"I'm not a complete pacifist. There are occasions when action is necessary. But I'm talking carefully planned surgical strikes like Operation Jubilee or Operation Neptune Spear, not farces like Operation Enduring Freedom. *Freedom*," Ro snorted. "They got the 'enduring' part right, but thirteen years after it started, still nobody was fucking free. They simply renamed it and started over. Troops go home, and then they come right back again." He glanced sideways. "Sorry. As you can probably tell, I feel quite strongly about these things."

That was better than being a warmonger, at least. "Okay."

"Are you? Okay, I mean."

My eyes prickled again, and I pressed my veil against them to blot the tears. Before Ro, the last person to ask if I was okay had been Grandma. She used to hug me whenever I felt down. Yafir used to hug me too when he was younger, but since he'd grown into a teenager, he'd become ever more distant.

"Of course I'm not okay. How can I be? I don't have a home anymore. Or money, or food."

"I'll take care of all that. The next few days might be a bit dicey, but we'll get through them."

"What's 'dicey'?"

"Unpredictable. Perhaps a little dangerous. I realise I have no right to ask this, but please, will you trust me?"

"I don't have a choice, do I?"

"From now on, you'll always have a choice. It would just make life easier if we weren't fighting each other as well as Tabesh's men, the Mujahideen, the Taliban, the Afghan army, and whoever else we happen across between here and Kabul."

"We're going to Kabul?"

"It's either that or head through the Khyber Pass to Pakistan. And I'm more familiar with Kabul."

Well, I'd never travelled farther than Jalalabad. No matter what Ro might have said about choices, I really didn't have any other options, not at the moment.

"Is there anything else you've lied to me about?"

The silence was deafening. A tangible thing that spread through the cab and pushed its way into my lungs.

"Tell me."

"There's more," he confirmed. "But I can't tell you. Not right now."

"You're asking me to trust you, but you won't trust me?"

"No, that's not it. That's not it at all. Ziya, it's for your own protection. If you don't know anything, then nobody can force it out of you."

My breath hitched, and a chill ran through me. This was bad. Really bad. Why all the secrecy? There was only one reason I could think of. Since I'd jumped to the wrong conclusion earlier, I forced myself to slow down. To run through the possibilities instead of just reacting. But every path I went along, I still ended up back at the same place.

"You're a spy," I whispered. "A freaking spy. Aren't you?"

His answer was to stomp on the brakes.

"What are you doing?" I shrieked as I slid forward in my seat, one arm over my stomach.

"Stopping before you try to send us into outer space again."

"I'm not going to do that. But you *are* a spy, aren't you? Ro? Is your name even Robert?"

"Rohan." The word came out of him grudgingly, barbed wire that stuck in his throat.

"Rohan. Ro?"

"Still Ro," he confirmed. "And I'm not a spy. Not in the conventional sense. I just...listen out for things. Information. Like your tip about the woman Tabesh sent to Deraz."

"You've reported it already? Someone will rescue her?"

"Not yet. I'll call my contact as soon as we have enough breathing space to stop."

He *was* a spy. Maybe a junior spy, but a spy nonetheless. Yes, I understood why he couldn't tell me all the details. I wasn't even sure I wanted to know them, but it still hurt to be left in the dark. Perhaps I should also have been upset that he was working against Afghanistan, but my country was a shell of what it had once been. And the blonde woman's cries… I couldn't get them out of my head.

"Why not call it in as we go?"

"Some conversations need to happen in private."

That knife he'd jabbed into my back twisted. *So many secrets. So many lies.*

"What about the rest? Do you really go canoeing on the weekends? What about Tinker? Is she dead?"

"Tinker?"

"Your dog. Or should I say imaginary dog? Please, will you just stop lying?" For the first time in public, I flipped my veil back over my head, feeling a freedom I hadn't experienced since my days in Jalalabad when I wore a chador instead of a full burqa. Then I looked Ro in the eye. "Do you think I'm dead from the neck up?"

As soon as the words left my lips, I froze. They'd just popped out. If I'd spoken that way in front of Tabesh, I'd have been black and blue by now. But Ro only laughed. Perhaps for all of his faults, he wasn't absolutely awful.

"Sorry," I whispered.

"Nothing to be sorry for." Ro cleared his throat. "I'm not keen on canoeing. And I've never lived in Swindon. Or grown my own vegetables. And my preferred mode of transport is a motorcycle."

"I always thought you weren't very good at planting things."

When he'd helped in the fields on that first visit, he'd gotten confused between weeds and corn. And he didn't know how to harness a donkey either.

"Ouch."

"So, just to be clear—you've lied about, well, everything, but I'm supposed to trust you anyway because otherwise I'm a dead woman walking?"

He shrugged, almost apologetically it seemed. "I won't lie again. There may be things I can't discuss, but I promise I won't lie. That's the best I can do at the moment."

The words he didn't say spoke volumes. Yes, I'd die without his help.

"As I said, I have no choice but to accept your terms." I flipped down my veil and folded my arms over my bump. "*Now* can we carry on?"

CHAPTER 12

RO

Sometimes, I forgot just how smart Ziya could be. And how persuasive. I'd broken the number-one rule of espionage by revealing my identity, and all because of her charms. Sure, it had been tempting to carry on lying, but if I did, I'd kiss any chance of a future with her goodbye. And I wanted a future with her. I couldn't stay away. The fire that smouldered inside her was a beacon to my soul, even though I knew I'd get burned.

I pulled back onto the road. At the moment, I had one goal—to get us both to a place of safety—and I had to focus on that.

"What about my brother?" Ziya asked softly.

Ah, fuck.

"Treasure, we don't even know where he is." Or whether he was still alive, for that matter.

"I'm the only family he has left."

"Exactly. So we need to keep you safe."

"What if he tries to look for me? At Tabesh's home?"

Potentially, that could be a problem. If Tabesh saw a possibility of getting to Ziya through Yafir, he wouldn't hesitate to use the boy as leverage. But since Yafir had no idea where Ziya was, it wouldn't do Tabesh any good. Would he hurt Yafir out of spite? Possibly.

"Has Yafir been in touch since you got married?"

"Not that I know of. But maybe he tried and Tabesh didn't tell me?"

"In which case, he thinks you don't care enough to contact him back. So is he likely to try again?"

A muffled sob came from Ziya, and she pressed her hands to her eyes once more. Did she think I hadn't noticed the damp patches on the fabric? I hated seeing her so upset, but there wasn't a hell of a lot I could do about it at this particular moment.

"Ziya? I understand it hurts, but we need to talk this through."

"I don't know! I don't know whether he'd try again."

"But you know your brother."

"Not anymore. He changed after the shooting. Did you realise he was meant to be in the truck that day instead of Malyar? He feels that he could have saved Baba if he'd been there."

"He couldn't."

Another sob. "Well, he told me he would have tried, and that if he failed, at least he would have died with honour."

I wanted to stop again, to give Ziya a hug, but firstly, we didn't have time for that, and secondly, I'd probably lose my testicles. Right now, I had to be happy with the fact that she was reasonably calm. Later, I could attempt to patch up our damaged relationship, such that it was.

"If I were in Yafir's position, I'd go to Balaguri first, especially if I'd heard rumours of the fighting. Once you're safe, I'll go back there and leave a message for him."

"What if he's already been?"

I didn't have an answer for that, not one Ziya would want to hear, anyway. "We'd better hope he hasn't. Let's hurry up and get to Kabul, okay?"

"Don't you need to sleep? You've been awake all night."

"If I get tired, I'll catnap for twenty minutes. But I've got caffeine pills and energy bars—those'll keep me going for now. You should sleep if you can, though. If I do take a rest, I'll need you to keep watch."

"I don't think I'll be able to sleep."

"Try. Please, Zizi."

The nickname slipped out, but she didn't call me on it this time. Was this progress? I certainly hoped so.

The sun was climbing higher in a brilliant blue sky now, its pale light coating the stark scenery like honey. This country was a land of contradictions—snow-capped mountains and lush green valleys and sandy deserts, quiet villages and colourful, bustling cities, bitter war and friendly hospitality from locals just trying to get on with their lives in the midst of chaos. After we left, would I ever come back here?

A half hour later, I found a shady spot behind a clump of evergreens and tucked the Land Rover under the branches. Time for a nap, but first I needed to speak to Marina. Despite Ziya's claims, she *had* drifted off, and rather than wake her, I closed the door quietly behind me and stepped a few feet away, standing guard. No harm would come to her on my watch.

I turned on the satellite phone. It was five a.m. in the UK, but Marina didn't keep regular office hours. And she'd told me to call her any time, day or night, so I didn't feel too guilty.

"It's Ro."

"Bit early for you, isn't it?" From the drowsiness in

Marina's voice, I guessed it was a bit early for her as well. "To what do I owe the pleasure?"

Marina was originally from Northern Ireland, and she hadn't lost the accent. But she did have a way of sounding perpetually peeved, even when things were going her way. And if things went my way today, she'd go from peeved to properly pissed off.

"I've got a lead on the American journalist who got kidnapped."

"What kind of a lead?"

"One of my contacts knows where she's been taken."

"Where?" Marina was fully awake now.

"See, now here's the thing. The information isn't free. There's a trade involved."

"A trade? We don't negotiate with terrorists."

"She's not a terrorist."

"She?"

"Women play a role in war. You of all people should understand that."

"Yes, but in Afghanistan? She's probably playing *you.* Everybody lies out there."

"I trust her."

A sigh from Marina. "Go on then, what does she want?"

"Safe passage to the UK, asylum when she gets there."

Marina gave a low whistle. "Not asking for much, then. Who is this woman?"

"I'm not sure—"

"Not that girl you installed the water pipe for?"

"Water pump," I said automatically, then bit my lip hard as the full meaning of Marina's words sank in. She knew about Ziya?

"Figures. Don't try to bullshit me, okay? I thought you

had more honour than that. And, quite frankly, it's insulting."

Fuck and double fuck. Yes, Marina was definitely annoyed now. "How do you even know about her?"

Marina's cackle only intensified the feeling of nausea. "You're not the only sleeper agent in Afghanistan. And the others tend to be more communicative."

"I'm sorry."

Marina ignored my half-arsed apology. "Didn't she get married? To a drug guy? Take my advice—if you're still in touch with her, make sure you stay under the radar because I hear we're running short on body bags over there."

"Might be a bit late for that," I muttered.

"Oh, for feck's sake. What happened?"

"She left him last night."

Marina let fly with a string of curses that would make a sailor blush. "And I suppose you helped her?"

"What can I say? I'm not one to leave a lady in distress."

"And they told me you'd be one of the easy ones to manage... Those arseholes." The *click, click, click* of a lighter told me Marina hadn't been successful in her attempts to quit smoking. "The drug guy—what's he called? Siddiqui?"

"Tabesh Siddiqui."

"He was involved in Katie Waller's abduction?"

"Seems that way. She was at his compound for a brief period."

"So your girl's info might well be good," Marina murmured, almost to herself. "But even if it is, I doubt I can do anything with it."

My stomach dropped like a cannonball from a diving board. "When I signed up, you sold the Foundation as a middleman whose members thought outside the box. And I know damn well you're connected to some powerful people." Rumours had abounded for years. Even before I'd been approached to work with the Mansfield Foundation, I'd known of their reputation. I'd met several of their operatives, or at least, I strongly suspected I had. The guy who'd guided my team to an arms dealer's stronghold one dark night in Iraq. The pair who'd delivered a trussed-up terrorist to us at an airstrip in Eritrea. A woman who'd passed me a flash drive in Libya. "Don't the Americans want to get their citizen back?"

"True, they do, but I doubt they'd take too kindly to one of our operatives negotiating himself a mail-order bride."

"She's not a mail-order bride," I snapped back.

"Whatever, it doesn't matter. Haven't you heard about the attacks?"

"What attacks?"

"A joint US/British patrol in Helmand province got ambushed by an armed militia last night. Plus the US and British embassies in Kabul got hit by suicide bombers, and word on the street says there's more fun and games planned for today and tomorrow. Every tinker, tailor, soldier, and spy in Afghanistan is hunting down the culprits right now. Nobody's got time to play knight in shining armour for a journalist who disobeyed government advice and strayed into the wrong place."

"Can't the Americans fly another team in?"

"In the next twenty-four hours? With President Indecisive at the helm? He's probably too busy playing golf to even take a briefing."

President McDonald had campaigned on a promise to get tough on enemies of the United States, but two years into his first term, he seemed more interested in photo ops than actual work. Which, to be fair, was probably for the best. Hell, last week he'd announced the US was sending troops to Oman when he meant Yemen, a mistake that nearly caused an international incident.

"I know the first twenty-four hours are the most critical, but even if a rescue team arrived in the next day or two, that's better than not coming at all."

"Feck, you really are out of the loop, aren't you? Guess you missed today's other news as well—the Jala Mujahideen say they'll behead Katie Waller at sunrise tomorrow unless the US releases seventeen prisoners currently being held at Camp Garzon. And clearly, the Yanks aren't going to."

"Of course not." If they did, it would be open season on foreigners.

"Well, not unless that idiot McDonald gets involved," Marina carried on. "If he starts negotiating, the Mujahideen'll end up with the prisoners, a dozen Stinger missiles, and a couple of BearCats."

"Let's assume he sticks with golf. What other options are there for Katie Waller?"

And Ziya, for that matter. I wouldn't give up. Going the semi-legal route would certainly have been the most straightforward option, but there were other ways. The black market thrived in Afghanistan. British documents were hard to come by, but Greek and Italian passports were easier possibilities. I wouldn't mind living in Italy. With all the time I had on my hands after I either resigned or got fired, whichever came first, I'd be able to renovate a property. One of those rustic little cottages in a remote village, a grove of olive trees—

"I do have one idea. How far away is Waller? And don't try to tell me you don't fecking know."

"About a hundred miles from Kabul," I admitted. "As the crow flies."

"And how far away from you?"

"Maybe twenty or—" It suddenly dawned on me why Marina was asking. "No. No way. I retired from all that."

"Come now, Rohan. You were among the best E Squadron had to offer."

"'Were' being the operative word there. Past tense."

"No, I think 'operative' is the one we want to focus on."

"You've got to be kidding me."

Marina's voice hardened. "There's nobody else available."

"Let me get this straight. You want one man—me—to creep into what's most likely a Mujahideen stronghold, sneak past a team of heavily armed fighters, rescue a female journalist who may or may not be in a fit state to walk, and you want me to do all of this by sunrise tomorrow?"

"Basically, yes."

"How about no."

Quite apart from the fact I wasn't feeling suicidal, Ziya would be upset if I even considered it. I'd seen her reaction to the handgun. If she found out about the M16 or grenades I'd brought with me from Kabul, she'd go from upset to furious.

"You're the only thing standing between Katie Waller and certain death."

"Oh, please. Spare me the movie lines. And the guilt trip."

"Doesn't every little boy want to be Superman?"

"I've been Superman. Now I want to be Clark Kent."

Even as the words left my mouth, they sounded hollow. I didn't want Katie Waller to die. But I needed to get Ziya out of Afghanistan, and that would be a big enough challenge as it was. We'd have to take one of the smuggling routes, and quickly because she was almost five months pregnant. We couldn't afford to waste even a day.

But Marina wasn't done yet.

"How about this?" She adopted what I assumed was meant to be a cajoling tone, but it didn't work well for her. "If you can pull off this one little job—just fetch Katie Waller and drop her off at the US embassy—I'll fix it so your 'friend' doesn't only get asylum, she gets full British citizenship."

I had to hand it to Marina. Not only was she a conniving bitch, but she was a conniving bitch who knew how to push my buttons too. Immediate citizenship for Ziya was something I hadn't even dreamed of, and it would solve a whole lot of problems, the most significant being the avoidance of a difficult journey through Iran, Turkey, and Greece. *Could* I get Katie Waller out? Once upon a time, perhaps, but now? Fuck me, I couldn't believe I was even considering it.

"I'd need more ammo," I said, half to myself. "Ideally door charges too."

"There's a cache near Alikhel. Another near Jaba."

"Anything near Baru?"

"How about Rowdat? Is that a yes?"

It wouldn't be the first time I'd rescued a hostage. It would, however, be the first time I'd attempted it alone.

I looked through the window at Ziya, her hands folded over her stomach as she slept. Over her baby. *Our* baby. Whatever decision I made, it had to be the one with the best outcome for my girl and my child. And Ziya *was* mine. No matter what she thought, that connection between us wasn't getting severed without a fight. I'd walk through fire to show her how much she meant to me.

"Two conditions."

"Name them."

"One: if I make it out of there, you provide transport to London for both of us. Two: if I don't come back, you send a driver to pick up Ziya from a prearranged location, you fly her to the UK, and you personally help her to process her citizenship application."

"You strike a hard bargain, Ro."

"I'd say it's you who's getting the better end of the deal. It's me who has to walk into the lion's den."

"Sometimes, I wish it was still me," Marina whispered, then huffed out a breath as if she was angry with herself for slipping out of character. "Fine. Fine, I'll do it. But you'd better not fecking die. I bloody hate paperwork."

CHAPTER 13

ZIYA

"What do you mean, you have to run an errand?"

"The girl you heard at Tabesh's place—I need to go and get her."

"Get her? I don't understand. How can you just 'get her'?"

If Tabesh's friends were holding her prisoner, they wouldn't simply hand her over. And they had guns, lots of guns.

"No need for you to worry about the details."

"Are you joking with me?"

I'd woken when Ro climbed back into the truck a minute ago, and although he smiled, I'd seen the creases in his forehead. Those little lines around his eyes. And now I heard the tension in his voice, even as he tried to brush away my fears.

"I realise this isn't an ideal situation."

Not an ideal... Had something got lost in translation? It wasn't just "not ideal." Ro was going to die. And although I very much hoped the blonde American lady would be okay, I wanted—no, *needed*—Ro to stay with me because if he didn't, it wouldn't only be he who lost his life. I had no hope of surviving without him, and neither did my baby.

"P-p-please don't go."

"I'll only be away for one night, and we'll find somewhere safe for you to hide. I've got survival gear in the back. Food, water, warm clothing."

"But what if something happens? What if you don't return?"

"I've got every intention of returning, but if I don't make it, an acquaintance will come to get you. It might take a day or two because there's a bit of trouble in Kabul at the moment, but I'll leave you with the satellite phone. All you have to do is sit tight."

"What trouble?"

"A bomb or two. Nothing unusual, sadly, but it means that anyone who might be able to help is indisposed."

Fear had been coiled in my belly like a snake, but now it slithered up my throat and threatened to choke me. How did Ro stay so calm? Disaster after disaster had happened, and yet he was so...so...what was the word? Stoic? Yes, stoic.

And me? I wanted to cry and scream and beg him to drive me far, far away from Nangarhar province right now because darkness was spreading. I felt it in my bones. Grandma had warned me. She said there'd be a tipping point in the battle of good and evil, and that it would be soon. I worried that humanity would be on the losing side, and now Ro wanted to wade into a fight that wasn't even his? No matter the lies he'd told me, I didn't want him to die.

"The people in Deraz, they're dangerous. And they have weapons. I know this. Tabesh said that only two groups in

Nangarhar have missiles—the Taliban and the Jala Mujahideen.”

He hadn't told that to me, obviously, but he and his men tended to forget that women had ears and also brains to process the information they heard. They'd been talking about Deraz last month. Apparently, the Mujahideen's leader was building a house even bigger than Tabesh's, so Tabesh was considering adding more rooms to his in what Nancy would have called the Afghan equivalent of a dick-measuring contest.

“I know,” Ro said.

“Then why do you insist on going?”

On doing something so incredibly foolish? Ro had never struck me as stupid, but his pig-headedness over this situation was making me reconsider my assessment.

“For you. For us. Ziya, I care about you, and I care about your baby. Our baby, I hope. No matter what you might think of me, I won't let you do this alone. My ultimate goal is to get us both to England, or Europe at least, but that won't be easy. And whether we ultimately live together or apart, I'll ensure you're supported.”

Tears prickled at my eyes. No man had ever said such things to me, not outside of my dreams, but a noble speech couldn't repair the damage Ro had done. Or the damage he was about to do.

“How does you walking into a storm of bullets help with that?”

“Because I negotiated an exchange.”

“What exchange?”

“Your British citizenship and passage to England in exchange for returning Katie Waller alive to the US embassy.”

That…that was crazy. And impossible. I didn't know

whether to be more shocked at the revelation that Ro knew people able to offer such a deal or at the idea that he believed he could rescue a woman from the Jala Mujahideen single-handedly.

If it had just been me in the truck with Ro, I would have forced him to leave Nangarhar and accepted my fate at Tabesh's hands, but it *wasn't* just me. There was a baby too, a baby stuck in the middle of this situation through no fault of his own, and I saw no way for all three of us to survive. I would give up my life for my child in a heartbeat. Did Ro feel the same way?

If he did, I realised I had no way of talking him out of this insane plan.

All I could do was pray to a god who'd proven not to be as merciful as I'd once been led to believe.

~

"This looks like a good spot."

Under these circumstances, "good" was of course relative. Ro backed the truck into a sheltered nook at the base of a steep hill, surrounded on two sides by rocks and on a third by trees. An hour ago, the *crack* of thunder had heralded the arrival of a storm as we stopped in Rowdat to pick up...well, Ro wouldn't tell me what it was, and judging by the size and weight of the two boxes he'd carried out of a disused hut and loaded into the back of the truck, I didn't want to know anyway. The rain hadn't stopped since.

Almost everything that could have gone wrong over the past twenty-four hours *had* gone wrong.

Ro and I hadn't spoken much on the journey. What would we say? I did glance across at him from time to time, and once or twice I'd seen his lips moving, heard the softest of whispers as he talked to himself too quietly for me to make out the words. A prayer? A plan? A pep talk? I now understood that I didn't know him well enough to guess.

Ro the soldier.

Ro the spy.

Ro the trickster who'd manipulated me so smoothly I'd never suspected a thing.

"Yes, an absolutely perfect spot."

"Ziya..."

I turned away from him, and the truck shifted on its suspension as he climbed out and kicked the door shut. I half expected him to march around to the passenger side to teach me some manners, but he just strode off into the trees. That was it? He was leaving? A tremor ran through me. I was on my own?

The clock on the dash ticked by for ten long minutes, and I began to take an inventory. There were two dozen bottles of water stacked behind the driver's seat, and a bag with plastic-wrapped food—nuts and dried fruit and energy bars. I wouldn't starve, but I felt too sick to eat. A canvas backpack contained clothing, matches, a compass, woven cord, candles, wire, and a first aid kit, among other things. At least one of us had come prepared. All I had was photos of my family and a necklace. How would those help me to survive?

Then I found the box. The box with the gun.

The slim case was tucked under the passenger seat, and when I opened it, I found a black pistol and enough ammunition to kill dozens of men.

Holy goats!

I shut the lid hastily, but then curiosity got the better of me and I opened it again. Was that black cylinder a silencer? The gun was heavier than I thought. I'd never held one before because a woman's place was in the kitchen, not on the battlefield, wasn't it?

The passenger door opening made me jump out of my skin. I swung around, heart pounding, and Ro grabbed the gun before I could blink.

"Not a good idea to point that at me, treasure. It's loaded."

I dropped it as if I'd been burned. "Sorry! I'm so sorry!" Then the tears came. "I didn't mean…"

"I know you didn't, but it seems that now's a good time for a lesson in gun safety."

"No, no, I'm never touching it again."

"I wish I could say that wasn't necessary, but since you'll be here alone, you should know how to handle a weapon."

"Why? I'll never shoot anyone."

My whole adult life had been about learning how to save people, not kill them.

"Humour me."

"Humour you? There's nothing funny about this situation."

"It's a figure of speech. Please, Ziya."

What choice did I have? My life wasn't my own. It never had been.

"Fine."

I listened while Ro showed me how to chamber a round, switch the safety on and off, reload the magazine, and use the sights to aim. As if that would help. Even now, my hands were shaking. If a man was close enough for me to hit, I'd be dead already.

After the gun, Ro taught me the basics of survival. How to make a shelter out of a poncho, purify water using tablets, and light a fire with kindling. Again, it was a nice thought, but if we got to the stage where I needed to use any of those skills, I'd already be living on borrowed time. Sooner or later, if I didn't die of exposure, someone would find me and take me back to Tabesh.

"But remember, all of this is a last resort," Ro said. "I intend to be back by sunrise. Deraz is two miles away in a straight line, but nearly four miles by road. I've brushed over the tyre tracks leading here." So that was why he'd left me on my own in the truck. "The Mujahideen would have to cover a lot of ground in a short time before they found you, and from what I've heard, they're not as organised or well trained as they'd like to think."

"They still manage to kill hundreds of people. The bombs in Kabul—was that them?"

"Probably the KLA, but I don't know for sure yet. Ziya, I want you to stay in the Land Rover unless you feel you're in imminent danger. The cliff means nobody can easily sneak up from behind."

"What if there *is* danger?"

"If someone comes, hide in the woods. They'll probably be in a vehicle. You'll hear the engine. See the headlights."

"Shouldn't I run?"

"Not if it's dark. They'll be more likely to find you if you're crashing through the trees than if you stand silently. Remember, they don't know who I am. Nobody knows we're together. If somebody stumbles across the truck and it's empty, they won't suspect you're nearby." He pressed a phone into my hand, a chunky black thing. "If I'm not back by midday tomorrow, you'll need to call my boss. There's a number you need to memorise."

I wanted to pinch myself. To wake up and find myself back in my shared room with the D-Team arguing over whose turn it was to prepare dinner. For months, I'd wished for escape, but now that I was freer than I'd ever been, I longed for my old life back. At least then, there'd been a tiny chance my baby and I would survive.

Now? No matter how calm Ro stayed, I didn't see how this could be anything other than the end. The end of our messed-up relationship, the end of hope, the end of our lives.

And if the darkness that filled my soul kept encroaching, maybe even the end of everything.

"Time for you to get some sleep," Ro said after he'd made me repeat the number back to him ten times. "I'll keep watch."

Sleep? How could I sleep?

And more importantly, what was the point?

I'd have plenty of time to rest when I was dead.

CHAPTER 14

RO

There were so many things I'd wanted to say to Ziya, but I couldn't. Time was of the essence. I'd had to stick with survival basics and leave the apologies and grovelling until later. Yes, I'd blown my chances with her, I understood that—accepted it—but I still wanted her to have the life she deserved, and our child too. All this upheaval surely wouldn't be good for the baby. Avoiding stress entirely wasn't possible, but I needed to keep it to a minimum.

While Ziya slept, I prepared the equipment I needed and packed it into my bergen. The cache near Rowdat had yielded a well-oiled AK-47 that some enterprising soul had decorated with a camo pattern, half a dozen fragmentation grenades, a couple of flashbangs, a folding knife, and a first aid kit. The knife was starting to go rusty, but the gun seemed good, and there was more ammo for the AK than I had for the M16—enough to take down a herd of wild terrorists if I was careful. The first aid kit only contained bandages and out-of-date painkillers. If I needed the former, I had bigger problems than the latter, but I'd brought my own medical supplies in any event.

What would actually have come in useful at that particular point in time was a damn good set of waterproofs. Mention Afghanistan to most people, and they thought of a barren sandpit because that's what they'd seen on the TV, but many regions were quite fertile. Deforestation had been a problem for decades, with most of the trees cut down for lumber exports, but a government tree-planting program was attempting to reverse that. The area around Deraz was lush, mainly arable fields surrounded by patchy trees with bare mountains rising in the background. Today, the weather reminded me of my training back in Hereford. Rain, rain, always bloody rain. On the plus side, there were no men chasing me with dogs. But on the minus side, if I got caught, I wouldn't be rewarded with three days of stress positions followed by a mock-interrogation and a nice cup of tea. No, I'd be killed. Possibly in glorious technicolour.

Earlier, Marina had sent me photos of Katie Waller as well as a copy of her hostage video debut. The "before" pictures showed a smiling blue-eyed blonde, one snap taken at a family barbecue and another that appeared to be work-related since she was wearing a *Natural World* T-shirt with a mob of kangaroos in the background.

Even from the blurry video footage, it was obvious she hadn't been treated well by her captors. Bruises marred her face and arms, tears streaked her cheeks, and she'd barely been able to choke out her own name. I'd winced when a scar-faced member of the Mujahideen slapped her. I never went into battle hoping to hurt people, but there would be some poetic justice if that motherfucker wound up in my sights.

I only hoped Waller hadn't deteriorated further by the

time I arrived. If I had to carry her back to the Land Rover, that would only hinder our escape, and we were on a wing and a prayer as it was.

But Waller's condition wasn't my main focus when I watched the video. I was looking for something—anything —that might help me to get a fix on her location within Deraz. I rewound the footage a dozen times, studying every frame for clues. The pale green concrete walls suggested the building was reasonably well constructed, and the quiet rumble of a vehicle fading in and out of earshot told me it was near a through-road. But my biggest clue came from a window high up on the wall behind Waller. When the camera tilted for a second, I glimpsed a view of sky and mountains, and one of the peaks in particular tapered to a distinctive point. Waller was being held in a room that faced east, and as I hunkered down in the mud half a mile away and studied Deraz through my binoculars, I narrowed down her likely location to a dozen possibilities—one cluster of five houses at the north end of the village, and a row of seven in the centre.

The question was, how could I pinpoint Waller's prison?

As dusk fell, I began a slow recce of Deraz, keeping to the shadows of trees and bushes and whatever cover I could find as I circled the village. The rain hadn't eased, and water seeped down the back of my neck and mingled with the sweat trickling along my spine. If I could get a look at the rear of the houses, I might be able to recognise the shape of the window.

The centre group of properties yielded one strong possibility, which was something of a shame. The location was far from ideal, and I could have groaned at the amount of foot traffic going in and out of the house next door. Who lived there? A big shot in the Mujahideen? The local opium dealer? Either way, I didn't fancy getting closer to find out.

I almost sighed with relief when the second cluster of buildings also had a property that would fit the bill. Almost, but not quite. Because as I watched, a furry crocodile ran around the corner of the house, barking at a kid who dared to walk past on the road outside. Fantastic. Just what I needed. A canine bloody herald.

What the hell are you doing here, Rohan?

When I was a kid at St. Peter's Primary School, we'd had to do a project on what we wanted to be when we grew up. Mrs. Grimshaw next door had recently got a schnauzer puppy, and she liked to follow me around, yipping. The puppy, not Mrs. Grimshaw. So I said I wanted to train dogs. I even taught Binky Grimshaw to track using a book from the library and my foster brother Bryan, and despite Bryan complaining the whole time, Binky had become quite proficient at following his scent trails around the village. She'd even found the little scrote who nicked Bryan's bicycle from outside the newsagent one afternoon, and I exchanged the shiny blue six-speed for a black eye plus a warning not to touch it again.

Yet even after all that effort, I'd somehow ended up in the army. I should have stuck with the bloody dog training.

I rounded a rocky outcrop, slowly, slowly, my camouflage jacket blending in with the scenery. Unlike the women. I stopped dead at the sight of light-blue burqas not thirty yards ahead. What were they doing? Just standing there?

Yes, because they were dead.

Eleven women in a row, and as I got closer, the ground turned soft underfoot. The grim realisation hit like a brick to the gut. I was walking on a grave. A mass grave. These women had been lined up and shot, nine in the forehead and two in the chest. They'd died where they fell, and now they'd watch over Deraz for eternity. I felt them following me with their eyes as I crept past, heard their whispers on the breeze.

"Who is he?"

"He doesn't look like the Taliban."

"A foreigner?"

"Maybe he will shoot those sons of donkeys?"

"Hellfire is too good for them."

"Is Dagar there?"

Dagar? According to Marina's notes, he was the Jala Mujahideen's head honcho.

"Yes, his truck is behind his house, see? I hope he dies."

Hmm... It seemed the women watched the goings-on in Deraz, and they also liked to gossip. Better still, they weren't fond of the Jala Mujahideen. Perhaps I could use this to my advantage?

"Good evening, ladies," I said in Pashto, keeping my voice low.

Eleven figures spun to face me, rigid in shock. Their body language told me what their veiled faces couldn't— that I'd surprised the hell out of them. Nobody replied, their collective voices silent in life and now in death.

"I mean you no harm. Just passing through."

A voice spoke. I wasn't sure who it belonged to because I couldn't see a mouth moving. "Are you...are you human? Or one of us?"

"I'm human."

"Then how do you see us?"

"Honestly? I'm not sure. And no, I'm not one of the Electi. I have absolutely no idea who they are or how to find them either."

"Then who are you? Why are you here?"

"My name's Rohan, and I'm looking for a young lady who's been kidnapped by the Jala Mujahideen. I'm hoping you can help me with that."

"How?" a different voice wailed. "How can we help? We're dead. They killed us all."

"You watch the village, don't you? Did you see a blonde woman arrive? Would have been the day before yesterday."

"They carried somebody into Pasoon's old home." The figure second from the left pointed towards the single-storey dwelling I'd identified at the end of the village. "He died last year, and it's been empty since then. But now there are people in there."

Bingo.

"You're here to rescue her?" another woman asked.

"That's the plan."

"Where are the rest of your people?"

"It's just me."

"Just you? There are a hundred men down there, and they're all as mean as wolves."

"Thanks for the warning."

"You're going to die."

Where had I heard that before? One woman laughed, and then the others joined in, their cackles echoing in my ears as I skirted the grave and crept closer to the village.

"You're leaving us?" one of them called, and I ignored her. "There's plenty of space for you here. Soon, you will be back for eternity."

Not if I could help it. I hadn't spent a decade training with the Regiment's finest to get slotted by some junior terrorist with a shoddily maintained AK.

Time to go FISHing.

CHAPTER 15

RO

If Binky Grimshaw had taught me one thing, it was that dogs liked food, and the skinny mutt outside Waller's prison was no exception. The first two times I crept close enough to toss it a chunk of energy bar, a guard came to investigate the barking. I'd covered myself in warpaint so I blended into the shadows, and I held my breath as the muzzle of his rifle pointed in my direction. Guess his eyesight wasn't too good. The third time, the dog got a kick in the ribs and leapt back, yelping. I cursed the guard under my breath. With any luck, karma would repay the favour later.

The fourth time, the dog licked my hand, then grabbed the rest of the snack and retreated into the darkness as I carried on towards the house. I'd been watching the place for most of the night, waiting until the current pair of guards had been on duty for seven hours straight. Undisciplined as they were, they'd grown fidgety and complacent, and now the two of them were sprawled out in lawn chairs, chatting, with their weapons dumped at their feet.

At least there were no bloody chickens here.

I toyed with the idea of slotting them, but I didn't want to start a war. I wasn't fucking Rambo. The best battles were the ones that no one knew had been fought. My only goal was to get Katie Waller and then get the hell out of Afghanistan, as quickly and as quietly as possible.

The back door was unlocked, the house still. Enough moonlight filtered in through uncurtained windows that I could see where to put my feet and avoid tripping over the pile of flip-flops left in the hallway. Snores came from behind a door to my left. The relief shift?

For the second time in two nights, I stole through an unfamiliar house, searching for a woman. I'd got lucky finding Ziya. Would Waller present more of a challenge?

Yes and no.

I found the room where she was being held easily enough. It was the only one with a padlock on the door. But now I had to work out how to get the damn thing off. My old mate Leatherman—we called him that because he was a complete tool—used to carry a set of lock picks in his pocket, and I'd always let him do the honours because my own lock-picking skills were, let's face it, shit. Five a.m. in hostile territory wasn't the best time to practise, and shooting off padlocks didn't work the way it did in the movies. In reality, it was more a game of Russian roulette. You were just as likely to take an eye out with a ricochet as you were to blow the shackle apart. Plus you'd alert every enemy soldier within a mile radius.

No, there was nothing for it. I took out my multitool, which had ironically been a parting gift from Leatherman himself, and began undoing the rusty screws.

What seemed like an hour later, but which was actually only two minutes, I wiggled the entire bolt assembly clear of the door and placed it gently onto the floor. Was Waller awake? The last thing I needed was to startle her into screaming.

The door squeaked on its hinges as I pushed it open, and I sucked in a breath, waiting.

Nothing.

Another inch. Two. Three... The gap grew big enough for me to slip inside, hoping the whole time that some enterprising kidnapper hadn't decided to chain Ms. Waller to the wall out of thoroughness.

She watched wide-eyed as I approached, cowering in the farthest corner. What had the fuckers done to her? Only a small amount of light seeped in through the filthy window, but I suspected the dark streaks on her pale shirt were blood. The coppery tang was all too familiar. She wore hiking boots and jeans, but when I realised the jeans were gaping open at the waist, anger burned through my veins. *Those animals.*

I put a finger to my lips, and when she nodded her understanding, I worked the gag out of her mouth.

"Can you walk out of here?" I whispered.

Another quick nod. Thank goodness for small mercies.

Luckily, the men had just handcuffed her and tied her ankles with rope, neither of which were a problem because I carried a universal cuff key on my zipper pull and a bloody sharp knife on my belt. Freeing her took moments. But as I pulled her to her feet, I heard the dreaded squeak of hinges.

Ah, fiddlesticks.

The snores had stopped. Was it changeover time? Or did one of the tangos need to take a leak?

Either way, footsteps sounded in the hallway outside. Bare feet. Followed by the unmistakable clatter of a pissed-off mujahid stumbling over the door bolt and uttering the requisite curses.

The door flew open, and I was already halfway across the room when an Afghan man stumbled in. More of a boy really, dressed in a kurta he seemed to be wearing as a nightgown. Who took a rifle to the toilet? It wasn't a bloody security blanket.

No matter, I twisted the gun out of his hands and clamped a hand over his mouth before he could yell to his pals. This was like the chicken chap all over again, except when this lad woke up, he found a wiry strength his compatriot hadn't possessed. I hung on for grim death as he thrashed back and forth. I was about to try switching my grip and snapping his neck when the muzzle of the rifle prodded his temple, and before I could get a word out, Katie Waller pulled the trigger.

Flesh, skull, and brain splattered everywhere, and the noise was deafening. For the love of *fuck*. I grabbed the gun before she managed to do any more damage, and she stumbled backward, arms flailing, then landed on her arse.

"What the hell are you playing at?"

"You looked like you were struggling. I—"

She didn't have time to finish before one set of footsteps turned into a dozen, coming from every direction. I dragged Waller to her feet again and hauled her towards the door.

"Stay behind me, and don't touch the bloody gun."

I'd hoped to get out of Deraz without having to kill anyone, but alas, it wasn't to be. Ziya was going to be distinctly unimpressed, wasn't she? I raised the AK-47 and took out the first guy to round the corner with a double-tap to the head, and he dropped in a heartbeat. His buddy fell behind him, and I half lifted Waller over the bodies, heading for the back door. How long since I'd been in a gunfight? Nearly two years. I only hoped I hadn't lost my touch.

Muscle memory took over, and all those drills in the killing house at Pontrilas let me assess each sound and movement, react, and neutralise each threat on instinct rather than forming conscious thoughts.

Go left, go left.

Duck!

Aim, fire, aim, fire, aim, fire.

Cover... Get to cover...

I shoved Waller behind a metal water trough as a shadow emerged from the back door. Being alone in this shitshow did have one advantage: everyone else was a bad guy. The shadow crumpled before he got his gun up. Another spirit rose jerkily from its former body.

"Move. Move!"

I practically threw Waller over the low earth bank separating Pasoon's old home from the next building, and already the Mujahideen were swarming like ants towards us. At least in pale nightshirts, they were easy to pick off. The sound of running boots came from inside the building we were sheltering behind, and I cursed under my breath. How much ammo did I have left? Two full magazines on my belt, approximately half of one in the AK. Plus my pistol. No backup, no radio. No air support.

No problem.

"Run," I told Waller. "Towards the trees. I'll cover you."

When she hesitated, I gave her a shove.

"Now!"

She took off like a baby fawn, wobbly with legs all over the place, and her bloody jeans started to fall down. Fucking hell. I had to trust she'd somehow get to the treeline as I turned to take out a couple more tangos. This wasn't what I'd intended, not at all, but in a quiet moment between bursts of gunfire, I heard whoops of delight from the watching women on the hillside. At least somebody was happy.

The boots were getting closer, and I counted down in my head. Three, two, one... The instant the back door opened, I flicked out the pin on a frag grenade and tossed it inside. Then I ran like hell after Waller, pausing to fire at a muzzle flash on my right.

The first *bang* was expected. The secondary explosion was not.

Fuck me, what had they been storing in there? The house lifted clean off its foundations, the shock wave punched me into Waller, and we both tumbled into a hole that, judging from the size and shape, was intended to be her grave.

I took a second—but only a second—to gather my thoughts. My ears were ringing. Military confetti fell all around, and the smell of burning flesh was enough to put me off barbecuing for life. Had I stayed in one piece? I levered myself off Waller and stretched out each limb in turn. Sore as hell, a bunch of cuts and scrapes, but nothing life-threatening.

"You okay?"

"What?" She tried again, louder. "What?"

"Keep your voice down." I put a finger to my lips again. "Are. You. Okay?"

"I... I..."

"Is anything broken?"

"I..." She quickly shook her head. "I don't think so."

"Good. We need to run again."

The sides of the hole crumbled as I scrabbled my way out, adding a few more grazes to the collection. Did the AK still work? No, the muzzle was bloody bent. I tossed it away and reached down to lift Waller clear of the pit. Right now, the remaining Mujahideen were in shock, and those who weren't wandering aimlessly were trying to put out fires and rescue their screaming comrades. We had a short window to get clear before they came after us again.

"Let's go."

Barking made me spin around, and I saw my furry mate giving the guard who'd kicked him earlier a mouthful. The arsehole wouldn't be kicking him again, not with only one leg, but he still had a gun. When he pointed it in my direction, I whipped out my pistol and put a bullet through his forehead.

Thanks for the warning, buddy.

Katie Waller vomited.

"We don't have time for that, love. Come on."

When she didn't move, I wrapped an olive-green poncho around her shoulders and cinched the hood under her chin. That white T-shirt was basically a target. Then I scuttled across to take the dead guard's AK as a substitute for my own, scooped Waller into a fireman's carry, and headed for the hills. It was time to find Ziya. The bloody dog followed, trotting along at my heels, and I didn't have the heart to send it away. It would be safer in the countryside than in the village in any case.

"Who *are* you?" Waller mumbled, upside down.

"Just a guy. It's not important."

And it really wasn't. What *was* important was getting back to Ziya and reaching Kabul. I'd need to wipe off my warpaint and change back into my shalwar kameez, perhaps ditch some of the extra goodies I'd picked up from the cache in case anyone searched the back of the Land Rover. With any luck, every militant within fifty miles would focus on the explosion at Deraz. It would take an hour or two for the survivors to calm down and mount an appropriate response. I doubted I'd tagged Dagar, and if he was alive, he couldn't afford not to retaliate. His honour would be at stake.

If only I'd had more time to prepare, I'd have found another burqa for Waller to wear. A disguise. As things were, she'd have to curl up in one of the rear footwells under a blanket if we came across a checkpoint. We were half a mile from the vehicle now, and my hearing was gradually returning. I'd worried about a perforated eardrum, but it seemed I'd been lucky.

Or not.

A low rumble vibrated through me, starting at my feet and working upwards. What the hell...?

Then I realised.

And I began to run.

CHAPTER 16

ZIYA

I'd always thought I knew what fear was, but the low-level anxiety I'd lived with during my time at Tabesh's barely registered on the scale compared to the outright terror I felt when I heard the explosion. The sky lit up to the east, a sunburst before dawn, and a few seconds later, the truck rocked.

Ro.

I was halfway out the door before I stopped myself. What could I do? Nothing. Yes, Ro had left me a gun, but I didn't know how to use it, not really. I was more likely to shoot myself in the foot than hit a member of the Jala Mujahideen. Was Ro still alive? In my world, explosions were never good.

Think, Ziya. Think!

My heart thudded against my ribcage as I went through Ro's instructions in my head. *Gather the gear. Look out for company. Escape to the woods. Hide.* I twisted as far as I could with my belly getting in the way and managed to snag the bag from the back and drag it through the gap between the seats. Then I added as much of the food as would fit and tucked bottles of water into the side pockets. How long should I wait?

Deraz was two miles away, farther if Ro didn't take a direct route. If he *had* survived, even if he ran straight here, it would take him twenty minutes at least. *Breathe, Ziya.* And if he'd managed to find Katie Waller, then she would slow him down, wouldn't she? I couldn't cover that distance in less than forty minutes.

Forty-five minutes. I'd give him that long before I began to panic properly. The clock on the dash said 05:28. Until a quarter past six, I'd stay where I was. The men from Deraz wouldn't find me in such a short time. Ro had hidden the truck well, I was certain of that much. He might not have been as good a man as I'd once thought, but he was a good soldier. I could tell from the way he moved, the way he watched our surroundings, the way he spoke. The way he'd killed Azeez. Quiet and efficient, none of the macho posturing of the idiots who visited Tabesh.

Time ticked by so slowly. So *painfully* slowly. Feelings tumbled around in my brain, a stew of confusion. I was angry with Ro, but I couldn't bring myself to hate him. If the story he'd told about my father was true, then he'd only been trying to help. And yes, if he'd been honest in the first place, my uncle would have sent him away. Would Balaguri have got its well? Maybe, but the children would have missed out on all the other gifts Ro brought. The boys would have missed out on his company and his laughter. And I'd have missed out on...was it love? I'd thought so at the time, but I'd been wrong about so many things...

As if to remind me of my stupidity, the baby booted me in the stomach. Was he trying to tell me something else? What if...? What if...?

Don't think about it, Ziya.

Another five minutes passed. Ten. Wind whipped through the trees, and every time a bough moved, I wondered if Ro had returned to me, even though I knew it was too soon. Would somebody really come to my rescue? Ro had promised, but I didn't trust anyone anymore. Not my so-called husband, not the father of my baby, and certainly not some unnamed spy boss from a country I'd never visited.

Everybody lied.

Then everybody died.

Tick, tock, tick, tock, tick, tock...

The baby kicked me again. Hard. If nothing else, perhaps he could have a career in football? And he didn't let up. What did he want?

I heard it first. A strange popping followed by a loud *crack* that made the hairs on the back of my neck stand on end. Because I'd heard that noise once before, many years ago in Balaguri. I'd been playing with my brother on the hillside at the end of the village when the goats around us started running, and my grandma's yells still echoed in my ears.

Come here, Ziya. Come here! Get down from there.

I'd heard the alarm in her voice and hurtled towards her as fast as my legs could carry me with Yafir in my arms, and we'd reached the yard just as a mass of earth detached from the mountain and slid over the spot where we'd been standing moments before. If Grandma hadn't called to me, my brother and I would both have been buried.

Today, I didn't hesitate, just grabbed the bag and tumbled out of the car, tripping over the bottom of my burqa and my own feet as I ran into the forest. The trees would protect me. I had to believe that.

Pebbles pelted my back, and the *pop*s and *crack*s turned into a dull roar as the front of the cliff gave way, chasing me as I stumbled through the trees. Only when the noise subsided did I stop.

Was it over? I couldn't hold the bag any longer, and I bent forward, hands on my knees as I sucked in air.

My life was officially jinxed.

I tried not to freak out as I took stock of the situation. The truck was gone, buried under a thousand tons of rock and mud. It was still raining. I'd left the gun behind, and... oh, hell...the phone. I'd left the satellite phone on the dash.

Rising terror threatened to overwhelm me, and I fought against it, tried to swallow it down. *Breathe.* Giving in to the urge to cry, to sit on the ground and rock, that would get me nowhere. Five months ago, perhaps I'd have accepted my fate, but now I had a baby to think about. He had a heartbeat, a soul, and for sure he had an attitude. It was up to me to make sure he had a future too.

Use your head, Ziya.

We wouldn't starve, not right away. I had food and water, and apart from a twisted ankle, I'd come through the latest disaster unscathed. Plus I had a magic number stored in my head. All I needed to do was get to another phone and call it. Easier said than done, but I wouldn't give up.

Should I start walking straight away? Or rest first? If I strapped up my ankle and—

"Ziya!"

Was I hearing things?

Or worse, was it a trap?

I shrank back into the trees, assessing. Honestly, I wasn't cut out for this. I was a housewife, and not even a particularly good one if Dina and Delal were to be believed.

The shout came again. "Ziya! Are you there?"

This time, I recognised Ro's voice, and then I saw a silhouette moving through the trees like a wraith. A sort of...lumpy wraith. What was he carrying? Was that an arm? He'd got the girl? And behind him... No, that couldn't be a dog, could it?

"Ro, I'm here."

I ran towards him. He dumped his bundle on the ground, and then I was in his arms. Yes, I was still angry with him, but it was the only place I wanted to be right then. Ro's strength gave me hope.

"Zizi, are you okay? I saw the hillside give way, and..."

"I'm okay. Are *you* okay?"

"A few dings and dents, but that's nothing new."

When I leaned back to check him over, I found that once again, Ro had lied. His handsome face was covered in greasy brown-and-green make-up, and I couldn't see much damage there, but his left leg was a different story. A two-inch gash in his calf was oozing blood.

"This needs stitches."

"Can you do it? I have sutures."

"Yes, but I don't have any anaesthetic."

"I'll cope."

It would hurt, and I hated to inflict more pain on Ro, but I had no choice. "Then I can do it. What was the explosion?"

"That's a long story, but for now, we need to get moving."

"What about...?"

I pointed at the woman on the ground. She'd scrambled into a sitting position, and now she was staring up at me, eyes white in the moonlight as she hugged her knees. The dog licked her face.

"Seems intact."

"*Seems intact?*" I glared at Ro, then wriggled free from his embrace and dropped into a crouch. This woman was far from intact. Maybe physically she was all right, but agony was etched into every line on her face.

"You're Katie?"

After a second's hesitation, she managed a nod.

"My name's Ziya, and I'm a doctor." Well, not quite, but I'd been damn close. "Are you hurt?"

I'd thought she was covered in dirt like Ro, but up close, I saw that many of the dark patches were bruises. Dried blood crusted at the corner of her mouth. But the way she shrank away, even from me, suggested there were deeper problems.

"Everything hurts," she whispered.

Where her poncho had ridden up, a nasty cut snaked along one forearm. The edges of the wound were already starting to knit together, but they looked pink. There was ointment in the first aid kit that would help.

"I need the bag."

"The bag?" Ro asked. "From the truck? It's buried under a landslide, treasure. We can't dig it out."

"No, I brought it."

"You did?"

Why did he sound so surprised? I might have been a fool in many areas of my life, but I wasn't totally stupid.

"Yes, it's over..." Okay, perhaps I wasn't totally smart either because I couldn't remember where I'd left it. I waved in what I hoped was the right direction. "Over there. Somewhere."

"I'll find it."

Time to confess. "But I lost the phone. Sorry."

Ro started to sigh, but he quickly cut it off. "You're alive, and that's the most important thing."

"But how long for?"

"Until we both grow old and grey if I've got anything to do with it. Don't worry; I've been in worse situations."

Really? Right now, the only worse place I could think of was hell itself.

CHAPTER 17

RO

I'd promised Ziya I'd never lie to her again, and I'd lied about that too. Quite frankly, I was a prize-winning arsehole.

This was by far the worst situation I'd ever been in. Sure, I'd endured greater physical hardships myself, like those nights in Wales when I'd been tossed out the back of a truck with a tin can of survival gear and a World War II-era uniform and told to find my way to a rendezvous point by morning, but never had I been stuck in hostile territory with no means of communication and two civilian women, one of whom was very likely carrying my child and another who was barely capable of speaking. Alone, I'd have stood a good chance of getting home, but could I keep all three of us alive? Four if you counted the damn dog. It had followed us here, and now it was sitting beside Waller, who glared at me as if this was all my fault.

In a way, it was. It was me who'd started the ball rolling that first night I'd crept out of my bed in Balaguri to speak with Ziya. Whichever dickhead came up with the motto "Who Dares Wins" was a bigger fucking liar than me.

No backward, only forward.

Losing the satellite phone was a huge blow. Of course, I wouldn't tell Ziya that because I didn't want her to feel worse than she did already, but it left us pretty much fucked. And to make matters worse, I'd smashed the regular backup phone when I fell into that bloody hole in Deraz.

All we had was the gear Ziya had managed to rescue and the snapshot of the map Marina had sent me that I'd burned into my brain. Better than nothing, and we'd have to make it work. Somehow. Our first task was to get out of the immediate area. We had a small head start on what remained of the Jala Mujahideen, but not only did they have vehicles, they'd be out for my blood too. Once they regrouped, our tiny advantage would evaporate like a puddle in the summer sun. And I was worried about Ziya. She might have been tough, far tougher than she believed, but there were limits to what she could handle. And as for Katie Waller... Part of me wished Ziya and I had taken our chances making our own way to Europe. I was glad Waller was alive, but damn, she was going to hinder our journey.

Ziya was checking her over, speaking softly. Listening in felt intrusive, so I made myself useful and went to look for the bergen. That Ziya had had the presence of mind to bring anything from the Land Rover, let alone a heavy bag, made me love her more with every passing second. It didn't take long to find the kit where she'd dropped it under a tree, and I schlepped it back to where the girls were waiting. Ziya's suspicions were correct—Katie Waller *was* in bad shape, and I'd deserved the look of contempt Ziya had given me earlier.

"Would something to eat help?" I suggested.

"We should all eat."

"Might as well die with a full stomach," Waller muttered.

"Nobody's going to die," Ziya told her, but she didn't sound convinced, and I couldn't blame her for that. "Ro, what happens now?"

Good question.

Right now, we were midway between Jalalabad and the Khyber Pass, around twenty-five miles to the east and west respectively. The main road was to the south-west, and that was the first place our pursuers would look for us. Did they know we were on foot now? The Land Rover was well and truly buried, so they might not realise straight away.

In the meantime, I had a decision to make. Should we try to cross the border into Pakistan or head deeper into Afghanistan? If we managed to reach Jalalabad, I could try to buy or borrow a vehicle. Steal one if necessary. But Kabul was another hundred miles from Jalalabad by road, and who knew what dangers lay along the route?

Pakistan would be more of a gamble. Assuming we managed to sneak across the border, there was still a possibility that people would be looking for us, and within a day, there'd be a price on our heads. I didn't know the country so well, and Islamabad, where the US embassy was located, was farther than Kabul.

Decisions, decisions... If I were on my own, it would be easy. I could tab to Jalalabad in a day, then stow away on a truck heading for the capital. From there, I'd head to my apartment and collect what I needed, sanitise the place, and be back in Blighty for tea and crumpets by Monday.

"Ziya, do you still have friends in Jalalabad?"

"I-I'm not sure. Nancy will have gone home to England, but the other girls... Maybe."

"Have you ever mentioned them to Tabesh?"

"I-I-I can't remember." Which meant we couldn't take a chance on calling them. "Why?"

"Because I'm trying to decide where to go now. Losing the Land Rover screwed with my plan. That bloody shock wave…"

I wasn't a hundred percent certain it had caused the landslide—the weather had played a big part—but it sure hadn't helped.

"Sorry I shot the guy," Waller whispered, and Ziya gasped.

"Don't dwell on it."

"You shot a man?" Ziya asked.

"I was only trying to help."

"There was a small miscommunication."

There, that sounded better than Waller simply not realising the amount of time it took to choke a man with bare hands, didn't it?

But Ziya didn't let it go. "You did it on purpose?"

Waller nodded, then turned to me. "Your name is Ro?"

"Yes."

"Ro was taking ages to strangle him. *Ages.* Like, I thought he was never gonna die."

For fuck's sake…

"The man, he's dead now?" Ziya asked.

Another nod. "Yes, and he totally deserved it. The pig threatened to rape me before he killed me."

"Threatened? So he didn't actually…"

"Rape me? No, but he was going to. I just know it."

"I thought from your trousers…"

"The fastener broke. Those pants cost me two hundred bucks, and it fell right off. I'm gonna complain to the store manager when I get home."

"You were lucky."

"Lucky? *Lucky*? They locked me in a cave for months, then they stuffed me into the trunk of a car and drove me over a bunch of rocks. I told those animals that if they came near me, I was gonna rip their dicks off."

Waller's words were tough, but a heartbeat later, she burst into great racking sobs. It was at that moment I began to regret the amount of focus the army put on hard skills rather than soft ones. I could put a bullet between a man's eyes at six hundred yards and assemble an IED out of common household objects, but I had no idea how to convince a distraught woman to stop crying. Usually, at this point in a mission, we were on a helicopter out of the hot zone, and I could simply hand her over to someone more equipped to deal with the problem before I headed off for drinks with the boys.

Thankfully, Ziya took charge, first offering a hug, and then removing her veil to comfort Waller with words too soft for me to hear. Even the dog had better people skills than I did, and he managed to get a wretched laugh out of Waller as he tried to scramble into her lap.

How long should I give them? Five minutes? Ten? At the very least, curious locals would wander over soon to see how much damage the landslide had done, and I wanted to be well clear of the area before they arrived. I shrugged out of my jacket and wrapped it around Ziya's shoulders. It had started leaking, but it was better than nothing.

Dammit, she didn't deserve this.

An hour and a half later, we hunkered down in a clump of trees as the sun rose higher. Ziya had stitched my leg up, and with a little cajoling, Waller had managed to walk a mile or so north between the two of us, Ziya holding one arm, me holding the other, and the dog trotting along behind. Ziya had also helped Waller to make a belt out of paracord to hold up her jeans.

Once I'd found a suitable resting place, we shared a packet of dried apricots and some water, turned our backs for awkward bathroom breaks, and settled in for a few hours. I took first watch. Waller had passed out from sheer exhaustion, curled against my right side to share body heat. I'd insisted the girls borrow my clothing, but I wrapped myself in a camo-print survival blanket to stave off hypothermia until the sun warmed us up. Ziya leaned her head on my left shoulder, and that was the only bright spot in an otherwise dark day.

"At least the rain's stopped now," Ziya said.

I groaned before I could stop myself.

"That isn't a good thing?"

"It was washing away our tracks." Her face fell, and I wished I'd kept my damn mouth shut. "Don't worry; the explosion must have set the Mujahideen back. If we keep moving, chances are they won't catch up."

"Are you going to tell me about the explosion yet?"

"Are you sure you want to know?"

"Yes. No. I don't know. Where are we going? Have you decided?"

"Jalalabad. I fully expect spies to be watching for us, but we both know Afghanistan better than Pakistan. And a border crossing brings a whole new set of risks." A quiet gasp from Ziya made me stiffen. "What is it? Are you all right?"

"The baby kicked again."

"What does that mean? It's okay?"

"He's fine. He just likes to wake me up every now and

again. Before the landslide, he was using me as a punching bag."

"He? You know it's a boy?"

She nodded.

"You had a scan? Everything's all right?"

"No, there was no scan. Can you imagine Tabesh wasting his time with such frivolities?"

"Then how did you find out?"

"You'll think I'm crazy."

I was the man who talked to ghosts when nobody else was around. "Crazy" was a relative term.

"Try me."

"My grandma told me."

"Your Grandma Bushra? But I thought…"

"She came to me in a dream. Laugh if you want, but I'm certain what she said is true."

"I believe you."

"You do?"

"Sometimes, things happen that we can't explain."

If only I'd known how prescient my words were, I'd have picked up both girls and used every last ounce of my strength to carry them to the Khyber Pass. But as it was, I just tucked away the strands of hair that had escaped from Ziya's hood, scritched the dog's head as he tucked himself in between us, and leaned back against the tree to rest.

CHAPTER 18

RO

The good news was that I knew where we were.

The bad news? I knew where we were.

The steep-sided valley wasn't named on any map, but the locals called it Dead Man's Pass. Rumour said a person could walk in there and never be seen again. I'd always written the stories off as hyperbole, but now I understood how the spot got its name. Spirits hovered as far as the eye could see, some in groups, some on their own, everyone from Perry's colleagues to elderly nomads to modern-day jihadists. So, why had we chosen to come this way? Firstly, because it was direct, and secondly, because the locals tended to avoid it.

Beside me, Ziya shuddered. "This place is creepy."

"Let's hurry up and get to the other end, then we can find somewhere to rest."

In places, the pass narrowed so much I had to take off the bergens—I carried one on my back and one on my front —and hold them above my head while I sidestepped through the gaps. A claustrophobic's worst nightmare, and trickles of water still ran through from last night's storm. Ziya's borrowed trainers were soaked.

Then the path would widen, and Ziya would hold my hand as she hurried along at my side. Waller seemed to prefer hanging onto the straps of the bergen on my back for support as she stumbled along behind. The AK hung alongside the bergen, but it was an awkward set-up. Thankfully, I still had the spare Glock I'd taken to Deraz securely tucked into a holster on my belt.

The sun hung low over the mountains now, the sky clear and the shadows long. After a brief discussion this morning, we'd decided to take a phased approach—an hour or so of walking followed by a rest. Rinse and repeat. Two months of imprisonment had left Waller weak, and she let us know how exhausted she was with every other step. Did she ever stop complaining? Ziya barely spoke a word, and although she was strong, she admitted she tired more easily now. All of which meant we had to move in daylight as well as darkness if we wanted to reach our destination before we ran out of food. Far from ideal, but at least we wouldn't be spending hours in one place. Everything was a trade-off. And when I'd offered to supplement our rations by trapping a rabbit or a hare, Waller had burst into tears and informed us she was a vegetarian.

We'd covered around five miles, mostly heading north before turning west for Jalalabad. So far, we'd managed to avoid getting close to civilisation. A few people passed in the distance, and Ziya was wearing a full burqa again so as not to raise eyebrows. Waller, we couldn't do much about other than keep her behind us. If anyone got close, we hid, and the dog had proven himself useful on those occasions because he tended to growl if any humans came near. It seemed that now he'd found himself a meal ticket, he wanted to protect it. Another trade-off, but it was worth sacrificing some of our food in exchange for the early-warning system.

"We should give the dog a name," Ziya said. "We can't keep calling him Dog."

Was that really a good idea?

"We can't keep him," I told her gently.

"I know." Shit, I hated the sadness in her voice. "But for the next few days, he's one of us, so he deserves a name."

"What about Bandit?" Waller suggested. "He stole a guard's lunch once."

"Tinker?" Ziya asked, her voice saccharine. "Tinker the Second?"

Another punch to the gut, and I noted Ziya had mastered the art of understated sarcasm. I suspected the snark had gone right over Tabesh's head, which was probably the only reason she'd got away with it.

Waller didn't pick up on it either. "I know, I know—Yoda. He's small and clever, and he must be practically immortal to have survived the bomb."

I didn't agree with Waller on much, but I had to concede it was an appropriate name.

"Yoda works. His ears stick out."

"What's a Yoda?" Ziya asked.

Oh, my sweet girl. "You watched *The Only Way is Essex*, but you never saw Star Wars?"

Waller's turn to be puzzled. "What's *The Only Way is Essex*? Is that something to do with your royal family?"

"No, that's Wessex. Which doesn't actually exist. Essex is—"

Tinker, Yoda, whatever his name was, growled. The girls were getting good at this now. They headed straight for the nearest boulder while I stepped behind an outcrop and looked in the direction the dog's ears had swivelled. Yoda it was. They really were abnormally large.

A shadow flitted across the pass, so quickly I almost missed it, and my sixth sense tingled. That wasn't the movement of an innocent shepherd or even a jihadi taking a shortcut. Not a ghost either. Whoever it was, they were two hundred yards behind, and we had an equal distance to go to the end of the pass.

"Keep going. Move. Move!"

To give Waller her credit, she shared my sense of urgency when it came to getting out of nasty situations. She started walking. Ziya was the one who paused, and I grabbed her hand.

"Need to hurry, treasure."

Up ahead, a group of spirits chatted among themselves, blood dripping from a collection of wounds. One had lost his head, quite literally. What had he been shot with? 7.62 NATO? An RPG? Like most lost souls or whatever they were, they paid humans scant attention.

I could feel our pursuers getting closer. I didn't need to look. My Glock found its way into my hand, its weight so familiar. Not so familiar? Ziya's slim fingers and the way they gripped mine ever more tightly.

"There are men behind us, and they're getting closer." I spoke Pashto now because I didn't want to panic Waller. "We need to run."

The words had barely left my mouth when the gunfire started. So much for avoiding panic. If we took cover behind the rocks, we'd end up in a standoff we couldn't win. Running was our only option. All we could do was hope our pursuers were terrible shots. I fired a couple of rounds, enough to make them hesitate, and I was pretty sure I clipped one of them in the shoulder and another in the leg. But I didn't have enough ammo to win an all-out gunfight.

We ran.

Shit, shit, shit. There was another man ahead, a rifle in his hands. I double-tapped him and he crumpled to the ground, his soul sitting up almost immediately like something out of a video game. Good. One less motherfucker to worry about.

Ziya yelped as she tripped, but I pulled her up and kept going. I'd carry her if I had to. That gap at the end of the pass was our only hope of escape. Our only hope of a life together with our son. Of Katie Waller going home to her family.

And a second later, that hope was lost.

More men appeared, a dozen at least, all with guns aimed at us. I could take out some, maybe even most of them, but it would be a bloodbath. They'd fire back, and Ziya would get hurt. Negotiation was the only option we had left.

Except these arseholes didn't seem so keen to negotiate, and when one of them grabbed Ziya, I wanted to tear his head off with my bare hands.

"Drop the gun!" the de facto leader barked in Pashto.

I did as instructed. I still had the Colt strapped to my ankle and the AK on my back. Hopefully, Waller wouldn't get tempted to use it and do even more damage.

"On your knees!"

Okay, this wasn't ideal. Yes, it brought me within reach of my backup gun, but it also felt an awful lot like I was about to be shot in the head. What would the others do if I took out their boss? Would they hesitate long enough for me to spray the lot of them? I could hardly miss at this range. They were starting to relax a little now. Muzzles were lowering, all except the bossman's. No, his was coming up again, and I didn't like the glint in his eye. Did he have orders to kill me? Or take me back to what was left of Deraz? Unfortunately, I suspected the former.

Ziya shifted her weight to the left. She knew what was going to happen, didn't she? Her inbuilt sense of preservation was taking over now, instinct telling her to save herself and the baby. Behind me, I felt rather than saw Waller lean forward. She was ready to go for the gun, wasn't she? Yoda growled too.

A strange numbness settled over me, an acceptance of my own fate. But underneath that flowed a grim determination to take as many of these fuckers with me to hell as I could. To give Ziya a chance to survive, no matter how slim. Time slowed. If Waller took the AK, we'd be two against thirteen. Unlucky for some. I reached towards my ankle.

And then suddenly, it didn't matter anymore.

Because the man who was about to kill me died.

Just like that.

He died.

And behind him, the other men died too, all except one.

Death had been a part of life for me. I'd seen a hundred men perish, and it always happened the same way. The body stilled, and the soul rose. Looked around. Blinked in confusion.

But this time, what emerged wasn't a facsimile of their mortal remains. No, these men's insides were as black as night, and they swelled and pulsed and then finally dissipated into every corner of the valley. Nothing was left but flesh and blood, and the latter was still contained within their bodies.

Of all the arseholes I'd watched meet their maker, none had gone quite like this.

Clearly, the one remaining foot soldier—a lad who couldn't have been more than sixteen—hadn't seen anything like it either because he dropped his rifle and sprinted towards the other end of the valley, yelling about Iblis and *shayatin*.

"Holy fuck. What just happened?"

Ziya started screaming and Waller began crying, but as I herded them to the safety of a large boulder, it was Yoda's growls that caught my attention. Two more men with guns were slinking towards us from the east, their attention focused on the bodies of their comrades. But the moment a muzzle swung in our direction, I shot the pair of them. No quarter given, not today.

As the bodies crumpled and two regular, full-colour souls stayed standing, Ziya's screams turned to wails of horror, and she began backing away from me.

"Ziya, don't go out in the open." Thankfully, Waller grabbed her hand and hung on. "Treasure, I'm sorry. It was them or us."

"What did you do to them?"

I glanced at the AK-47 in my hand. Wasn't it obvious? "I...shot them?"

"Not them! The others." She waved a hand at the dozen twitching corpses lying at our feet. "That boy, he said you're the devil and we're your demons."

"Honestly, I have no idea what happened. I swear I didn't do a thing."

"People don't just die that way. Maybe one from an aneurysm, but not ten."

Twelve, but I wasn't about to correct her. And she was right. People didn't just die that way. Not without help. The question was, what kind of help?

And would we be next?

CHAPTER 19
ZIYA

"Zizi, you were standing right next to me. I was on my knees."

Ro was right, but those men... *I* hadn't killed them. And Katie...? No, she'd been behind us, and now she was more upset even than me. My eyes struggled to believe what was in front of me. All those men, dead, and there wasn't a mark on them. No bullet wounds, no blood, no bruises. Nothing. The first man Ro had shot, he'd bled. I'd seen the wound in his head, a small opening, but definitely a bullet hole.

Was cardiac arrest a possibility? My own heart was pounding against my ribcage, and I feared I might join them. *Think, Ziya.* I'd once watched a horror movie with Nancy where five teenagers had died at the same time, and they'd been electrocuted. But we were in the middle of nowhere. There were no generators, no cables, not even a battery.

"As I walk through the valley of the shadow of death," Katie said, her voice trembling, "I will fear no evil."

"I'm not sure prayer is the answer here," Ro muttered.

Then what *was* the answer? *Wait they for nought else than that Allah should come unto them in the shadows of the clouds with the angels? Then the case would be already judged. All cases go back to Allah.*

I didn't know what to believe anymore. Nothing made sense. *Could* there be a higher power at work here? What other answer was there?

"You have a better idea?" Katie asked.

"We watch, and we wait."

"Wait for what? Until we die too?"

"No, until whoever killed those men reveals themselves."

"You think it was a human?" Katie's voice grew higher, and I worried she was going to lose her reason.

"Well, it wasn't a bloody ghost." Ro blew out a breath. "Sorry. Can we just have some quiet here?"

"Shh, shh," I tried, taking Katie's hand in mine. "Let's sit."

Ro shook his head. "Don't sit. Be ready to run."

The cliff above us overhung slightly so nobody could look down on us, and a huge rock gave us cover from the east. Ro stood between us and the path to the west. We were safe for now, but we couldn't stay there forever. Or maybe we could? There were bones on the ground, and I recognised one as a metacarpal, another as a vertebra. I shifted so they were hidden by my burqa. Katie had been through enough without finding out we were in a cemetery. Yoda settled at my feet, content just to sleep. Life must be so much easier as a dog.

After fifteen minutes, I risked a whisper. "What are you looking for?"

"Something out of place."

"Like what?"

"Movement. A glint of light. A rock that's the wrong colour. An alarmed animal. Anything that's not meant to be there."

"You really think there's somebody watching us?"

"It's the only rational explanation. When I was in the army..." He paused. Sighed. "Ziya, I'm not supposed to be telling anyone any of this."

"I won't say anything."

"You wouldn't voluntarily." Ah, so we were back to the "for your protection" thing. That was comforting. "And then there's..." He nodded sideways at Katie.

Her eyes widened. "What? I won't say anything about anything either." She mimed zipping up her mouth and throwing away the key. "I promise."

"You're a journalist."

"Not anymore. I totally quit."

"A juicy story can prove quite tempting."

"I never wanted to be a journalist in the first place, but do you know how many jobs are out there for biology grads at the moment? None. So I had to suck it up and work for my daddy."

"Your father owns *Natural World* magazine?"

"Yes, plus three local newspapers and a radio station."

"And he sent you to Afghanistan?"

"No, that was my idea. Well, originally I planned to go to Russia. Daddy was worried, but my brother's the editor of *Natural World*, and he thought it was a great idea. Like, he even booked my ticket. The other staff were super supportive too."

"Why Russia?"

"I was going to write an article on Siberian musk deer. But a week before my flight, Sandy Canales from *Really Wild* posted on Twitter that *she* was writing an article on

Siberian musk deer, and I'd look like a total idiot if mine came out a month later."

"So...Afghanistan?"

"I was watching this news segment, like, super late at night, and the reporter was in a market in Jalalabad, interviewing a shopkeeper. He mostly sold onions, but there was a cage in the background and I was almost certain I spotted a pygmy jerboa, so—"

"A pygmy what?"

"Jerboa."

"You're going to have to explain."

"Jerboas are rodents, but they look more like mini kangaroos. And I thought that maybe, just maybe, it was a Thomas's pygmy jerboa, and so little is known about those. Like, there's literally one type specimen, and..."

Ro zoned out. I watched him do it. And I struggled to follow everything Katie was saying because when she started talking, the words flowed like floodwater in the rainy season. Perhaps it was a good thing because her passion was helping to take her mind off the horrors she'd endured, although I didn't quite understand her excitement over the jumping mice. There were hundreds of them in the hills beyond Balaguri.

What was Ro looking for? What was I missing? The only movement came from a vulture circling high above the pile of bodies in front of us, and I prayed we'd get out of the valley before it landed. I'd attended plenty of autopsies during my time as a medical student, but I still didn't want to see corpses being torn apart by beaks and talons.

"So I thought that if I could rediscover a lost species and give *Natural World* the scoop, then Daddy might finally be proud of me."

A tear rolled down Katie's cheek. Oh, no. Not again.

"Did you find these, uh, pygmy gerbils?" Ro asked.

"*Jerboas*. Yes! The onion seller still had the one he kept as a pet, and he told me there were plenty hopping around in the desert near Tangar. The translator Daddy hired found us a guide, so we went to look for them."

"It didn't at any point occur to you that this might not be a good idea?"

"I had two bodyguards. Daddy insisted. Ex-marines who came with me from the US. They told me...they said nothing would get past them."

"And where are they now?"

Katie buried her face against my shoulder, and I glared at Ro. Couldn't he show the tiniest bit of tact? Yes, Katie had been incredibly stupid in leaving the relative safety of Kabul, but what was done was done and was there really any point in making her feel even worse than she already did?

"Those marines should have known better," he muttered. "Bloody idiots, letting their egos and their greed override all sensibilities."

My shoulder was wet now. Katie's tears had soaked through my burqa, and Ro wasn't helping.

"Can we focus on the important things?" I asked. "What aren't you meant to tell us?"

Silence.

"Are we going to stay here forever while you think about it?"

Ro let out the longest sigh. "This place *feels* empty. Over the years, I've learned to trust my instincts on these things, and while I fully admit the last few days have been one long series of fuck-ups, my gut's been fairly reliable in the past."

"That's good." Or so I thought, but his expression said otherwise. "Isn't it?"

"No, it's not. It means whoever's out there is better than me. And they've got more sophisticated toys than I've ever come across." He paused, then came to a decision. "In the army, I was privy to the occasional whisper, and rumour said the Americans were developing sonic weapons. Next-gen nerve agents too, although if those men were gassed, it would surely have affected us too."

"What if it happened at the other end of the valley?" Katie sniffed. "Maybe they tried to set a trap for us and it went wrong, and they had some kind of delayed reaction? Like with...you know, what's that stuff the Russians used in England?"

"Novichok?"

"Or the other one...polonium? The men who kidnapped me have stuff like that, and for sure they work with those assholes you rescued me from."

"Wait a second... I thought you were a wildlife journalist?"

"I am."

"Then how the hell do you know about radioactive isotopes in Afghanistan?"

"Because of the jerboas." Katie wiped her nose with what was left of her T-shirt hem. "Those poor little creatures."

Ro spoke again, this time through gritted teeth, and I could tell he was working hard to keep his cool. Although being honest, Katie's rambling was starting to get on my nerves too.

"What *about* the jerboas?"

"So, they're super rare, but I've studied other jerboas, and these were different. We set up cameras and stuff, you know, to monitor their numbers and behaviours, but after a few days, we realised they were sick."

"Sick?"

"Losing weight, lethargic, unable to open their eyes properly. Their fur was all ruffled. Sometimes they'd recover, and sometimes they wouldn't."

"How long were you there for?"

"Nearly a month. Our translator rented a house from a local guy." Katie snorted. "A house. It was made of mud, and it didn't even have a faucet. How do these people live like—" She suddenly remembered whose shoulder she was crying on. "Uh, sorry. So, anyhow, the jerboas were acting really weird, and you know what they reminded me of?"

"I couldn't possibly guess," Ro said.

"When I was at college, this guy I totally hated did his thesis on the effects of irradiation in rodents. And the jerboas, they looked just like mice he used. Always tired, and some of the babies had deformed tails. It was awful."

"And you think these gerbils—"

"Jerboas."

Ro took a calming breath. "Jerboas. You think they had radiation sickness?"

"Not just the jerboas. The guy whose shack we rented, his nephew got sick too. Like, he was puking everywhere and he had a fever. Everyone thought he ate something bad, but then his skin started peeling off."

"Ah, fuck. Did he say where he'd been? What he was doing?"

"He said he only went to work."

"And where did he work?"

"I don't know. He didn't really say. I mean, he was kind of delirious by the time I saw him."

"Didn't *really* say? What does that mean? Did he give any clues? Be specific."

Katie's bottom lip quivered, and I knew what was coming. Not only the inevitable tears, but also something much, much worse. Her story had set alarm bells clanging. I'd studied the symptoms of radiation sickness too. With the constant threats of war against my country, my teachers at medical school had considered it a matter of importance. Which led to the question I wasn't sure I wanted to know the answer to—where in Tangar had a man stumbled across a source of radiation?

"He mentioned a guy called Dane? Like, I think that was his boss."

"Dane? Do you mean Dayyin?"

Katie shrugged. "Maybe."

One blow after another, and now I was on my knees. Literally. My legs buckled under me, and I fell to the dusty ground.

"Ziya!" Ro was beside me in an instant, keeping me from falling any farther. "It's okay. It'll be okay."

"What's wrong with her?" Katie asked. "*I* was the one who got kidnapped."

I'd felt so sorry for Katie when we first met. She'd seen the very worst of mankind and survived, which was why I felt guilty that now my hand itched to slap that pale face of hers.

"Dayyin Rouhani is the leader of the Khyber Liberation Army," Ro told her. "And it's possible Ziya's brother is involved with them."

Katie's eyes hardened into two chips of stone. "Your brother is one of those beasts? Do you know what they did to me?"

"My brother's not a beast! He's only fifteen years old."

Ro stepped in. "Let's not argue, eh? That doesn't get us anywhere. I heard Yafir did some scut work for the KLA because he needed the money. He's hardly a hardened terrorist."

"Yafir? A boy? I think I met him, but I thought he was more like twelve."

"He's small for his age."

Katie had met Yafir? "Where? Where did you see him? Was he okay?"

"They kept me in this tiny dark room with walls made of rock. He brought me food. Look, if you're worried about him getting irradiated, he's probably fine. He said he was gonna travel to Europe."

Europe? No, no, no. Yafir always said he wanted to stay in Afghanistan. He'd dreamed first of becoming a poet, and then a teacher, and then an artist. But that was before our parents died, and after... I couldn't remember when we'd last talked about the future. Had he really changed so much that he'd leave without saying goodbye?

"Are you sure?" My voice sounded weak, even to my own ears. I'd tried to stay strong, for Ro, for the baby, but now... The last of my energy leaked away into the dusty valley, soon to be scattered by the wind.

"He seemed nicer than the others. I figured that if I, you know, built up a rapport, maybe he'd bring me more food. I hardly got given anything, and my pants started to fall down, then those filthy pigs tore my shirt, and—"

"Katie, what did the boy say?" Ro asked. "We need to know everything you can remember."

"Why does it matter? We're all gonna die anyway."

"Stop! Just stop!" I cried.

"What? I'm only being realistic."

Ro's turn to glare, and fortunately it wasn't aimed at me because that look could melt steel.

"How about we try being optimistic?"

Katie rolled her eyes and huffed, but she did at least get back to the subject of Yafir.

"What did he say about Europe? Not a whole lot. I asked one day if I'd be able to go home to my family, and he said he didn't know. So I tried asking about *his* family, and he said he didn't have a family or a home either. Are you sure you're his sister?"

A tiny bud of hope sprouted in my chest. Perhaps there were two boys called Yafir? It was a common enough name, after all. There'd been a Yafir in my class at university, another at the market where my father used to sell our produce.

"Let's assume for now that she is," Ro said, and now it was he who was being negative.

"The kid said he was going to Europe for a new start."

"Alone?"

"No, I don't think so. He said 'we' once or twice."

"Did he mention which country?"

"He asked if I'd been to Greece, and when I said that I had, he asked if I knew a café in Athens... What was it called? Nostima, Nostimo, something like that."

"And did you know it?"

"I went to Mykonos. It's nowhere near Athens."

If Yafir had gone to Europe, would that be such a bad thing? It hurt, the thought of him leaving without telling me, oh did it hurt, but if he and a friend had seen a way to a better life, could I really be angry at him for taking it? He thought I'd abandoned him, and to all intents and purposes, I had.

"I suppose I should be thankful if he's escaped Tangar."

Shouldn't I? The flash of horror in Ro's eyes before he slammed his mask back into place told me I should be anything but.

CHAPTER 20

RO

It never rained but it poured.

I realised now that we were in the eye of the hurricane, and the worst was yet to come. If Dayyin Rouhani was facilitating passage to Europe for Yafir—and I couldn't see how the boy would get to Greece otherwise—there was only one reason. He needed cannon fodder.

The KLA had been on a bombing spree around Afghanistan in recent months, but according to rumour—and Marina—they had bigger ambitions. Today Kabul, tomorrow the world. Suicide bombers were a favourite tactic. I didn't want to worry Ziya, but *fuck*.

And the radioactive material? That bomb was going to be dirty.

"We need to consider making a move," I said.

"About time," Waller muttered, and deep down, a tiny part of me regretted not leaving her in that bloody grave. Now that she'd stopped weeping, every time she opened her mouth she upset Ziya more.

"Do you have a plan?" Ziya asked, speaking so softly I could barely hear her.

"We'll start moving as darkness falls. There's a possibility the enemy might have night vision goggles or thermal imaging equipment, but if we don't take a chance, we'll never get out of here." I fished around in my pocket for an energy bar. "But first, I want to try something."

I broke off the end and tossed it at the pile of bodies. As predicted, Yoda quickly followed. Not as predicted, Katie ran after him, shrieking.

"What are you doing, you jerk?"

For the love of all that was holy...

"I'm checking to see if whatever killed those men is likely to kill us too." Waller grabbed a pissed-off dog and dragged him back to the safety of the rock. "Guess not."

"That was cruel!"

"Would you rather one of us died instead?"

"I'm not even sure I want to go anywhere with you now."

"Well, love, you're very welcome to make your own way to Kabul. I'm sure the folks at what's left of the embassy will be overjoyed to see you."

The fact that Waller was alive and kicking—and pouting—meant we should try to leave. We'd have to backtrack along Dead Man's Pass, detour around it, and then restrict our travel to the hours of darkness. Walking through the night would be hell on the girls, and it would take several days for us to reach Jalalabad, but we were out of other options. And the worst part? That was only the first phase of the battle.

We were in a race against time, and for this leg of the journey, we weren't the only participants.

"Stay there."

"What, on my own? I thought you were joking about that."

Tiredness had seeped into my bones by the time we approached Jalalabad nearly three days later, and the last thing I needed was more of Waller's incessant whining. We'd already discussed this—Ziya and I couldn't just waltz into town with a filthy, blonde-haired, blue-eyed American in tow. We might as well paint targets on our backs. No, Waller had to hole up for an hour until Ziya could pick out a nice burqa for her, and then we'd see about organising food and transport. Plus I needed a nap. I'd managed to snatch a few hours of sleep during the trek, but not enough that I could safely drive to Kabul.

"No, he wasn't joking," Ziya said, her exasperation loud and clear. To me, at least. Katie Waller seemed oblivious to everything but her own discomfort.

Ziya was exhausted too. I'd been powerless to help as she tossed and turned in her sleep, and the lines around her eyes had grown deeper, more pronounced. A week ago, I'd have held her in my arms and promised her everything would be okay, but now that my lies had come to light, she was keeping her distance. Yoda was the one to offer comfort. Perhaps it was irrational to be jealous of a dog, but when he curled up with her each time we took a break, I couldn't help wishing it was me at her side. Waller wasn't happy about the sleeping arrangements either. She'd taken a shine to the mutt, and I was sure he'd be thrilled when he realised she wanted to take him back to the US and keep him as an "emotional support animal," whatever one of those was. Years might have passed since I studied canine body language, but there was no mistaking how cheesed off he was with all the affection she showered on him.

"We'll be back soon. Just stay here, okay? Don't wander off."

"I'm not stupid."

That was debatable. "Nobody's suggesting you are."

"What if someone finds me?"

"You're tucked away between an abandoned house and several overgrown bushes. It's highly unlikely."

"Yoda will look after you," Ziya added.

Waller tightened her grip on the collar she'd made for him out of braided paracord. "Fine. Just hurry up. I need a shower."

"You'll get a shower when we get to Kabul."

"What? But Jalalabad's, like, a city. Doesn't it have hotels?"

"We're trying to keep a low profile."

"Yeah, so just book a room in your name and we'll sneak in."

"A man on his own will still get extra scrutiny. The Jala Mujahideen's looking for both of us, together or alone."

"So tell them you're with Ziya. An Afghan married couple. Nobody's looking for *her*."

Not entirely true. Tabesh was still lurking in the background. But much as I hated to admit it, Waller's idea wasn't actually terrible. Tabesh didn't know Ziya was with me. The only witnesses to our antics that night were a dead guard and Dina, and Ziya had been the one who clonked Dina over the head. With any luck, she wouldn't even remember I'd been there.

Should we risk it?

Usually, Ziya had excellent posture, almost regal, but the past few days had worn her down, and when she hunched, the baby bump wasn't quite so noticeable. Would a poorly paid desk clerk pay much attention? If she wore a burqa and said a few words at check-in so there was no mistaking her for an American, we might just get away with a night in an out-of-the-way hotel. And we all desperately needed the rest.

"We'll see what we can do."

The dog whined as Ziya and I walked away, and I felt slightly guilty for leaving him behind. But that guilt was tempered by the relief of being alone with Ziya for the first time in days.

"Are we really going to a hotel?" she asked once we were out of Waller's earshot.

"If there's somewhere suitable. You know Jalalabad better than me—can you think of a quiet place with a side entrance we can sneak Waller through?"

"And Yoda?"

"I suppose."

Yoda had grown on me, much to my regret. I should have known better. It was always harder to say goodbye when you cared. Ziya was a case in point—my obsession with her had already proven to be my downfall.

"Thank you," she said softly before pausing to ponder my question. "There's the Silver Star Hotel. We went to the restaurant for Nancy's birthday, and when she wanted to smoke, she went out another door down an alley to the side. And there's also the Desert Suites on the edge of the city. I've never been inside, but I used to go to the café opposite sometimes. I remember it has a main building with tiny houses behind it instead of regular rooms."

"Is there a second way in?"

"Maybe? There's a parking lot at the back."

Even though we'd cleaned up as best we could with the last of the bottled water, we still got pitying looks when we swung by the local bazaar to pick up clothes. But no trader was going to turn down the handfuls of crumpled afghani notes I'd retrieved from the bergen Ziya grabbed from the Land Rover. They'd have liked the dollar bills even more, but spending those would be too conspicuous.

The Silver Star Hotel was a no-go. A wedding party had taken over the entire place, and Ziya tensed at the sound of the music leaking out from the ill-fitting doors. The last wedding she'd been to was her own, and that marriage hadn't ended well. In fact, it technically hadn't ended at all. She was still hitched to that double-crossing bastard.

The Desert Suites was a dump, but at least it was quiet. And porous. Half of the back wall had fallen down, which didn't bode well for the rest of the place, but we only needed to spend one night there. It'd do. Tomorrow, I'd beg, borrow, or steal a vehicle that would get us to Kabul, and with any luck, none of us would have to set foot in Jalalabad again.

"About time," Waller griped when we returned. "Yoda hates it here."

Couldn't possibly be something to do with the company, could it?

"Don't worry; it's time to go for a walk. We bought you a nice new outfit."

Ziya held out the plastic carrier bag, and Waller tore into it with the excitement of a kid on Christmas morning. But her face soon fell when she shook out the light-blue burqa.

"Oh. You were really serious about me wearing one of these."

"Yes."

"It's way too long. How am I meant to walk in it?"

"Carefully."

"They didn't sell shorter ones?"

"You'd rather somebody saw your little white feet sticking out the bottom?"

She opened her mouth to retort, couldn't think of anything to say, and closed it again. Thank fuck for that. If I'd been gifted the ability to time travel rather than chat with ghosts, I'd have left Waller behind in Deraz and brought one of the Mujahideen along for company instead.

"Hurry up and get dressed. If you stand out in the open much longer, we might as well write your obituary."

We'd also picked up two new canvas bags, blue with thin white stripes, and I stuffed the bergens into them. Walking into town like an advert for a military surplus store would only draw attention we didn't want.

Ziya was staring at me, and I raised an eyebrow.

"Uh..."

"What do you need?"

"Could you...?" She made a spinning motion with her fingers. "Please?"

"Right. Sorry."

I turned so she could swap her black burqa for a twin of Waller's, and my heart sank a little lower. Our relationship, if you could call it that, seemed to be going backward. I'd almost preferred the righteous anger to the polite wariness she'd defaulted to over the past two days.

Back in Hereford, my old mate Albert—his name wasn't really Albert, but he'd taken a wrong turn into a piercing parlour on a night out, and the moniker stuck even if the dick decor didn't—had once told me that a good woman would bring me to my knees. I'd been twenty-five or twenty-six at the time, more accustomed to women kneeling for me than the other way around. So of course, I'd laughed. Now? Now I owed him an apology. Ziya had got under my skin, and I'd crawl to the ends of the earth to make things right between us again.

But would it be enough?

Today, I could only offer a thin mattress in a run-down hotel room, one that was in no way commensurate with the three shiny gold stars on the sign outside. The heater didn't work, I removed three cockroaches within five minutes of unlocking the door, and there was a crack in the wall wide enough to see the stars twinkling above.

"Someone needs to report this place," Waller grumbled. "Three stars my ass. There's no hot water. Can we get a manager over here? A maintenance guy?"

"Which part of 'keep a low profile' are you struggling with?"

"There's no need to be snippy. Cut me some slack, okay? I got kidnapped."

Yes, so she kept reminding us. The stitches in my leg were starting to itch now, not that I was bitter or anything.

"You should be grateful there's water at all," Ziya told her. "Thousands of people don't have access to a tap."

Waller folded her arms and turned away in a huff. She couldn't argue with that logic.

"Thank you," I mouthed at Ziya. Her face was hidden under the burqa, but I very much suspected she was rolling her eyes.

"Is there any food left?" she asked after a pause. "And we should still purify the water here if there are any more tablets."

"I'll go out in a minute and buy us something to eat. Any requests?"

Ziya shook her head, but of course Waller had a whole list. Next time, I wouldn't bother asking.

"Bars of chocolate. And potato chips. And a vegetarian

meal, but get something pre-packaged because I don't want food poisoning. And coffee. A latte made with skim milk."

"Nobody drinks coffee here, and they sure as hell don't know what a latte is."

"This is ridiculous. I just want to go home."

"Well, that makes two of us," Ziya snapped back in that beautiful sing-song voice of hers with the merest hint of an Essex accent. "I just want you to go home as well."

It was the dog that woke me.

After supper—rice and stew for Ziya and me, plastic-wrapped cheese croissants that I knew from experience tasted awful for Waller—we'd settled down to rest. The rickety closet had yielded extra blankets, and I'd unfolded one to lie on beside Ziya's bed. Yoda had curled up next to me with his cold, wet nose pressed against my hand.

And now he was growling.

Very softly, but years of training had made me a light sleeper, and I was alert in an instant. I checked my watch—eleven p.m. Moonlight filtered through the dirty glass above my head, and I saw Yoda's ears were jammed forward in the "what the hell?" position, his eyes fixed on the door.

Then I heard it too. A faint scuff, as if someone had shifted from foot to foot.

Fuck.

I'd already ballsed things up once in Dead Man's Pass,

and I wasn't about to do it a second time. No, now it was my turn to go on the offensive.

"Ziya."

I whispered her name softly as I nudged her shoulder, one hand poised over her mouth in case I needed to shush her. Her dark hair was spread out across the pillow, and I wished I had a moment to drink in her beauty. But no such luck.

"Wha…?"

I put a finger to her lips and leaned closer. "Somebody's outside. Go into the bathroom."

Ziya rose silently and tiptoed away. Some might even say she moved like a ghost, but I knew that was a lie.

Waller presented more of a challenge. Wake her nicely, and she wouldn't be able to resist talking. In the end, I opted for the quick and dirty approach—just clamped a hand over her mouth and kept it there until I'd deposited her in the bathroom with Ziya. Yoda followed, and Ziya crouched beside him, holding his makeshift collar. He seemed to understand the need to stay quiet. Smart dog.

Then I slipped out of the rear window. Earlier, I'd checked that it opened properly and even greased the hinges with a little oil from the top of the stew. And before I'd gone to the café, I'd mooched around the hotel grounds to get a handle on the lie of the land. Thirteen bungalows surrounded a patchy lawn, but as far as I could ascertain, only ours and three others were occupied. Scrappy trees and bushes provided plenty of hiding places, which was both a blessing and a curse. They meant I could creep around unnoticed and flank the enemy, but they also provided cover for any unwanted visitors.

I paused at the corner of the next building, half-hidden by a walnut tree, breathing steadily as I scanned the grounds. Movement by our room caught my eye—three men were gathered under the rotten pergola, examining the door. Shit. Although I'd never met him in person, the profile of the one in the middle looked remarkably like photos I'd seen of Tabesh Siddiqui. How the hell had he found us?

I was about to surprise him with that very question when the hairs on the back of my neck prickled.

Danger, danger, danger.

I stayed stock-still, letting my vision adjust to the dim light from the moon and the yellowed lamps that illuminated the path to the main building, and two more silhouettes became apparent in the gloom, standing in the shadow of a tree between Tabesh's crew and me. Their clothing said backpackers, but their bearing said military. The shorter of the two—which was only relative because he was still at least six feet tall—had something in his hand. A knife? Whoever they were, their attention was on the trio by the door. A metallic scrape reached my ears. Tabesh was fiddling with the lock. I had to act, and I had to act quickly or they'd be inside.

The guy with the knife stiffened as I closed the distance between us, even though my movements were silent. He was the one with the instincts. The one I had to watch out for. I stopped six feet behind the pair, out of arm's reach, and ground my heel into a dry leaf. The noise wasn't loud enough to alert Tabesh's band of goons, but it sure got the attention of the pair in front.

Knife-Guy had the right moves, but they came too late. He saw the gun in my hand an instant before he sprang, and quickly thought the better of it.

And then he surprised me.

"We're on your side," he whispered.

Was he? Was he really? A flicker of recognition niggled

at the back of my brain as he dropped the knife into a pile of dirt, and in the pale moonlight, I saw that same puzzlement reflected back at me. Who was he? Where had I seen him before? One thing was for sure—I didn't have time to consider the question further at that moment because there were still twenty feet between me and Tabesh and that motherfucker had one hand on the doorknob.

And a gun in his other hand.

Fuck.

I lunged forward, ready to risk a shot because even if it woke everyone in the complex, it was still better than Ziya getting into that bastard's hands.

But then he died.

Tabesh died, and so did the men on either side of him. Their souls rose, blacker than the darkness around them, then scattered into the night.

That was the first time in a decade I'd truly felt scared. Gripped by an all-consuming fear because something I didn't understand was in play, and that something could very well be about to kill me.

Knife-Guy... I suddenly remembered where I'd seen him before. Kandahar, five years ago. No, six. The mess hall at Camp Garzon. The place had been packed, and we'd shared a table. My team had been on a mission to mark enemy targets for air strikes, and his was tasked with eliminating a high-value target if British intel was to be believed. What was his name? Bennett? No, Beckett. Beckett Sinclair, 75th Ranger Regiment.

An operator.

Tier 2 to my former Tier 1, but definitely not to be underestimated. Guess now I knew who'd been playing with deadly high-tech toys. The question was, where was the damn weapon?

I spun back to face Beckett and his friend. Neither had moved, and I kept my sights trained on his head. If those hands moved again...

"Where is it?"

"Where's what?"

"Don't bullshit me. Your weapon—where's your weapon?"

He cut his eyes to the side. "I dropped it."

"Your other weapon."

"I have a knife in my pocket," the other guy volunteered. "That's it. We flew commercial, and we haven't had time to go shopping."

"A knife didn't kill those three men."

"You're sure they're dead?"

"Don't try to twist this. We both know they're dead."

Beckett's jaw dropped. "Holy shit, I just remembered where I've seen you before. Camp Garzon, right?"

His mate looked puzzled. "You know him?"

"Not know him, exactly, but we've met. Rohan? It's Rohan, isn't it? You helped me to break up a fight between two infantrymen who couldn't hold their liquor." He shook his head, seemingly incredulous. "Of all the people I might've expected to see, you sure weren't him."

"What are you talking about? You've been following us for days."

"Yes and no."

"We only arrived in Kabul yesterday," the other guy said. "Getting visas delayed us."

"Yesterday? Forgive me if I smell bullshit. Whoever just killed those men used the same weapon in Dead Man's Pass three days ago. If it wasn't you, then who was it? And where is it?"

"You don't understand, do you? You really don't know?"

"Know what?"

"You're the weapon, Ro."

Had I fallen into an alternate bloody universe? "I'm quite certain I didn't kill them. Believe me, I'm familiar with death and how to cause it."

"Not with your own hands, but you facilitated the act. Tell me, did you notice anything strange about their souls as they rose?"

I nearly dropped the gun. For sure, it wobbled in my hand. Beckett had to be bluffing. *Had* to be. He didn't know my secret. He *couldn't.*

"Have you been taking drugs?"

"Not even caffeine, unfortunately. And we've been too busy chasing your ass all over Jalalabad to get any sleep. Look, buddy, we know what you see, and we know why you see them. So you can carry on sidestepping the issue, or we can sit down and work out how to get your girlfriend and that annoying blonde to Kabul."

Was there any possibility I was still asleep? Having a nightmare? I focused on the ground beneath my feet, on the stones under my boots. No, I was definitely awake. And Beckett Sinclair was standing in front of me, claiming he knew my deepest secrets. None of this made any sense. Including the three bodies lying motionless just feet away.

"If you know so much, then tell me what I see. Explain that." I pointed at Tabesh. "Because I'm at a loss."

"Do you want to find somewhere more private, or...?"

"We should probably move the bodies," his friend said. "I'm Reed, by the way. Don't suppose you'd consider putting the gun away?"

Was it nuts that I was actually considering his suggestion? Neither of the men had made any worrying moves, but Beckett was Special Operations. Those guys were trained to be unpredictable.

"How many more of you are there?"

"In Afghanistan? It's just us."

"The US Army sent you here without backup? Now, why don't I believe that?"

Beckett spoke up again. "Neither of us is in the army anymore. I got a medical discharge, and Reed left to join the police force."

"A medical discharge? And yet here you are in Afghanistan?"

"It's a long story, and I'll tell it when we have more time. But Reed's right—we need to move these bodies first. Are any more of those idiots likely to show up? We only saw three arrive, but there could be more elsewhere."

"You saw them arrive?"

"Yeah, we were on our way out to get a late dinner when we heard the chunky one asking the guy at the desk about the pregnant lady. They seemed to know each other."

Dammit all to hell. Tabesh had a better network than I'd suspected.

"You're certain of that?"

"My Farsi's rusty, but your visitor called him *daadaash*. That's 'brother,' isn't it?"

"More like 'bro.'" I blew out a long breath. There'd probably been money involved, and Tabesh wasn't short of a bob or two. "The chunky one was the ringleader. If there *are* more of them, there's no one to tell them what to do."

"Good. Let's stash the bodies in one of these empty villas. The place isn't exactly buzzing, so I doubt anybody'll find them until after we're gone." When I didn't answer, Beckett shrugged. "Hey, you can stand there with the gun if you want, but we can't leave them lying on the damn terrace."

"Are you okay to carry them?" Reed asked. "Will your back hold up?"

"I'll deal."

Beckett had a back injury? Was that why he'd been medically discharged? Perhaps I should offer to help? If the pair of them or whoever they were in cahoots with had come to harm us, they'd had ample opportunity during the past few days. *Were* they working against us? When I'd met Beckett in Kandahar, he'd never struck me as an arsehole, but if I let him risk further injury by carrying Tabesh, then I definitely would be one. And I had to concede that both sets of deaths, no matter how shocking, had been to our benefit. Hmm... Shocking... You know what I didn't see when Tabesh and his pals carked it? Any surprise from Beckett or Reed. They'd known it was going to happen.

And that only piqued my curiosity more.

"This is my mess; I'll help. But I'll need to pat you down first. I'm sure you understand why."

Beckett merely shrugged again. "Sure, buddy. Do what you need to do."

I didn't find any additional weapons besides the knife Reed had told me about, but once I got closer, it didn't take me long to spot the earpieces both men wore. Wireless units, presumably connected to the satellite phones in their pockets.

"Who are you talking to?"

"Our girlfriends," Reed said.

"Be serious," I snapped, fast reaching the end of my patience with this escapade. Another pile of bodies had left me feeling just a little bit tetchy.

"I am. We'll explain, okay? As soon as we clear up this mess."

The strange thing was, I almost believed him. This night had got beyond insane, but now that the immediate danger had passed, my thoughts turned back to Ziya.

"I need to speak to my companions."

"Be my guest. Need a hand getting the door open? The skinny guy's blocking it."

Shit, he was.

"Thanks."

How was I meant to explain any of this? I'd promised Ziya I wouldn't lie to her, but would she even believe the truth?

CHAPTER 22

RO

"Everything's fine out there. Sorry for the excitement—you can both go back to sleep now."

Yoda was sniffing around the front door, tail wagging. What did he think he was, a bloody cadaver dog?

"Are you sure?" Ziya asked. "I thought I heard voices."

"There are a couple of Americans staying here. That was them coming back. Turns out I actually know one of them, sort of. Our paths crossed on a base a few years ago. I'm just going to catch up with him over a drink, and then I'll be straight back."

"We'll be on our own?"

"I'll be right outside, treasure. I promise. I wouldn't leave you alone if I thought there might be a problem."

"Shouldn't you, like, not be drinking?" Waller asked. "How can you shoot people if you're drunk?"

Did she think I was an idiot? "I'm not planning to drink alcohol. Or shoot anyone, for that matter."

Apparently, I didn't even need a gun to kill people anymore. What the hell had Beckett meant with his "you're the weapon" comment? Well, there was only one way to find out.

In the garden, Reed was stowing a set of lock picks after opening the room next door. At least he'd done the honours —we'd have been there all night if I'd made an attempt. One or more of the dead men had voided his bowels, and I kept my fingers crossed the smell wouldn't seep under our door and invite more bloody questions from the two girls.

"Head or feet?" Reed asked.

Did it matter? I grabbed the nearest pair of hands— Tabesh's—and waited for Reed to take the other end. Even in death, Tabesh managed to look like a smug son of a bitch. How he'd ever thought he was good enough for Ziya was beyond me.

"Any idea who these assholes are?" Beckett asked as he held the door open for us. "Is one of them Tabesh?"

Tabesh's head cracked off the tiled floor when I dropped him to stare at Beckett.

"How do you know about Tabesh?"

"You've been discussing him with Ziya. But you never mentioned a surname, so we couldn't work out exactly who he was."

"You've been eavesdropping on my private conversations? Who the fuck do you think you are?"

"Chill, buddy. It wasn't something we set out to do, but we didn't have a lot of choice."

"I'm not your damn buddy. How did you get close enough? What did you use? A parabolic microphone?"

"I'm not even sure you're going to believe me when I tell you."

"Not that I can talk about it, but I saw some pretty interesting things during my military years."

"It's nothing to do with the military."

"What about the spooks?"

"Spooks? Kind of. Not the CIA or the DIA or the NSA or any other acronym. You think we should put these assholes in the bathroom? Or just leave them here in the bedroom?"

"Does it really matter?"

I was getting sick of all the smoke and mirrors. Why wouldn't Beckett give me a straight answer? Was it an issue with security clearance? I still maintained mine at the highest level in the UK thanks to my work with the Mansfield Foundation, although that might not help in this particular setting. Finally, we got the last body into the empty room, and Reed locked the door again. Now would they tell me what the hell was going on?

"Drink?" Beckett offered. "We didn't make it out for dinner, but we've got snacks."

"What I want is some answers."

Their room was opposite ours, and I positioned myself on a chair in the doorway so I could watch for movement. I'd jammed the rear window shut when I went back to talk to the girls so nobody would be able to sneak in that way, but the threat level was still high. Just because we'd cut the head off one snake didn't mean there weren't others. The remains of the Jala Mujahideen were still out there, plus the KLA and dozens of other smaller groups. The Afghan authorities could also be problematic, and every country had opportunist thieves...

"Where to start..." Beckett mused. "I suppose the best place is with my own death."

"I'm sorry?"

"The medics brought me back. But for three minutes and twenty-eight seconds in the operating theatre at Camp Garzon, I saw what you see. The spirits. I spoke to them, met a spirit guide. And then I got pulled back into my body and woke up two days later."

"Huh?"

"You said you wanted answers."

"Yes, but..." Could it be true? Admittedly, the tale sounded plausible, but how on earth did Beckett know *I* saw ghosts all the damn time? "Go on."

"The spirit guide told me about the Electi. You must've heard of them, right?"

"Hypothetically, let's say I have."

"Hypothetically, sure. So you understand that the only way a spirit can be freed from earth is if one of the Electi kills the person who killed them."

Was that a question? Did he expect me to answer? I shrugged, non-committal.

"An ex-girlfriend of mine was murdered, and after my own brush with death, I realised her soul was trapped on earth. I spent years looking for the Electi, *years*, and then one fell into my lap by accident."

Beckett had met one of the Electi? I sat up a little straighter.

"Ah, now you're interested."

He just laughed at my scowl, and Reed took over the story.

"It's taken a while, but we've finally got all four of the Electi together again. And it wasn't until we found the fourth that we realised you even existed. So many pieces of knowledge have been lost over the years. Iris knows more than the others, but—"

"Wait, wait. Iris?" The cogs were turning slowly, but suddenly it clicked. *Their girlfriends.* "Is that who you're talking to? The Electi?"

"Some of the time. There're a couple of others with them."

"If they're...what...supernatural assassins, why didn't they come themselves? Why send you?"

Reed's bark of laughter was unexpected. "The girls and Afghanistan wouldn't be a good mix. I doubt we'd even get Kim to leave the airport." He tilted his head to one side, listening. "Sweetheart, it's true." A pause. "She says she might consider visiting the bazaar."

"The girls want these powers about as much as you do," Beckett explained. "They're not assassins. Rania's the only one who comes close, but now she's a private investigator. Nicole's a scientist, Iris owns a garden centre, and Kimberly's a wedding planner."

A wedding planner? "Are you kidding me?"

"Wish I was."

"Then how do they do their jobs?" Honestly, I couldn't believe I'd even asked that question.

"Historically, they haven't. Rania made an attempt when she lived in Syria, but one woman against a nation at war? The odds were impossible. There've been a few accidents through the years, enough that the girls knew the curse, gift, whatever, it worked. But for the most part, they tried to ignore it."

"And now? Why are you here?"

"Because last week, everything changed. We found Iris late last year. The final piece of the puzzle, or so we thought. The girls, they have this...this..."

"Connection?" Reed suggested.

"Yeah, a connection. They say it's like a shared soul. Nicole, Kimberly, and Rania just wanted to find their missing sister and get to know her, but then we tried putting their gold pieces together, and—"

"Their what?"

"Each of them has a gold talisman. Like a medallion? They seem to be linked to their powers in some way, and—"

Enchanted medallions? This was bullshit. Somehow, they'd found out enough about my weird ability to spin a fairly convincing story, one I might even have fallen for if they hadn't veered off into the realms of fairy tales.

"We're done here."

Reed got to his feet at the same time as I did. "Please, just hear us out. I realise this sounds crazy, and believe me, I thought the same thing when I first found out about it. You have a gold medallion, right?"

"Do I look like the sort of man who wears jewellery?"

"Maybe it's at home? Your father would have given it to you. They're supposed to stay with their owners come hell or high water."

Clearly, they hadn't done that good a job on their homework. D-minus.

"Nice try. I'm adopted, and I have no idea who my birth father is."

"Well, shit."

"Just leave me alone."

"Don't you want to find out why people keep dying?" Beckett asked.

I did, but not at the expense of my sanity. Curiosity killed the cat, and possibly the former SAS corporal if I let my guard down.

"You've got one minute."

Rather than sit down again, I leaned against the doorjamb, arms folded. The clock was ticking.

Beckett shrugged, but in a "you asked for it" manner rather than a dismissive one.

"We found out that when the girls and their medallions link together, they can see through your eyes. And when they all wish a person dead at the same time, that person dies if they've killed somebody in the past. That's what you saw—their black souls being banished. Kind of like the regular Electi mechanism, but on steroids."

Holy fuck, these men needed help.

"Well, nice meeting you. I have to go now, but I can provide the number of a good psychiatrist if you feel you want to talk about this further."

"There's already a psychiatrist on the team. He's dating Iris."

"Great. He can have you all sectioned."

When I turned to move off, Beckett put a hand on my shoulder, and I removed it pretty damn quickly. He landed on his arse, and when Reed stepped forward, I thought he might try the same thing, but instead he offered me his earpiece.

"The girls want to talk to you."

I paused mid-stride. The girls might have wanted to speak to me, but did I want to speak to them? Did they even exist? The rest of the story was so obviously bullshit. Had this team really gone so far as to bring a quartet of women in on this pantomime? I snatched the earpiece and jammed it into my ear, if for no other reason than to give them a piece of my mind.

The first voice I heard was English. "It's rude to joke about mental health."

"What makes you think I was joking?"

"After everything you've seen—"

I heard rustling, and a hissed, "Iris!" Then a new voice spoke. This time, the British accent was underpinned by something else. Something Middle Eastern. I was going to hazard a guess and say it was Rania.

"Please don't run. I know this isn't easy. If we felt we could have waited, then we would have, but we saw you were in danger."

"Well, the danger's passed now."

"If you won't listen for yourself, then do it for your son."

"Don't you dare bring my child into this."

"He'll inherit this curse. And in eight or nine years, when your powers gradually transfer, it'll be your job to teach him how to use them. But if you die sooner because you won't accept help, then that transfer will happen in an instant. One day, all the ghosts will be there, and he won't understand why or how or what to do about it."

My blood turned to ice as a vision of *that* day flashed into my mind. The first ghost I saw. An old man, or at least he'd looked that way to six-year-old me. At that age, anyone over thirty seemed ancient, and besides, I hadn't been paying much attention to his face. No, I'd been more concerned with his olive-green uniform and the knife sticking out of his chest. More of a small sword, really. A dark splodge of blood seeped out from the wound, soaking all the way down to his trousers. I'd gasped. Screamed. Begged my foster mum to help him. Then finally cried my eyes out as she dragged me to school, warning me that making up tales wouldn't excuse me from doing PE.

And now...this woman I'd never met was telling me that the reason I'd gone through that hell, the reason I'd spent my early years thinking I was a freak and a monster, was because the man who'd donated half of my DNA had died?

The thought left me frozen.

I'd never abandon my own son, not in a million years,

but say he did inherit this curse, as she called it... What was I meant to tell him? Whether I liked it or not, these strangers seemed to know more about me than I knew about myself.

"Which way did it happen for you, Rohan? Was it sudden, or was it gradual?"

"Sudden." The word clawed its way from my throat.

"I'm so sorry."

"It's not as if I ever knew him."

And if nothing else, the revelation blew away those last romanticised thoughts about my abandonment. The notion that perhaps my biological father had died before I was born and my birth mother, penniless and consumed with grief, had chosen to send me off to a better life. No, he'd been alive at that point. He just hadn't cared.

"I'm sorry for that too. Rohan, we'd like to meet you. To get to know you. But that's your choice. Whether you accept your destiny, that's also your choice. Whichever decision you make, I can't imagine it'll be easy, and we're still learning about the process ourselves by trial and error. But we can make choices too, and until you and Ziya get to England, we're going to be in your head, doing everything we can to keep you safe. If that includes more men dying, then so be it."

"How can you be in my head? That's impossible."

"We don't understand it either, and yet we're there. We see what you see and hear what you hear, but we don't know what you're thinking."

They could do that with hidden cameras. Microphones. Had they bugged me unnoticed? Put a miniaturised device in one of the bags? I'd picked the smaller one up from the cache, so it was entirely possible. I needed to rip the damn thing apart.

When I didn't answer, Rania carried on talking. "I

understand you're sceptical, so let's do a test, okay? Beck has a notepad. Write something, and I'll tell you what it says."

"Fine. *Fine.* Let's settle this once and for all. But I'll use my own notepad."

Beckett's could have hidden sensors. Technology evolved every day. Marina had a jotter that took her handwriting and converted it to type—she said it was faster than a secretary and more accurate too. Secretly, I thought she was just a control freak.

"As you wish."

Neither Beckett nor Reed moved when I strode back across the threadbare lawn. I didn't trust them. I didn't trust anyone here except Ziya, and she didn't trust me. It suddenly struck me just how alone I was. How alone I'd always been. Since I left the army, I'd barely even socialised with my old brothers in arms. Perhaps I should have made more effort, but at the time, I'd simply wanted to leave that life behind.

"What are you doing?" Ziya asked when I started rummaging through our bags of stuff.

"Just looking for something. Nothing to worry about."

"Do you need help?"

I was beginning to think so.

"No, no, all under control. Won't be long."

I found a pencil and a notepad I'd brought with me from Kabul. When I got outside again, I pulled off my shirt and took off my jeans, just in case there was any funny business. Should I lose my underwear too? No, but I felt carefully around the waistband and then removed my boots. Think I was being paranoid? Fifteen dead men said otherwise. The stakes were too high not to be thorough.

Beckett and Reed watched in silence as I walked to the

far end of the garden. The full moon lit the way, and a yellowed streetlight cast enough of a glow to see what I was writing.

Mulberry.

Flannel.

Skidoo.

"Mulberry, flannel, Skidoo," Rania recited. "What's 'Skidoo'? Is that even a word?"

Holy fuck.

An American voice spoke in the background. "It's like a snowmobile."

"There are no Skidoos in England."

"That's because we don't have enough snow," an English voice explained. Iris? "A few flakes, and everyone freaks out and stays home."

"I fell off a Skidoo in Vermont," another American said. "A moose jumped out in front of me."

"Shh, shhh. So, we saw your words," Rania said. "Now do you believe us?"

Somebody giggled. Iris again. "Nice underpants, by the way, but you didn't have to dress up specially."

There I was, standing half-naked in the grounds of a run-down Afghan hotel, and my whole world had just been turned on its head. And the only sentence I could manage to utter was, "You'd better not have been watching me in the shower."

"I second that," Beckett said from behind.

When I turned, Reed held out my trousers.

"You might need these. Don't worry; we've all worn that look." When I made no move to take them, he gave me a sympathetic pat on the shoulder. "You all right?"

No. No, I wasn't. And at that moment, I wasn't sure I ever would be.

CHAPTER 23

ZIYA

Mother of a goatherd, it was worse than I thought.

I realised Ro had been under a lot of strain these past few days, but until this evening, I thought he'd been holding it together. His nightmares had worried me, and now? Now, he'd cracked. Why else would he be standing in the hotel garden in his underwear? And who were those two men with him? The Americans he'd mentioned earlier?

I shrank back into the shadows as they headed in my direction. The black burqa I'd hurriedly pulled on made me all but invisible, but I still held my breath as they passed within six feet of me.

"Come and sit down, buddy," the dark-haired man carrying Ro's clothes said. "It might not be as bad as you think."

The other guy steered Ro across the lawn towards the only room with a light on. Should I offer to help? Would Ro even want me to? I'd be lying if I said it didn't hurt that he'd sought the comfort of strangers instead of talking to me.

Did he think I was too fragile? Because that stung too. Hadn't I proven that I was strong enough to cope during the journey from Deraz?

I used the cover of the scrawny trees as I crept closer and closer to the men's room. A light breeze whispered through the overhanging branches, and I shivered, partly from the cold but mostly out of worry. On any other day, Ro would have sensed my presence, but tonight, he was oblivious. We still needed to travel to Kabul. How could we get there if Ro had lost his mind? The familiar sense of panic slithered its way up my throat, and for the thousandth time, I cursed Afghan men in general and Tabesh in particular. Without his deceit, we wouldn't be in this position.

Inside, the strangers' room looked the same as ours, except they had extra chairs and a small table. And a laptop, a slim, expensive-looking one. Did everyone from America have fancy computers? Even backpackers?

"Are they still watching?" Ro asked.

Who was "they"? I glanced around, but the only movement came from a bird swooping low towards the main building. Even the street sounds from outside seemed muted.

"Does it feel like they are?" the blond-haired man asked.

"How am I supposed to know? Twitchy is my normal operating state."

Uh-oh. This didn't sound good. Was he hearing voices? Seeing things? Ro snatched his trousers and began putting them on, and I definitely shouldn't have felt that pang of disappointment. This was the first time I'd got a good look at his body, and I'd probably committed a thousand sins in the process.

What's one more added to the list, Ziya?

"I'm not sure of the answer to that. Want a cup of tea?"

"The kettle doesn't work," the dark-haired man pointed out.

"Cola? Lemonade?"

"I don't want a bloody drink; I want to scoop my eyeballs out with a spoon."

This got worse and worse. Several years ago, I'd read a case study where a psychiatric patient tried to do just that. Doctors managed to save the sight in one of his eyes, but he had to spend years in a hospital afterwards.

"They'll still be able to hear you."

No, no, no! Don't feed into the fantasies.

"Are they going to be in my head for the rest of my life?"

"Not at all. Everybody needs to sleep."

"This isn't fucking funny."

No, it wasn't, not one bit.

"Sorry."

Ro turned to a corner—an empty corner—with his hands on his hips. "And you can stop laughing too."

"There's a ghost in here?"

"Yes, there's a bloody ghost. They're everywhere, especially in this graveyard of a country."

Ghost? Now we were onto ghosts? I was way, way out of my depth here. Perhaps if I could make it to the university and find my old psychology teacher, we might be able to get Ro the help he needed? Therapy sessions, a proper diagnosis, maybe some pills?

If I came out of hiding, would Tabesh find me? There was a good chance—he had spies everywhere. But Ro was too important for me to shy away from trying. Yes, we'd had a rocky patch, but the trials of the journey to Jalalabad had shown me his true character. Ro was selfless. He cared. I'd had time to think about the lies he'd told and consider his reasons for telling them, and I realised now that an attempt to do the right thing for Balaguri had snowballed into an avalanche of untruths when we'd grown close.

I forgave him.

But could I save him from himself?

"Look, how about we try a different method of talking to them?" The dark-haired guy waved a hand at the laptop. "Skype? FaceTime?"

Had they *all* lost their minds?

"Stop. Just stop!" I couldn't take it any longer. "You should be ashamed of yourselves. Can't you see he's unwell?"

The look of abject horror on Ro's face when he turned and saw me made my heart seize. I tore off my veil and gripped his hands.

"Don't listen to these people. Please, come back to our room and we can talk about this." I'd toss that whiny American woman out of the window if necessary. "I understand you're under a lot of stress."

The blond-haired man stepped forward, reaching towards me. "Hey, what's this?"

I smacked his hand away as it reached for my necklace, then flinched on instinct, waiting for the blow to land. But it didn't. Ro got between us, snorting like an angry bull, and then he had the would-be thief pinned against the wall.

"Don't you dare fucking touch her."

"Chill, dude. I didn't mean to— Don't...don't you get it?" The words were difficult to make out over the choking sounds. "That's the medallion I was t-t-talking about."

Ro pressed the hand that wasn't around the man's throat against his own ear. "Shut up. Just shut the fuck up!"

I tried a hand on his arm, ready to jump back if I needed to. "Please, Ro. Let him go. Too many people have been hurt already."

The effect was instantaneous. Ro released his prey and stumbled backward. "Sorry. Ziya, I'm so sorry." He glared at the other men. "Do *not* touch her."

Meanwhile, the dark-haired man had been fiddling with his phone, and now he held up the screen.

"We won't touch her, buddy, but you need to look at this. Beck's right. Your girl has the missing piece. It *did* find its way back to you."

I looked at the phone too, and the hot panic that had been coursing through me turned glacial. On the screen were four gold pieces, arranged together in a perfect circle. But there was a gap in the middle. And that gap was the exact same shape as Grandma's talisman.

"I...I don't understand."

"We're still working out the puzzle ourselves," the blond-haired guy said. Beck? "But your boyfriend is a big part of the answer, and so is your necklace."

Ro squeezed my hand. "I haven't got a bloody clue what's going on."

And then all at once I *did* understand. The realisation hit me like a fist to the face. Ro had saved me, and he'd saved Katie Waller. *He* was the saviour Grandma had told me about. And now he was meant to do the same for mankind. The talisman belonged to him. It made horrifying, perfect sense.

"You're him," I whispered. "You're the traveller."

Three men stared at me.

"The what?" they asked as one.

A tear rolled down my cheek. I couldn't hold it in.

"Grandma told me you'd come for the necklace one day." I fumbled to pull it off over my head. "Here. It's yours."

Ro tried to give it back. "Zizi, what are you talking about?"

"I was only ever looking after it. Grandma told me to keep it safe until you came."

"Treasure…"

"Don't you get it? *I'm* not your treasure. You didn't come to me, not at Balaguri and not at Tabesh's house. You only wanted the necklace. *That's* your treasure."

"That's not true."

My cheeks were wet now, damp with grief at losing not only a man I cared deeply for but hope as well. It turned out there were three elements in our relationship, and I was the spare part. Ro had been heeding the siren's call of the golden charm around my neck, whether he knew it or not.

"Then how, out of all the places in the world you could have gone, out of all the women you could have met, did you end up with me, the one who was wearing the key to your destiny?"

"I…" Ro's voice dropped to a whisper. "I don't know."

Sometimes, being right was the worst thing of all.

Beck and his friend fidgeted uncomfortably. Who were they, exactly? I realised now that they were connected to Grandma's prophecy, but why were they here? Why today?

"What did your grandma tell you about the medallion?" Beck asked. "About Rohan?"

"Almost nothing! Just that she'd been its guardian and now I had to take over. That it would help to save the world when its owner returned."

"The traveller?"

"That's what she called him."

"We know Rohan as the Judge."

Ro threw up his hands, still bare-chested. "The only thing I've ever judged is the poor choices of recruits coming through selection. And as for travelling, yes, I'm well versed in the joys of military transport, but that hardly makes me unique. This necklace belongs to Ziya. I don't want it or need it. What I *do* need is sleep, because tomorrow..." He checked his watch. "Today, I need to get to Kabul. I've got an entitled American journalist to deliver to the embassy, and I need to get ahold of my contacts in intelligence because as I'm sure you know from eavesdropping on my conversations, there's a KLA dirty bomb out there some- where, most likely with an innocent target's name on it."

A sob burst from my throat. Mention of the KLA reminded me that Yafir was out there too, and he was also a victim of those monsters. My baby brother didn't have a bad heart. But he was young and naive, too trusting, just like me. That he'd been bringing food to Katie showed they'd already corrupted him. What else would they make him do?

"We can give you a ride to Kabul," Beck offered. "We have a truck."

"The Jala Mujahideen is after us. It's not as simple as just hitching a lift."

"The Jala Mujahideen's fucked. You took out their leader in Deraz, and their number two died in the valley. According to my sources, the third and fourth in command are fighting about who's gonna take over, and they've forgotten you entirely. Plus the only checkpoints between here and Kabul at the moment are manned by the US Army, and I've still got friends in low, low places."

"Nobody's looking for five people travelling together," Reed added. "And we'll also have the Electi on our side."

"Just what we need," Ro muttered. "More dead bodies."

Huh? Dead bodies?

"What's the Electi?" I asked.

Was it somehow connected to the fatalities in the pass? I'd been at a loss for an explanation, but if the supernatural was involved... Perhaps it was strange to believe in such things, especially since I'd spent so long studying science, but there was so much that science couldn't explain. Grandma had taught me to be open-minded. When she was younger, many had shunned her for her beliefs because those beliefs didn't fit with their own views of religion or the world, but they hadn't been able to change her mind. Even my own father had warned me she was a few goats short of a full herd, and as for the Taliban... She'd learned to keep quiet about her thoughts. But in the evenings, we'd talk for hours, and she told me stories that had been passed down through generations. Tales of the traveller, of ghosts and vampires and shape-shifting wolves, of realms that existed beyond the earth.

Everyone told her she was wrong, and perhaps even I'd thought her tales were a little far-fetched.

But Ro was proof that she'd been right.

The men all looked at each other, and it was Beck who spoke.

"The Electi are basically supernatural law enforcement. Judges, jury, and executioners."

"But you said Ro was the judge."

"We think he's a different kind of judge. Kind of like a Supreme Court justice."

"You think? You're not sure?"

"We're all learning as we go."

Ro rubbed his eyes. "This is a horror story."

"Can't say I disagree with you there. So, Kabul? You gonna take the bus?"

Silence was Ro's answer.

"Thought not. What time do you want to leave?"

CHAPTER 24
RO

This was the nightmare that never ended.

Tuesday morning found me sitting behind Beckett as the truck bumped over pothole after pothole towards Kabul. My underwear was still damp from when I'd showered in it, and Ziya had climbed into the other side of the back seat in silence. Which meant Waller was squashed next to me in the middle, complaining as usual.

"The US gives, like, millions to these people, and they can't even build proper roads? I don't get it."

Reed seemed the more amenable of our two new companions, but I'd noticed a muscle twitched in his neck every time Waller spoke.

"Because feeding people is more important than renewing the pavement," he said.

"You think? My daddy says all the money gets lost to government corruption."

"If you already knew the answer, then why'd you ask the question?"

Forty miles to Kabul, and I was counting down the

minutes until we could ditch the bitch. That moment couldn't come soon enough. In an ideal world, I'd have got rid of Beckett and Reed as well, but I had a feeling they'd just pop up again like bad pennies.

After Ziya's appearance last night, I'd told Rania and the other girls that our discussion would have to wait. Whatever they had to say, Ziya was more important. After all, I'd carried this curse, as Rania called it, with me for twenty-seven years. One more day wouldn't matter. And Ziya... She thought I was only with her for a bloody necklace? Of course that wasn't true. Was it?

If a month ago, somebody had asked why I was attracted to her, I could have reeled off a whole list of attributes—she was smart, kind, courageous, beautiful inside and out. But there were any number of women who met those criteria. What made Ziya so special? Honestly, I couldn't give an answer. She just *was*. The charm she wore around her neck was a lump of metal. An inanimate object. A shiny gold *thing*.

Unless Beckett was to be believed, in which case, it could be so much more.

This was such a fucked-up mess.

Made all the more complicated by a child, most likely mine, who would be arriving in four short months through no fault of his own.

Perhaps I *should* have stayed up to talk last night because sleep hadn't come easily. I'd heard Ziya fidgeting too and longed to reach out to her, but she hadn't spoken, and I had no idea what to say. And now we couldn't talk because Waller was still whining and she obviously had no idea who Beckett and Reed truly were or why they were there. We'd told her they were old friends of mine from my military days, here to help out with a ride to the embassy.

The dog rested his head on my knee, staring up with doleful eyes. The uncertainty in them reflected my own. He didn't know it yet, but he was off to America to be dressed up in fancy collars and spoiled with expensive food and treats. Poor bugger. Waller was already planning out posts for his Instagram account.

And Waller didn't know it yet, but she wouldn't be flying straight back home on Daddy's dime as she intended. When we got to Kabul, we'd be making a detour via my apartment so I could pick up a secure phone and brief Marina Carrigan before we drove to the embassy. Whatever Waller knew about radioactivity in the desert around Tangar, she'd be spilling the details to any number of intelligence agencies, not posting it all over Facebook. I pitied whoever had to question her, but I sure was glad it wouldn't be me.

Four hours later, we hit our first snag. It was about time. The trip from Jalalabad had gone suspiciously well so far. Beckett's mates had waved us through both checkpoints, we'd made it to my apartment, and I'd caught Marina between meetings to give her an update. Her sharp intake of breath followed by a string of expletives suggested the information was new and somewhat unexpected.

"Well, that's a twist in the fucking tale, isn't it? Bollocking arseholes."

"Don't shoot the messenger."

"Where the hell did the KLA get radioactive material?"

"I'm fairly sure the answer to that is above my pay grade."

"What does Katie Waller know?"

"I doubt she's privy to many details, but she should be able to give you a rundown on the area she was poking around in. I'd also suggest warning our American friends to keep her away from social media."

"Noted. Get her to the US embassy, and then you need to head to our embassy for a debrief."

"What about Ziya? We had a deal."

"Yes, and I don't break my word. Is your cover blown?"

"Blown? I don't think so. Dead men tell no tales."

Not to the authorities, anyway. The only man left living was the hotel receptionist, and as we'd found out, he'd been more interested in Ziya than in me. As long as I trimmed my beard and cleaned up, he wouldn't recognise my ugly mug.

"Good, good. It'll take a few weeks to sort out the paperwork. Your girl can hole up in your apartment until we make the arrangements, and you can keep your ear to the ground at the university."

"Go back to work as normal?"

"Is there any reason why not?"

A thousand reasons. Nothing was normal anymore. But I could hardly discuss the issues with Marina because she'd send me straight to a shrink.

"No."

"Excellent. And Ro?"

"Yes?"

Marina's voice softened just a little. "Great work out there."

High praise indeed from a woman who held onto compliments as if releasing one into the wild might make her physically ill.

I took my time changing my clothes to give Marina the opportunity to cue up her American colleagues, and then we piled into the truck again for the trip to the US embassy.

Technically, I could have gone alone, but I didn't yet trust Beckett and Reed, not to be alone in my apartment and certainly not to take care of Ziya.

And now I wanted to sink into the ground as Waller argued with the deputy chief of mission.

"What do you mean, dogs aren't allowed here? Yoda's my emotional support animal, and under US legislation, you can't discriminate against him. And this…" She stomped one foot. "Is US soil."

"Ma'am, it's not an issue of discrimination. The ambassador's wife has a severe fur allergy."

"Can't she stay at home? It's not as if I'll be here for long. I can book a flight, like, tomorrow."

"I'm afraid that's not possible. We have people here who want to ask you questions, and we'll need your help with identifying the area where you spotted the radioactivity."

"You can't keep me here."

"Well, actually…"

"So I'm a prisoner?"

"Ma'am, this is a matter of national security."

"You can't kick Yoda out onto the streets." Waller knelt and flung her arms around the poor mutt's neck. "He saved my life."

That was a stretch, but I'd developed a soft spot for the dog, and although Ziya hadn't said so in as many words, I knew she was fond of him too.

"I can take the dog."

Waller beamed up at me. "You will?"

"Yes."

"Like, permanently?"

"Uh…"

"Because I love him and everything, but I already have a

cat, and I don't even know if he likes cats." She didn't think of this earlier? "You promise you won't abandon him?"

My life was going to hell in a handbasket.

"Scout's honour."

"Okay, fine. Where can I get a shower in this place? And is there any proper food? What the people eat here, it's inhumane."

One issue resolved, one new challenge to face. Although I had to admit, Yoda did make much better company than Waller. Out in the car park, Beckett raised an eyebrow when I loaded the dog back into the truck.

"Don't say a bloody word, okay?"

Yoda curled up in the middle of the seat between Ziya and me, and she sighed contentedly as she scritched his head. That alone made the decision to keep him worth it. Now all I had to do was buy dog food and a leash, work out how to transport an animal to England, rent a house that allowed pets, and somehow convince Ziya to give me a second chance.

No fucking problem.

CHAPTER 25

ZIYA

Ro's apartment could best be described as minimalist. Clean, tidy, and plain, with none of the tacky decorations Tabesh had been so fond of. My husband. Now my ex-husband, I very much suspected. And why did I think that? Because I'd found Tabesh's keys outside the hotel room in Jalalabad this morning, half-hidden by a straggly bush. Three keys on a metal ring—front door, back door, gate—with a plastic tag. Just in case I might have been mistaken, the plastic tag was printed with a photo of him grinning as he held up a rifle in one hand and a gold cup of what was most likely vodka in the other.

Yes, Tabesh had been close, and Ro had been outside.

Now Ro was here, and Tabesh was nowhere to be seen.

Perhaps I should have been more upset at his disappearance, but I couldn't bring myself to be devastated about the probable death of a man who'd raped me over and over again and then treated me as a human incubator. Being honest, I was more disappointed that Ro had kept yet another secret from me.

I lay back on his bed and stared at the plain white ceiling. Ro had insisted I take his bedroom while he slept on the couch, and Yoda had also decided that the huge double bed with its springy mattress was the most comfortable place in the apartment. The two Americans were in a guest room along the hallway.

What would happen next? Ro said we needed to stay here until the papers came for me to go to England, but now that the immediate danger was over and I had the time and space to think, the future terrified me. I had nothing. No home, no family. At the thought of Yafir, a sob welled up in my throat. Where was he? Ro had promised to leave a message for him in Balaguri, but if Yafir was in Europe, he wouldn't find it, and I'd never see my brother again. Yoda crept along on his belly and licked my tears. I tried to push him away, but he only snuggled closer.

"Stop, shh, shh."

A soft knock at the door sounded. "Ziya?"

Ro. I knew we had to talk, but I'd hoped to put it off for a few more hours.

"Yes?"

"Can I come in?"

It was his room. I could hardly say no. "Okay."

When he stepped inside and saw my tears, the panic on his face was all too clear, and I thought he was going to run right out again. But no, he fidgeted inside the door, hands in his pockets.

"Why are you crying? What's wrong?"

"Nothing."

Everything.

"I don't have a handkerchief. Maybe I should..."

"It's fine." I wiped my face with a sleeve. "I just...I just don't know what to do."

"At the moment, you don't have to do a thing. Rest, and I'll let you know when it's time for dinner."

Dinner! How late was it? I scrambled to get up. "I should start preparing now. What do you want me to make?"

"Zizi, I'm not expecting you to cook."

"But...but what will we eat?"

"Either I'll buy something in the market, or I'll cook a meal myself."

Ro would cook? The idea was foreign to me. My father had never cooked. My brother had never cooked. And Tabesh certainly hadn't cooked, although he did occasionally throw dishes when the food wasn't to his liking.

"Any preferences?" Ro asked. "Kofta? Chicken? Something with vegetables? *Badenjan*?"

He'd remembered that eggplants were my favourite? I quickly nodded.

"Great. I'll call you when it's ready."

"What about tomorrow?" I blurted.

"Tomorrow? We can have *badenjan* again if you want."

"I meant with us. What happens with us?"

The strained smile slipped off Ro's face completely as he stepped farther into the room and perched on the edge of the bed.

"We just need to sit tight for a week or two. Then we can head to England, and I'll rent a place in the short term while we come up with a plan."

"You want us to live together?"

"I'd like us to try. If ultimately things don't work out, then at least we'll have no regrets."

"But we barely know each other! We didn't sleep together out of love, Ro. It was desperation on my part and pity on yours."

"What about all those nights we spent talking?"

"I..."

"You can't deny that there was something more."

"But the necklace..."

"Forget the necklace."

"It led you to me."

"What if it led *you* to *me*? If you're such a believer in fate, then who's to say that gold charm wasn't in both of our destinies?"

I'd never really thought of it that way. Could Ro be right? How did the gold piece get into our family in the first place? Grandma had never said. I'm not sure she even knew. But by some cosmic fluke, it had ended up in my hands, and then Ro had walked into my life.

"Maybe."

"Maybe? Ziya, there's no 'maybe' about it. We were meant to be together, and I'll do anything to prove I'm not the arsehole you think I am."

"You'll do anything? Like killing my husband?"

The words just fell out. I gasped, Ro froze, and I wished I could snatch my stupidity back and swallow it down. I couldn't afford to alienate him, not when I relied on him for everything.

"Fuck." At least he didn't try to deny it. "How did you find out Tabesh was dead?"

"His keys were on the ground outside the hotel room."

A long, low groan escaped Ro's lips. "I wasn't thinking straight. I should have spotted them. But Ziya, I didn't kill him, not with my own hands. Remember in the valley, the way those men just died?"

"I'm unlikely to ever forget that."

"Of course you're not. Forgive me. I'm an idiot." Ro swallowed hard. "Well, it happened again. Reed and

Beckett were watching Tabesh and his two friends, and I was watching all of them. Then I realised Beckett had a knife. So I dealt with that, and it seemed the Electi decided to help out with the Tabesh issue."

"The Electi? They're here in Afghanistan?"

"Not in body, but possibly in spirit."

"I don't understand."

"That makes two of us. The Electi have promised to explain, but I've had more important things to deal with." Ro reached out to tuck a lock of hair behind my ear. "*You're more important.*"

A shiver ran through me at his touch. For the most part, he'd kept his hands off me, but even as reservations hammered inside my brain, my body craved his.

"I'm a nobody."

"You're the woman who's been haunting my dreams for months. You're clever and brave and beautiful, and soon you'll be the mother of our child. That's not 'nobody.'" Ro leaned forward to kiss me on the forehead. "Try to get some sleep before dinner, Zizi? I see in your eyes how tired you are."

"I can't sleep. Every time I close my eyes, I worry about Yafir. Will you... You said you'd leave a note for him at Balaguri? I don't think he'll go back there, but just in case..."

I wasn't sure about the "brave" or "beautiful" parts from Ro's little speech—most of the time, I wanted to curl up in a ball and hide—but I knew I wasn't stupid. Naive like my brother, perhaps, but not stupid. And my gut told me that if he was involved with the KLA, there could be no good outcome. When my father worked for them, they'd been a small group of idealists, all bark and no bite, but now... Living with Tabesh, I'd heard more about the Afghan underworld than most. Those guards sure had liked to gossip. And I knew that the KLA had morphed from propaganda and posturing into action. If my brother was still alive, he was on borrowed time.

"I'll leave the note."

It was all I could ask for.

CHAPTER 26

RO

It wasn't only exhaustion I'd seen in Ziya's eyes. Sorrow lurked there too, and I knew why. She'd lost so much. Her home, her family, and her brother. Yes, I'd leave a message for Yafir in Balaguri, but if Waller was right and he'd seen a path to Europe, he wouldn't be going back to the village. And since the KLA would only facilitate passage to Europe if there was something in it for them, that meant we'd be attending either a jury trial or a funeral in the near future. Unless I managed to get to Athens and find Yafir before it was too late.

But how could I? Time was of the essence, and Ziya's papers wouldn't come through for weeks. Leaving her behind in Kabul wasn't an option I wanted to contemplate. Even if she stayed in the apartment with a stockpile of food and a fully charged phone, there was still a risk somebody might get to her.

"Penny for them?"

I glanced up an instant before I walked into Beck—I figured I should be calling him Beck now, seeing as we were past the formalities.

"Just contemplating the pros and cons of another act of stupidity."

"Yeah, I know that feeling. Are you ready to talk to the girls yet? I've held them off for as long as I can, but Kim's not the most patient girl in the world, and if she doesn't get some answers, she's gonna volunteer Rania to visit in person."

Reed appeared behind him. "The only reason she hasn't done that yet is because the four girls have to stay together to activate their death-stare thing."

"Then perhaps Rania *should* come here," I said, then sighed. "Okay, fine, I'll speak to them. Better to get it over with."

By the time I'd made a mug of tea, Reed had his laptop set up on the dining table. As I took my first sip, the Electi appeared on screen, the quartet squashed onto a three-seater sofa. I wasn't sure quite what I'd been expecting, but they all looked remarkably...normal.

Rania was easy to pick out. Dark hair, dark skin, dark eyes whose inherent wariness came through even on a screen. Out of the four women, she seemed the most relaxed. Or should I say resigned? Almost as if she'd accepted her fate, whatever that fate may be.

Kimberly sat next to her, the American princess. Everything about her screamed high-maintenance. Reed was dating her? He was a braver man than me.

That left a blonde and a petite brunette. Since the blonde was gripping the hand of the man perched on the arm beside her, I figured she must be Iris. Nicole gave us a nervous wave as another chap wandered into view. Rania's other half? He sat on the other arm next to her, so that was a fair assumption.

"So, I guess we should start with introductions?"

Kimberly said, and then proceeded to tell me what I'd already worked out. "And you're Rohan? It's weird that Beck had already met you, don't you think?"

Before I could answer, Iris did. "It's fate. All of this is fate. So you're a soldier? That's definitely more useful than being a gardener. For our job, anyway. Not that any of us want to do the job. I mean, those people who died in the valley? It was a complete accident, I swear."

"None of us knew they'd die," Nicole said.

"We thought *you* were going to die."

"I had a plan," I muttered, even if it hadn't been a very good one. "Why did you let one of them live?"

Rania finally spoke, her voice soft and measured. "We didn't. As Iris said, it wasn't a conscious decision. We all simply willed those men dead, and twelve of them obliged. Our assumption is that this new...ability works the same way as the Electi curse. So if the person we direct our thoughts at has killed before, his black soul will rise, and if he hasn't, then nothing happens."

Right. Beck had mentioned something similar before. And if I abandoned rational thought and forgot everything I'd learned about the laws of physics, I could grudgingly agree that the explanation made a certain amount of sense. The mujahid who'd run off had been little more than a boy.

"If you think we all have magical powers, then why do the souls scatter for you and not for me?" I'd killed murderers before. Their spirits hung around as normal. "Why do the souls turn black? I've never seen that before."

"Because our powers aren't the same. You're the Judge."

"So I've been told. But who am I meant to judge?"

"Us."

What the hell? "*You?*"

"It was a surprise to us, too. Only Iris even knew of your existence, but we didn't find her until last September."

"Now do you see why this is fate?" Iris asked. "We've spent centuries apart, and now in the space of a year and a half, we're all back together again."

"We think that maybe the build-up of trapped souls here on earth finally triggered a reaction, and that reaction resulted in our reunion," Nicole said. "Believe it or not, their presence is detectable. Each soul emits a low level of high-frequency electromagnetic radiation, measurable if you know what you're looking for, but undetectable to the human eye or ear."

"Bad juju," Iris added.

"That's the non-scientific term. We believe that these waves have a negative impact on human emotions, and possibly on the earth itself. Look around you—war, hate, division, fires, earthquakes, ice storms, famine... What's the one thing that links them? Trapped souls. And it's a self-perpetuating cycle—directly or indirectly, each of those events causes more violence, which leads to more souls being tethered, which leads to even more disasters."

"And we're the ones who are meant to fix this?"

"Yes."

"How? I heard that you're meant to avenge people's deaths to release the souls. Unless you plan to hunt down every murderer on earth and blast them with thought waves, I'd say we're shit out of luck. And many of these souls are centuries old. Their killers are long gone."

"That's where you come in."

I suppose I should have guessed.

"And exactly what am I meant to do?"

"We're not entirely sure, but we think that we have to present a soul's case to you, and if you judge that there's nothing more we can do to get justice for them, then you can…I don't know, send them to the next plane or something?"

"Which takes us back to the 'how' question."

"It'll involve your gold piece."

"If you mean Ziya's gold piece, then I'm not taking it from her. It's all she has left from her grandma."

"Ziya inherited it?" Iris asked. "Maybe she's descended from the original line of guardians?"

"The what?"

"The Electi were split up during the witch hunts of the fourteenth century and sent to different parts of the world for our own safety. We were all just children then. With each generation, our souls and gold pieces got passed on, but knowledge got lost and it seems you did too."

"At some point, one of your ancestors must have died without having a son," Nicole said. "So your soul ended up in a new family line. As far as we can ascertain, suitable hosts have a particular genetic marker, for the Electi at least. I'd love to get a look at your DNA too."

"I'm not a bloody lab rat."

Nicole's face fell, and I felt a pang of guilt for that, but I hadn't asked for any part in this. Although the story wasn't entirely far-fetched. Could Ziya be descended from the original Judge? I was beginning to suspect that anything was possible. I thought back to my days in Balaguri—not my recent trip, but happier times. Ziya called me the traveller, and I remembered Shaykha Bushra mentioning the term in some of the stories she'd told. She'd spoken of a wandering soul who brought peace to mankind, and only after the earth was at rest could he find peace within himself. I'd always assumed it was a fairy tale. A myth. If I truly was the traveller, was that why I always felt unsettled? Why I grew more troubled with every passing season? Fuck. There were thousands of lost souls on earth. *Millions.* How was I meant to get rid of them all? And Ziya's grandma had spoken about more than just the traveller. Did vampires and werewolves exist too? Because that wasn't a possibility I wanted to contemplate.

"Maybe I could borrow the gold piece," I suggested. "As long as it wouldn't get damaged."

Kimberly beamed at me. "They don't get damaged. We only have to put them together so they're touching. They seem to act as some kind of supernatural switch."

"Good. So that's sorted out. If you leave me a contact number, I'll call you when I'm free. And in the meantime, do you think you could stop looking through my eyes? I'd like to be able to take a shit without an audience."

And kiss Ziya if she ever let me near her again.

Rania shook her head. "As I said, while you're in Afghanistan, we're in your head. We've come too far to risk you dying unnecessarily. But compromise is possible. Since we have other means of communicating now, you can let us know if you need to use the bathroom."

"That's not much of a compromise. That's you doing whatever you want ninety-five percent of the time."

"Only in the short term."

"When are you going to England?" Kimberly asked. "We'll meet you there, and then we can begin putting the rest of the puzzle pieces together. Whereabouts do you live?"

"Right now? I live in Kabul. And after I leave here, I have another trip to make straight away, so as *I* said, I'll call you when I'm available."

"What trip? Where are you going?"

I wanted to tell Kimberly it was none of her business,

but I was all too aware that my destination would stay secret for about five minutes.

"Athens."

"Athens?"

"He's going to look for Ziya's brother," Rania said. "Isn't it obvious?"

"Aw, that's sweet. Maybe we could come to help? I've never visited Greece before."

A wedding planner tagging along? That was the last thing I needed.

"It's not a vacation."

"Sure, I know that. But we're good at finding people. We found Iris, and that was like looking for a needle in a haystack. One person in a crowd of seven billion."

"More like three and a half billion," Rania pointed out. "We knew she was female. But Kimberly's right—Will, Reed, and I are private investigators, and Beck used to work as a bounty hunter." Seriously? "We've got access to networks and resources that you most likely don't have."

It shouldn't have irked me that Rania was right, but it did. These people had ridden roughshod into my life, and now they were hell-bent on turning it upside down. But they'd also helped me out of several tricky situations, and whether I liked it or not, I couldn't simply walk away from them. Giving the Electi the slip would be impossible. So perhaps I should make use of their dubious talents?

"I barely know you. Why should I trust you?"

"Did Beck or Reed do anything underhand? No. Have we lied to you? No. We've been completely transparent, whether you appreciate that or not."

Another point I couldn't refute.

"Fine," I said on a sigh. "Fine. If you're going to keep interfering in my life, then you might as well help."

Kimberly's smile was a touch too smug for my liking. "Superb. I'll start making the arrangements. When are you planning to leave?"

"To leave Kabul? Not for weeks. As I'm sure you already know, I rescued Katie Waller in exchange for Ziya's British citizenship, and we're waiting for her papers to come through."

"You shouldn't wait that long," Rania said. "We started researching the KLA, and rumour says they're planning action in Europe. If Ziya's brother is involved, a few weeks' delay could be fatal."

"You think I don't know that?"

Rania merely watched me.

"Sorry." I shouldn't have snapped. "Yes, I'm all too aware of the ticking clock, but I'm not leaving Ziya behind. She's nearly five months pregnant, for pity's sake."

"So we need to get her temporary papers."

"Oh, and we just magic those out of thin air, do we?"

"What are you thinking?" Reed asked.

Rania leaned forward to look at Nicole, whose horrified expression told me I was missing a significant part of the story.

"Oh, no. No, no, no. A thousand times no."

"He's out of jail now, and there's no way a slippery little worm like Corey Harmon went straight."

"Who's Corey Harmon?" I whispered to Reed.

"Before Nicole met Beck, she accidentally dated a master forger. Since the prisons are all full, they let him out with an electronic tag."

Nicole was still shaking her head. "I don't want to speak to him ever again."

"He owes you a favour," Kimberly said. "And we could pay him."

Even Beck chimed in. "The guy's an asshole, sprite, but he does source quality passports. And I don't want to hang around in Afghanistan either."

Nicole folded her arms, obviously unhappy, but also resigned. "Okay, okay. I'll call him. But somebody would still need to take the papers to Kabul."

"I'll go," Rania said.

Will shook his head. "No way."

"I'm perfectly capable."

"Nia, I know you are. Believe me, I know. But we need to keep the four of you together. The Electi can't work properly if there are only three. We tried it, remember? I'll go."

"But—"

"I'll only be in Afghanistan for a few hours. Plus I've visited Athens before. When we get there, it might be advantageous to have someone on the ground who's familiar with the city."

Rania relented with a quiet, "Okay," but she didn't look happy about it. I couldn't blame her. I was far from happy either.

"While you're in the mood to assist, would you be able to find a safe place for Ziya in the UK until I get back?"

This time, Iris grinned. "Sure. Rania has a spare room. She can stay with us."

And so it was arranged. My life wasn't my own anymore, and soon I'd set off across Europe on a mission I gave only a slim chance of success.

CHAPTER 27
RO

Four days later, I'd discovered that weddings weren't the only thing Kimberly could plan. Will had arrived with not only a passport for Ziya, but also a full set of travel papers for Yoda. Apparently, Nicole's slug of an ex had tried to charge rush rates, but Nicole had reminded him that he stole her TV, and he'd grudgingly agreed to provide the documentation at cost. Now we were Roger and Zineb Kent, both with British passports, and I had to concede they were top-notch work. Will had also brought two suitcases full of equipment—spare phones, cameras, clothes for Ziya and me, and even a selection of collars for the dog. We had a pet-friendly hotel reservation —thankfully, Yoda had been quick to pick up the concept of house-training—and a rental car waiting at Athens International Airport.

My decision to trust Beck and Reed had so far proven to be the right one. Beck had travelled with me to Balaguri while Reed stayed at the apartment with Ziya, but the village had still been deserted. The spirits hanging around the well told me that occasionally a passer-by stopped to use the tap, but there'd been no sign of Yafir. I'd left a note in what remained of his house, pinned to the wall in the kitchen. Like Ziya, I had my doubts that he'd return, but at least we'd covered all bases.

Beck and Reed had also stood guard while I went back to the university. I'd spoken with Marina first to let her know what I was doing—I felt I owed it to her since she'd been supportive in the main—and although she couldn't condone my rescue mission officially, I got the impression that she privately supported the attempt to rescue Yafir. She'd signed off on a month of "personal leave" and warned me not to do anything stupid.

Based on recent form, I couldn't make any guarantees. I'd already omitted to mention that Ziya, Beck, and Reed were coming with me.

Marina also delivered a snippet of bad news—sources suggested Dayyin Rouhani had left Afghanistan a week ago, but the intelligence services had lost track of the man they suspected to be him after he landed in Rome. He'd flown on an Italian passport. If he was in Europe, that made our mission all the more urgent.

I hadn't wanted Ziya to go to Greece. My original plan meant escorting her to Will and Rania's home in England so she could stay safe with the Electi while I headed to Europe, but she'd wanted to go to Athens, so we'd talked about it over cups of tea, and now she was coming to Athens. I might have been able to withstand the most barbaric of interrogators, but give me a pleading Ziya and I'd back down every time.

When I went to collect the files from my office, I told Faruq I had a family emergency to deal with. I wasn't lying. Ziya was my family now, and Yafir's situation certainly qualified as an emergency. What I didn't tell Faruq was that

I wouldn't be returning. I did say goodbye to Perry, though. I figured he deserved an explanation.

"You're going to be a father? Then I suppose I should offer my congratulations, old chap."

"Thank you."

"When are you leaving?"

"Saturday, if all goes according to plan."

"On one of those magic air-boats?"

The concept of planes had also been a difficult one for Perry to grasp.

"That's right.

"Can't say I won't miss our chats. Dr. Bashir spends far too much time talking about death, in my opinion, and I've seen enough of that to last me an eternity." He chortled at his own joke. "But I suppose all good things come to an end."

I didn't mention the possibility of freedom—in my eyes, giving a man false hope was as bad as leaving him with no hope at all. Instead, I mumbled my agreement, packed the last of my bits and pieces into a cardboard box, and left. No farewell party, no fanfare. That was the way I preferred things, to be honest.

I'd miss Kabul. The hustle and bustle of the city, my colleagues and students at the university, the friendliness of ordinary Afghans. Nothing was ever too much trouble. Corruption, war, and religious extremism had brought the country to its knees, but I had hopes that the forces of good would rise again. Perhaps one day soon, if the Electi's tale was to be believed.

But for now, I was on a plane bound for Athens with Ziya at my side. And somebody in my new circle of friends obviously had money because we were sitting in business class. I'd bet on Kimberly, although Will's plummy accent suggested a public-school upbringing as well. You could take the boy out of Eton, but you couldn't take Eton out of the boy.

"Would you like drinks before take-off?" the air hostess asked.

Since it was an Afghan carrier, the flight was dry, but she had three kinds of fruit juice on a tray. I took a glass of what might have been orange or mango, but Ziya shook her head. She was nervous. How did I know that, you ask? Because her nails were digging into my palm. But I didn't mind. She was holding my hand, and with our relationship still teetering on the rocks, I'd take any crumb of progress I could get.

CHAPTER 28
ZIYA

Ro breathed softly next to me, but I struggled to sleep. Instead, I watched the rise and fall of his chest, his face finally at peace. The furrows in his brow had grown deeper with every passing day. I'd been the one to cause most of that stress, first with my escape from Tabesh and now with this trip to search for Yafir. Guilt ate away at me, but when Ro had said he'd go to Greece, I couldn't turn the offer down.

And so many other people were helping us too—Reed, Beck, and Will on the plane, plus the Electi on their way to England from America. Inside, I was a mess of remorse and gratitude and fear that we'd be too late. Plus just a tiny bit nervous to be flying. At least my ears had stopped popping now. Ro had shown me how to wiggle my jaw to relieve the discomfort.

What would Athens be like? I'd studied the city along-side Reed while Ro and Beck went out, although I hadn't been able to focus on anything the day they'd travelled to Balaguri. I'd almost flung my arms around Ro when he came back in one piece, but I'd stopped myself at the last second. What if I made him uncomfortable? He'd been keeping his distance all week.

From what I'd seen, Athens seemed to be a city of many faces, much like Jalalabad. They both had their beauty—from the Mausoleum of King Amanullah Khan and the many mosques to the Acropolis and the Parthenon. But there was also a dark underbelly most tourists didn't see. And by bad luck or intention, Café Nostima—the only place in the city with a name like the one Yafir had mentioned to Katie Waller—was located on a seedy street near Omonia Square, one Ro said I'd go near over his dead body. Since I quite liked him alive, that meant I'd be staying in the hotel while he went to search for my brother. Ro had given in to me going to Athens in the first place; I wasn't about to argue for more.

But I was still worried about fitting in. Kimberly had sent a whole selection of maternity clothes made from the softest fabrics with beautiful patterns, and Ro had bought me a choice of chadors from the market to wear outside. Technically, I should have worn them inside too since I was neither related nor married to any of the men I was sharing an apartment with, but my inner rebel made me leave the cloak in the bedroom.

Grandma used to tell me tales of old Afghanistan, before war broke out. She'd worked in Kabul, and she'd worn short skirts and gone to the cinema with her friends. Headscarves had been optional. Until the fighting started, women's rights had been on a par with those in western countries—indeed, Afghan women were eligible to vote a year before women in the USA, and gender segregation was abolished in the 1950s. But then the Mujahideen began their battle with the government and the Taliban took over, which left women the biggest losers of all. Almost every scrap of progress we'd fought for got rolled back, and simply for being born female, we were punished worse than murderers.

The Taliban banned us from studying, from working, from leaving the house without a male relative acting as chaperone. We weren't allowed to show our skin in public or speak to an audience, and transgressions were punishable by anything from flogging to death. The situation had improved since the Taliban lost power, but that improvement was relative. We still had a long way to go before we got back the freedoms we'd had in the 1970s. Men like Tabesh forgot that in Islam, the sexes were equal, just as they forgot that killing was a sin unless one was following a lawful process.

So for now, we were still beholden to our fathers, to our brothers, to our husbands, and Afghan men had evolved to believe that beauty in a woman meant being plain and modest. Therefore we had to stay at home and cover up. A wife should look after the house, not indulge in frivolities like fashion.

But I wasn't in Afghanistan anymore.

Under my navy-blue chador, I'd worn a pair of jeans with a stretchy panel at the front, and a loose, flowery blouse with frilly cuffs and a bow at the neck. I'd loved the outfit as soon as I put it on, and it was the first time since I left Balaguri that I'd worn anything but a dress. Tabesh had hated women in trousers with a passion.

Careful not to wake Ro, I stood and folded up my chador. Then a lady from the cabin crew helped me to get my borrowed suitcase out of the overhead locker, and I swapped the shapeless cloak for a silky lightweight scarf that I draped over my hair.

Then I lay back in my seat and tried to sleep.

Ro's eyes widened when he woke and saw my new outfit, and I suddenly felt half-naked.

"You took off the chador?"

"Do you mind me wearing this? In public, I mean."

"You should dress for yourself, Zizi, not for me. *Be* yourself. Are you comfortable?"

"Uh, I think so? I mean, yes?"

"Then why would I mind you wearing jeans and a shirt? You need to put on your seat belt, though. We're descending to land."

And that was that. I did up my seat belt, slipped my hand into Ro's, then wiggled my jaw as I got my first look at Europe.

At first, I thought we'd got lost and ended up at a palace. The marble facade of the building gleamed under purple and white lights, a masterpiece against the darkening sky. But then I read the sign. *The Olympia Hotel and Suites.* Wait, we were staying here? I kept quiet as the car drew to a halt outside, desperately trying to pretend that all this was normal. Mrs. Zineb Kent wouldn't gawp in shock, and that was who I had to be this week. Ro had picked our names, and he explained that he'd kept them close to our real identities so we could carry on calling each other Ro and Zizi. I appreciated the thought—my brain was so frazzled that if

I'd had to call him James or Ben or Charlie, I'd have slipped up for sure.

Kimberly had apologised in advance for the hotel being on the outskirts of the city, but apparently there was a celebrity awards show and almost everywhere was booked up. This place was too, but she'd asked for a favour from her friend Katia, and the staff had found us two rooms, one with a small garden terrace for Yoda. And the way Kimberly told it, having a friend whose father owned hotels all over the world was perfectly normal.

"The room only has a double bed," Ro whispered after he'd checked us in, and heat flashed through me in an instant. "I thought it would be weird if I asked for a cot, but don't worry; I'll just sleep on the floor."

Well, that was...disappointing. But also gentlemanly, so I could hardly complain.

"Won't that be uncomfortable?"

"I've slept in far worse places, treasure." He handed me an envelope. "And Kimberly's friend sent this for you."

"What is it?"

"I have no idea. It's got your name on it, not mine."

Spa vouchers. She'd sent me spa vouchers. And in the room, we found a fancy box of doggie treats for Yoda, a platter of fresh fruit, and a bottle of non-alcoholic champagne. When I saw the gift basket in the bathroom, I burst into tears. Everything was just so...so...

"Zizi? What's wrong? You don't like bubble bath?"

Ro's words only made the tears flow faster.

"Shall I get rid of it? I'll get rid of it." Before I could blink, he'd scooped up the basket and tossed it out of the terrace doors. "All gone."

That was when I started to laugh. Uncontrollably. Possibly even hysterically. And now Ro's expression was a cross between puzzled and worried, and I couldn't say a word. So I threw caution to the wind and simply hugged him. And slowly, tentatively, he hugged me back. I rested my cheek against his solid chest, trying to swallow my giggles, and that was the moment I saw a glimmer of hope. Hope that someday, somehow, we'd find our way through the darkness together and reach the light.

"I've never used bubble bath," I mumbled into his T-shirt. "I just feel...overwhelmed? Is that the right word? Everybody's being so kind, and I don't know how I'll ever repay them."

"Don't worry about that."

"How can I not?"

"Because worrying is my job. The only thing you need to focus on is keeping yourself and our baby happy and healthy. Which means resting while I do the necessary. The danger's receded for the moment, so you can wander around the hotel and make use of those spa vouchers."

"I've never been to a spa either."

Ro gifted me another of those sweet forehead kisses. "Then now seems like a good time to start, don't you think? The receptionist told me they do a mother-to-be package—something about a face scrub and a pedicure. And I'll pick up some vitamins tomorrow. The internet mentioned folic acid. Should you be taking that?"

"That's most important during the first trimester, and I've been eating plenty of chickpeas and green vegetables. But extra vitamins would be good."

"I'll get them. Do you need anything else?"

I quickly shook my head. The lump in my throat wouldn't let me speak. My emotions had been on a roller coaster lately, all over the place, and I wasn't sure if it was due to hormones or the situation or Ro. *Ro.* I'd once fallen in love with Ro the mild-mannered waste disposal executive, but now that the true meaning of his job title had become clear along with his character, I thought I might actually prefer the new Ro. Yes, he'd been a military man, but underneath the tough exterior, he was kind and fair. I didn't even mind the fierceness anymore because it meant he'd defend his child—our child—to his dying breath.

That flame of hope grew a little brighter.

CHAPTER 29

RO

Leaving the hotel took an effort. Not because of the three-page room-service menu or the putting green or the Turkish barber attached to the spa, but because of Ziya. With her hug, I'd finally felt a spark of what we used to have, and I wanted to sit out on the terrace with cups of tea and the dog and talk all night.

But I couldn't, not when I had an altogether more unpleasant errand to run. According to our research, Café Nostima was a run-down establishment with a nautical theme. Blue and white paint peeled from the facade, and boat-shaped planters surrounded an outdoor seating area that spilled onto the pavement. A cannon took pride of place outside the entrance, and judging by the crime levels in that locale, they probably kept the damn thing loaded. There was no website or Facebook page, and snippets of information on the internet suggested the café was favoured by locals rather than tourists.

Our flight hadn't landed until six o'clock, and by the time we'd collected Yoda and our luggage and checked in at the hotel, the café was closed. But Will, who'd had far more experience at finding people than me, insisted that this was the perfect time to visit because although there would be no patrons to talk to, the spirits would still be awake. They never slept. And all they had to do with their days was watch people, which made them the perfect witnesses.

Will and Beck were coming with me so I wouldn't look like an idiot chatting to myself, and Reed had volunteered to stay behind at the hotel in case Ziya had a problem. Plus, I suspected, he wanted to pay a visit to the Turkish barber.

When I'd spent some time in Istanbul in the dim and distant past, I used to go to the local barber most days for a shave, and also because Rekan, who ran the place, was the best source of gossip in the area. My fellow troopers had ripped the piss out of me over the hot towel treatments until Rekan let slip details that led us to a Kurdish resistance network. Those guys and girls had been among our best assets for years to come. So in all honesty, I couldn't knock Reed for wanting a little "me" time.

And even better, treatments at the hotel were free. When I'd offered to repay Reed for whatever the stay cost, he'd explained that Katia wasn't just a friend of Kimberly's, she'd been kidnapped by a madman the previous year and he and Kimberly had played a part in her rescue, along with Will and Rania. They'd refused the reward on offer, and now Katia's father practically insisted that they take vacations in his hotels, all expenses paid. That certainly explained why we were getting the white-glove treatment at the Olympia, and I had to admit, it beat huddling in a bivvy bag in three inches of mud.

"Ready to go?" Beck asked, materialising behind me in the lobby with Will at his side.

"As ready as I'll ever be. But what happens if we find a ghost and they only speak Greek?"

"Easy." Will waved his phone. "Voice translator app. You just have to repeat what they say."

"Right. Of course."

"Not our first rodeo, mate."

Half an hour later, we walked towards Café Nostima to begin my first premeditated attempt at paranormal investigation. There was still a tiny kernel of doubt within me, a festering fear that any moment, a camera crew would jump out from behind a bus stop and announce I'd been Punk'd. If Will and Beck truly believed in the spirits, they had a hell of a lot of faith, that was all I could say.

"This is the place," Will said.

The photos on the internet must have been several years old judging by the state of decay. One of the planters had split in half, spilling soil across the pavement, and the others were filled with weeds. At first, I thought the place had closed down for good, but then I spotted a woman with a mop shuffling back and forth behind the grimy windows.

"Should we knock on the door?" I asked.

"Nah. She looks like the night shift. See any spirits?"

A rainbow of graffiti decorated the cannon, and I knew instinctively that if we ran the words through Will's translation app, none of them would be pleasant. The ghost who sat swinging his legs on the barrel didn't seem too thrilled to see us either. Even without the scowl, his face wasn't the most appealing, marred as it was by several fresh knife wounds and the associated blood trails.

"Just one, right outside the door." I spun in a slow circle. "Wait. There's another over there, I think. In the doorway beside the grocery store. It might be a homeless person, but the movements aren't quite right."

Once they got used to their new bodies—or rather, the lack of them—ghosts moved in a sort of...liquid way.

Smoothly. Probably because they were weightless. I'd learned a lot about their habits on surveillance ops when watching them had kept me awake.

"Let's try the one in the doorway while we wait for the cleaner to finish."

Will's idea seemed sensible, but when we got closer, I quickly realised we were on a hiding to nothing. The lady in the doorway wore the grubby layers of a long-time street person, and I felt a deep sadness that only once she'd died had she found a place to call home. If she'd still been alive, I'd have taken her for a bacon sandwich and a coffee, but now... There was nothing I could do.

Or so I'd assumed for most of my life. What if I *was* able to give her another chance?

"Try speaking to him?" Will suggested.

No need. This spirit wouldn't be able to help us. She wasn't all there, quite literally.

"Her. And she's blind."

"Are you sure?"

"Her eyes are missing."

Part of her face too. It looked as if she'd been eaten. Alive, since as far as I'd been able to ascertain, each spirit was a snapshot of a person's body at the moment of death.

"Oh," Will said. "Rats."

Very likely, judging by the abundance of droppings. Mental note: don't buy Ziya's vitamins or anything else from the store next door.

"We'll have to try the chap on the cannon."

Which meant hanging around in this delightful part of town until the lights inside the café blinked off. A youth approached us, and although I couldn't understand his words, I figured he was trying to sell us drugs. When we shrugged, he shuffled off along the street, head down.

Finally, the café went dark.

The guy on the cannon watched with undisguised curiosity as we approached, and I took that as a good sign. Will nodded to our left.

"There's a security camera just under the roofline."

Well, it wasn't illegal to talk to thin air, was it? I took point and stopped two feet from the ghost, Will and Beck on either side of me.

"Good evening," I said. "Uh, *kalispera*."

The ghost's expression didn't change. I consulted the translation app and tried out pidgin Greek.

"I see you, on the cannon."

Nothing. Shit. We'd already had a blind ghost—don't tell me we had a deaf one too?

A menu in the window caught my eye, not because of the dishes listed but rather the languages they were listed in. Farsi as well as Greek. This wasn't an establishment frequented by locals as we'd assumed; it catered to immigrants.

I switched to Farsi. "Hey, friend. You, sitting on the cannon."

Now his eyes widened, and he pointed to his chest in a "Me?" gesture.

"Yes, you. What's your name?"

"Musa."

"Musa, I'm Ro. I'm hoping you might be able to help me."

Musa snorted out a laugh. "How can I help you? I am dead." Then his one-and-a-half remaining eyebrows pinched together. "How do you see me? You are also dead? How do you move around? I am stuck here."

"No, no, I'm still alive."

"Then... Wait! You are an Elected? You are here to avenge my death? Why are you not glowing?"

"I'm not one of the Electi."

"Then why are you here?"

"As I said, I'm hoping you can help me."

"With what?"

"I'm looking for someone. A boy, from Afghanistan. I heard he was on his way here."

The ghost waved one bloody hand dismissively. "Boys from Afghanistan come here every day."

"Were you one of them?"

A shrug.

I pulled my phone out of my pocket. When Ziya left Tabesh's compound, she'd only taken two things in addition to the clothes on her back—the gold charm and the few photos she had of her family. Three were of Yafir, and I'd once again thanked my lucky stars that she'd had the presence of mind to grab what was important. I showed them to Musa, scrolling through them slowly.

"This is him—his name's Yafir. We're not sure if he's been here already or whether he's still on his way. Have you seen him?"

"Maybe."

"Maybe?"

"Why should I help you?"

"We're trying to save Yafir's life. We believe he's in danger."

"What will you do for me in return?"

"Won't you consider helping out of the goodness of your heart?"

"Nothing in this world is free, my friend. Everything has a price."

"And what's yours?"

"You will find one of the Electeds and they will take vengeance on the man who killed me." Musa folded his arms and smiled. "Then I will help you."

Oh, Musa didn't want much, did he? I suppose I couldn't blame him for trying.

"The Electi aren't hired guns. I can't just order them to kill somebody. There are rules about that sort of thing."

"But it is their job. They should have done it already."

"The world's changed since they were created."

"Maybe so, yet I am still stuck here."

I had to admit he made a good point. "Musa, what is it you actually want more—revenge or freedom?"

"Both."

"That's not possible, but I might be able to offer you a way out of here."

"How?"

"Freeing trapped souls is *my* job."

According to rumour, at least. It wasn't as if I had any idea how to do it or if it was even possible.

"Really?" Musa frowned, sort of. "The face in the mist did not mention you."

I had to assume he was talking about the spirit guide. From what I'd heard, "face in the mist" wasn't a bad description.

"That's because the guides aren't privy to that information. My existence is known only to the Electi."

And now Musa, it seemed. Was I meant to be a secret from everyone? Or had the Judge's job description merely been temporarily misplaced in the sands of time? Either way, the cat was out of the bag now.

"So you *do* know the Electeds?"

"Yes."

"Then I wish to speak with one of them."

Musa's attitude was starting to grate. Yes, any information he had could be extremely useful, but he wasn't in the best position to be making demands. Did Will and Beck understand any of this conversation? Will maintained an expression of mild interest, but Beck's slight smirk suggested he got the gist.

"Well, you can't speak with the Electi," I told Musa. "They're all abroad at the moment, and by the time one of them got here, it would be too late."

"They can't fly?"

"Not without an aeroplane."

"Too late for what?"

To save Yafir.

"To make the trip worthwhile. Tomorrow, I can come back when the café's open and speak to live witnesses. And then the chances are that I won't need your information anymore. So, Musa, this is a one-time offer. You can trust me and tell me what you know, and if it checks out, I'll come back and release you. Or you can hold your peace. Forever."

I took his fidgeting as a good sign. He knew something, and he also suspected that if I did return in the morning, I'd find out what it was. So I stayed silent. Gave him space. And as I'd hoped, he came to the right decision.

"Okay, okay. I will tell you if you give me your word that you will set me free."

"Yes, I'll give you my word." I only hoped I wouldn't have to break that promise. "Did you see the boy?"

"Two days ago, he was here, and again today. With another man, older."

So near, yet so fucking far.

"What time today?"

"This afternoon? I do not have a watch."

"Did you hear anything they said? Do you know who the man was? What did he look like?"

Musa shook his head. "I never saw him before. He wore jeans and a blue jacket, and he had a big beard." Musa mimed with his hands. "But they went inside and spoke with Abbas. Abbas, he is here every day, and he gave the man a package. He is...how is it called? A fixer?"

"What kind of a package?"

"Thin. Like a big envelope. Now will you free me?"

"As I said, I'll need to check the information first. What time does Abbas usually get here?"

"Lunchtime. Always he orders the chicken sandwich. You should try it."

"Thanks for the tip."

If only we'd reached Athens a day sooner... Ziya was going to be disappointed, but at least we knew we were on the right track. Yafir was alive, and he was in Europe.

CHAPTER 30

RO

I'd hoped that Ziya might take Katia up on her spa offer, but of course she didn't. Nor did she sleep well. I heard her tossing and turning all night, and in the end, she got up and shut herself in the bathroom. Five minutes passed. Ten. Fifteen, and I heard a quiet sniffle.

"Zizi? Are you okay?"

A pause. "I'm fine."

"And I'm worried about you."

The door opened, and I found I was right to be concerned. Fresh tears streaked Ziya's cheeks, and the look on her face was one of utter misery. When I opened my arms, she walked straight into them. Where she belonged.

"I'm just scared we won't find Yafir," she whispered.

"We'll find him."

"But Europe is such a big place."

"He was here only yesterday. He can't have gone far." Pressed against Ziya, I felt the faintest flutter against my stomach and froze. "Was that…? Was that…?"

"The baby?" She managed a hesitant smile. "Yes. He likes to move around now."

That was the moment it hit home for me. I really was going to be a father. Which meant I shouldn't be gallivanting around Europe, and neither should Ziya. She ought to be in England, resting and going to hospital check-ups and attending baby classes. Probably I should be going to those too. We had to rent a house. Buy a car. Get all the things a baby needed. Bloody hell.

And first, we had to find Yafir.

This time when we approached, Musa grinned and pointed inside the café.

"Abbas, he is sitting at the back."

"In the red jacket?"

"Yes, yes."

Abbas was a rotund gentleman with curly black hair and a habit of waving what looked like a falafel sandwich in the air as he talked. The chap he was speaking with didn't seem particularly happy, but Abbas was smiling nonetheless in between mouthfuls.

"I'll wait outside," Beck murmured. "Three people might come across as intimidating."

Good plan. Plus he could keep an eye on the car. A kid was already eyeing it up with more than mild interest, and we needed to keep the wheels on it for the trip back to the hotel.

Abbas said something in Greek as we approached and beamed a grin at us. I shrugged in the universal language of "sorry, haven't a clue" and tried Farsi.

"Abbas? We were told you were the man to see if we had a problem."

"Always I fix problems." The grin grew wider. "For a

price, of course. Where are you from? You speak my language, but you are not Iranian."

"I've been living in Afghanistan."

That answer seemed to satisfy him, or maybe he was just used to dealing with questionable characters. "And what help are you needing?"

"Do you speak English?"

Abbas switched languages, which meant Will could follow the conversation too. "Yes, I speak English."

"I work at an office in Kabul, and the brother of one of my colleagues has gone missing." It seemed easier to bend the truth than to try and explain my and Ziya's car crash of a relationship. "She heard from a friend of his that he came here."

"To Athens?"

"He mentioned this café specifically."

"Many people come here from Afghanistan. It's a meeting place. A hub."

"Could you tell me if you've seen him? I have a picture."

Abbas studied the photos of Yafir, swiping between them, non-committal. But a glint of recognition sparked in his eyes.

"Does he look familiar?"

"It's possible I saw him."

"Possible?" I took out my wallet and tried a fifty-euro note. Would that be enough? I wasn't familiar with bribery in this part of the world. "Does this help to jog your memory?"

Seemed so, because Abbas nodded. "The boy, he was here yesterday. With his father."

Beside me, Will let out a relieved breath. The good news was that Musa had been absolutely right, and Yafir was definitely in Athens. The bad news was also that Musa had been right, and now I had to work out a way to send him wherever spirits went when they left earth.

But what was all this about a father?

"Yafir's father is dead."

"Well, the man said he was his father. The boy didn't disagree." A shrug. "Their papers say they are father and son."

The way he said it... Now I understood what the package Abbas handed over had contained—new identity documents for Yafir and his companion. And that only worried me more. False identities cost money—thousands for good papers, as I'd just found out first-hand—and men like Dayyin Rouhani weren't renowned for being charitable. What did he want from Yafir in return?

"I don't suppose you happened to notice the names on their papers?" I asked.

Another smile. Another fifty-euro note.

"The names were Vincenzo and Davide Conti."

"Italian? They're travelling on Italian documents?"

Bloody hell. When I'd met Yafir, he'd spoken Pashto and passable Dari, plus the basic English he'd learned from Ziya. Unless the KLA had been offering language lessons as part of their jihadi training course, Yafir was going to have an interesting challenge if anyone actually asked to see his new passport. At least we could safely assume he wouldn't be going through any airports.

"*Sì, sì, loro sono Italiani.*" Abbas cackled at his own non-joke. "Italy is a very nice country. Maybe you would like to visit?"

Abbas was a man who said a lot without saying much at all.

"Would I? Can you recommend anywhere in particular?"

"Such recommendations are very expensive."

He knew where Yafir had gone? I handed over fifty euros, but Abbas kept his hand out. Fine, another fifty. I'd have paid double.

"Ancona is a good place to go. Your friends, they took the bus to Igoumenitsa. The ferry runs once each day. It used to run twice, but there were not enough passengers. Cutbacks, always cutbacks. If you want to follow, the bus stop is at the end of the street."

"Thanks for your help."

"You want free advice? Try the falafel. It's always crispy." He gave his finger and thumb a chef's kiss. "*Perfetto.*"

I was already halfway to the car with Musa's shouts echoing in my ears.

~

Back at the Olympia, I headed to Will and Beck's room. Much as I wanted to see Ziya, I also didn't want to worry her before we'd worked out our next course of action.

"Right," Will said. "We know Yafir was in Athens yesterday. The ghost outside said in the afternoon?"

"Yes."

"And according to the timetable, the bus travels from Athens to Igoumenitsa three times a day at seven a.m., eleven a.m., and three p.m., and it takes nearly seven hours. So, even if they managed to get the three p.m. bus, they wouldn't have reached Igoumenitsa until ten o'clock in the evening."

Beck was busy thumbing through his phone. "The Igoumenitsa-to-Ancona ferry departs once a day at four p.m."

"Which means they wouldn't have made yesterday's ferry."

"So they must be on today's." Shit—they'd be boarding in an hour, and there was no way we could get there in time. "How long does the ferry take?"

"Sixteen hours."

"What's the fastest way to Ancona?"

The fastest way, it turned out, was to phone Kimberly. While I broke the news to Ziya and helped her to pack, our American queen chartered a private fucking jet. This whole bloody trip was going to bankrupt me, but when it came down to it, that didn't matter. I'd sell my soul to put a smile back on Ziya's face. And that meant being whisked through the airport, squashing myself into a flying cigar tube that came complete with champagne and a leggy stewardess to serve it, and praying Yafir Khalizai was on the damn boat.

CHAPTER 31
RO

At eleven a.m. on Monday, the five of us waited at the port in Ancona as the huge ferry slowly manoeuvred itself into place. Beck, Reed, and Will stayed in the background while I sat on a bench near the water with Ziya. Everyone except Ziya was wearing an earpiece, and I knew the Electi were watching. I'd discovered that when I relaxed, when I emptied my mind of day-to-day noise, I could feel them there in the background, a sort of…niggle at the edges of my brain. A hum.

I hadn't wanted Ziya to come at all. Kimberly had rented us a house in Camerano, and that's where Ziya should have been, catching up on rest with Yoda. But she'd insisted on joining us, and when Will pointed out that Yafir was less likely to run if his sister was there, I'd lost the argument.

"Are you okay?" Ziya asked softly.

"Shouldn't that be my question?"

"You've asked it a hundred times already."

Was I okay? Relatively speaking, yes. At least physically. I'd been through a thousand life-or-death situations, nearly given up the ghost more than once, and a jaunt around Europe should have been a cakewalk. But for all those years, it had just been me. If I'd died, my mates would've shown up for the funeral, but nobody else would have missed me. My parents—my adoptive parents—had died a decade ago, first my mum from cancer and then my dad soon afterwards from what the doctors termed cardiac arrest but which was in reality a broken heart. Before he passed, he'd told me that one day, I'd meet a girl who had the power to shatter me, but deep down, I'd thought he was just being melodramatic. Now I knew the truth.

No, I wasn't okay. Because Ziya wasn't okay.

But right now, she didn't need to know that, so I forced a smile.

"I'm fine, treasure."

She slipped a hand into mine, and that small gesture made my chest swell.

"When we find Yafir..." When, not if—I was trying to stay optimistic. "I need you to take him back to the car with Will, okay?"

"Why? Where are you going?"

"I want to have a chat with the man he's travelling with."

Beck had rented an extra SUV at the airport, and we'd stopped at a hardware store to stock up on the essentials— zip ties, duct tape, nylon cord, a couple of drop cloths. Knives, screwdrivers, a hammer. A blowtorch.

"A chat?" Ziya tried to move away, but I shuffled along the bench with her.

"Just a chat. We don't want to hurt him."

Only scare him, but I made no such promises on Marina's behalf. That was who I planned to hand the man over to if I got the slightest inkling he was anything more than an unwitting courier. Luckily, Ziya didn't press for more information.

The gangway was slowly manoeuvred into place alongside the behemoth of a ship, and Ziya's grip tightened as passengers slowly began to disembark. We waited, and we waited, and we waited. The stream of passengers stepping out into the sunshine slowed to a trickle, and Ziya began to fret.

"Where is he?"

I didn't have an answer. Could Abbas have been wrong? Or worse, had he deliberately sent us on a wild goose chase? Will muttered something about googling flights back to Athens—it seemed he'd had the same thought—but then Beck pointed at the top deck. On the open portion to the rear, a small group of people had gathered, and one man in particular seemed agitated, pointing inside, then down at the water. Now what had happened? The chap wore a blue jacket and jeans, and sported the same bushy beard that Musa had described. Could he be Yafir's "father"? If so, where the hell was Yafir?

I began to get a bad, bad feeling about this.

"Any idea what's going on?" I asked the boys.

"No, but there's a tour group heading in this direction," Will murmured. "I'll see if any of them speak English."

All of them spoke English. Very loudly and at the same time. The accents suggested the ladies of Liverpool had decided to venture farther afield.

"A boy's gone missing, so his dad says."

"Poof, vanished."

"It's a big ship, sure he'll turn up."

"Maybe he's messing around?"

"That nice German lady from the roulette table thinks

he fell overboard. Her friend saw the lad on the top deck, standing near the railing."

"Doubt anyone'll find him, then. That water's freezing."

"Big waves too."

"Where are we going first? The cathedral or a museum?"

The river of curses that flowed through my head would have made my entire SAS squadron blush, but I held them in. If Yafir *had* gone missing, I didn't want to panic Ziya.

"Do they know anything?" she asked. "What's happening?"

I wanted to tell her everything was fine, that maybe we'd got it wrong and Yafir wasn't on this ferry after all, but I'd also promised I wouldn't lie to her.

"One of the passengers told Will that a boy's gone missing."

Ziya, my smart Ziya, put two and two together straight away.

"Missing? How could Yafir go missing on a boat?" Then she looked up at the deck, where a man in a waiter's uniform was peering over the edge, and the colour drained out of her face. "They think... They think he fell?"

"It's too soon for anybody to be certain of anything. Perhaps he got lost? Those ships are like mazes."

We'd done several hostage rescue exercises on borrowed cruise liners during my years in the SAS, and they were an absolute fucking rabbit warren of corridors and dead ends and nooks and crannies. When we took part in a joint exercise with DEVGRU, I'd nearly got my head taken off by a SEAL-slash-terrorist who'd popped out from between two slot machines wielding a bottle of Bombay Sapphire.

Hope mingled with despair in Ziya's voice. "Do you truly believe that?"

"At the moment, I'm as clueless as everybody else. But Zizi, I need you to go to the house with Will."

"No! I have to stay here."

"Please, treasure. If Yafir doesn't turn up in the next few minutes, somebody's going to call the police, and that sketchy fellow in the blue jacket isn't going to hang around when they arrive. We need to intercept him as he leaves."

"But—"

"If Yafir *is* still alive, questioning that man is our best chance at finding him. And after we've picked him up, one of us can come back and talk to the ferry crew. Uh, I hate to ask this, Zizi, but can Yafir swim?"

Ziya bit her lip as she shook her head, her expression wretched. I wrapped an arm around her, and she didn't protest as I led her over to Will. Handing her to a virtual stranger hurt like hell, but right now, I had to focus on the end goals: finding out what had happened to Yafir, and stopping whatever atrocity Dayyin Rouhani had planned.

"Take her back to the house, mate. We'll join you shortly."

It didn't take long for people to start arriving at the ship—the police, a trio of guys in suits, and a group of men who walked over from the coastguard station. Reed nipped into a souvenir shop and bought a pair of binoculars that let us get a better look at the movements on board. One of the suits was on the lower deck, gesturing at a bunch of people in light-blue uniforms. Directing the cleaning staff to search?

"Where's Vincenzo Conti or whatever his name is?" Beck asked suddenly. "He's gone."

The answer? Scuttling down the gangway. Time to act.

I hurried after him as he skirted the harbour, and when he paused to check his phone, distracted, I caught up.

"*Vuoi un taxi? Prezzo più basso?*" My Italian came from Google, and my accent wasn't much better. I was banking on Yafir's fake father being neither Italian nor familiar with the language. "*Aeroporto? Stazione ferroviaria?*"

"Taxi? *La gare? Le train?*"

Gare? Le train? The railway station—that was French rather than Italian. I'd quite enjoyed French lessons at school, mainly because Mademoiselle Coubert had nice legs and the kind of breasts a fifteen-year-old boy pictured while he had his hand on his cock.

"*Oui, la gare. Je peux vous emmener à la gare. Suivez-moi.*"

He followed obediently, all the way to the car. I held the door open, and he was so engrossed with whatever was in his messages that he didn't realise anything was wrong until Beck and Reed climbed into the back seat on either side of him. He started screaming bloody murder, of course, but Beck stuffed a rag in his mouth, and ten seconds later, his hands and feet were taped securely. A blindfold finished the ensemble.

Well, that went more smoothly than I could have hoped. Still, I'd take the breaks when I got them. As we trundled along the streets of Ancona, I had a feeling that things would get worse before they got better.

The house Kimberly had rented definitely fell into the "luxury" category. On any other day, I might have paused to admire the swimming pool, the bocce pitch, the state-of-the-art kitchen, or the Michelangelo reproduction on the hall ceiling. But today, I only had eyes for the finished basement. Theoretically, it was meant to be a games room, complete with a pool table and ping-pong, but it also made an excellent torture chamber. Once we'd removed the net, the ping-pong table was the perfect size to tie a man spreadeagled, and the floor was tiled and therefore easy to clean if he pissed himself.

I locked the door. The last thing I wanted was for Ziya to wander downstairs and get a look at the prisoner's meat and two veg.

Were the theatrics necessary? I wasn't sure yet, but better to give the chap a scare to start with than go in too soft. He needed to believe we were serious. I'd been truthful with Ziya—I didn't *want* to hurt him, but want and need were two entirely different beasts. I'd do whatever it took to get the answers.

But some answers were easier to get than others.

"Pass his phone?" I said to Beck.

He did so, and I held it up to the guy's face. God bless facial recognition technology. In the good old days, we'd had to convince gents to tell us their PINs, and some of them were awfully reluctant. Hmm, what did we have? Emails? Coupons from a fast-food chain, a message from an African prince promising riches beyond his wildest dreams, and a reminder to update his profile on a dating website. I clicked through to that one.

"So, Farzad," I said in Dari. "You're a non-smoker who enjoys cooking, relaxing with friends, long walks in the fucking countryside, and trafficking minors across conti-nents. You'd love to meet a woman with similar interests." I sucked in a breath. "I'd say that could be a challenge."

"Trafficking children? No, no, I don't know what you're talking about."

"Really? Considering you just lost your 'son,' I'd have expected you to be more distraught."

Click, click, click... I could practically hear the cogs turning. Farzad was trying to figure out how long we'd been watching him.

"My son... Yes, of course I'm upset."

"And that's why you left the scene?"

"The boat captain told me to stay out of the way while they searched."

"I'm fairly sure he didn't mean for you to hop on a train out of town."

At least Farzad was talking. A chatterbox was easier to deal with than a man who clammed up, even if most of his words were lies. I took another look at the phone. A handful of bathroom selfies, a few artistic shots of the sea... This was a new phone, bought for the job. Nothing on it was more than a week old. Farzad had probably broken the rules by hooking up a personal email account, but I wasn't going to complain, not when it helped us.

The only apps he'd installed were Telegram—every terrorist's favourite because the messages were encrypted plus they self-destructed—and some football game. But I did find a rather interesting document in the notes folder. More of an itinerary, really, written in Farsi.

3 March - Meet boat.

4 March - Travel Athens.

5 March - Café Nostima, Athens. Meet Abbas 3 p.m. Stay Hercules Hotel.

6 March - Wait.

7 March - Meet Abbas.

8 March - Bus Athens to Igoumenitsa. Boat Igoumenitsa to Ancona 7 p.m.

9 March - Train Ancona to Torino to Lyon. Stay Hôtel Royale.

10 March - Train Lyon to Toulouse Matabiau. 2 p.m.

For the most part, the document merely confirmed what we'd already worked out, but the last two lines... Those were new. Toulouse was their final destination? What was in Toulouse?

I posed that question to Farzad. First, he went quiet, and then he shrugged as far as his bonds would let him.

"Nothing. I don't know."

"So why were you planning to go there?"

Another shrug. "I am just a man who does favours for people. Sometimes, I take friends of friends on a tour. To see the sights, yes?"

Ah, so we were going with the "I know nothing" defence.

"And what's the name of this 'friend' you're doing the favour for?"

"Uh, Mohammed?"

"Mohammed what?"

"I forget."

I didn't believe that for a moment. But the part about him being unaware of what waited in Toulouse was plausible. A man like Dayyin Rouhani wouldn't trust a low-level courier with any significant pieces of information, so what Farzad had been told was most likely on a need-to-know basis only. The bare minimum. Collect Yafir, take him from point A to point B via C, D, and E. The question was, why was Yafir so important?

The answer? I'd leave that to Marina. Whatever happened in Toulouse was her problem. Yafir hadn't made it out of Ancona, so I'd be staying here with Ziya to help with the search.

And thankfully, I didn't have a floor to mop.

Marina was mildly peeved that we'd kidnapped Farzad, but after her "which part of 'don't do anything stupid' did you not understand?" lecture, she did at least arrange for a pair of men to take him off our hands. And better still, she promised to send a team to Toulouse's main railway station tomorrow to see who showed up.

Which meant we were back to our original problem—where was Yafir?

Will and Reed had headed back to the port while Beck babysat Farzad and I comforted Ziya, but when Will reported in, the news wasn't good.

"We found a copper that spoke English, and he says the search of the ferry's almost finished."

"No sign of Yafir?"

"Nope. But apparently, several people saw him leaning over the railing on the top deck. One said he seemed fascinated by the waves."

"How far into the voyage?"

"Just before the captain asked everyone to vacate their cabins prior to docking. So about half an hour before the ship arrived."

"Has the coastguard gone out to search?"

"Yes, but I'm not sure how much luck they'll have in the dark."

"Yafir's a smart kid. If he stays calm and realises he can float…"

Now I was clutching at straws. I wouldn't even fancy my own chances overnight in a rough sea, especially at this time of year.

"There's another problem, mate."

Shit.

"What problem?"

"Reed got talking to one of the ferry crew. The police have realised old Farzad's done a runner, and they're starting to wonder whether he made up the whole story for attention or something worse."

"What could possibly be worse?"

"A rival ferry operator and a dirty tricks campaign were mentioned. They had to cancel today's sailing while the boat was searched, and that cost money."

Yes, that was worse. What if they stopped the search? It wasn't as if we could officially report Yafir missing ourselves. Where would we start? With his fake name? With the fact that he was an undocumented migrant? With Ziya, who was also in the country illegally?

I let out a groan.

"That's about right," Will said. "This place is in chaos. Hardly anyone got the message regarding the cancellation, and there're still pissed-off tourists trying to board."

"When's the ferry leaving again?"

"Tomorrow afternoon. Two o'clock."

We had less than a day to do something. But what?

CHAPTER 32
ZIYA

"Are you okay?"

Define "okay." I was sitting in the bathroom, crying. My brother was missing, the rest of my family was dead, and my home had been destroyed. Everything I'd known was gone. I was hopping my way across an unfamiliar continent with a bunch of men I barely knew, and if that wasn't bad enough, there was a lunatic with a dirty bomb on the loose. Dayyin Rouhani. I'd met him several times when I was a little girl. He'd grown up in a village not too far from Balaguri, and our fathers knew each other, but the Rouhani family had moved away when Mr. Rouhani got a new job working for a wealthy family in Jalalabad. How had Dayyin strayed so far from what was good? He was only four years older than me. What had happened between then and now to turn him against his fellow human beings?

"I'm f-f-fine," I called to Ro. He checked on me a lot. I kind of liked it, although I'd vetoed his suggestion of taking me to the hospital "just to be on the safe side" earlier. Yes, I'd been upset, but I didn't want to be prodded by strangers.

The baby was all right. He kicked every five minutes to let me know this.

I waited for Ro's footsteps to quiet on the tile, then slumped back against the wall. They'd given me my own bedroom, and it even came with an en suite. *On sweet.* I never used to understand how bathrooms could be sweet, but Nancy told me the words were French. Was it weird that bathrooms had become my sanctuary? Living with Tabesh, it'd been the only place where no one would disturb me, and I'd spent so much time in there that Dina had giggled about me being constipated. And she must have told Tabesh because he started buying me tins of prunes. In some small ways, he'd cared, but I really, really hated prunes and I never wanted to eat another as long as I lived.

What had happened to Dina? Had she woken up after I knocked her out? Even though I disliked her, I hoped so. And what would happen to her and the others now that Tabesh was dead? I wished Daneen would find happiness, but Dina and Delal? I didn't much care. They were a pair of mingebags.

I choked back another sob as I remembered all the lingo Nancy had taught me, words I'd never dared to utter out loud to anyone but her or Ro. I missed Nancy so, so much. She'd given me her email address before I left, but I hadn't had access to a computer, and a smartphone was way out of my budget. Now it was too late. Almost two years had passed since I last saw her.

But at least I had Ro. A man who protected me and frustrated me, sometimes in equal measure. A warrior. A man with a supernatural gift, and—I laid a hand on my belly—the father of my child. Together, we'd created a life, yet he'd never even kissed me properly.

Did I want to be kissed? Maybe. When Tabesh had slurped his way around my mouth, I'd fought not to gag, but Nancy had assured me kissing could be pleasurable when done properly.

I had no doubts that Ro knew how to do things properly.

The question was, would he ever want to? With me? I'd caused nothing but trouble for him so far.

So many questions, so few answers, and now my butt was going numb. I used the towel rail to pull myself to my feet and unlocked the door.

Then stopped dead in the doorway.

Ro was lying on my bed. Not *in* my bed, but on top of the covers. He'd taken off his boots, set them neatly beside the door, and now he had his eyes closed, breathing slowly and rhythmically with his mouth half-open. I wasn't sure whether to be annoyed that he'd hung around or get the warm fuzzies because he'd stayed to make sure that I really was okay.

Should I wake him? He looked so peaceful, and he'd hardly got any sleep over the past few days. Perhaps I could just...hmm...slide in beside him? It wasn't as if we'd actually be sleeping *together*-together. I'd be *under* the covers. Totally separate.

Yes, that would work.

Perfect.

~

No, Ziya, not perfect. If perfect was a cherry blossom, then I was a discarded pit.

The covers were twisted around my feet, which were tangled around Ro's legs. My swollen belly rested against his side, and somehow—*somehow*—my hand had ended up under his T-shirt. He sniffed a bit where my hair tickled his nose.

Bloody Nora.

Very slowly, very carefully, I tried to remove my hand and wriggle backward, but too late, I realised Ro's arm was wrapped firmly around my back. I was stuck. And he was waking up.

I froze as his eyes flickered open.

"Zizi?"

"Uh, hi?"

We stared at each other for a beat, the shock in Ro's eyes matching my own. I snatched my hand away from his chest, but he moved too, and it ended up in an even worse place. How in the name of a rabid goat had that ever fit inside me? Yes, I'd studied the textbooks, knew that things stretched, but still...

"Oh, bollocks," I muttered, and Ro snorted a laugh.

"For those, you need to go down a bit."

My cheeks burned. "Sorry, I'm so sorry."

"Zizi, how did we end up in bed together?"

"I think you fell asleep?"

"Yes, but why didn't you wake me?"

"You looked tired."

And I wanted to lie next to you, just for a night.

Ro cupped my cheek. "I promise it won't happen again." But my poker face must have needed work—probably because gambling was haram and I'd never held a playing card in my life—and Ro raised an eyebrow. "Unless...you want it to happen again?"

"I slept really well," I mumbled.

"Me too, treasure." He kissed me softly. On the forehead. Again. Was there something wrong with my lips? Or was it just the rest of me that was the problem? "I'll leave the sleeping arrangements up to you. No pressure. If you want to share my bed, then my door's always open. But in the meantime…" He glanced at his watch. "I need to make some calls."

The horrors of yesterday all came flooding back. Just for a moment, in my fairy-tale world, I'd managed to pretend my life wasn't a disaster and Yafir's fate wasn't a terrifying unknown.

"The harbour—I need to go to the harbour."

"I'm not sure that's a good idea, Zizi."

"I'll walk if I have to." Then, almost to myself, "Yafir's alive. I feel it."

At least, I didn't feel that he was dead. When my mother had died and then my father, the darkness had come out of nowhere, a heavy weight that settled in my gut, a deep-seated fatigue that left me struggling to move. And when Grandma died, even before I heard the news, her passing had left me breathless. I'd known. I'd just known.

But today, the only niggles were the baby's restlessness and a vague sense of unease over my relationship with Ro. Had he invited me into his bed? It sure seemed that way. But did he mean it? Or was he simply being polite? Nancy had once told me about the time she and her ex went to Spain and met a French couple at the hotel, and before they left, they'd said that wouldn't it be nice to catch up someday? A month later, when these people turned up on her doorstep, she'd had to hide behind the sofa because, apparently, when an English person said "let's meet up," what they meant was "let's share memes on Facebook and never speak again." I didn't use Facebook. I wasn't even totally sure what a meme was. Some sort of cartoon?

Ro studied me, and it wasn't difficult to read his

thoughts on one subject at least—he was trying to work out whether it would be more stressful to make me stay here alone or let me go with him to the harbour the way I wanted. In the end, he simply nodded.

"Give me five minutes to get dressed, and we'll go."

The port was quiet today. Disappointingly so. With my brother missing, I guess I'd expected, well, more than a single policeman leaning against a lamp post at the end of the pier and half a dozen early-morning joggers. Kimberly had sent a warm coat, soft plum-coloured wool lined with fleece, and I pulled it tighter around me, then quickly clutched at my hijab to stop it from blowing loose in the wind.

"Where is everybody?" I asked Ro.

"They're probably searching in the bowels of the ship. If Yafir's still on board, then he's either stuck somewhere or hiding for some reason. Uh, could you just...?" Ro nudged me three steps to my left. "Thanks."

"What was wrong with where I was standing?"

He dropped his voice to a whisper.

"There's a ghost there. An old lady. Your faces were mashed together, and it was weird."

Eurgh. Would I ever get used to the fact that Ro was able to see things I couldn't?

"Sorry," I told him, and then I turned to the ghost, just in case she thought it was weird too. "Sorry."

"Will and Reed have offered to take the ferry back to Athens later, on the off chance Yafir's still on board."

That was sweet of them—another kindness I had no

idea how to repay—but if a hundred people had searched already, would two more really make a difference?

"Do you think they should?"

Ro sighed. "No, she can't see you, but I can."

"Huh?"

He gestured towards the empty air on my right. Oh, the ghost.

"Yes, she *is* very sweet." Another sigh, followed by a smile. "I'm to tell you that you're sweet."

"Uh, thank you?"

"Sorry, no, I'm afraid I'm not one of the Electi. ... And I'm Ro. ... Forty years? That's a long time. ... A mugging? Yes, we'll be careful."

Forty years? The poor lady had been stuck there for forty years? At least there were things to watch in the port. I tried not to think of my father, trapped alone by the side of a road in Afghanistan. Part of me wished we hadn't had to leave, that we could visit every so often for Ro to let Baba know I hadn't forgotten him. That I'd *never* forget him. My uncle and aunt too. My cousin. Would Ro really be able to free them one day? I clung to that hope the way I clung to his arm.

Then Ro stiffened. "What rope? When? ... Are you sure? ... Can you describe him? ... Yes, yes, a teenager, but small for his age."

What was the lady saying? Had she seen something? Had she seen my brother? Ro glanced towards the street that ran behind the harbour.

"Thank you *very* much for your help. ... Yes, I promise I'll let you know."

Ro gripped my hand as we hurried towards the street.

"What's happening? What did she see?"

"As it was getting light, somebody climbed out of one of

the lifeboats and slid down a rope to the dock, and then he ran off."

That tiny ember of hope glowed brighter.

"And she thinks it was Yafir?"

"She couldn't make out much in the gloom, just that he had dark hair and was carrying a backpack. I guess it could have been a stowaway, but if I were a betting man…"

"It was him! It was Yafir!"

But why had he hidden in the first place? And in a city the size of Ancona, how on earth were we going to find him?

CHAPTER 33

RO

Tuesday had been a day of two halves.

First, I'd woken up in bed with Ziya. I'd only meant to rest for a few moments while I waited to check she really was okay, but tiredness had got the better of me. And Ziya... Well, she could grope me any time she wanted, but I only hoped I managed to keep my hands to myself because I didn't want to scare her off. I wanted her to feel safe with me, not nervous or pressured, and in the past month, she'd already been through more than any woman should in a lifetime.

And it wasn't over yet. The elation of finding out that Yafir was most likely alive had been replaced with desperation to find him, but so far, we'd had no luck on that front.

Beck, Reed, and Will had joined the search as soon as I called them. Yoda too. If we were going out walking, I figured we might as well bring him along. So far, we'd wandered the streets around the harbour, then tried Ancona's three mosques and four homeless shelters, and now we were visiting the churches. Will had gone to talk to a print shop to organise flyers, and I was starting to worry about Ziya. She hadn't said anything, but I could see her getting tired.

And then my phone rang.

"Do you want the bad news or the really fucking shit news?" Marina asked.

I muted the microphone for a moment. "Zizi, why don't you try that shop over there?"

She narrowed her eyes for the briefest second, then nodded and walked off, phone in hand. She'd learned the Italian phrases for "I'm looking for my brother" and "If you see this boy, please call this number," and everyone who saw her sad smile promised to help.

"What happened?"

"We sent a team to meet the courier you told us about."

"And? Did anyone show up?"

"Only Dayyin fucking Rouhani himself."

"Isn't that good news?"

"Would've been, if the sodding gendarmes knew their arses from their elbows. He legged it, they gave chase, and somehow—the details are still hazy—he drove into a bridge abutment."

Her tone told me he hadn't survived the impact.

"Ah, fuck."

"Bunch of bloody idiots. As you've said before, dead men can't fucking talk. But martyrs can sure as hell inspire their brainwashed followers."

"Did he say anything before he ran?"

"Not a word. Just made the undercover guys and bolted. But Ro, they found a Eurotunnel booking confirmation in his wallet, dated a week from now. If he was on his way to England..."

She didn't have to finish the sentence for me to understand the implications.

"Was he carrying anything else? A phone?"

"His phone got smashed in the crash. The tech guys are piecing it back together, but I understand it's not the work of five minutes. And there wasn't much else—a wad of euros, a key that looks as if it opens a house, and a receipt for drinks from La Pêche Parfaite."

The perfect peach? "Sounds like a classy joint."

"It's a strip club. Bunch of bloody hypocrites. The French sent a pair of gendarmes over, but the club's owner claims to know nothing. Doesn't remember seeing Rouhani, doesn't have any cameras."

"What about the girls?"

"They're not fond of talking either. Ro, I keep coming back to the boy. Why him? He's young, inexperienced. Unreliable."

It was a conundrum I'd been puzzling over as well. "Because he's easily expendable? Honestly, I don't know. But unless he had a growth spurt in the last year, he's small too. And sneaky—he managed to evade the search team on the ferry for hours. I'm wondering if they wanted him to slip into a place where an adult couldn't fit?"

"It's a possibility. MI5's compiling a list of likely targets, so I'll pass the information on. You really think this boy's still alive?"

"The witness we found believes so."

I'd given Marina an update this morning, obviously without mentioning that our witness was, in fact, dead.

"Find him. Find him, and find out what he knows."

"If he's out there, we will."

∽

I said that, but tracking down Yafir was proving to be far from easy. Will had obtained two thousand flyers for us to hand out, but I was reluctant to plaster "Missing" posters all over the city. Firstly, I worried they might scare Yafir even deeper into hiding, and secondly, if any of Rouhani's cohorts were hanging around, I didn't want them getting wind of the fact that Yafir might still be alive in case they decided to tie up loose ends. So we'd stuck with handing out the leaflets to shopkeepers, restaurant owners, street-sweepers, and traffic wardens with a plea to call us if they saw him.

That night, I held my breath as I lay in bed. This morning, I'd invited Ziya to join me, but would she? Did she even want to? Or had last night been a one-off? I hated the thought of her crying in the bathroom alone, but in the same way that I didn't want to pressure Yafir, I didn't want to push Ziya either. As my mum used to say, you caught more flies with honey.

I'd almost given up hope when the door handle moved a few minutes before midnight. Then the door opened wider, and my pulse sped up as Ziya stood there, looking for all the world as if she was going to run.

I flipped back the quilt on the empty half of the bed and waited.

And waited.

I'd never met Kimberly, and our initial conversations had been tense, but I was definitely warming towards her. The clothes she'd sent for Ziya looked stylish to my untrained eye, but they were also comfortable and modest. The loose, cat-covered pyjamas Ziya wore tonight were a case in point. Cute.

Ziya took one tentative step forward. I didn't need to be a genius to understand that she wasn't just at a crossroads in her life, she was trying to navigate Spaghetti Junction without a map or even a driver's licence. Her whole way of life had been yanked out from under her. Everything she believed in was under question. I could guide her, but she needed to decide on her own path.

I only hoped that path led to me.

She took another step, then another and another, a gazelle tiptoeing towards a lion.

I'd come to an arrangement with the Electi. When I finished for the day, I sent a text to let them know, and one of them confirmed receipt. When I was good to go in the mornings, I sent another message, and in between times, they'd promised not to jump into my head. During the day, I peed with my eyes closed.

Tonight, it was just Ziya and me.

Neither of us said a word as she slipped under the covers and arranged the quilt over herself. She left a gap between us, but that was okay. We'd take things slowly. My dick would lose its fucking head if she touched me, anyway.

"Are you okay?" I asked.

"No, but I hope that one day I might be."

At least she was honest.

CHAPTER 34

ZIYA

For the fourth morning in a row, I woke tangled up in Ro.

On the nights I'd had to share a bed with Tabesh, I'd instinctively lain as close to the edge as possible, trying not to touch him as he spread out and snored. Some mornings, I woke up half on the floor. But with Ro, the opposite was true. Even when I instructed myself to give him space, my body gravitated towards his, and he curled around me like a suit of armour, one hand resting on my belly as he breathed softly against the back of my neck. On his wrist, he still wore the bracelet I'd made him last year, although it was slightly frayed around the edges now. He'd kept it this whole time.

If only I hadn't been running from my past, I might have been able to enjoy the moment. If we hadn't been searching for my brother or hunting for information on a terror cell intent on stealing lives, I could have closed my eyes and gone back to sleep. But there was too much to do. My feet still hurt, but I'd walk the streets all day again.

Ro stirred behind me. Was he waking too? The first time

I felt his hard length pressed against my butt, I'd had to fight back the panic, but I'd quickly realised he was still asleep and certain parts of his anatomy had a mind of their own. Now, lying there as the sky lightened outside, I wondered what it would be like if he slid inside me again. Would it hurt as much as last time? In Balaguri, I'd been so tense, terrified that somebody would hear a noise and find us, but in this beautiful house in Italy... None of our temporary housemates had so much as raised an eyebrow when I'd held Ro's hand yesterday. They didn't judge what I did.

I closed my eyes again, only for a second, but they quickly flew open when the phone rang. Ro grabbed it in a heartbeat, instantly wide awake.

"Hello? *Buongiorno*?" A pause. "Ah, *sobh baxir*." Why was he speaking Farsi? "We're on our way. Thank you."

"What's happened?" I asked the second he hung up.

"Yafir just showed up at the mosque for Friday prayers."

Alhamdulilah. The fear that had coiled itself around my chest eased. *Yafir was alive.*

"Which mosque?"

"The one nearest to the port. Apparently, he's hungry."

"We need to go there."

I was already on my feet, in a daze as I unbuttoned my pyjama top and dropped it on the floor. Then I realised that I wasn't in my own bedroom, and Ro was staring at me open-mouthed.

"Uh... Uh..."

He tossed me his T-shirt. "You can do a striptease for me any time, but if you're planning to walk around the house naked, I'll have to poke the other guys' eyes out."

"Sorry! I'm sorry!"

"You're beautiful." Ro already had his trousers on. "Get dressed, treasure, and I'll meet you by the car."

The people at the mosque hadn't told Yafir we were coming. They'd just shown him into an empty room, called the number on the flyer, and waited outside the door for us to arrive.

"The boy is sick," the imam said, leading us in through a side entrance. "We gave him bread and cheese, but he does not eat."

Sick? My poor, poor brother. Yafir looked exhausted too. Hardly surprising if he'd been skulking around the back-streets of Ancona for three days. The dark red zip-up sweat-shirt he wore was several sizes too large and made him appear even smaller, and his eyes turned into dinner plates when we appeared in the doorway. I won't lie and say it didn't hurt when he looked around for a way to escape. Nor was it lost on me that Ro blocked the only exit while I stepped inside.

"Yafir…" Now that we'd found him, I didn't know what to say. "I… I missed you."

"Why are you here? Did he send you?"

"Nobody sent me, I promise. I found out you'd left Afghanistan, and I wanted to find you."

"How? You couldn't leave alone. Not without Tabesh's permission."

He spat my former husband's name, leaving me under no illusion how he felt about him.

"Tabesh died."

That shocked Yafir. He opened his mouth, then closed it again.

"How did he die?"

"He collapsed. Maybe a heart attack?" I mean, that was possibly true. Nobody quite knew how the Electi delivered justice. "Do you remember Ro? He offered to help me look for you."

Yafir focused on Ro for the first time, and then nodded. "Yes, I remember. Why would *he* help you?"

I wasn't about to dig into the mess of my relationship with Ro, not in the mosque and especially not with the imam watching from the doorway.

"Because he's a good person, and he's worried about you." I held out a hand. "We'll take you somewhere safe."

Yafir's face morphed from wariness into fear, and he shook his head violently. "Nowhere is safe. There...there are people looking for me."

"We've rented a house. Nobody will look for you there."

"You rented a house? With him?" Yafir glared at Ro. "That is haram."

"There are other people staying there too." All men, which actually made things worse, but we just needed to get away from the mosque before the imam started selling tickets to the show. "Are you hungry? There's plenty of food."

"You can take my room," Ro said. "I'll sleep on the couch."

It was a kind offer, but my heart sank. If Ro slept on the couch, then I'd be alone, and I probably wouldn't sleep at all. I'd quickly grown used to having Ro next to me at night. His presence made me feel safe.

"Where else would you go?" I asked. "You can't keep hiding forever."

Yafir's defiance melted away, and he looked much younger than his fifteen years. He wanted to think he was a grown-up, but he was still a child. And I sympathised. Even though I was eleven years older than him, I'd have given anything for a hug from my mother right then.

"Okay," he said softly, picking up the backpack on the floor beside him. "I'll come."

I thanked the imam on our way out and got a nod in return, while Ro got a handshake and a smile. Then we were driving back to the rented villa, through the streets of a city whose sidewalks I'd spent so many hours trudging in despair. I sat in the back seat with Yafir. He'd returned my hug, stiffly, but he didn't complain when I held his hand. Perhaps he realised I needed that closeness? Those months spent apart had been so hard. Was I happy now? Yes, but I knew it wasn't over. Yafir had questions to answer, and Dayyin Rouhani's men were still on the loose, possibly with a radioactive source.

"You're having a baby?" Yafir asked.

"Yes."

"Tabesh said so, but I thought he lied."

"Tabesh said so? When did you see Tabesh?"

Yafir shrugged, then yawned. How much sleep had he got during the past few days?

"A month ago? Two months? I wanted to ask you about going to Europe, but Tabesh, he said you didn't want to see me."

I gasped. And at that moment, I was sorry the Electi had killed Tabesh because I wanted to go back and do it myself. Slowly.

"Why? Why would he say that?"

"He said you wanted your new life and not your old one. That you were pregnant."

"May his soul be eaten by cockroaches."

Did cockroaches exist in the afterlife? I needed to ask Ro that question.

"Then you didn't shun me?"

"Of course not. Yafir, I've been following you across Europe."

"If Tabesh didn't tell you I left, how did you find out?"

"I met a lady called Katie. She said the KLA held her prisoner, and you brought her food. You spoke to her about Athens."

"Katie?" Yafir's eyes lit up. "Dayyin said she was an infidel, but she was nice to me. She is alive?"

"Yes. She went home to America."

"Dayyin said he would let her go, but I wasn't sure..." Yafir chewed his lip. "Maybe I have been wrong about more things."

"They didn't let her go. Ro—"

"I heard she escaped," Ro said from the driver's seat. "Rumour says she got passed to the Jala Mujahideen and they were planning to execute her, but she got away."

Yafir's shoulders slumped.

"This is true?" he asked me.

I owed it to Ro to keep his secrets. "Yes, it's true. Yafir, how did you get involved with these people?"

"We were hungry," he said simply. "The army destroyed the poppies, and we needed to buy food."

"Poppies? You were growing poppies?"

"Uncle Shafiq said they were worth more than wheat and potatoes."

Of course he did. My father had always been vehemently opposed to contributing to the country's opium problem, which had led to many arguments between him and Uncle Shafiq. Was I surprised that my uncle had dishonoured his brother's memory? No, just disappointed.

"Wheat and potatoes are legal."

"This was why he didn't tell you. He said you would be upset."

I took a calming breath. "What's done is done. But that still doesn't explain how you got involved with the KLA."

"Dawoud said the work was easy and that they paid more money than working in the fields."

This went from bad to worse. Dawoud lived in the next village. Yafir had gone to school with him.

"Dawoud is also working for the KLA?"

Yafir nodded.

"What did they make you do? Apart from feeding hostages?"

"Hostages?"

"Katie Waller?"

"Dayyin said she was a spy. I'm glad she's alive, but she brought soldiers into our territory."

"She's a wildlife journalist. She brought her bodyguards and a cameraman to look for jumping mice."

"Jumping mice? Why did she not look near Balaguri? There are many jumping mice there."

"Because somebody told her they were near Tangar. And she found the mice, but then the KLA kidnapped her."

"But Dayyin said—"

"Dayyin was a liar."

Yafir snatched his hand away and folded his arms, and I regretted being so blunt. He'd been on his own for days, scared and hungry, and now that I had my brother back, I didn't want to push him away again. But if Dayyin Rouhani had brainwashed him, he needed to hear the truth.

The car slowed, and Ro turned into the driveway of the rented house. Once again, I saw the shock in Yafir's eyes. It mirrored my own when I'd first caught sight of the Olympia Hotel in Athens. And this house was truly beautiful—a peach-coloured mansion with five bedrooms, a vast living room, and a kitchen that would make cooking a pleasure rather than a chore. Except I hadn't cooked a thing because Reed had prepared dinner every day.

And breakfast this morning, it turned out.

Ro hadn't called the others to tell them we were coming, but they knew. The Electi must have been watching again. A sweet aroma drifted around the hallway when Ro opened the front door, and I realised that Yafir wasn't the only one who hadn't been eating properly. My stomach grumbled, and the baby kicked me in the bladder.

"I need to use the bathroom," I whispered to Ro.

"Take your time. I'll move my stuff so Yafir can have my room, and we'll meet you in the kitchen."

Reed had made a huge stack of pancakes with syrup and fresh fruit, and when I walked into the kitchen, Yafir was picking at them, one small forkful at a time. I started to take off my headscarf because of the heat, then decided not to give Yafir yet another shock that day and wrapped it tighter instead.

"How many do you want, Ziya?" Reed asked, holding up a plate.

"Uh, three?" Then I remembered I was eating for two. "Four?"

"Coffee?" Ro asked.

"I'd rather have juice."

When I started towards the fridge, he waved me into a seat.

"I'll get it."

"Why aren't you cooking?" Yafir whispered as I sat down.

"Because they won't let me. What happened in Tangar, Yafir? Why did you come to Europe?"

The sooner we got answers, the sooner this nightmare would be over, and better for me to ask the questions than a stranger. I knew Ro would have been in touch with his contact in England already. He might have gone above and beyond the call of duty for me, but his loyalty was still to his country.

"Doesn't everyone want to come to Europe?"

"Many boys do, but why did the KLA help you to get here? Travel isn't cheap."

Yafir's fork clattered onto the plate. "They have money."

"But why did they spend it on you?"

"Stop asking these questions! You're not my father."

"No, I'm your sister."

"In Afghanistan, you would respect me."

"We're not in Afghanistan. And because of everything that's happened, we can't ever go back there. Just be thankful that we're both still alive."

To my horror, Yafir began to cry. Fifteen years old, a boy who wanted so desperately to become a man, and he broke down in tears. What could I do but hug him? At first, he tried to resist, but then he gave in and wrapped his arms around me. The only part of my Balaguri family that I had left.

"Dayyin said he wanted to give us a new start," Yafir sniffed. "That foreigners had ruined our country, so we should go out into the world and spread the word of Allah."

"And how were you going to do that?"

I couldn't see Dayyin Rouhani handing out pamphlets the way two brave but foolhardy Christian missionaries had done many years ago when they visited our village.

A shrug. "He didn't say. Just that he would give us somewhere to stay when we got here."

"So why did you run away?"

"Because...because I was scared."

"Scared of what?"

Yafir's voice dropped to the softest whisper, and I felt Ro moving closer to listen.

"The first man I travelled with, through Iran and Turkey, he was crazy. And in Ankara, I heard him on the phone, and he said that we were on our way and when I arrived, hellfire would rain down on the infidels and everyone would take the KLA's demands seriously."

My blood turned to frozen slush in my veins. "W-w-what did he mean?"

"I don't know! But I didn't want any part in hellfire. And Dayyin never mentioned attacking infidels, only educating them. So I think that maybe these men had their own plans." I didn't. I thought that Dayyin Rouhani had just been better than his minions at hiding his true intentions. "The first man was like a hawk, always watching, but the second man fell asleep on the boat, so I escaped and hid."

"In the lifeboat." My own words came out flat.

"How do you know?"

Sweat trickled down Yafir's temple, and when he pulled off the oversized sweatshirt, I saw he'd lost weight. But that wasn't all I saw. I grabbed his hand.

"What happened to your arm?"

"Nothing."

"It's gone red. And your skin's peeling."

He tried to snatch his hand away. "I don't know. It just started itching."

"When? Before you left Afghanistan?"

"No, a couple of days ago. I must have scratched it."

No. No, no, no. Would this never end? A tear rolled down my own cheek because I'd seen marks like that before, back when I was doing my medical training.

"Ziya?" Ro crouched next to me. "What's wrong?"

"I think... I think this is radiation dermatitis."

CHAPTER 35
RO

"Who do you think those guys are?"

Over four hours had passed since we'd evacuated our rented house, and information was still sketchy. I paused in my pacing as Reed stepped forward to squint at the small TV screen high up in the corner of the room they'd quarantined us in. This wing of the hospital was closed for refurbishment, and the air smelled of paint and plastic rather than antiseptic and death. It was quiet too. Eerily so.

Will and Beck leaned against the wall a few feet away, wearing blue scrubs that matched my own. They hadn't been able to find a set the right size for Reed, and every so often, he tugged at the seams as if that might stretch them bigger. Yoda lay at his feet, still damp from the shower. Technically, dogs weren't allowed in the building, but we weren't going to leave him behind, and the staff had more important things to worry about in the chaos.

On the local news station, a team of uniformed men climbed out of a blue-and-white truck with *Artificieri* written on the side. Fuck. The driveway of the rental house was visible in the background, and an excited female reporter was jabbering away in Italian, clearly thrilled that something so exciting was happening in a sleepy municipality near Ancona.

"Looks like the bomb squad," I told Reed.

Because a radioactive source alone wasn't bad enough.

Will gave a nervous laugh. "The bomb squad? That's just a precaution, right?"

Beck shrugged. "Guess we're gonna lose our security deposit."

Marina didn't do things by halves, I had to give her that.

"Mr. Kent?"

The nurse's heavily accented voice was muffled by a respirator, her body dwarfed by a bulky hazmat suit. All very necessary until we worked out exactly what we were dealing with, and I was glad they were taking the proper precautions, but the outfit didn't help to calm my nerves. While I was trying to work on the "no news is good news" principle, my stress levels had gone through the roof.

"How is she?"

I pictured Ziya hugging her brother again, the joy in her eyes before we realised he'd been carrying a silent killer. At the moment, we didn't know the form of the radioactive source, whether it was loose or sealed, whether he'd been contaminated or merely exposed. If Ziya had been badly affected, or the baby, somebody might as well carve out my heart and toss it into a black hole.

Yes, I might have been affected too, but I hadn't been as close to Yafir. Nor was I pregnant. A chap had checked me and the other guys over with a Geiger-Müller counter and pronounced us "near to background," so I was hoping we were only dealing with exposure, but since we'd all taken showers before the ambulance showed up, the doctors couldn't definitively confirm that right now.

"We have to wait for some test results to come back, but she's comfortable."

"Any possible contamination?"

"We don't believe so in your wife's case, and her exposure was most likely minimal. If you want to see her, I can take you now."

Thank goodness. And of course I bloody wanted to see her. But would she want to see me?

I lowered my voice. "And her brother?"

The nurse's eyes grew more serious. "He is still sick, but his headache is easing. We will know more tomorrow. But he is also very nervous, and we're having trouble communicating with him. I understand you speak Persian?"

"Dari, yes, and Pashto."

"Would you be able to translate when the specialists come?"

"No problem."

Although I wasn't sure Yafir would be happy to see me either. One minute he'd been eating pancakes, the next all hell had broken loose, and he'd been wailing as the response team bundled him into an ambulance.

Crinkles formed at the corners of the nurse's eyes as she smiled. "*Grazie*. I will take you to see your wife."

Ziya was lying in bed with the blankets pulled up to her chin, and while she scowled, she was also struggling to hold back tears. I couldn't blame her, not for either. Today had been terrifying for everyone involved, and I included myself in that.

"You locked me in the pool room," she muttered.

When Ziya had uttered the words "radiation dermatitis" in the kitchen, my brain had gone into overdrive. Yafir said the rash had only appeared in the last few days, which meant his exposure had been recent, and we knew Dayyin Rouhani had been messing about with radioactive material. Logic said the two issues had to be connected. But where was the source? Yafir had been travelling with the courier, but he seemed to be a minor player, and according to Marina, he'd been carrying nothing out of the ordinary on his person.

Which meant...

"Yafir, did anyone give you a package to bring with you to Europe? A box?"

"No package."

"A bag? Anything?"

"Only a camera. A big expensive camera. Mahdi said he trusted me to carry it to Dayyin." Yafir's face fell. "But it is broken."

"Broken?"

"After I ran away, I thought I could sell it to buy food, but it won't turn on." He attempted a smile. "Do you know how to fix it?"

No, but I did know that in the event of contamination by radiation, decontamination procedures were necessary. They'd been drilled into me during my army training, along with a thousand other pieces of information I hoped I'd never need to use. And my first thoughts were for Ziya and the baby. Before she had time to speak, I'd scooped her up in my arms and headed for the pool house at the back of the property.

"What are you doing? Put me down! Where are you going?"

"You need to shower, just in case. Use soap and tepid water."

Too cold, and your pores closed, trapping radioactive

particles. Too hot, and your pores opened and blood flow increased, boosting the risk of absorption. Funny the things a man remembered in an emergency, wasn't it?

"I need to help my brother!"

"And contaminate yourself further? No. I'll help Yafir. You're pregnant, Zizi. That's high risk."

Ziya stayed quiet because she knew I was right. She even stood still and let me strip her out of her clothes and help her into the shower cubicle. But then she started scrubbing at herself, her movements jerky and hurried, and I knew she'd be outside again as soon as she could dry herself. That was when I'd locked the door and pocketed the key.

"Yes, treasure, I did lock you in the pool house. And I'd do it again if, heaven forbid, the need ever arose." The nurse had left the room, and I took a seat on the high-backed chair at Ziya's bedside. "How are you feeling?"

"I... I... Despaired? Is that the right word?"

"In despair. And there's a good chance Yafir will be okay. He said he first vomited in the middle of the afternoon yesterday, and he was fiddling with the camera in the morning. If he got a high dose, he'd have thrown up more or less straight away."

"He was carrying that...that *thing* around. What if it kept leaking radiation?"

I didn't have an answer for that.

"We'll cross that bridge when we come to it. The nurse said they're running tests."

"Yes, cytogenic analysis."

"Right."

"It measures ab...ab...things that are wrong with the chromosomes to work out the dose he received."

"Abnormalities?"

"That wasn't the word the doctor said."

"Aberrations?"

"Yes. Those."

Usually, Ziya was pleased with herself when she learned a new word, although her English was pretty damn good now. But today, she just looked utterly miserable. I missed her smile.

"Once we can identify the source of the radiation, we'll have a better idea of the prognosis. People are working on that as we speak." The fucking bomb squad. "Did the doctor check the baby?"

Finally, I got a tentative smile.

"I heard his heartbeat. I know you wanted me to get checked in the hospital, but this was very drastic, even for you."

Relief flooded through me. If Ziya had managed to keep her sense of humour, then there was hope. I shifted from the chair to the edge of the bed so I could hold her, and she clung on tight. We stayed like that until my bloody phone rang, and I had to answer it because it was Marina. How did I know it was Marina? Because after my phone got confiscated for decontamination, a stranger had handed me the phone without a word before disappearing, and until I synced my data, there was only one number saved in the contacts.

"Tell me you've got some good news?"

I moved over to the window so Ziya couldn't overhear Marina's side of the conversation.

"It's one of those 'good news, bad news' situations, I'm afraid. Which do you want first?"

"Give me the good news."

Might as well have one brief moment of respite before the shit hit the fan again.

"It looks as if we're dealing with exposure only." A little of the tension left me. "From the provisional exam, the source looks to be an old teletherapy capsule. The—"

"A what?"

"It's used in hospitals for radiation therapy. You know, for cancer? And radiation's only emitted when the internal source is lined up with the aperture. The thing was hidden inside the telephoto lens, so if the boy was messing around with it, it's possible he switched the device to the 'on' position."

"What position did they find it in?"

"Off."

"Thank fuck for that." If Yafir had only been exposed to a narrow beam of radiation for a short period of time, then he had a good chance of survival. "So what's the other thing?"

"The body of the camera was packed with enough plastic explosive to blow up a car. PETN, judging by the colour."

Bloody hell, and Yafir had been merrily carrying it around Europe.

"Have they..." I dropped my voice to a whisper. "Have they disarmed it?"

"The technician's still working on that. Just thought you might like an update in the meantime." Marina's voice softened. "I know you've been worried about the boy."

"I appreciate it."

"And we appreciate everything you've done. Hell, if that thing had gone off... The explosion wouldn't have been huge in the great scheme of things, but the clean-up doesn't bear thinking about. If a bomb like that ended up on the Tube, the whole network would be shut down for months."

The damage wouldn't just have been physical, it would have been economic and psychological too. Who would have felt safe on the London Underground after that?

"You're welcome. Maybe the powers that be could show their thanks by putting a rush on Ziya's paperwork? And we need to deal with her brother too."

"An interesting challenge. If he's been radicalised, he'll need therapy. Deprogramming."

Deprogramming. I hated that term. Yafir was a human being, not a computer. Beck had mentioned that Iris was dating a psychiatrist—would he be able to help in a situation like this? And speaking of the Electi, where were they? They'd definitely been around when the drama kicked off at the house, but for the last couple of hours, I hadn't felt the niggle of their presence in my head. And now that I thought about it, their absence was odd.

"Don't forget it was his decision to leave the KLA handler."

"We'll take that into account. Have you spoken to him yet?"

"Not yet, but I will soon."

"Find out what he knows. The doctors are being difficult—they won't let our people in until he's been 'fully evaluated,' whatever that means."

Hadn't the poor kid been through enough?

"I'll see what I can do."

"Excellent. Got to go—there's a call on the other line."

Ziya was sitting up in bed when I turned around, her fists clenched. "What's the bad news?"

I'd been careful not to use that particular term. "Uh…"

"You asked what the good news was, which means there must be bad news too."

Sometimes, Ziya was too damn smart for her own good. "It's nothing that affects us at the moment."

"Just tell me. Please?"

"Don't you want to hear the good news? The capsule containing the radioactive material was still intact, and it appears Yafir's exposure was only temporary."

"What kind of radiation was it? Alpha? Beta? Gamma?"

"It seems to be a small unit used in radiotherapy."

Ziya closed her eyes and took a long breath. "Gamma and beta. The worst. And you say that's the good news?"

"It *is* good news, treasure. There's no contamination."

"So what's the bad news? You said you wouldn't lie to me, and not telling me something, that's like...like half a lie."

"Zizi..."

Her eyes shone with tears. "Not knowing is always worse than knowing."

Hadn't I been angry at Tabesh for keeping her in the dark about her uncle's death? About Balaguri? She was right; I had to tell her. We'd been through hell already—we'd get through this too.

"The camera was a bomb."

It took a few seconds for my words to sink in, and then Ziya was on her feet. "That man, he is a boil on a viper's arse. I'll kill him."

"If you mean Dayyin Rouhani, he's dead already, remember?"

She slumped back onto the bed. "Oh, yes."

"And I'm not sure that a viper actually has an arse."

A giggle burst out of her. "Then I hope Dayyin burns to ashes. Did he go to hell? Tell me he did."

"I'm still learning about all of this stuff. I guess I could ask the others."

Another giggle. "When can I see my brother?"

"I'll ask. They've asked me to assist with translation when the specialists arrive to talk to him. Will you be okay on your own for a short while?"

"Yes."

I leaned in to kiss Ziya on the forehead, but she grasped my face in both hands and pulled my head down so I got her lips instead. My turn to be stunned for a second. Was that intentional?

"Why do you only kiss my head?" she murmured.

"Because I don't want to push my luck and risk scaring you off."

"You don't scare me, Ro. Not anymore. One day, will you kiss me like the men in the movies that I absolutely didn't watch on Nancy's computer?"

"How about now?"

She closed her eyes, a sweet smile playing across her lips as she waited. Our first proper kiss, a year after we met. Even when we'd slept together, I hadn't kissed her on the lips. I'd been afraid of getting in too deep. Where would we have ended up if I *had* shown her how strong my feelings were that night? Would we have taken a different path?

There was no point in dwelling on the past, only in looking towards the future. Her lips were soft under mine, and when I ran the tip of my tongue along the seam, they parted with a soft gasp. It turned out that Ziya was a natural—breathy and pliable, sweet to taste. Not shy with her tongue either. Every day, I loved this woman more. So did my dick, unfortunately. I reached a hand down to adjust myself, but commando in a pair of scrubs, there wasn't an awful lot I could do to hide my erection.

Fortunately, a nurse quickly took care of that problem. Not literally, I hasten to add. No, she walked in without knocking and when she cleared her throat behind me, my dick deflated like a pricked balloon.

"Mr. Kent? Would you mind helping with the translation?"

"No, no, of course not." I gave Ziya's hand one last squeeze. "I'll be back soon."

CHAPTER 36

RO

I explained the situation to Yafir—that he'd been exposed to a currently unknown dosage of radiation, and he'd have to stay in the hospital for a few days while his white blood cells and skin were monitored—but I wasn't sure whether he shared Ziya's preference for knowing the details. Certainly, he didn't look happy afterwards.

The doctors said I could sit with him for a while, and much as I hated to do Marina's bidding, I knew I had to. The bomb-maker was still at large, as were other men who supported Rouhani's ideology. They all needed to be rounded up.

"You mentioned a man named Mahdi?" I asked. "Can you tell me more about him?"

"He is a friend of Dayyin."

I didn't bother to correct Yafir on his use of the present tense. "They spend a lot of time together?"

Yafir nodded. "I saw him at the caves often."

Tangar Caves. Not just caves, according to the satellite pictures of the area I'd seen, but a whole residential and

283

training compound set at the base of the mountain. Estimates said that there were fifty to a hundred men there at any one time, and if things got hairy, they could retreat into their network of tunnels. The original caves had been expanded into a giant anthill over the years, work that started back in the days when Ziya's father used to work for the KLA.

"Did he live there?"

"I don't think so. He came in a truck. A white truck."

That didn't narrow things down much. "Could you describe him? What did he look like?"

"Old. Very old."

"Sixty years? Seventy?"

"No, old like Ghazan."

Ghazan—the tailor from Balaguri—had been around forty, so not that old at all. But his beard had been greying. Was that what Yafir meant?

"He had black hair? Grey?"

"Black and grey."

Good thing I wasn't a police sketch artist, or we'd have been there all day. Wait a second... A sketch artist...

"If I got you pencils and paper, could you draw Mahdi?"

Another nod, this time accompanied by a smile. "Yes, I'll draw him. Will the soldiers go to Tangar?"

Too bloody right. "Somebody needs to make sure Mahdi doesn't send any more boys like you to Europe with radioactive cameras."

"I don't think he will send any more. I was the last."

What?

"The last?"

"The others left before me. Do you think they will be all right? Is somebody helping them also?"

Oh, hell. Bloody hell. There were more kids with bombs tripping around Italy?

"How many others?"

"I think..." He counted on his fingers. "Five. Five more. Dawoud left a week before me."

Honestly, I had no idea how Marina did it. How she sat in an office gathering information on potential terrorist attacks without being able to get out there and *do* anything about it. I'd spent my life in the thick of it. There'd always been some sort of action I could take, some practical step that would fix the problem, be that guiding in an air strike or getting my own hands dirty. Here, sitting in a hospital room with a child who didn't truly realise the magnitude of what he was telling me, the news was a punch to the chest.

"There are five more teenagers out there? Did Mahdi give them cameras to take to Dayyin too?"

"I don't know. Not Dawoud—he had a game box to carry."

"A game box."

"You hold it in your hands and you play the games."

Ah, a games console.

"Did you meet the other boys? Spend time with them?"

"Some, but they grew up far away. I didn't know them before they came to Tangar. So mostly I spoke to Dawoud and Waseem."

"Who's Waseem?"

"Another friend of Dayyin. He got me the job working at the caves."

"How did you meet him?"

"At the market. Every week, he went there, and he used to buy vegetables from my father. And after Baba was killed, he gave me money because he said his own father had died and he knew how hard it was to live afterwards. And he gave me a phone, and books."

"What did your uncle say about that?"

A shrug.

"You didn't tell him about Waseem?"

"Uncle saw me with Waseem and told me to stay away from him, but he was always busy in the fields. And Waseem, he said that Uncle just wanted me to work and make money for him instead of getting a better job."

"And then Waseem offered you that job?"

"It was a good job."

A good job. Well, I had to agree with that assessment. The way Waseem had groomed Yafir was textbook. He'd showered him with attention, provided him with access to selected information via the phone, demonised his family, then finally initiated control. The one thing he hadn't counted on was Yafir's conscience making an appearance at the last moment.

Rather than argue, I simply nodded. "Do you know your final destination? When you escaped from the man on the boat, you were on your way to meet Dayyin—where was he going to take you?"

"The man didn't say. He was taking me to meet Dayyin?"

Yafir's smile at the thought of seeing his old boss was problematic.

"Yes, he was. Did Dayyin give you any hints as to where you might live in Europe?" Or die. "England, perhaps?"

"England? No, no, France."

"France? You were going to stay in France?"

Another shrug. "Probably. Waseem taught me French."

"French?"

"*Oui.*" He smiled brightly. "*Je m'appelle Yafir. Un billet, s'il vous plaît. Où est la scène?*"

My name is Yafir. One ticket, please. Where is the stage?

Fuck. This just got worse and worse.

"A ticket. What was the ticket for?"

Yafir shrugged.

"The stage? Were you going to a concert? A play?"

Another shrug.

"If I bring you enough paper, can you draw Waseem and all the other boys as well?"

"Yes, yes. I like to draw."

As soon as I got into the corridor, I pulled out my phone.

"Marina, we've got a bloody big problem."

"Buddy, we've got a problem."

Those were exactly the words I didn't want to hear from Reed when I walked back into the quarantine room.

"You don't know the half of it."

I explained the conversation I'd just had with Yafir, and if anything, it sounded worse the third time around. Even Marina had been uncharacteristically speechless when I told her.

"So you're saying there might be another five of these devices out there?" Beck asked. "They could shut down a whole city."

"Marina assures me that by tomorrow, half of the intelligence operatives in the UK and Europe will be looking for these kids."

"Tomorrow? They could blow the bombs tonight."

"It's possible. Marina has people compiling a list of possible targets. Do any of you have family in France?"

"One of my cousins is working in a ski resort," Will said. "Chamonix, I think. I'll have to ask my aunt."

"You might want to suggest your cousin stays away from populated areas for a week or two."

"Yeah. What a bloody nightmare. Is there anything else we can do to help?"

"Marina wants me to stay here. She thinks Yafir might respond better to questioning if someone he knows is present, and I'm inclined to agree with her. He was twitchy even around the doctors. And I need to go out and buy art supplies so he can draw pictures of the suspects."

"He's drawing his own photofits? Don't the police use sketch artists in Italy?"

"He'll be better at drawing people than he is at describing them, trust me." Will's expression said he was still dubious, and I couldn't blame him. Yafir was a surprisingly good artist, but we'd be dependent on his memory as much as his drawing skills. "What was your news? There's another problem?"

"Four of them, actually," Reed said. "The good news is that Kim's found us a place to stay tonight. A damn palace."

"It's got a tennis court as well as a pool this time," Beck added.

As if we'd have time to use either. "Why is that a problem?"

"Because when I told Kim we'd have to stick around here for a few days, she also rented a plane. The girls will be here in..." He checked his watch. "Three and a half hours."

"You couldn't stop them?"

Will barked out a laugh. "Mate... You had to lock your girl in the pool house this morning."

"Okay, point taken."

"Rania said they've waited many lifetimes to meet you,

and they didn't want to leave it any longer. She hates war, but sometimes, it's worse watching from the sidelines. If it hadn't been for the fact that the four Electi need to stay together for their powers to work, she'd have been in Afghanistan with Beck."

"I guess I can understand that."

"Marcus is coming too. His daughter's gonna stay with RJ."

"Who's RJ?"

"My closest friend. And honestly, if you think our girls are a challenge, wait until you meet RJ's fiancée. He reckons he'll tame her one day, but it won't happen."

"He doesn't want it to happen," Reed said. "He's a closet masochist."

"Takes one to know one," Beck muttered.

"Kim's just a little uptight sometimes, that's all."

So this was it. I was finally going to meet the Electi. And I wasn't sure whether to embrace my destiny or jump on the nearest plane out of Italy.

One thing was for certain—once I did leave Ancona, life would be very, very different.

CHAPTER 37

RO

I'd prepared myself for meeting the Electi. I'd spoken with them on the video calls, talked on the phone. Hell, they'd been in my damn head. But what I hadn't been prepared for was seeing them in person. Because the quartet that walked off the plane weren't simply women, they were ethereal beings surrounded by white, pink, blue, and orange light that shimmered and pulsed as they walked. Ghosts I'd talked to had mentioned a glow, but this was practically a fireworks display.

"What the hell...?" I murmured. "Iris is on fire."

Will just laughed. "You can see their colours? I wondered if you'd be able to."

The girls didn't say a word. They didn't have to. The four of them simply wrapped their arms around me, and holy hell, that light was blinding.

And the connection was instant.

When I was a kid, I'd grown to appreciate the hugs my adoptive mum was so fond of dishing out, even if I pretended to hate them as a teenager. When I met Ziya, I'd discovered what it was like to love a woman romantically, to value her life more than my own. But in the middle of the Electi huddle, I felt as if I'd finally come home. As if I'd wandered the world forever and then found the place where I belonged. Even though we'd never met before, I was them and they were me.

"Do you feel it?" Iris whispered.

"Yes."

She rested her head against my shoulder and sighed. Kimberly was crying. Nicole's fingernails were digging into my arm, and Rania didn't move a muscle. The airport around us disappeared as we became one great ball of light and energy, and at that moment, I truly believed we could do anything. That together, we *could* change the world.

Then Iris's boyfriend cleared his throat and held out a hand. "Marcus."

The moment passed. The spell was broken.

For now.

I offered a hand in return. "Ro."

"So, you're the saviour of mankind?"

"Apparently so. Disappointing, isn't it? I don't even have a cape."

"Kimberly's probably got one in her luggage," Beck said. "Want me to take some of those suitcases?"

"A cape? No way." Iris looped her arm through mine. "The Green Lantern doesn't wear a cape."

"Why is Ro the Green Lantern? The Green Lantern isn't even in the top ten when it comes to superheroes."

"Number one, that's a lie because Ryan Reynolds is hot, and number two, he's green."

"That's just make-up."

"Not Ryan Reynolds, you idiot. Ro."

"Ro's green?"

"Yup." Iris waved her free hand over my face. "He

sparkles too. We're glowing stupidly bright today. Making a joke about a nuclear reactor would be in really bad taste, wouldn't it?"

"Probably."

"Okay, then I won't. Hey, it's cool having a brother."

I was green? I looked at my arm, but it didn't look any different to me. Nicole saw what I was doing and smiled.

"We don't know what causes it. Not yet, anyway. The glow doesn't seem to have any particular purpose other than allowing us to recognise each other, but it's interesting that it's become so much more intense today. I wonder if there's a way of measuring it?"

"The whole is greater than the sum of the parts," Rania said. "We don't need to measure it, not when we can feel it."

Kimberly kissed me on the cheek. "I'm glad we could finally meet. I had no idea you even existed until a few months ago."

"The ghosts told me about the Electi, but I wasn't convinced you were real."

"We're definitely real." Iris poked me with a finger. "See? Where did you park the cars? We have work to do, and I'm starving. Can we pick up food on the way to the house?"

"And where's Ziya?" Kimberly asked. "Is she still in the hospital? We brought her more clothes."

"Yes, she's in the hospital. They want to keep her there overnight, and I need to go back to sit with her brother."

"I'll come with you," Rania said, a statement rather than a question. Although if she'd asked, I'd have agreed. From what I'd heard, she was as tough as me under her slightly standoffish exterior. My kind of girl.

"Ziya could use a friend."

"We'll all be there for both of you. The Judge and the Electi, our souls are linked. But the others—Ziya, Will, Reed, Beck, and Marcus—fate led their souls to ours, and now the ten of us are joined, at least for this life. We're a team. Sometimes we'll disagree, sometimes we'll get annoyed with each other, but we're a team. We'll love one another, support one another, and do our best to follow the path our creator laid out for us."

"Legally," Nicole added.

Rania just shrugged. "We'll make sure we don't get caught doing anything illegal."

Yes, I rather liked Rania.

CHAPTER 38

ZIYA

"Hello."

The girl in my hospital room was beautiful. Dark hair tumbled around her shoulders, flawless skin stretched over high cheekbones, and she wore tight jeans and a tailored burgundy jacket that I'd never have the courage to put on. But her eyes gave her away. They scanned me from head to toe, assessing. Under the pretty exterior, she was tough. Her gaze paused on my belly for a second before snapping back up to meet mine.

This was Rania.

I hoped my smile wasn't too nervous. "Hello."

What was I meant to say to her? Ro had told me on the phone that she was coming to Italy, but he hadn't said she'd be at the hospital.

The ice was broken when she spotted my necklace and reached out a hand. "May I?"

I took it off over my head and held it out to her, only for her to mirror me with her own gold piece. Two treasures twinkling under the lights. Hers was slightly bigger, and it lined up perfectly with the edges of mine. *With Ro's.* I was just the guardian.

"The final pieces of the puzzle," she murmured.

"Pieces? I only had one piece."

"You, Ro, and the medallion. Ten souls, five gold talismans. We've all played our parts in getting them back together, and now we have one goal to achieve."

Rania took my hand, and her smile transformed her whole being. That was the moment I realised what I'd been missing. When I'd found out the purpose of the gold piece, that it belonged to Ro and it had brought us together, I'd feared that I was disposable. A tiny cog in the wheel of eternity that could be discarded once I'd served my purpose. I'd been terrified of losing Ro, but now I understood. I hadn't lost him, and I never would. But I had just gained four sisters and four brothers.

I wasn't alone anymore, and I never would be.

"*Sì*, it is definitely a boy."

Grandma had been absolutely right, and now the doctor had confirmed it. I ignored the slimy goo on my belly and the fact that I really needed to pee and focused on the screen. On the grey blob fidgeting because he couldn't escape for another four months. On Ro's hand as it gripped mine. On his fascinated expression when he leaned in to take a closer look at our baby's genitals.

This early-morning scan was a tiny respite, a chink of light in the darkness. The shadows under Ro's eyes gave away the fact that he'd been awake for most of the night, and I hadn't slept well either despite the police guard outside my door. Every couple of hours, Ro had come with another drawing from my brother, asking if I knew any of the subjects. Five boys, two men. I recognised Dawoud Gulwal, of course, although he'd grown older since I last saw him. Not just in body, but in spirit.

The others? I'd never set eyes on any of them.

The older man, Mahdi, looked so ordinary. So average. Short hair, a long beard, a thin face with protruding eyes. His bushy eyebrows were perhaps his most notable feature. But this man… If he'd built the bombs used by the KLA, he was responsible for a hundred deaths. Bodies broken, families torn apart. What made a person want to destroy things rather than fix them? I couldn't understand.

The baby moved again, raised one tiny arm, and it looked for all the world as if he was waving. Ro snapped a picture of the screen with his phone, grinning.

"Think I'll frame that one."

"Can I have a copy?"

The doctor beamed. "I'll print it for you, Mrs. Kent."

Mrs. Kent. It wasn't my real name or even Ro's, but I liked it all the same. A month ago, I'd been terrified that Tabesh would kill the baby and me as well, but I'd been widowed and reunited with Ro. I'd lost my home and gained a family. Happiness was within reach as long as we could avert the impending apocalypse set in motion by Dayyin Rouhani.

When the doctor left the room, Ro traced my smile with a fingertip. A shiver ran through me, but a good shiver.

"You like being Mrs. Kent?"

"Even with the death and destruction, it's still a million times better than being Mrs. Siddiqui."

Ro squeezed my hand. Why did he suddenly look so nervous?

"How about being Mrs. Keyes?"

"Is...that an option?"

"Do I win the prize for the worst proposal ever?"

Quite honestly, it was just nice to be asked rather than told.

"I'd love to be Mrs. Keyes."

Ro tunnelled his fingers through my hair and leaned in, his eyes fixed on mine. Before he kissed me for the first time, I'd been worried I'd mess it up. That I wouldn't know what to do. But it turned out that all I had to do was follow his lead and try not to hyperventilate as heat flooded through my veins. My hands... I wasn't sure what to do with them, so I rested them against his chest, feeling his hard muscles twitch through his shirt. If we hadn't been in a hospital, maybe I'd have slipped my hands underneath, skin on skin.

He did that thing with his tongue again, then tugged on my bottom lip with his teeth. Unexpected, but I liked it. The mix of hard and soft, tough and sweet. Fierce and not-quite-relaxed-but-almost.

Then a doctor cleared his throat behind us. Again.

"Uh, Mrs. Kent? I have your discharge papers. You can go home now."

Home? Not quite, but I couldn't wait to get out of there. I liked working in a hospital, but I didn't enjoy being a patient.

"Ready to leave?" Ro asked, resting his forehead against mine. He had ultrasound gel all over his shirt, but he didn't seem to care.

"Can I come back later to see Yafir?"

My brother was sleeping now, but when he woke, he'd want to see me. The doctors said he'd be in the hospital for three more days at least so they could monitor him.

"I'll ask the staff to call us when he's awake." Ro grabbed a roll of paper towel and began to wipe my stomach clean, showing that sweet side again. "In the meantime, we have work to do."

So much work. But would it be enough?

CHAPTER 39

RO

"The Electi meets CSI," I muttered to Ziya. We'd been in the new house for less than a day, and already Kimberly had managed to find half a dozen giant whiteboards. According to Reed, she'd brought all the pens and Post-it notes with her. Now the living room resembled a police squad room, with link charts and laptops and cups of cold coffee everywhere. Plus a whole collection of paperclip animals, also courtesy of Kimberly. Every time I looked, she was twisting wire with her fingers.

"CSI? Nancy used to watch that."

"I didn't realise she liked detective dramas."

"She didn't, not really. She had a weird crush on one of the actors in it. One time, he replied to a comment of hers on Twitter. We were walking in Jalalabad when she saw it, and I had to pull her out of the road before a taxi hit her."

Hmm... Perhaps Nancy wasn't the best influence on Ziya, after all.

"I don't think anyone here will have that problem." And

certainly not when we had much bigger issues to deal with. "Do you want to rest while we work?"

Ziya leaned into me when I kissed her hair. For a confirmed bachelor, I'd certainly got used to this "relationship" idea quickly. Wrapping my arm around her waist felt as natural as breathing now, but that half-arsed proposal earlier... Where had it come from? Yes, I'd always assumed we'd get married eventually, but the words had just popped out of my mouth. So now it seemed I was engaged. No ring, no announcement, no real clue what I was doing. And a wedding didn't seem like the sort of event a man should try to muddle through. I wanted to give Ziya the world.

Assuming, of course, that it still existed after Rouhani's teenage army had done their worst.

"I want to help, not rest," Ziya said. "I don't know much about computers, but I can make food and carry things."

"You're *not* carrying things."

She gave me a tight little smile. "Then what would you like to eat?"

Honestly? I leaned down to whisper in Ziya's ear, and her cheeks turned scarlet as she gasped.

"Men...do that? Are you joking with me?"

Definitely not, but nor was I about to elaborate because everyone's ears had pricked up at the sound of the gasp. Now they were all listening while pretending they weren't.

"We can discuss that later. A sandwich would be super if it's not too much trouble."

Marina had emailed the list of potential targets. Over a hundred of them. When Yafir woke up, she wanted me to go back to the hospital and talk with him, mention each place in turn to see if anything jogged his memory. And it had to be me—when Marina's spooks had gone in alone earlier, he'd clammed up and refused to say a word.

In the meantime, we were taking a look at the list ourselves, and it read like a horror story. A motor race in Pau. The shrine at Lourdes. A parade in Tarbes. A charity extravaganza in Nice. The US ambassador had been advised to cut short his ski trip to Biarritz, and the airbase at Toulouse was on high alert, as was the nuclear power plant in Golfech. Any place where people gathered was considered a risk—shopping malls, markets, theme parks, concerts, schools, places of worship. If a dirty bomb exploded at one of those locations, there would be hundreds of casualties over the coming weeks as the radiation did its damage, and the clean-up costs would run into millions.

Yafir had mentioned a ticket and a stage, but Rouhani's remaining kids potentially had five devices. Where were they headed? To the same place? Or did each have a different set of instructions?

My phone screen lit up, and I walked through to the giant conservatory. Marina again.

"Is he awake?" Her men were watching Yafir at the hospital. "Do I need to head back?"

"Not yet. Thought you might want an update on the bomb."

"Not particularly, but go on."

"It was PETN, as we thought. Just over three hundred grams." Enough to blow up three cars, then. Or a concert hall, or a packed restaurant, or... "Remotely detonated once armed. By encrypted radio signal, not phone, which means there's no SIM card for us to trace and we couldn't bar it. No fingerprints, and apart from the radioactive source, no components that are easy to trace. This guy's good."

"And by 'good,' you mean 'terrible'?"

"One has to admire his technical ability if not his morals."

"You sound as if you're planning to offer him a job."

"I think that's unlikely," she replied in all seriousness. Marina sounded tired today. Judging by her croakiness, she'd had less sleep than Yafir.

"Where did the source come from? You managed to trace that?"

"Like so many orphan sources, it seems to have originated in Russia. A relic from the eighties, but caesium-137 has a half-life of thirty years, so it's still fecking dangerous. Originally, it belonged to a radiotherapy clinic near Vladivostok that went out of business. We're trying to trace the former owner, but you know what the Russians are like when it comes to cooperating."

They protected their own.

"Any idea of the range of the device? The radio detonator, I mean."

"Several kilometres."

Bloody hell. "So if Rouhani did have a partner, and that partner's carrying on with the plan, he could send in the kids, blow them to kingdom come, and live to fight another day?"

"Potentially. But we'll catch him, Ro. We *will* catch him."

"Yes, but will we catch him in time?"

"Don't be so negative."

Click. Marina was gone.

I tried to focus on the positives: I was going to be a father. I was engaged. I'd finally found my family. But if we couldn't fix this, what sort of world would my son grow up in? The initial attack had the potential to be one of the worst terrorist atrocities in the world, and radiation was the gift that kept on giving.

"You look pensive." Rania appeared beside me, silent as a wily viper. "That was your English friend? Did she have bad news?"

"Is there any other kind at the moment?"

"I see how it can feel that way, but things will get better. We're back together now. Once you start releasing the spirits—"

"Which I have no idea how to do."

"We'll work it out. Maybe you could start with the one in the master bedroom upstairs?"

"This place is haunted?"

"She only speaks Italian, but we think her name is Juliana. She talks at a hundred miles an hour and shrieks a lot. Kimberly slept on the sofa last night."

"Princess Kimberly? I bet she was thrilled about that."

"Once you get to know her, you'll find that she isn't as much of a princess as you think. But she does have a backache now."

"Well, we'll try to work out the Judge thing, but not until we've found Rouhani's army. That takes priority right now."

"We all agree on that." Rania held up a phone with a grainy picture of two men. One was Rouhani, and he looked pissed. The other was more jovial, relaxed with a drink in his hand and his dress shirt open at the collar. Their faces were a little fuzzy, but the woman in her underwear behind them was in perfect focus.

"Where was this taken?"

"Remember how Rouhani had the receipt for a bar in his pocket when he crashed? This is the place."

"But Marina said there were no cameras?"

"No CCTV, and taking pictures is forbidden, but since when do people pay attention to the rules?"

"How did you find it?"

"Messaged everyone who checked in at La Pêche Parfaite on Facebook that night. The fifth guy we spoke to sent us the photo. There are more, but this is the best one."

So simple, yet so effective. Marina was probably still arranging wiretaps and coordinating intelligence agencies when all she'd had to do was check social media for horny arseholes.

"Well?" Rania asked. "Do you recognise him?"

"Unfortunately not, but I need to send this to the boss."

Marina would consult with MI6 and run it through the database. Maybe we'd get lucky?

"Will's already sent it to your email. And Ziya made sandwiches. As in, she *made* sandwiches."

Rania wasn't kidding. I'd suggested a sandwich because it was easy—even I could put a slice of cheese between two pieces of bread—but I'd forgotten that wasn't how they did sandwiches in Afghanistan. Pre-sliced bread was unheard of in Balaguri. Ziya had made flatbread from scratch, fried lamb, mixed it with spicy tomato sauce, and served it with French fries and sweet tea.

"Oh, treasure, this wasn't what I meant."

Ziya's face fell. "You don't like it?"

"I'm sure it's delicious, but I didn't want you to go to so much trouble."

"It's no trouble. And the kitchen is magic. Did you know there's a tap that boils water and a machine that makes ice? *Magic.* I think I will live there."

Sometimes, I forgot how little Ziya had seen of the world. She'd taken this month's upheaval in her stride, but her childlike wonder at the little things made me smile.

"You can design your own kitchen when we get to England. Not right away—we'll have to rent to start with—but once we get settled and decide where we want to live, we can buy a place."

"You can have the cottage soon," Iris said with her mouth full. "Once our house is renovated, it'll be empty."

"What cottage?"

"Rania and Will have a cottage in their garden."

"You can't just offer us somebody else's house."

"Rania?"

Rania shrugged. "As soon as Iris, Marcus, and Cassie move out, you're welcome to use it. But until then, there's a spare bedroom in the main house."

"Teddy would love a friend too," Iris said, scratching Yoda's head. He'd taken all the moves in his stride as well.

"Who's Teddy?"

"Our dog. How are your DIY skills? I mean, we know you can handle a gun, but what about a paintbrush?"

"I haven't had to paint anything for over a decade, but I'm sure it'll come back."

While I spoke, I opened the email on my borrowed laptop, saved the photo Will had sent, then attached it to a new email for Marina. The faster she received it, the sooner we might get an answer. Except Ziya had other ideas.

"Why do you have a picture of Dayyin and Hamza? And who is the naked girl? Surely that is haram?"

"I'm sorry?"

"They're both Muslim. A woman shouldn't be naked around a man like that unless he's her husband, and she can't be married to both of them. That is also haram."

"No, no, I mean Hamza. Who's Hamza?"

"Dayyin's friend."

Holy shit.

"You know him?" I jabbed the screen with a finger. "You know this man?"

Ziya leaned closer and squinted until I enlarged the picture. Then she stepped backward and fell onto my lap. No complaints.

"Yes, I mean, I think so. I haven't seen him for a few years, but I'm almost certain."

"And his name is Hamza? Do you know his surname?"

"Lodi. Hamza Lodi. Dayyin's father used to work for Hamza's father."

"You're sure?"

"That's why they moved to the city. The Lodi family is rich. Really rich. They have a huge house in Jalalabad, near the university."

"What else do you know about them? Are they hard-line?"

"Not that I ever heard. I think they just sell drugs. Hamza doesn't even live in Afghanistan anymore. He went to school in England, and now he only comes back to visit. Sometimes in Jalalabad, I used to see him driving in a big black car. Nobody else could afford such a vehicle."

Will was already typing the name into his laptop. Whatever search program he used, it wasn't Google, I knew that much. Now he gave a low whistle.

"Hamza Lodi is loaded. After university, he went into investment banking, and now he runs his own hedge fund."

"How did you find that out so fast?"

Will turned his screen to face me. "It's on his website."

Sure enough, there he was, smiling in a suit, arms folded in a power pose. I compared the face to the slightly blurred man from the strip club, and Ziya was right—if it wasn't Lodi with his head a foot from the blonde's gyrating crotch, then it was his doppelgänger.

Beck snorted out a laugh. "Your folks in England are scouring the terrorist watch lists, and they should have been checking *The Times*'s 'Forty Under Forty.'"

"You're serious?"

"Yup. He's number thirty-two on last year's list of the UK's up-and-coming businessmen."

Reed was also tapping away. "Here he is falling out of a bar with two blondes. And a nightclub. Brunettes this time."

"Anyone want to watch his speech to London's Young Entrepreneur Society?" Rania asked. "It's on YouTube."

Could we be barking up completely the wrong tree? I'd come across hundreds of terrorists and a number of sympathisers in my life, but none whose lifestyle was quite so at odds with the KLA's values. Rouhani had been a dangerous ideologue. Lodi? He seemed to be more of a playboy. Perhaps the meeting at La Pêche Parfaite had been nothing more than a reunion between two old friends? Or should I downgrade that to acquaintances? Rouhani certainly hadn't looked thrilled to be there.

"I should pass this on to the boss."

"You think Lodi's involved in the bomb plot?" Beck asked. "The guy's halfway to being a billionaire. Why would he risk losing that by going to prison?"

"Who knows?"

"Wait a second..." Reed said. "There's an article on him in *The Isis* magazine."

Beck raised an eyebrow. "Islamic State has its own magazine?"

I knew the answer to that question. "They did—it was called *Dabiq*, but it folded a while ago."

"Oh, wait... It says here that *The Isis* is the student magazine of Oxford University. Why would they call it that?"

"Because the River Isis runs through Oxford," Will told him. "I'm pretty sure the magazine's been around for longer than Islamic State."

"Right. Well, Hamza Lodi was on the fencing team. See? They even won a medal."

Will leaned forward. "Hey, I know that guy."

"Lodi?"

"No, the fellow next to him. Archie Bradshaw—we went to school together. I haven't seen him in years, but my mother was good friends with his mother. If I'm honest, Archie was a bit of a dick—always pratting around—but I might be able to get in touch."

"What have we got to lose?"

In the meantime, I'd send everything we had to Marina. Running background checks was her specialty, not mine, and I had an appointment at the hospital.

CHAPTER 40
ZIYA

Yafir yawned as I hugged him goodbye, and I couldn't blame him. After trekking across two continents, he was probably feeling the same bone-weary tiredness as me. This evening's session had gone on for hours, every word carefully monitored by a doctor and a man in a suit who said nothing. A camera in the corner let nameless people around the world watch too, and Ro wore two earpieces—one linked to his boss and the other to Marcus, Iris's boyfriend. Apparently, his professional qualifications had convinced whoever was in charge that he should be permitted to offer advice. My job was to be encouraging while Ro probed deep into the recesses of Yafir's mind for something, anything that might tell us the target.

The biggest clue had come when Ro asked Yafir how he'd been chosen to travel to Europe.

"How many boys were at the Tangar Caves?"

"All of them. Women were not allowed."

"I mean younger boys, your age."

"Sometimes twenty, sometimes thirty. They come, they go."

"Why do they go?"

No answer.

"Do they go home?"

Yafir didn't like that question. He'd got that same sulky look when he was told off by our father.

"Please answer, Yafir," I said. "Nobody will be upset with you."

"Dawoud said they martyred themselves."

"And still you stayed there?"

"Dawoud, sometimes he lied. And even if he told the truth, what choice did I have? The government is corrupt. It has failed us. There are two laws in Afghanistan—one for the rich and one for the poor. People like me, we have no opportunities there. I just wanted to help to change the system."

The system. The government had been promising for decades that ordinary Afghans would have a better life, but those promises had been broken time after time. Little changed. Only private efforts such as Ro's gave us services like water and school buildings. Having men from the KLA in charge wasn't a good solution either, but at the moment, there were no other alternatives.

"Martyrs don't change the system. They just create more division."

"This was why I wanted to come to Europe instead."

"Did you volunteer?" Ro asked.

"Yes, but at first I was not selected. Dayyin said I needed to spend longer at the caves first."

Because he wasn't fully indoctrinated?

"What changed?"

"Shabir."

"Shabir changed?"

"Dayyin said he couldn't go anymore."

"Do you know why?"

"No."

"You don't have any idea at all? Shabir didn't say anything?"

"No, but he got scared."

"Scared? Of what he was meant to do in Europe?"

"He was scared in the mountains. Mahdi made us climb with new wires for the solar panels, and Shabir couldn't do it. He got stuck."

"Stuck?"

"He wouldn't go up and he wouldn't go down."

"Vertigo? A fear of heights?"

"Maybe. The next day, Dayyin said I would go to Europe instead."

Was the target high up? Was that why Yafir had been sent instead of Shabir? The Eiffel Tower was on the list, and so was a cable car in the Pyrenees.

Yafir was talking freely, and for that I had to be thankful. He'd been treated well so far. I was under no illusion that he'd get away with what he'd done—he'd been carrying a radioactive bomb, however unknowingly—but at least he wasn't wearing handcuffs. He had pencils and paper, people brought him healthy food, and the guards outside the door were polite.

And most importantly, he was alive.

It could have been so much worse.

"What do you think will happen to my brother?" I asked Ro on the way back to the house. We had another rental car, a red one this time. "Will he go to prison?"

"I don't think so. What would that achieve? He's more likely to get radicalised in prison than anywhere else, plus he's as much a victim in this as anyone. But the authorities will want to be sure he isn't dangerous before they let him loose on the streets."

"Will they send him back to Afghanistan? He's got nobody there. And if people find out he betrayed Dayyin..."

"I hope not. If he keeps talking and the people I work with think he might be useful, they'll make arrangements to bring him to the UK. He'll probably have to go through some kind of treatment program."

That was the best thing I could hope for. Above all, I wanted my brother to be safe, and I won't lie and say I wasn't worried that he'd got tangled up with Dayyin Rouhani in the first place. Perhaps naivety ran in the family? I'd been taken in by Ro, hadn't I? Although that had turned out a lot better.

"Thank you," I murmured.

"For what?"

"For everything. For building the well in Balaguri, for that night in the goat house, for coming back to me. For rescuing Katie Waller and for caring enough to help me find Yafir."

Ro took my hand and brought it to his lips. His beard tickled my skin as heat burned through me. One touch, and I melted.

"When you love somebody, you'll do anything for them."

"You...you love me?"

"Of course I love you. Zizi, I asked you to marry me."

"In my world, love and marriage don't always go together. Wait, why are we stopping?"

"So I can do this."

Ro unclipped both of our seat belts, leaned over, and cupped my cheeks in his hands. Then he kissed me, and if he'd made my knees weak before, today my legs turned to noodles. Was this normal? Stopping at the side of the road to make out?

"What if someone sees us?"

"We're not doing anything illegal. Yet," he added under his breath. "I could be tempted."

"I don't think—"

That was it. I didn't think. Not when he kissed me again. All rational thoughts scattered as one of his hands tangled in my hair and the other slid down to cup my breast.

"What don't you think?"

I just curled both hands into his shirt and pulled his lips onto mine again, kissing him until I was breathless. When I paused for air, Ro pressed his lips to my forehead the way he always used to do.

"In case there's any doubt, I love you, Zizi."

"I love you too."

"I know, but it's nice to hear the words."

"You're so cocky."

He guided my hand downwards, and I nearly choked when it landed in his lap. But he just laughed.

"Yes, I am."

"Uh, what were these illegal things you mentioned?"

"I was thinking public indecency, unless you have a better idea?"

Luckily it was dark because my cheeks were on fire. "That thing you said last night about being hungry... That was a joke, yes?"

Ro clipped my seat belt back into place, then his own, and started the engine.

"Ten minutes, and I'll show you."

~

Ten minutes, Ro said, but when we got back to the house, he disappeared into the bathroom and stayed there. Was he getting cold feet? Hiding? Because wasn't that what I always did?

I was lying under the quilt naked, and now my own feet were getting chilly. Was he expecting this? I'd always worn pyjamas in bed before, and I began to worry that I might have misinterpreted something.

I'd spent the past week questioning myself. Lying awake, wondering if I was behaving appropriately. I'd swapped my dresses for trousers, and I hadn't covered my hair since the day we found Yafir at the mosque. Nobody had said anything, but what were they thinking? Were they judging me?

Certainly I'd been judging myself.

Then the bathroom door opened and Ro appeared. Underwear, no shirt. And where had his beard gone? He lay on the bed next to me, his head propped up on one arm.

"What's up?"

"What do you mean?"

"You look worried. Which means I'm worried."

"I'm fine."

"That's not a proper answer."

Sometimes, Ro was too observant for comfort.

"I just... Am I doing this right?"

"Doing what right?"

"This. Everything. What I'm wearing, the way I'm behaving... Is it right?"

"Perfect. You're perfect."

"Because everything's different here. I don't understand

all the rules. And so many things that I was taught were the truth... Now I'm not sure anymore."

"Are you talking about your faith?"

"Yes, in part."

"Faith... I suppose I'm in, well, not quite a unique position, but certainly an unusual one. The way I see it is there are over four thousand organised religions in the world, and logic says there's no way they can all be right. But maybe parts of them are? There's a higher power out there. I've glimpsed parts of it. I don't know how or why or what, but we're not alone."

"I guess that makes sense."

"When it comes down to it, I just do what I feel is right."

"You've killed people."

"Only in pursuit of a greater good, and I have plenty of regrets. If everyone made kindness their religion and love their goal, the world would be a better place." Ro brushed a lock of hair away from my face. "This is all getting very serious, Zizi."

"I don't want to mess this up."

"You won't. If you're worried about anything, we can always talk. I won't judge."

"You're literally the Judge."

"Not with you, treasure. With you, I'm just Ro. Fiancé, dork, soon-to-be father."

"You're not a dork."

"Sometimes I feel like one. What do you want to do tonight, my love? We can just sleep if you want."

"You're not hungry anymore?"

"I'm ravenous."

I slowly pushed the quilt down, watching Ro's face as I

did so. His eyes darkened, and his sharp intake of breath told me he wasn't quite as controlled as he made out.

My blood turned to lava as he sucked one nipple and then the other, teasing them into stiff peaks, and my heart beat loud in my ears. Chills followed as he trailed his tongue over my skin, goosebumps popping up in its wake. The only sounds in the room were our mingling breaths. Was it weird to just lie there? I felt guilty that Ro was doing all the work, but it felt so good that I didn't want to move.

And then he spread my legs and dipped his head between them, and I *couldn't* move.

When Nancy used to joke about sex, I'd get embarrassed, and she'd laugh and tell me I didn't know what I'd been missing.

Well, now I did, and it was no laughing matter. It was more of a screaming, sobbing, mind-blowing matter, and when my world exploded and left me limp on the mattress, I couldn't even think. All I could do was curl myself up in Ro's arms and thank the stars above that Balaguri spent so many years without a water well.

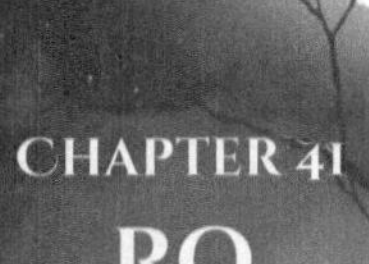

CHAPTER 41
RO

Sunday morning, and there was no rest for the wicked as Rania handed me a mug of coffee.

"You shaved?"

Yes, because I hadn't wanted to give Ziya beard rash. She'd been through quite enough in the last month without having to deal with chafed thighs as well. And fuck, it had been worth the effort. My sweet, innocent Zizi. Despite my earlier warnings, she'd been shocked when I buried my face between her legs, squealed when I ran my tongue over her folds. She'd tasted every bit as delicious as I knew she would, and her breathy little gasps had left me hard as a rock. Painfully so. And when she screamed and nearly crushed my head as her hands tugged at my hair, I realised this was all even newer to her than I thought.

"W-w-what?" she'd stuttered. "What happened?"

That selfish bastard had never made her come before? Not once?

What an arsehole.

Still, I'd liked being the first.

"Fancied a change," I told Rania. "Thanks for the

317

coffee."

"What time are you going back to the hospital?"

"Around eleven. Whenever I get the call." Which meant I had an hour or so to lend a hand here. "The doctors wanted to run more tests this morning. I sense a power struggle between the medical staff and the spooks."

"Do you think Yafir knows anything more?"

"I'm not sure. Marcus says that if I keep asking questions, talking over Yafir's time at the caves, he might recall additional details. There's a possibility the target's high up. Another kid got bumped from the team after he froze on a climb."

"Maybe that had more to do with his lack of courage than his aptitude for a particular task?"

"Who knows? Anything's possible."

Rania shrugged. "We'll keep poking around, but I'm not sure we'll be able to add much when all the police in Europe are on the case."

"Better to do something than nothing," Will said from behind her. "If we can't go home, we might as well investigate."

Kimberly appeared in the doorway. "We could go sightseeing."

"Do you really want to do that?"

"I guess not." She sighed as she took a seat at the table. "I've picked up more groceries, plus extra art supplies for Yafir. What else should I do today?"

"If you take—" Will's phone rang, and he held up a hand. "Hold on a sec. Archie? Thanks for calling me back. No, I'm in Italy." He turned the phone onto speaker so the rest of us could listen too. Easier than repeating the conversation later. "Do you happen to remember a chap called Hamza Lodi from your Oxford days?"

"Old Hamza? Yes, of course I remember him. An excellent business mind, but not much of a sense of humour. We tried punting on the river in our first term, and when he fell in, he did *not* see the funny side. Why on earth are you asking about him?"

"His name came up in connection with a case."

"Oh, yes, right—Mother said you'd become a private investigator. What's he done? Money laundering?"

"Money laundering? Why would you say that?"

Archie gave a nervous laugh. "No particular reason. He just seemed the type, that's all."

"What type?"

"Smart, but not particularly moralistic. I see he made *The Times*'s 'Forty Under Forty' list last year, so I imagine he's doing quite well for himself, and that start-up capital had to come from somewhere."

Interesting.

"I'm not looking into his business dealings, more of a personal matter. Did you spend much time with him?"

"Well, we were both in the fencing club, and sometimes he hung around on the fringes of our little group. But he used to fly home to visit his family during the holidays rather than join us on our jaunts, so I didn't get to know him as well as I did the others."

"What did you think of him as a person?"

"Always serious," Archie said. "Quite boring, really, at least until our final year when he went off the rails a bit."

"What do you mean? Was it something to do with religion?"

"Religion? What do you mean?"

"The case I mentioned is centred around religious extremism."

Archie chuckled. "Must be a different Hamza Lodi, then.

The chap I knew wasn't religious in the slightest. Oh, he used to tell his father he went to the mosque and all that palaver, but you were more likely to find him in the Cricketer's Arms."

"So how did he go off the rails?"

"Over a woman. Plain old-fashioned jealousy. He'd been on a handful of dates with a rather attractive undergrad named Alice, and it seemed he believed the affair was a lot more serious than she did."

"What happened?"

"He saw her kissing Pierre in the Junior Common Room and hit the roof. Broke Pierre's nose, Alice was screaming... It was quite something. First, Hamza kept yelling about betrayal, then he went deathly quiet, walked right up to Pierre, toe to toe, and told him he'd pay for stealing his woman. *His* woman. As if Alice was property. She was not impressed, let me tell you. I thought *she* was going to punch *him* on the nose, but she just informed him that their relationship had been casual and if he was going to act like a complete pillock, she never wanted to see him again anyway. Then she walked out with Pierre, and if looks could kill..."

"Did Hamza take things any further?"

"That was a question I always asked myself."

"Why?"

"Hamza stopped hanging out with us after that day, but a week before finals, four men jumped Pierre on his way back from visiting a friend at Balliol. He'd come in the rear gate, and the path was deserted at that time of night. I wondered if Hamza was involved. I mean, he'd never get his own hands dirty, but somebody had to have given those thugs the code to get into the college grounds."

"Was Pierre badly hurt?"

"Thomas was out for a late jog and heard the noise, and since he was president of the aikido club at the time, the attackers came off worse than he and Pierre did. But the police never found the men."

"That was the only incident?"

"The only incident that I know of. We graduated, and I headed to Australia. Originally, it was only supposed to be for six weeks, but then I met John, and we stayed for a year."

"How long have you been married now?"

"Five years next month."

"Congratulations in advance."

"Thanks, old chap."

"Did you keep in touch with either of them? Hamza or Pierre?"

"Hamza? Of course not, not after that incident. I wouldn't invest a penny in his hedge fund either. I hear it's volatile, just like him. But I still see Pierre from time to time. He and Alice got married not too long after John and me. We were guests at their wedding. As a matter of fact... Hang on..." There was a *clonk*, as if Archie had dropped the phone. "Yes, it *was* this weekend. Pierre invited us to France for a few days, but John's gallery had a new exhibition opening so we couldn't make it."

"Special occasion?"

"Yes, three incredibly talented young modern artists— ninety percent of the paintings sold on the first night."

"I meant Pierre's invitation."

"Oh, of course. Yes, he had an opening too. Parc Aventure. If I recall correctly, he sketched out the original idea when we were in our second year at Oxford. His family owned some land in the Pyrenees, and he thought it would be the perfect spot for a family-friendly attraction."

The atmosphere in the room went from relaxed to "holy fuck" in a split second. Reed dove across and tore the list of targets off the wall while Rania's fingers flew over the keyboard.

"It's here," Reed said. "We had it in the 'unlikely' group."

"What's Pierre's surname?" Rania whispered, and Will relayed the question to Archie.

"De Guillebon. Do you want me to spell it?"

No need. Rania hit a key, and the press release for today's grand opening projected onto the white wall opposite. A life-sized Pierre de Guillebon grinned down at us, the snowy vista of Parc Aventure in the background. France's tallest roller coaster, a toboggan ride, an ice-skating rink, a big wheel, a year-round Christmas market... Two hotels, six restaurants, a snow field for the little kids.

Kids.

If this was the target, Hamza Lodi was a bigger monster than we'd ever suspected. Would he really risk so much collateral damage for petty revenge? Had his rage festered and grown to such an extent that he'd kill hundreds? I struggled to believe a man could be so cruel.

But if he'd joined forces with Dayyin Rouhani... Two agendas, one goal: to make a statement.

It was possible, wasn't it? And the pieces fit. Rouhani's teenage foot soldiers would blend in perfectly at a theme park, and vertigo wouldn't mix well with the rides. Rouhani had been in Toulouse. Yafir had talked about tickets and a stage, and the press release billed a big speech by de Guillebon at eleven a.m.

Half an hour from now.

Fuck, I had to call Marina.

CHAPTER 42

RO

"Hamza Lodi?" Marina said. "The investor guy? As far as I know, he hasn't come up on any of our watch lists."

"That's because you're looking for religious extremists, and this isn't about religion. It's about revenge. Plain, simple, dirty revenge."

"A bit drastic, don't you think?"

"But if he's working with Dayyin Rouhani, a man who was hardly known for his subtlety..." Even now, remembering the aftermath of his Kabul car bombs made me feel sick. All those broken kids... "The KLA suddenly started getting money, and none of my Afghan sources had a clue where it came from. Lodi has money and, rumour says, dubious ethics. Plus he could funnel it through his father's businesses."

"It's a stretch."

"Lodi knew Rouhani, and he knew de Guillebon. Those facts are indisputable."

"I'll look into it. See if we can trace Lodi."

"Hurry. If it *is* Lodi, he's most likely going to act today."

"Understood."

Marina hung up, and I began pacing. It was a bad habit, and one born out of helplessness. A madman was planning mass murder, I was hundreds of miles away, and all I could do was wait. And pray. I thought back to my discussion with Ziya last night. Was somebody up there listening? Despite what I'd said about a higher power, I had difficulty believing my own words. Why would they allow so much suffering in the world? If there was a God, it seemed they treated the human race as a science project.

While I was speaking, the four Electi had appeared, plus their significant others. Even Yoda was sitting to attention. The only person missing was Ziya, but she'd been so tired last night. Better to let her sleep.

"What should we do next?" Kimberly asked.

Why was everyone looking at me?

"What *can* we do? We need to find Hamza Lodi, and we're in the wrong damn country."

"Where's his website? I'll try phoning. Say I'm interested in investing and I want to speak with him."

"It's Sunday. The office will be closed."

"If you have enough money, the office is always open. Rich people don't like waiting."

Kimberly scrolled through the website until she found a number for Lodi, and as predicted, someone picked up. Not Lodi—I could make out the high pitch of a woman's voice, even if I couldn't hear the words themselves.

"Is Hamza available? ... No, I really don't want to speak to anyone else. Hamza came very highly recommended. ... On vacation? Oh, that's a shame. I have funds maturing in the next few days, and I need to find a home for them. ...

How much? Several million. More in six months if the investment performs well. ... You will?" Kimberly's voice turned syrupy sweet. "I'd very much appreciate that." She tossed the phone back onto the table. "Hamza's on vacation."

"We got that, sweetheart," Reed said. "Did she say where?"

"No, and I'm not sure she even knows. She said he was incommunicado, but she's going to try calling him anyway. So if RJ can get a look at her phone records and see what number she dials in the next few minutes, we can track that and find Hamza. Right?"

"Nice work," Will said. "I'll call RJ."

RJ was a friend of his, that much I recalled. "How will RJ find the phone records?"

Will waved a hand. "RJ has tentacles in all sorts of databases. Let me know if you ever need a speeding ticket revoked."

"Thanks, I'll bear that in mind. How long will he take?"

"Ten minutes? I'll tell him it's urgent."

But Marina beat him to it. She called back in five, and I knew straight away that the news wasn't good. In the year and a half I'd known her, I'd never heard so much as a hint of panic in her voice, but today, she couldn't hide it. The tension in the room ratcheted up a notch.

"You were right. Hamza Lodi was in the south of France."

"Was?"

"His private jet just took off from Toulouse-Blagnac. We were ten minutes too late to stop it."

"He's leaving? Where's he going?"

"His pilot filed a flight plan for Zaragoza."

Spain? "Why is he going there?"

"I don't think it matters."

"What do you mean?"

"Do you have a map handy?"

"Give me a second."

Rania was on it already. A map popped up on the wall, Toulouse highlighted in red and Zaragoza in blue. A dotted line connected the two, and that line went right over...

"Fuck."

"Exactly."

"What's the range of that detonator again?"

"We think he'll be close enough. It's only a short hop from Toulouse to Zaragoza, so he'll be flying low."

The motherfucker would get a front-row seat for the show. He could watch the fireworks from the air and stay out of danger himself.

"How can we stop it?"

"The French Air Force is scrambling interceptors, but we're not sure they'll make it in time. If Lodi gets an inkling that we're onto his plan, he can blow the bombs as soon as he's within range rather than waiting until he's overhead. And if the pilot's as crazy as Lodi, we'd have to shoot the plane down to stop it anyway."

"Can't you do that? There's plenty of open countryside."

"As I said earlier, we've made a hell of a lot of assumptions to get to this position. There's no concrete evidence. Shooting down a foreign businessman's civilian plane would spark an international incident, and if we're wrong..."

"There must be some way of stopping him. Can't you evacuate the park? Send people in to look for the kids?"

"It's a seven-hundred-acre park, there are three thousand people there, and we've got less than fifteen minutes. Ro, I need to go and deal with this."

Silence fell in the room. We knew what was going to happen, and we knew who was going to make it happen, and there wasn't a damn thing anyone could do apart from arrest Lodi when he landed in Zaragoza. By that point, tens, hundreds of people would be dead and a large chunk of southern France would be contaminated with caesium-137. People said that hell hath no fury like a woman scorned, but it turned out that a man scorned could be even worse.

"What happened?"

I spun to find Ziya standing by the door, wearing one of my T-shirts and a pair of sweatpants. She'd never looked more beautiful.

"Did somebody die?" she asked.

"Not yet, but they're about to. And there's nothing we can do to stop it."

I gave her a quick recap of events, and her face morphed from puzzlement to horror.

"They should shoot down the plane," she said. "It's two lives or two hundred."

"The people who'd make the ultimate decision are notoriously risk-averse, plus the pilot might be innocent."

"So they'll let families die?"

"Yes, because if that happens, it's easier to blame somebody else."

"It's a shame you can't get on the plane with him," Iris said. "If Hamza's killed before, we could do our thing and..." She made a cutting motion across her neck with one hand. "Buh-bye."

"It's not feasible, even if I was in the same country."

We'd actually experimented with shit like that in the military. Wing-walking on a Typhoon. It was bloody terrifying, and also impossible to blow a hole in the pressurised fuselage of a jet without endangering the chase aircraft and everyone in it.

"Maybe it *is* feasible," Ziya said.

"No, treasure. Trust me, it's been tried."

"Has it?" She lifted her necklace over her head and held it out. "Has it been tried this way?"

CHAPTER 43

RO

"What are you talking about?" I asked Ziya. "What's the necklace got to do with anything?"

"My grandma, she always said you were the traveller, and I don't think she meant on foot."

"Zizi, I can't just hop onto a plane mid-flight."

"How do you know?"

"Well, logic says..."

"I'm not sure logic applies to the Electi," Beck pointed out. "A month ago, if somebody had said the Electi could see through your eyes and kill people with their thoughts, would you have believed them?"

He did have a point.

"No, but—"

"What do you have to lose by trying?" Ziya asked softly.

Nothing. We had nothing to lose, and if we did nothing, we'd lose everything anyway.

"How does it work?" I asked the other girls. "When you see through me, how do you do it?"

All I knew was that they had to be together, and I'd

made damn sure that Kimberly was asleep on the sofa yesterday evening before I went down on Ziya. An audience was the last thing I'd wanted for that little show.

"We need to be in a circle," Iris said.

She pulled off her own gold piece, detached it from its cord, and passed it to Marcus. The other girls followed suit. He was in charge of this part? Seemed so, and now wasn't the time to question it. The four Electi sat down on the floor cross-legged and held hands.

"As far as we can work out, the holes in the medallions represent our heads, which means you need to be in the middle."

Okay, fine. I stepped into the circle, and although I felt that strange rush of togetherness again, nothing happened.

"I don't think this is working."

But I'd spoken too soon. Marcus pushed four of the gold pieces together on the nearest coffee table to form a circle, and the niggle came back. That odd buzz that told me the girls were seeing through my eyes.

"You're inside my head now?"

"They don't tend to talk to us when they're under," Marcus said. "Only to themselves. Ready?"

He held up Ziya's gold piece, and I nodded. Time to find out what all the fuss was about.

Fuuuuuck.

The instant the circle was complete, I felt myself falling. Reed and Beck rushed forward to catch my body as it crumpled to the floor in the middle of the Electi, but at the same time, I stayed standing. The girls were standing too, watching curiously.

And they were also sitting.

Their bodies were sitting, and their souls were standing.

What the actual hell?

I opened my mouth to speak, but then I realised I didn't have to. Their thoughts were my thoughts, and mine were theirs. We could hold a conversation in our heads. Did my voice still work? I tried speaking, saw my seated body's mouth open. Heard myself, but in the distance.

"Freaky, isn't it?" Iris thought. "Don't worry, though. Marcus is good at judging when to bring us back."

"Now what?" Nicole asked. "Usually, we just end up where you are, but this is different. Today, we can see each other."

"And you," Kimberly added. "Your aura's more intense now."

"Why don't we try walking around?" I suggested. "See if we can move?"

"Where to?"

"The swimming pool? Let's go out to the swimming pool."

We didn't walk. We didn't need to. I thought "swimming pool," and there we were, floating above the water next to the steps. Iris tried dipping a toe in, but the surface didn't so much as ripple. Through the floor-to-ceiling windows, I could see the others standing around, the four men and Ziya. Yoda looked confused. He was licking Nicole's leg, but her body didn't react and her soul didn't seem to notice either.

"Well, that was a rush," Iris said-slash-thought. "Who knew we could walk on water?"

Rania scanned the sky. "Fun, but we need to find Lodi's plane. How do we get there?"

Good question. I spotted a passenger plane high in the sky, a tiny speck, and suddenly we were standing on the wing. There was no rush of wind, no chill from the altitude.

Just the five of us, riding on a fucking Airbus. Then we were inside, standing in the aisle as a member of the cabin crew pushed a drinks cart through us.

"This is the wrong plane," Rania said.

"Yes, I think I got that."

"You seem to be in charge."

"That's debatable."

"Reckon we can float on a cloud?" Iris asked.

No. The answer was a very definite no. I thought "cloud," and we found ourselves hurtling towards the earth at a hundred miles an hour. Somebody screamed, and my first thought was "Ziya." Then we were back in the living room at the rented house, Ziya was staring at Kimberly with her eyes wide, and Marcus had his hand hovering above the gold pieces. Slowly, he lowered it to the table again.

"I think they're okay. Kimberly gets nervous sometimes."

"Kimberly gets nervous? I'm terrified."

Reed put an arm around Ziya, and I found I wasn't jealous, just grateful that he was there to offer her comfort.

"We don't have time to stand around," Rania warned. "At least we know that we can get onto planes now."

"I guess we're like the spirits," Kimberly said. "They get stuck to their spots on earth, but they can also be tethered to larger objects. Cars, buses, planes, that sort of thing."

"Have you ever even been on a bus?" Nicole asked.

"No, but I came across a dead girl in a car once."

Where was Lodi's plane? In the south of France, somewhere between Toulouse-Blagnac Airport and Parc Aventure. I didn't know how to get to the airport, and how many planes were in the sky in that area? No idea. But if I focused on the theme park... I'd been looking at it on the satellite map, I could picture it, and— There we were. A shrieking child hurled a snowball straight through the middle of me.

Rania gave a rare smile. "Now, this is more like it."

"Watch for the plane. It'll be coming from the north."

I looked north. Rania looked north. The others looked confused. I guess wedding planners didn't do much orienteering. I turned Kimberly around and pointed at the sky.

"That direction."

"Maybe we should look for the kids as well?" Iris said. "You know, cover all bases?"

She tried to jog away and made it roughly three paces before she turned into MC Hammer doing the Running Man.

"Hey, I'm stuck."

Rania snorted a laugh. "I guess the spirits aren't the only ones who have rules to follow. We can travel, but we have to do it together. No turning renegade."

"That sucks."

"There's a plane," Kimberly said. "See?"

"Too big and too high."

Nicole pointed skywards. "There's another one following. A smaller one. It just went behind a cloud."

I glanced at Rania for a second opinion, and she nodded. "Get us up there."

Dubious morals sure did let a man travel in comfort. Lodi's jet was tastefully furnished with cream leather seats, a walnut table, and cashmere blankets. Crime paid, it seemed. The man himself was kneeling on a fancy couch, his nose pressed to one of the windows as the plane approached Parc Aventure. Nobody else was in the cabin, and the door to the cockpit was closed.

"He's got the detonator in his hand," Rania whispered.

So he did. A small black box with a flip switch. We'd

been absolutely right. There was no other reason for the odd position Lodi had adopted, for his palpable excitement as the man who'd stolen the object of his affections grew closer. Ordinarily at a time like this, I'd have expected to feel the changes in myself—a racing heart, a trickle of sweat down my spine. Hyperfocus as I worked out the best way to eliminate my target.

But I had no body, none of the usual visceral reactions. And killing this man wasn't my job.

"So I guess you do your thing now?" I said to the Electi.

"Yes."

I heard their thoughts, one after the other.

"Die."

"Die."

"Die."

"Die."

But Lodi didn't die. He stayed on his knees, one finger poised to flick the switch.

"Why is he still alive?" Iris asked, panicked. "Doesn't it work if Ro's here with us?"

"Perhaps he hasn't killed anyone personally before," Rania said. "Will's friend said Hamza didn't like getting his hands dirty."

Kimberly took Iris's panic and raised it to sheer horror. "So we have to stand here and watch him kill people, and only *then* can we banish his soul? That's insane. It makes a mockery of our whole job."

"Maybe we're working within a rule-based system rather than a principle-based system," Nicole said. "It's not as if whoever created us provided an instruction manual. We definitely can't...I don't know, grab him or something?"

I lunged forward on the off chance with Rania at my

side, but our hands went straight through him. He didn't flinch.

"That's a no."

Iris folded her arms. "The man's a monster. He deserves to die."

"Right now," Kimberly added.

Nicole looked close to tears. "He's the perfect candidate for hell or wherever the black souls go."

"He should be punished," Rania said.

Never had I felt so helpless, and the clock was ticking, unhurried yet inevitable. "Yes, I agree he should die, but—"

Lodi died.

His regular soul, the image of his living self, bulged out of his flesh. Fought free of its mortal bounds. Then it darkened, frayed around the edges, and scattered into the clouds outside. His body slumped sideways on the couch, and the detonator slid away under a plush leather seat.

"Is...is he dead?" Iris asked.

"We saw his soul burst," Rania pointed out.

Kimberly kept her gaze fixed on Lodi, eyes wide. "What happened? I don't understand."

But Rania did. "It's so obvious now. Don't you see? Ro's the judge. We put forward a case, however rudimentary, and he issued his judgement."

Kimberly stared blankly.

"We wanted Lodi to die, but his soul was still normal. Think of the black souls as judged already—all we do is send them on their way. To dispatch a regular soul, to pre-judge them for what they're about to do, that takes an extra step."

"Like a safeguard?" Nicole asked.

"Exactly like a safeguard. And I bet when it comes to the tethered souls, it'll be a similar process. We tell Ro why they should be released, and if he agrees with us, they can leave."

Could it really be that simple?

Only time would tell, but the evidence, in part, was lying on the couch in front of us. This was why I saw spirits, and why they couldn't pick me out the way they could the Electi. Why only the Electi saw my aura. I wasn't *meant* to mix with the spirits. My role was to judge the Electi, to act as a fail-safe to stop them from killing the wrong person, whether in error or on purpose. To ensure they didn't go rogue. One girl could dispatch a black soul alone, but she had to do it the hard way. When all four acted together, they could take a shortcut. They had the power, and I stopped them from abusing it.

Alone, I was nothing.

Together? We were everything.

CHAPTER 44

RO

We stayed on the plane until the authorities raided it in Zaragoza because none of us wanted to take the risk that Lodi would wake up again. As I said, we were still learning the rules in this strange new existence of ours.

But he stayed dead, and when the plane landed, it was directed to a quarantine area—the out-of-the-way spot they'd use in the event of a hostage situation—and the pilot exited at gunpoint. The poor guy seemed totally unaware of what Lodi had been planning, and when he saw the body, he vomited on the carpet. Good thing the jet hadn't been shot down. Another innocent life had been saved.

Then we headed back to the villa, and when Iris began fidgeting, Marcus brought us back to reality. Or rather, one of our realities. We'd been gifted with the ability to exist in two separate planes, so it appeared.

"What happened?" Beck asked. "We've been watching the news and nothing blew up."

"Peacefully dispatched. We learned a thing or two about ourselves up there."

"Up there? You're saying you managed to get on the damn plane?"

"Two planes." I held up a hand. "Don't ask—the first one was a navigational error."

"Whoa."

The other men began asking questions, but before I attempted to answer them, I had something more important to do. I let the girls take centre stage while I hurried to Ziya.

"Zizi? Are you okay?"

Unlike the others, she hadn't said a word since we got back. Or woke up. What was the correct term for arriving home when you went travelling without moving? We were in uncharted territory.

"That should be my question," she said softly.

"I'm fine. Actually, I'm better than fine."

And I was. I'd last felt this heady combination of relief, satisfaction, and elation years ago, and back in those days, I usually had a few dings, dents, and scratches to go with it. Today, we'd carried out a precision execution and prevented a terrorist attack without even breaking a sweat. There'd been no danger, only salvation.

"You were in a trance. And I..." Ziya shook her head and bit her lip.

"You were scared?"

"Yes."

"There's no reason to be. Lodi couldn't even see us, and now here we are." I wrapped my arms around her, and after a moment's hesitation, she returned the hug. "Your quick thinking saved hundreds of lives today."

"It was definitely Hamza behind it?"

"He had the detonator in his hand."

Ziya gave a soft sigh and went limp in my arms as the relief hit her too. Yes, I'd told her there was no need to fret, but until we came back, she couldn't have been sure we were safe. And do you know what? The selfish part of me was glad she'd been worried because it meant she cared. I'd missed having people who cared. Yes, my fellow soldiers had shared the same desire to come home alive, but it was different. The connection with Ziya ran deeper.

Mrs. Keyes.

The lads used to kid that I'd be a bachelor for life, that I'd run the Fan Dance three times backward before I'd walk down the aisle, but oddly, I found myself looking forward to kissing the bride.

The chatter from behind me grew louder.

"It might be over, but I still can't believe it," Iris said. "The motive, I mean. That a man would murder kids because a hook-up fell in love with another guy? And people call *me* crazy..."

"Murder always comes down to four overarching motives," Will reminded her. "Money, lust, power, or revenge. It shouldn't really surprise us. And Rouhani had his own motives for participating in the plot."

"Revenge with a side of religious extremism," Beck muttered. "A powerful combination."

"And a healthy dose of manipulation."

"Scary how close they got."

Will leaned back against the wall and surveyed the room. "Yes, but the Electi stopped them. The sixty-four-thousand-dollar question is what happens next?"

"My boss's people will pick up the kids from Parc Aventure. Plus they have two more names and descriptions from Yafir—the suspected bomb-maker and the man who groomed him—and they know roughly where to find them."

"What if you and the Electi got there first?"

"That's not our…"

I trailed off because it was exactly our job, wasn't it? In the SAS, I'd hated the fact that faceless bureaucrats got to act as judge and jury from their ivory towers while my men and I were expected to do their bidding as executioners. But now? Now, I was the judge. The backstop.

"Consider it, Ro," Rania said quietly. "We've both seen war. We've both seen good men and women lose their lives trying to do what we could do in seconds. A surgical strike. Cut out the cancer."

"Maybe it would be okay to leave the groomer," Kimberly said. "But the bomb-maker, he tried to kill kids. *Kids*. I can't stop thinking about all those people in the park."

We'd seen them from the air as we flew over—hundreds of tiny specks milling around below. I couldn't stop thinking about them either.

And now Iris ganged up too. "We'd probably need you to agree to him dying. I mean, he doesn't kill people with his own hands, and perhaps he never has. He just provides the tools. Like, I don't think we could order a blacksmith to die because a lunatic beheaded someone with a sword he made."

"Nicole?" Kimberly asked.

"I guess. But do we know that we can repeat what we did on the plane? What if it was a fluke? An anomaly?"

"There's only one way to find out."

"Then we should also start understanding what else we can do."

"Like releasing the spirits, you mean?"

Nicole shrugged. "I'm just saying that we should get a handle on the basics before we go flying off to the other side of the world."

"So let's try it. If we can get rid of the dead woman in the bedroom, maybe I won't have to sleep on the couch tonight?"

"Wait a second," Marcus said. "One step at a time. You've only just got back from...wherever the hell you went. Don't you want to take a break?"

Iris rolled her eyes. "It's not even lunchtime, and all we've done is sit on the floor."

"That's not the point I was trying to make."

"I know, and I really do appreciate it, but I'm fine. Honestly."

"Ro?" Kimberly asked. "What do you think? Can we try?"

"You mean free the woman upstairs?"

"Unless you'd rather take a trip to Afghanistan right now?"

"As Marcus said, let's take one step at a time. Do you know who the woman is? Shouldn't we try to talk to her first? If the person who killed her is still on the loose, then surely we should get that information and do something about it?"

"You mean...kill them?"

"No, I mean report it to the police. Somehow."

"We could call in with an anonymous tip," Nicole suggested. "That's what I used to do."

"We can't just let her go?" Kimberly asked.

"How long has she been dead? Because if she's been dead for a century, then yes, we can just let her go because her killer's dead too. Unless they're a vampire, but that doesn't bear thinking about."

"Her clothing looks modern. A pink satin negligee. If I had to guess, I'd say she died around the time *Friends* was on because she's got the same hairstyle as Rachel."

Will grabbed his laptop from the table. "Then I bet there's something online. A rich lady dying in suspicious circumstances? That won't have flown under the radar."

It turned out she wasn't rich. Juliana Ricci had been a prostitute, and the wife of the man she'd been in bed with hadn't been at all happy to find her there. The wife had also been a champion markswoman, and in her rage, she hadn't hesitated to put a round between Juliana's eyes. Now she was serving a life sentence in prison.

"Motives two and four," Will said. "Lust and revenge."

Iris nodded her agreement. "So I guess it's safe to send Juliana wherever, then."

I couldn't argue with that.

"Do we have to go upstairs? Or should we do the circle thing again?"

Rania picked up a cushion from the couch. "The circle—that's how it works. But let's make it a bit more comfortable this time."

As with the dispatch of Lodi, the actual event was somewhat anticlimactic. At least, it seemed that way to me. We all flitted upstairs, each of the girls voiced their opinion that Juliana should be allowed to leave, and I concurred. Then she just faded away to nothing.

Gone.

More interesting was the fact that after I climbed into the circle, we ended up upstairs before I'd even thought about travelling. How had we got there? Well, a brief discussion while we waited for Marcus to bring us back revealed it had been Kimberly's doing. In her eagerness to sleep in a proper bed again, she'd imagined us upstairs, and boom, there we were.

So it appeared that one person needed to lead each session, but I didn't have to be responsible for directions all the time. Good. That took some of the pressure off.

While I'd found the release of Juliana a rather mundane process, not so the girls. I guess they'd spent more time speaking with the spirits over the years than I had. They were closer to them. And once we got back to the living room, the chatter began immediately.

"You know what this means?" Kimberly said. "We can let Margaret go."

"Who's Margaret?" I asked.

"She lives in my house."

Nicole's eyes shone. "Herman can leave as well, and Anna. And that poor girl who helped me to find you, the one whose child ran her over by accident."

"And Helene," Rania said. "She was a pain, but she wasn't malicious, and she doesn't deserve to be stuck in a hallway for the rest of her immortal life."

Iris shrugged. "I guess we should set the victims from Lakeview free as well. Except maybe Archie. He was a real prick."

I didn't know who those people were, but we could help them, and we would. And I also needed to keep my promises to Musa at the café and the lady who'd seen Yafir escape from the ferry. But before all that, there was somebody else I needed to visit. A man I needed to speak to and release. I caught Ziya's eye, and she managed a sad smile because she knew exactly what I was thinking.

"Ladies, we have another trip to make first."

Half an hour later, we found ourselves hovering by the side of a road in Afghanistan, at the spot where I'd decided to change the course of my life. Ziya's father was right where I'd seen him last, but he'd changed. Before, he'd been getting over the shock of dying while growing used to the new normal. Now? Now his shoulders were hunched, and his entire demeanour spoke of resignation. Of loneliness. I'd seen it before—the thought of spending eternity alone weighed heavy on a man. When ten days became ten weeks, then ten months. Ten years. The girls talked about negative energy being a burden on the earth, and maybe it was caused by sadness?

"Hello, Adil."

"Rohan? You came back!"

"Not in body, but in spirit."

"And these...these are the Electi?"

I glanced at the girls standing either side of me, their glowing auras surrounding us.

"How did you guess?"

"You came to avenge my death?"

"Not quite." I wasn't about to send a fellow soldier to wherever those black souls ended up. He was as much a victim of a flawed system as Adil had been. "We're here to help you move on."

Adil's gap-toothed smile said that wasn't such a bad option. "Move on to where?"

"To a new life. But before you go, I have a message from Ziya."

His smile stretched into a grin. "You found Ziya?"

Ziya and I had spent much of the half hour before I "departed" for Afghanistan discussing what to tell her father. Above all, she wanted him to pass to the next plane in peace, which meant glossing over the Tabesh debacle and the fate of Balaguri.

"I did. She's in Europe now, and she's engaged to be married."

"To a good man?"

"I'd like to think so. She wants you to know that you'll be walking down the aisle with her in spirit, and she'll always carry memories of you in her heart."

"And I of her. My Ziya... Her mother would be so proud. Her grandmothers too. And Yafir? Did you see Yafir?"

"He's also in Europe."

"With Ziya?"

"Yes, with Ziya."

Now Adil's expression was one of peace. "Then I can leave as a happy man."

The actual act took only seconds, and unlike with Juliana, I felt a twinge in my chest as Adil faded. Perhaps because I'd known him, however briefly, this release felt less like a job and more like the loss of a loved one. But he was in a better place now. I truly believed that.

Ziya was quiet as we followed the day's events on the TV. Reporters made no connection between the attempted terrorist attack at a French theme park and the mysterious death of a wealthy businessman in Spain, but they took the number one and two spots respectively on every news show. The authorities had rounded up "a number of suspects" and "removed several suspicious devices."

Marina called before dinner with another update, her voice hoarse but upbeat.

"You've been watching the news?" she asked.

"What else would I be doing on this fine March day? I see Lodi popped his clogs."

"What a stroke of fucking luck."

"Any idea how he died?"

Because I had to admit, I was curious.

"Not yet. Post-mortem's tomorrow. But he was alone in the cabin and there wasn't a mark on him, so maybe he stroked out from the excitement?"

"Karma at its finest. What about the kids?"

"We got them all," she said. "The five boys plus two women who were with them. They claim they had no idea about Lodi's motives. Apparently, he'd promised to help the teenagers start new lives in France—sort of like an unofficial adoption. The women were employees, one French, one British. Paid chaperones. They were hired to shuttle the kids around, cook for them, that sort of thing. They're being questioned, of course. How's Yafir?"

We'd made a quick trip to the hospital in the afternoon. Obviously, the urgency had gone out of questioning him now, but he was still being detained.

"Seems bright enough. The doctors didn't raise any concerns."

"That's good news. We'll have to look at moving him soon."

"To the UK?"

"That's the plan. I have a number of colleagues who want to chat with him."

"Are we talking custody?"

"Prison? No. More like enforced hospitality, for a few months at least. We'll want to be sure he isn't a threat."

That was the deal I'd been expecting. Cooperation in exchange for a chance at a future. Ziya and I would have to keep Yafir on track and ensure he told all he knew, but I had hope we'd get through this. Together.

"Five devices?" I asked. "They've been defused?"

"Three cameras and two handheld games consoles." Marina's voice cracked. "The smallest kid was twelve years old, Ro. Twelve years old."

"Bloody hell."

"It very nearly was. But we stopped it. Obviously we don't dish out medals at Mansfield, but know that my superiors are very grateful for everything you've done. And keen for you to carry on doing it."

"About the job..."

"I thought that's what you'd say. The girl?"

"She's pregnant."

"So I heard. Yours?"

"Yes."

Ziya might not have been certain, but I was. The bond, that other-worldly thread that linked me to my son, I felt it already.

"You're a dark horse, Rohan Keyes. But not all of Mansfield's roles involve fieldwork. Come and see me when you get back, okay? We'll talk."

"Okay."

One chapter of my life was over, and a new one was beginning. I had Ziya, I'd found my family, and I was about to become a father. Life...it wasn't too bad.

Plus Reed had offered to cook dinner, which was a bonus.

Yes, I'd sleep soundly tonight.

We can sleep well tonight.

Those were the last words Kimberly had said before we all headed upstairs, and I'd smiled and nodded my agreement. But I'd lied.

I couldn't sleep.

I couldn't even close my eyes.

Ro was in the bathroom, and I was praying to whoever might be up there that when the door opened, he would walk out naked. I wanted another helping of what he'd given me last night. No, I wanted more than that. I wanted everything. I wanted *him*.

Now that the end of the Rouhani/Lodi nightmare was in sight, my mind had switched onto a different track. But was Ro's travelling in the same direction?

The water shut off, and I froze. I'd arranged myself on the bed in my underwear, but now I was second-guessing myself. What did I know about the art of seduction? Only what I'd learned from Nancy, and her tactics relied on nightclubs and cocktails. I couldn't dance, and even if I weren't pregnant, I still wouldn't drink alcohol. This was a bad, bad idea. I was about to get up and grab my pyjamas when the bathroom door opened and Ro's silhouette appeared in the doorway. Wearing boxer shorts.

Uh-oh.

"Zizi, are you feeling okay? Too hot? Shall I turn the heating down?"

"No, no, I'm—"

I definitely wasn't fine because when I tried to burrow under the covers, my foot got tangled in the quilt and I tumbled off the bed. Instinct made me curl around my bump and close my eyes as the tiled floor rushed to meet me.

But the *crunch* never happened. And perhaps I should have fallen off the bed more often if Ro's arms was where I ended up?

"I'm sorry," I whispered.

Those arms tightened around me. "I'm not."

His heart beat against my chest, and was it me or did his pulse not seem as steady as it usually was? I took a moment to study him in the glow from the bedside lamp. He'd shaved again. When we ate dinner, he'd had a five o'clock shadow, but now when I ran my fingertips over his jaw, his skin was smooth, and it smelled faintly of soap.

He leaned into my touch, eyes half-closed, and I did what I should have done five long, long months ago.

Erased all those regrets for good.

If our past kisses had been intense, then this one was off the charts. For once, there was no sweetness from Ro, only darkness and fire and raw power. As his tongue clashed with mine, a little of that power began pulsing through my veins as well, and I shifted so my legs were wrapped around his waist. Then I clung on until I was breathless.

"Holy fuck," he murmured when we came up for air. "Who are you and what have you done with Ziya?"

"You said you wanted me to be myself." I shrugged. "So I think... I guess maybe this is who I am?"

Ro lowered me onto the bed, spread my legs, and knelt between them. I craved the sweet caress of his tongue, but a sudden chill crept up my spine when he leaned forward to kiss me. I blinked to banish the image of Tabesh looming over me like that, right before he'd flop down and shove his dick inside.

"What's wrong, treasure?" Ro stilled, his weight supported on one arm.

"Nothing. It's nothing."

"Zizi..."

"Just a bad memory, that's all."

"Of *him*?"

"He only knew one way to have sex, and that was it."

"On behalf of mankind, I'm sorry. I'm so sorry you went through that."

"I don't want to think about him anymore, only us. But maybe there's another way we could...you know?"

"Make love?"

It sounded so much nicer when he put it like that. I nodded.

"Missionary position isn't good for the baby anyway. I looked it up on the internet."

He did? That was...sweet. Thoughtful. Every day, Ro managed to surprise me.

"So there is another way?"

"There're plenty of other ways." Ro dropped onto his side and paused to kiss my shoulder. "And when you're ready, we'll try them all."

"I think... I think I'm ready."

Although admittedly, there was an element of wanting to get it over with. I loved the connection I felt with Ro, craved the closeness, but the act itself? Yes, I was nervous. I wanted to make Ro happy, but I was also a tiny bit scared.

"'Think' isn't good enough, Zizi. We'll wait until you're sure."

"But—"

"Shh." Ro put a finger to my lips, then replaced it with a kiss. "We've got all the time in the world now."

A moment later, he shifted down the bed and gifted me his tongue again. This time, I knew what to expect, and a contented sigh escaped my lips as I lay back. Ro called me his treasure, but I was the one who'd struck gold. I'd found the man who was always meant for me.

Fate had finally come through.

This was the nicest way to wake up in the morning. Wrapped in Ro, lying in a comfortable bed with sun streaming through the windows. It took me back to my childhood. In those days, I'd loved the clear blue skies, but as I grew older, I'd learned to embrace the rain clouds because when the skies were grey, the drones didn't come. Life in Afghanistan had been hard. Still was hard for all those left behind. But perhaps now, this tiny team I'd found myself a part of might be able to do something about that. Turn darkness into light.

Ro stirred behind me, and his stubble tickled my skin as he dropped soft kisses across the back of my shoulders. One hand left my stomach, and he cupped my breast, then circled the nipple with a fingertip. I felt the tip harden under his touch.

And that wasn't the only thing that was hard. My breath hitched as he pressed his hips against my butt, but rather than feeling trepidation or dread or fear, this morning, I felt only want. *Need.* Ro always gave, never took, and now I wanted him to give me *that.*

"Ro?"

"Mmm?"

"I've been thinking, and what I—"

"Shh... You're tense. Just relax. No need to think this morning."

"But..."

His hand moved up, and he pressed one finger against my bottom lip until I opened my mouth.

"Suck."

What could I do but obey? And how could such a simple act send a jolt of heat through me the way it did? I shuddered and arched back against Ro, pressed against his hard chest, those muscles as solid as brick, as protective as a wall.

His finger left my mouth with a quiet *pop*, and now his hand moved downwards. *All* the way down. My legs parted of their own accord as it slid between them, and jumping jerboas, Ro's finger was every bit as good as his tongue. He was a magician, a living god, and me? I was a mess. A coiled, sweaty spring. By the time stars burst behind my eyes, my thighs were slick and gibberish was flowing from my mouth. What language was I even speaking?

"I love you too, treasure," Ro whispered.

Had I said I loved him? Phew. Perhaps my word vomit hadn't been as bad as I thought.

"The part about a good rogering..." he continued. "Did you get that from Nancy?"

"Oh, bollocks."

Ro's soft chuckle vibrated against my skin. "You've got quite a mouth on you."

"Sorry."

"Don't be sorry. I like that in a woman."

"You do?"

"Absolutely. The filthier the better, my darling."

Wow, really?

"So, about that rogering..." I started, and Ro stiffened behind me. Not just his dick, all of him. "I'm ready. I'm definitely ready. I want that. Now."

Ro didn't speak, and for a moment, I thought I'd have to beg, but then I felt that delicious length nudge between my legs. Slowly, slowly, he slid the whole way in, giving me time to adjust to his size. I won't lie and say it didn't make me gasp, but it also felt good. Right. As if we'd joined not only our bodies but our souls as well.

This was so, so different from our first fumbled attempt in the goat house. This morning, Ro stroked smoothly in and out of me, almost lazily, pausing every so often to whisper his own dirty thoughts into my ear. His finger found its way between my legs again, and that blissful ache built once more as he fisted the other hand in my hair. This man...he was everything. And he was mine.

Ro thrust harder, then grunted and stilled as the wave crashed over me, this one so powerful I thought I might drown. A sumptuous heat spread through my belly, and I realised my limbs wouldn't move anymore. I was a week-old spinach leaf, limp in Ro's arms.

His lips ghosted across my skin, as soft as his whisper. "I love you."

"What's more than love? Because that's what I'm feeling at the moment."

"Us."

It really was that simple. Us. Two broken pieces, one perfect whole. Soon we'd be three, four if you counted Yoda, and we'd made it against all the odds. Yes, we still had challenges to come—taking care of my brother, getting to England, finding a permanent home—but we'd do it together.

Together.

EPILOGUE - ZIYA

F*ive months later...*

"They're here!" Iris yelled, and Yoda started barking. Teddy quickly joined in, and both dogs raced out the back door of the White House—that wasn't its official name, but everyone called it that—and zoomed around the garden. They'd been a little wary of each other at first, but now they were the best of friends. Partners in crime too. Teddy had taught Yoda how to swim, and in return, Yoda taught Teddy how to dig holes. Muddy footprints had become the norm.

"Coming," I called.

We hadn't seen Kimberly, Nicole, Beck, and Reed for nearly two months. Work commitments meant Team Electi couldn't stay together all the time at the moment, although we spoke every day. Zoom calls, WhatsApp, emails—technology was our friend. But I had another friend too, and that was perhaps the most wonderful surprise I'd ever had.

"Bloody Nora, you're gonna have to help me." Nancy held her hands out, and I hauled her off the sofa. Yes, Nancy, and her belly was even bigger than mine had been.

I'd only been in England for a week when she'd arrived at my new home with Ro. He'd teamed up with Will and Rania to find her, and none of them had told me a thing. Not even a whisper. After Nancy left Afghanistan, she'd taken a job at Southend Hospital, started dating a doctor, got pregnant, dumped the doctor, transferred to St. Albans City Hospital, and rented a flat just half an hour away from the White House. She'd held my hand while I gave birth a month ago, and I'd return the favour in two weeks or so. Ro had been there too, and I'm not sure who'd looked sicker through the whole process, him or Nancy.

My wedding ring glinted in the sunlight streaming through the window as Nancy got her balance. Yes, I was married already. Why wait? As soon as Ro's boss made good on her promise of paperwork, we'd headed to the local registry office with the others to tie the knot. Kimberly had offered to organise us "the mother of all weddings," but I'd already had one of those and I didn't want another, thank you very much. The three-day party Tabesh insisted on had tainted my view of weddings forever. I'd wanted to be married to Ro, that was all, and he made sure it happened exactly the way I wished. A short ceremony, a kiss, a few photos, and a meal at a local Italian restaurant. Pizza was my new favourite food. When I was pregnant, I'd piled it high with bananas and pickles while everyone looked on in horror, but now I'd progressed to regular toppings. If I ever saw another pickle, I might just throw up.

Yafir had been at the wedding too. The people Ro worked for had allowed him out of their facility for the day, and if everything went according to plan, soon he'd be released permanently. He wasn't in prison, more of a halfway house along with the other boys who'd been found at Parc Aventure. The questioning had more or less finished now, and Yafir's therapist was pleased with his progress. Weirdly, my relationship with my brother was better than ever. Twice a week, Ro drove me to visit him, and we talked, really talked. Yafir had been harbouring a lot of bitterness towards the men who'd killed our family as well as the world in general. Today, the bitterness had mostly been replaced by grief, and he was gradually healing. Like me, he understood that nothing we did could bring our loved ones back, and by allowing that darkness to fester and grow, we'd only end up hurting ourselves. Our friends too.

And thanks to Ro, I knew my father was okay. Balaguri was empty too. Still and quiet, free of its spirits.

Team Electi, as we'd started calling ourselves, had been busy in the weeks after we left Italy. The bomb-maker was gone, his soul banished, and Waseem, the man who'd groomed my brother, had been captured alive by coalition soldiers. We didn't know all the details, but Ro's boss said he was spilling his guts. I hoped she meant metaphorically rather than physically, although having met Marina when she came for dinner one night, I wouldn't have put anything past her. That woman made me very nervous.

Marina had also given us an update on Katie Waller. She'd been released after a thorough debriefing, and now she was back in the United States. Apparently, she'd promised to keep her mouth shut. The bodies of her bodyguards and cameraman had also been located and returned home for a proper burial. Those loose ends were finally getting tied up. Nancy had checked Katie's Instagram page the other day, and there wasn't a single mention of

Afghanistan or jumping mice or being kidnapped, just a thousand photos of her new puppy and her new boyfriend.

"Poor sod looks as if he wants to run a mile," Nancy said.

"The puppy or the boyfriend?"

"Both."

And who could blame them?

Through the window, I saw Ro walking over from the little cottage at the end of the garden carrying our baby. Charlie Adil Keyes, named after both of our fathers. Ro said he considered the couple who'd adopted him—Charles and Marion—to be his parents. He rarely mentioned his birth parents, and when he did, there was always a hint of bitterness.

We'd only been living in the cottage for two months, but already it felt like a home, a space where we could be happy until we found a bigger house. Yafir would have his own bedroom, and Charlie shared with Ro and me. Iris and Marcus had moved into their new house too, a bigger cottage that we'd all helped to decorate. Our next job would be renovating a stable block because Marcus's daughter insisted she wanted a pony. I'd overheard Marcus telling Ro that he was lucky to have a boy, but I knew Marcus didn't mean it. He adored Cassie.

In the hallway, Kimberly burst through the door with hugs and gifts for everybody.

"Where's the baby? Where is he?"

"Here," Ro said, and then he dropped his voice. "But he's sleepy."

Kimberly held out her arms. "Please?"

Ro handed our son over, and Kimberly rocked him gently. She wanted a baby of her own, I knew she did, but I also knew why she was waiting. Although we learned more about the workings of the Electi every month, there were still unknowns, and I couldn't deny that I worried about Charlie taking on Ro's responsibilities, especially if the powers transferred before he reached puberty as the girls' had. Nicole and a professor friend of hers were working on a way to slow the process, and they thought they were close, but we wouldn't know the outcome for sure until Charlie grew older. Did I worry about my son being a guinea pig for her experiments? Of course, but I trusted her, and the alternative—that he'd be expected to carry the weight of the world on his shoulders at the age of eight—was worse.

Speaking of Nicole, there she was. I hugged her, then Reed and Beck, trying not to show how strange that still felt after years of forced segregation. With Charlie the centre of attention, I took advantage of Ro's empty arms and pressed against his side, sighing out loud when he wrapped an arm around me.

Finally, I had everything I'd ever dreamed of.

EPILOGUE - RO

Since the sun was shining, we'd decided to sit in the garden today. With Kimberly and Nicole visiting, we'd taken last night to eat, drink, and make merry, but now it was time for more serious matters.

Work.

Technically, I was on paternity leave, but that only covered one of my jobs. Yes, I was still working for the Mansfield Foundation. Oh, I'd tried to quit, but Marina had offered me a desk job, and the country estate they'd adopted as their headquarters was only fifteen miles from the White House, so... I'd agreed to annualised hours, three days a week on average. Marina thought she'd get me back in the field one day—I saw the gleam in her eye every time we crossed paths in the company gym—but for now, being a father was my priority.

As well as trying to make the world a better place for my son to grow up in.

Kimberly had bought us fancy cushions, and I waited for the girls to get comfortable before I took my place in the middle of the circle. We had a system now. A plan. Since the

Electi couldn't be together all the time, not physically, we had to use the hours we did spend as a quintet wisely. That meant research and a schedule.

We'd made more discoveries since our initial bumbling attempts in Italy, the most important one being that Ziya's fifth gold piece really was the key. As long as the circle was complete, the girls could travel in pairs or as a trio. They couldn't dispatch souls that way, but they could talk to them. That meant Iris and Rania could visit spirits all over the world, hear their cases, and take any necessary action before the full team went to release them. Will, Reed, and Beck helped with the investigative work, as did Will's friend RJ and RJ's fiancée, Shannon. They'd been engaged for six months now. Would they ever get married? Possibly, if they ever stopped arguing about the logistics. Even Kimberly backed away slowly whenever the subject of their nuptials came up.

Speaking of Kimberly, occasionally she and Nicole got together stateside and lent a hand with the spirits, but they had more important things to do. Division of labour and all that. Nicole was researching the Electi at a genetic level, and Kimberly was our money girl. As well as her trust fund, the wedding planning business was doing well, and she wanted to build it up with a view to taking a step back in two years. By then, her assistants should be able to run things with minimal input from her.

Two years, that was our goal. Enough time for Nicole to finish her current research project, for the team to get our finances sorted, for us to decide on a permanent base of operations. In the meantime, my job at Mansfield gave me access to intelligence we wouldn't otherwise have, allowing us to target our efforts and carry out the occasional pre-emptive strike, the way we had with Hamza Lodi.

Marcus still worked three days a week as a psychiatrist, plus he and Iris had recently opened a small garden centre. They had a similar two-year plan to Kimberly in regard to building up the business, but for the moment, we all used the place as a getaway. Pottering around with plants gave us an escape, and for me, it brought back memories too. My mum had loved her garden. She'd have loved Ziya and Charlie as well, and I was sorry my parents would never get to meet them, but I took comfort in knowing they'd moved on.

"Ready?" Kimberly asked. "Is everyone wearing sunblock?"

Iris rolled her eyes. "Yes, Mum."

Kimberly only nagged because she cared.

"Who begged me to make an emergency pharmacy visit for after-sun lotion last week?" I asked.

Iris turned sheepish. "I fell asleep on the sunlounger, okay? Can we go now?"

Working on the theory that a build-up of spirits caused negative energy and therefore led to more violence and death, we'd decided to focus our initial efforts on a small number of high-crime areas where we might be able to make a measurable difference. City ghettoes with a high ratio of spirits to flesh-and-blood humans. And it seemed to be working. We'd spent our previous get-together clearing out a corner of Chicago, and in the past two months, crime rates had fallen to their lowest levels in three decades. Today we were off to New York. If nothing else, the travel perks were great with this career.

Rania led the way, and we found ourselves in Brownsville, strolling among ghosts, locals, and the occasional tourist who'd strayed away from the usual haunts. The girls had already checked out the area and marked the spirits we needed to release on a map. Our efficiency had improved—now we could do one every thirty seconds. We'd stay under for an hour, then take a break to stretch our legs. The cushions might have been packed with memory foam, but sitting cross-legged for any longer gave Kimberly pins and needles and started Iris fidgeting.

We made good time in this first session. Perhaps we'd even fit in a few extras? Or so I thought. I was considering the logistics when I saw her, and the sight stopped me dead in my tracks.

"What?" Rania asked. "Why have you stopped? We need to turn left here."

"Have you ever seen anything like that before?"

Rania squinted in the direction I pointed. "Is that a costume?"

"I don't think so."

The focus of my attention looked to be around Iris's age, a pretty woman wearing tight jeans and a blue-and-green striped sweater. Her hunched shoulders spoke of the problems that weighed her down, and she seemed oblivious to all around her as she hurried along the sidewalk. But that wasn't what had caught my eye. No, the reason I'd stopped to stare was the ring of light that floated above her head, a halo, silvery white as it flickered and sparkled. Light balled around her hands too, sparking as she walked. I'd never seen anything like it, and judging by the other girls' stunned expressions, they hadn't either.

The woman wasn't one of us, but instinct told me she wasn't entirely human either. Rania moved first, sprinting through a car as Kimberly gasped in shock.

"I hate it when she does that," Iris muttered.

"Hello?" Rania got in front of the angel-like creature, but the woman didn't stop. Didn't react at all. Up close, the light surrounding her head and hands was even more vibrant, fizzing like sparklers on a dark night. "Who are you? Where did you come from?"

No answer.

Either the woman couldn't hear us, or she had a better poker face than anyone I'd ever met. I added a query of my own into the mix: *what are you?* We followed her into a run-down building, up the stairs to the seventh floor, and into a tiny apartment.

Just as we'd solved one mystery, it seemed we'd found another. The question was, what—if anything—were we going to do about it?

GLOSSARY

British military slang

Bergen - a large backpack.

Bivvy bag - an alternative to a tent. Basically a waterproof bag that you sleep in.

DEVGRU - the US Naval Special Warfare Development Group, aka SEAL Team Six.

Fan Dance - a fifteen-mile load-bearing march over the mountain Pen y Fan, part of SAS selection.

FISHing - urban warfare (Fighting In Someone's House).

Furry crocodile - a dog.

Kalashnikov - a Russian-made assault rifle. The most common is the AK-47 (AK stands for *Avtomat Kalashnikova*, or automatic Kalashnikov)

Military confetti - shrapnel.

Recce - reconnaissance.

Slot - to shoot someone.

Tab - to march with full kit and a weapon.

Other British slang

Bloody Nora - general expression of surprise.

Feck - Irish version of "fuck."

Hen do - a bachelorette party.

Mingebag - a bad person.

Paralytic - extremely drunk.

Scrote - an obnoxious person, also known as a gobshite or a toerag.

Tosser - an asshole.

Sectioned - kept in hospital under the Mental Health Act, being involuntarily committed.

Short of a bob or two - short of cash (a "bob" was the nickname for a shilling, which was an old British coin).

Notes on Afghanistan

Two main languages are spoken in Afghanistan—Pashto in the south and east, and Dari elsewhere. Dari is the Afghan variant of Farsi, also known as Persian. All are based on the Arabic alphabet, but the languages themselves are quite different from Arabic.

Burqa - a dress that covers the whole body and head, with a mesh panel to see through.

Gaday bacheeay - in Pashto, this means "daughter of a sheep."

Hijab - a veil or scarf worn by Muslim women to cover their hair and neck, and sometimes their face too.

Imam - the person who leads prayers in a mosque, kind of like a priest.

Mujahideen - a person engaged in jihad. In the West, we tend to interpret this as holy war, but in Arabic, it simply means "struggle"—a believer's internal struggle to live by their faith, the struggle to build a good Muslim society, and the struggle to defend Islam. The original Mujahideen were members of guerrilla groups who fought during the Afghan War.

WHAT'S NEXT?

Are you wondering where the Electi came from? Or who the girl with the halo might be? A little of that story is told in *A Vampire in Vegas*, the first book in the Planes series...

A Vampire in Vegas

When nightclub hostess Vee Pelletier stumbles across singer Serenity Strange's body in a storeroom at Club Dead, the search begins to find her killer...but it won't be easy. The list of suspects is longer than the line of beautiful people waiting to get in.

Detective Jack Callahan has earned a reputation for solving the unsolvable, but this case may be beyond even his formidable skills. The deeper he digs, the darker the trail gets. And Serenity's killer isn't the only person with secrets. Vee's keeping a devilish one of her own...

Find out more here: www.elise-noble.com/vampire

~

You might also enjoy *Coco du Ciel*, a standalone novel set in the same world as the Electi series...

Coco du Ciel

Could you solve your own murder?

When Rhys Evans agrees to house-sit for his uncle, the last thing he expects is to find a strange girl hiding in the greenhouse. A girl with no memory of her past and no chance at a future unless he helps her.

A freak of nature has given Coco a second chance at life, but before she can live it, she needs to find out who she is and where she came from. The answers aren't quite what either of them were expecting...

For more details: www.elise-noble.com/coco

~

And if you like romantic suspense without supernatural elements, why not give my Blackwood series a try? The story starts in *Pitch Black*...

What happens when an assassin has a nervous breakdown?

After the owner of a security company is murdered, his sharp-edged wife goes on the run. Forced to abandon everything she holds dear—her home, her friends, her job in special ops—she builds a new life for herself in England. As Ashlyn Hale, she meets Luke, a handsome local who makes her realise just how lonely she is.

Yet, even in the sleepy village of Lower Foxford, the dark

side of life dogs Diamond's trail when the unthinkable strikes. Forced out of hiding, she races against time to save those she cares about. But is it too little, too late?

Pitch Black is currently available FREE.
For more details: www.elise-noble.com/pitch-black

~

If you enjoyed *Judged*, please consider leaving a review.

For an author, every review is incredibly important. Not only do they make us feel warm and fuzzy inside, readers consider them when making their decision whether or not to buy a book. Even a line saying you enjoyed the book or what your favourite part was helps a lot.

WANT TO STALK ME?

For updates on my new releases, giveaways, and other random stuff, you can sign up for my newsletter on my website:
www.elise-noble.com

If you're on Facebook, you might also like to join Team Blackwood for exclusive giveaways, sneak previews, and book-related chat. Be the first to find out about new stories, and you might even see your name or one of your suggestions make it into print!

And if you'd like to read my books for FREE, you can also find details of how to join my advance review team.

Would you like to join Team Blackwood?

www.elise-noble.com/team-blackwood

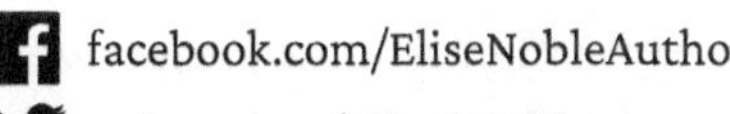

facebook.com/EliseNobleAuthor
twitter.com/EliseANoble
instagram.com/elise_noble

END-OF-BOOK STUFF

The inscription on Ro's watch in the opening scene —*Always a little further*—comes from a poem by James Elroy Flecker called "The Golden Journey to Samarkand":

We are the Pilgrims, Master; we shall go
Always a little further; it may be
Beyond that last blue mountain barred with snow,
Across that angry or that glimmering sea.

This excerpt is engraved on the clock tower of the 22 SAS regiment's barracks in Hereford, and it's also the philosophy Ro can't help continuing to live by, even though he left the army in search of a quieter life. Fate had other ideas. And yes, it's "further" rather than "farther" because we're British, lol.

Thankfully, Tabesh is fictional, but during my research, I found that Afghanistan really isn't a great place to be a woman. Domestic violence is very real. Oppression is very real. There are some men who love their wives very much, but many others who treat them like property. Things are gradually easing in Kabul, where there are now a few cafés that don't require men and women to be segregated, but out in the sticks, women definitely still get the raw end of the deal. Will things ever change? Only time will tell.

While I was reading, I came across one particular story that stayed with me. Ali and Zakia are a young Afghan couple, the children of neighbouring farmers, who fell in love working in the fields. He'd sneak over to her house at night and recite poetry to her while she sat on the roof.

Although they're both Muslim, they come from rival sects—Shia and Sunni—so her family forbade them to marry. Zakia was meant to marry a cousin, but when she refused, she had to stay in a women's shelter because her family threatened to kill her. Yes, honour killings are very real too. But their love wouldn't die, so she eloped with Ali, and they went on the run. A journalist broke all the rules to help them escape, and eventually they fled to America as refugees. A modern love story. Even though Zakia couldn't read, she'd grown up hearing old love stories—Afghan girls would pass them around secretly by word of mouth, even while the elders were preaching against it. And eventually hers came true.

And finally, I have a blooper confession. I live in England, and I went to grammar school, which is a state school but selective. Not as posh as a private school and definitely not as posh as a public school (we call our super posh private schools "public schools" because...who the hell knows?) but still a little bit posh. Anyhow, this partic-ular school offered the choice of learning German or Latin, and because when I was twelve I wanted to be a veterinar-ian, I picked Latin. Big mistake. The Latin teachers were... not good, and worse, there are NO SWEAR WORDS in Latin. I somehow managed to get a B in my GCSE, and then promptly forgot the entire language. Which wasn't a problem until I decided I needed to use a little bit of Latin in this series of books.

Latin is a language where the endings are everything— the order of the words doesn't matter so much. Which is quite cool when it comes to poetry because you can move the words around to paint a picture, and...never mind. My memory of the endings is rusty. *Really* rusty. So what I'm basically trying to say is that if I'd had my brain in gear, the Electi would actually have been called the Electae because that's the feminine ending. I'm just going to go with the story that Uncle Tiberius (more about him in *A Vampire in Vegas*, which also contains a hint about the identity of the angel-like woman in New York) was also shit at either Latin or spelling :)

My next book will be *Coco du Ciel*, which is a standalone novel also set in the Planes world, and another result of Uncle Tiberius's crackpot experiments.

Finally, thanks to the awesome team who helped me with this book... To Nikki for editing, to Abi for designing the cover, to John, Lizbeth, and Debi for proofreading, and to Jeff, Renata, Terri, Musi, David, Stacia, Jessica, Nikita, Quenby, Jody, and Sandra for beta reading.

And thanks to you for reading!

Elise

P.S. If you're wondering what "qui audet adipiscitur" from the epigraph means, it's Latin for "Who dares, wins."

ALSO BY ELISE NOBLE

Blackwood Security

For the Love of Animals (Nate & Carmen - Prequel)

Black is My Heart (Diamond & Snow - Prequel)

Pitch Black

Into the Black

Forever Black

Gold Rush

Gray is My Heart

Neon (novella)

Out of the Blue

Ultraviolet

Glitter (novella)

Red Alert

White Hot

Sphere (novella)

The Scarlet Affair

Spirit (novella)

Quicksilver

The Girl with the Emerald Ring

Red After Dark

When the Shadows Fall

Phantom (novella) (2023)

Pretties in Pink

Chimera

Secret Weapon (Crossover with Baldwin's Shore)

The Devil and the Deep Blue Sea (2023)

Blackwood Elements

Oxygen

Lithium

Carbon

Rhodium

Platinum

Lead

Copper

Bronze

Nickel

Hydrogen

Blackwood UK

Joker in the Pack

Cherry on Top

Roses are Dead

Shallow Graves

Indigo Rain

Pass the Parcel (TBA)

Blackwood Casefiles

Stolen Hearts

Burning Love (TBA)

Baldwin's Shore

Dirty Little Secrets

Secrets, Lies, and Family Ties

Buried Secrets

Secret Weapon (Crossover with Blackwood Security)

A Secret to Die For (TBA)

Blackstone House

Hard Lines

Blurred Lines (2023)

Hard Tide

Hard Limits (2023)

Hard Luck (TBA)

The Electi

Cursed

Spooked

Possessed

Demented

Judged

The Planes

A Vampire in Vegas

A Devil in the Dark (TBA)

The Trouble Series

Trouble in Paradise

Nothing but Trouble

24 Hours of Trouble

Standalone

Life

Coco du Ciel

A Very Happy Christmas (novella)

Twisted (short stories)

Books with clean versions available (no swearing and no on-the-page sex)

Pitch Black

Into the Black

Forever Black

Gold Rush

Gray is My Heart

Audiobooks

Black is My Heart (Diamond & Snow - Prequel)

Pitch Black

Into the Black

Forever Black

Gold Rush

Gray is My Heart

Neon (novella)

www.ingramcontent.com/pod-product-compliance
Lightning Source LLC
Chambersburg PA
CBHW060733190726
48285CB00001B/189